Praise for bestselling

"Palmer proves that love ~~and passion can be found~~ even in the most dangerous situations."
—*Publishers Weekly* on *Untamed*

"You just can't do better than a Diana Palmer story to make your heart lighter and smile brighter."
—*Fresh Fiction* on *Wyoming Rugged*

"Diana Palmer is a mesmerizing storyteller who captures the essence of what a romance should be."
—*Affaire de Coeur*

"The popular Palmer has penned another winning novel, a perfect blend of romance and suspense."
—*Booklist* on *Lawman*

"Diana Palmer's characters leap off the page. She captures their emotions and scars beautifully and makes them come alive for readers."
—*RT Book Reviews* on *Lawless*

NEW YORK TIMES BESTSELLING AUTHOR

DIANA PALMER

COWBOY TRUE

Previously published as *Maggie's Dad* and *Champagne Girl*

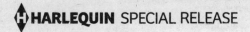 HARLEQUIN SPECIAL RELEASE

If you purchased this book without a cover you should be aware that this book is stolen property. It was reported as "unsold and destroyed" to the publisher, and neither the author nor the publisher has received any payment for this "stripped book."

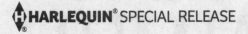 **HARLEQUIN**® SPECIAL RELEASE

ISBN-13: 978-1-335-46315-9

Recycling programs for this product may not exist in your area.

Cowboy True

Copyright © 2021 by Harlequin Books S.A.

Maggie's Dad
First published in 1995. This edition published in 2021.
Copyright © 1995 by Diana Palmer

Champagne Girl
First published in 1986. This edition published in 2021.
Copyright © 2015 by Diana Palmer

All rights reserved. No part of this book may be used or reproduced in any manner whatsoever without written permission except in the case of brief quotations embodied in critical articles and reviews.

This is a work of fiction. Names, characters, places and incidents are either the product of the author's imagination or are used fictitiously. Any resemblance to actual persons, living or dead, businesses, companies, events or locales is entirely coincidental.

This edition published by arrangement with Harlequin Books S.A.

For questions and comments about the quality of this book, please contact us at CustomerService@Harlequin.com.

Harlequin Enterprises ULC
22 Adelaide St. West, 40th Floor
Toronto, Ontario M5H 4E3, Canada
www.Harlequin.com

Printed in Spain

CONTENTS

A prolific author of more than one hundred books, **Diana Palmer** got her start as a newspaper reporter. A *New York Times* bestselling author and voted one of the top ten romance writers in America, she has a gift for telling the most sensual tales with charm and humor. Diana lives with her family in Cornelia, Georgia. Visit her website at dianapalmer.com.

Books by Diana Palmer

Long, Tall Texans

Fearless
Heartless
Dangerous
Merciless
Courageous
Protector
Invincible
Untamed
Defender
Undaunted

The Wyoming Men

Wyoming Tough
Wyoming Fierce
Wyoming Bold
Wyoming Strong
Wyoming Rugged
Wyoming Brave

Morcai Battalion

The Morcai Battalion
The Morcai Battalion: The Recruit
The Morcai Battalion: Invictus
The Morcai Battalion: The Rescue

Visit the Author Profile page
at Harlequin.com for more titles.

MAGGIE'S DAD

PROLOGUE

RAIN WAS PEPPERING down on the roof of the small house where Antonia Hayes's parents lived. It was a cold rain, and Antonia thought absently that she was very glad it was summer, because by early autumn that soft rain would turn to sleet or snow. Bighorn, a small town in northwestern Wyoming, was not an easy town to leave once it was covered in ice. It was rural and despite having three thousand inhabitants, it was too small to offer the transportation choices of a larger town. There wasn't even an airport; only a bus station. The railroad ran through it, too, but the trains were spaced too far apart to do Antonia much good.

She was about to begin her sophomore year in college, at the University of Arizona in Tucson, and snow was fairly rare in that area in winter, except up in the mountains. The desert floor had light dustings, but not enough to inconvenience anyone. Besides, Antonia—having just finished her first year there—had been much too busy trying to pass her core courses and heal a broken heart to notice the weather. She did notice the summer heat now, though, she mused, and thanked God for air-conditioning.

The clock sounded and Antonia turned, her short, blond hair perky and her gray eyes full of sadness at having to leave. But fall semester started in less than a week, and she had to get back into her dorm room and set up some sort of schedule. The only comforting thing about going back was that George Rutherford's stepdaughter, Barrie Bell, was her dorm roommate, and they got along very well indeed.

"It's been lovely having you home for a whole week," her mother, Jessica, said warmly. "I do wish you could have stayed the whole summer…"

Her voice trailed off. She knew, as did Antonia and Ben, her husband, why Antonia couldn't stay in Bighorn very long. It was a source of great sadness to all of them, but they didn't discuss it. It still hurt too much, and the gossip hadn't quite died down even now, almost a year after the fact. George Rutherford's abrupt move to France a few months after Antonia's departure had quelled the remaining gossip.

Despite what had happened, George had remained a good, true friend to Antonia and her family. Her college education was his gift to her. She would pay him back every penny, but right now the money was a godsend. Her parents were well regarded in the community, but lacked the resources to swing her tuition. George had been determined to help, and his kindness had cost them both so much.

But George's son, Dawson, and his stepdaughter, Barrie, had rallied around Antonia, defending her against the talk.

It was comforting to know that the two people closest to George didn't believe he was Antonia's sugar daddy. And of course, it helped that Dawson and Powell Long were rivals for a strip of land that separated their respective Bighorn ranch holdings. George had lived on his Bighorn ranch until the scandal. Then he went back to the family home he shared with Dawson in Sheridan, hoping to stem the gossip. It hadn't happened. So he'd moved to France, leaving more bitterness between Dawson and Powell Long. There was no love lost there.

But even with George out of the country, and despite

the support of friends and family, Sally Long had done so much damage to Antonia's reputation that she was sure she would never be able to come home again.

Her mind came back to the remark her mother had just made. "I took classes this summer," she murmured absently. "I'm really sorry, but I thought I'd better, and some of my new friends went, too. It was nice, although I do miss being home. I miss both of you."

Jessica hugged her warmly. "And we miss you."

"That damn fool Sally Long," Ben muttered as he also hugged his daughter. "Spreading lies so that she could take Powell away from you. And that damn fool Powell Long, believing them, marrying her, and that baby born just seven months later...!"

Antonia's face went pale, but she smiled gamely. "Now, Dad," she said gently. "It's all over," she added with what she hoped was a reassuring smile, "they're married and they have a daughter now. I hope he's happy."

"Happy! After the way he treated you?"

Antonia closed her eyes. The memories were still painful. Powell had been the center of her life. She'd never imagined she could feel a love so sweeping, so powerful. He'd never said he loved her, but she'd been so sure that he did. Looking back now, though, she knew that he'd never really loved her. He wanted her, of course, but he had always drawn back. *We'll wait for marriage*, he'd said.

And waiting had been a good thing, considering how it had all turned out.

At the time, Antonia had wanted him desperately, but she'd put him off. Even now, over a year later, she could still see his black eyes and dark hair and thin, wide mouth. That image lived in her heart despite the fact that he'd canceled their wedding the day before it was to take place.

People who hadn't been notified in time were sitting in the church, waiting. She shuddered faintly, remembering her humiliation.

Ben was still muttering about Sally.

"That's enough, Ben." Jessica laid a hand on her husband's arm. "It's water under the bridge," she said firmly. Her voice was so tranquil that it was hard for Antonia to believe that the scandal had caused her mother to have heart problems. She'd done very well, and Antonia had done everything possible to avoid the subject so that her mother wouldn't be upset.

"I wouldn't say Powell was happy," Ben continued, unabashed. "He's never home, and we never see him out with Sally in public. In fact, we never see Sally much at all. If she's happy, she doesn't let it show." He studied his daughter's pale, rigid face. "She called here one day before Easter and asked for your address. Did she write to you?"

"She wrote me."

"Well?" he prompted, curious.

"I returned the letter without opening it," Antonia said tightly, even paler now. She looked down at her shoes. "It's ancient history."

"She might have wanted to apologize," Jessica ventured.

Antonia sighed. "Some things go beyond apologies," she said quietly. "I loved him, you know," she added with a faint smile. "But he never loved me. If he did, he didn't say so in all the time we went together. He believed everything Sally told him. He just told me what he thought of me, called off the wedding and walked away. I had to leave. It hurt too much to stay." She could picture in her mind that long, straight back, the rigid set of his dark head. The pain had been terrible. It still was.

"As if George was that sort of man," Jessica said wearily. "He's the kindest man in the world, and he adores you."

"Not the sort to play around with young girls," Ben agreed. "Idiots, people who could believe that about him. I know that's why he moved out of the country, to spare us any more gossip."

"Since he and I are both gone, there's not much to gossip about," Antonia said pointedly. She smiled. "I'm working hard on my grades. I want George to be proud of me."

"He will be. And we already are," Jessica said warmly.

"Well, it serves Powell Long right that he ended up with that selfish little madam," Ben persisted irritably. "He thinks he's going to get rich by building up that cattle ranch, but he's just a dreamer," Ben scoffed. "His father was a gambler, and his mother was a doormat. Imagine him thinking he's got enough sense to make money with cattle!"

"He does seem to be making strides," his wife said gently. "He just bought a late-model truck, and they say a string of ranches up in Montana have given him a contract to supply them with seed bulls. You remember, Ben, when his big purebred Angus bull was in the paper, it won some national award."

"One bull doesn't make an empire," Ben scoffed.

Antonia felt the words all the way to her heart. Powell had told her his dreams, and they'd planned that ranch together, discussed having the best Angus bulls in the territory…

"Could we not…talk about him, please?" Antonia asked finally. She forced a smile. "It still stings a little."

"Of course it does. We're sorry," Jessica said, her voice soft now. "Can you come home for Christmas?"

"I'll try. I really will."

She had one small suitcase. She carried it out to the car

and hugged her mother one last time before she climbed in beside her father for the short ride to the bus depot downtown.

It was morning, but still sweltering hot. She got out of the car and picked up her suitcase as she waited on the sidewalk for her father to get her ticket from the office inside the little grocery store. There was a line. She'd just turned her attention back to the street when her eyes froze on an approaching pedestrian; a cold, quiet ghost from the past.

He was just as lean and dark as she remembered him. The suit was better than the ones he'd worn when they were dating, and he looked thinner. But it was the same Powell Long.

She'd lost everything to him except her pride. She still had it, and she forced her gray eyes up to his as he walked down the sidewalk with that slow, elegant stride that was particularly his own. She wouldn't let him see how badly his distrust had hurt her, even now.

His expression gave away nothing that he was feeling. He paused when he reached her, glancing at the suitcase.

"Well, well," he drawled, watching her face. "I heard you were here. The chicken came home to roost, did she?"

"I'm not here to stay," she replied coolly. "I've been to visit my parents. I'm on my way to Arizona, back to college."

"By bus?" he taunted. "Couldn't your sugar daddy afford a plane ticket? Or did he leave you high and dry when he hightailed it to France?"

She kicked him right in the shin. It wasn't premeditated, and he looked as shocked as she did when he bent to rub the painful spot where her shoe had landed.

"I wish I'd been wearing steel-toed combat boots like one of the girls in my dorm," she said hotly. "And if you ever so much as speak to me again, Powell Long, I'll break your leg the next time!"

She brushed past him and went into the depot.

Her father had just paid for the ticket when his attention was captured by the scene outside the depot. He started outside, but Antonia pushed him back into the building.

"We can wait for the bus in here, Dad," she said, her face still red and hot with anger.

He glanced past her to where Powell had straightened to send a speaking look toward the depot.

"Well, he seems to have learned to control that hot temper, at least. A year ago, he'd have been in here, right through the window," Ben Hayes remarked coldly. "I hope you crippled him."

She managed a wan smile. "No such luck. You can't wound something that ornery."

Powell had started back down the street, his back stiff with outrage.

"I hope Sally asks him how he hurt his leg," Antonia said under her breath.

"Here, girl, the bus is coming." He shepherded her outside, grateful that the ticket agent hadn't been paying attention and that none of the other passengers seemed interested in the byplay out the window. All they needed was some more gossip.

Antonia hugged her father before she climbed aboard. She wanted to look down the street, to see if Powell was limping. But even though the windows were dark, she wouldn't risk having him catch her watching him. She closed her eyes as the bus pulled away from the depot and spent the rest of the journey trying to forget the pain of seeing Powell Long again.

CHAPTER ONE

"THAT'S VERY GOOD, Martin, but you've left out something, haven't you?" Antonia prompted gently. She smiled, too, because Martin was very shy even for a nine-year-old and she didn't want to embarrass him in front of her other fourth graders. "The secret weapon the Greeks used in battle…a military formation?"

"Secret weapon," he murmured to himself. Then his dark eyes lit up and he grinned. "The phalanx!" he said at once.

"Yes," she replied. "Very good!"

He beamed, glancing smugly at his worst enemy in the second row over, who was hoping Martin would miss the question and looked very depressed indeed that he hadn't.

Antonia glanced at her watch. It was almost time to dismiss class for the day, and the week. Odd, she thought, how loose that watch was on her wrist.

"It's time to start putting things away," she told her students. "Jack, will you erase the board for me, please? And, Mary, please close the windows."

They rushed to obey, because they liked Miss Hayes. Mary glanced at her with a smile. Miss Hayes smiled back. She wasn't as pretty as Miss Bell down the hall, and she dressed in a very backward sort of way, always wearing suits or pantsuits, not miniskirts and frilly blouses. She had pretty long blond hair, though, when she took it out of that awful bun, and her gray eyes were like the December sky. It would be Christmas soon, and in a week they could all go home for the holidays. Mary wondered what Miss Hayes would do. She never went anywhere exciting for holidays. She never talked about her family, either. Maybe she didn't have one.

The bell rang and Antonia smiled and waved as her students marched out to waiting buses and cars. She tidied her desk with steady hands and wondered if her father would come for Christmas this year. It was very lonely for both of them since her mother's death last year. It had been hard, coping with the loss. It had been harder having to go home for the funeral. He was there. He, and his daughter. Antonia shivered just remembering the look on his dark, hard face. Powell hadn't softened even then, even when her mother was being buried. He still hated Antonia after nine years. She'd barely glanced at the sullen, dark-haired little girl by his side. The child was like a knife through her heart, a reminder that Powell had been sleeping with Sally even while he and Antonia were engaged to be married; because the little girl had been born only seven months after Powell married Sally. Antonia had glanced at them once, only once, to meet Powell's hateful stare. She hadn't looked toward the pew where they sat again.

Incredible how he could hate Antonia after marriage and a child, when everyone must have told him the truth ten times over in the years between. He was rich now. He had money and power and a fine home. His wife had died only three years after their wedding, and he hadn't remarried. Antonia imagined it was because he missed Sally so much. She didn't. She hated even the memory of her one-time best friend. Sally had cost her everything she loved, even her home, and she'd done it with deliberate lies. Of course, Powell had believed the lies. That was what had hurt most.

Antonia was over it now. It had been nine years. It hardly hurt at all, in fact, to remember him.

She blinked as someone knocked at the door, interrupting her train of thought. It was Barrie, her good friend and the Miss Bell of the miniskirt who taught math, grinning at her. Barrie was gorgeous. She was slender and had beautiful long legs. Her hair was almost black, like a wavy curtain down her back. She had green eyes with mischief in them, and a ready smile.

"You could stay with me at Christmas," Barrie invited merrily, her green eyes twinkling.

"In Sheridan?" she asked idly, because that was where Barrie's stepfather's home was, where George Rutherford and her stepbrother, Dawson Rutherford, and Barrie and her late mother had lived before she left home and began teaching with Antonia in Tucson.

"No," Barrie said tightly. "Not ever there. In my apartment here in Tucson," she added, forcing a smile to her face. "I have four boyfriends. We can split them, two each. We'll have a merry whirl!"

Antonia only smiled. "I'm twenty-seven, too old for merry whirls, and my father will probably come here for Christmas. But thanks anyway."

"Honestly, Annie, you're not old, even if you do dress like someone's maiden aunt!" she said explosively. "Look at you!" she added, sweeping her hand toward the gray suit and white blouse that was indicative of the kind of clothes Antonia favored. "And your hair in that infernal bun… you look like a holdover from the Victorians! You need to loose that glorious blond hair and put on a miniskirt and some makeup and look for a man before you get too old! And you need to eat! You're so thin that you're beginning to look like skin and bones."

Antonia knew that. She'd lost ten pounds in the past month or so and she'd finally gotten worried enough to make an appointment with her doctor. It was probably nothing, she thought, but it wouldn't hurt to check. Her iron might be low. She said as much to Barrie.

"That's true. You've had a hard year, what with losing your mother and then that awful scare with the student who brought his dad's pistol to school and held everybody at bay for an hour last month."

"Teaching is becoming the world's most dangerous profession," Antonia agreed. She smiled sadly at Barrie. "Perhaps if we advertised it that way, we'd attract more brave souls to boost our numbers."

"That's an idea," came the dry agreement. "Want adventure? Try teaching! I can see the slogan now—"

"I'm going home," Antonia interrupted her.

"Ah, well, I suppose I will, too. I have a date tonight."

"Who is it this time?"

"Bob. He's nice and we get along well. But sometimes I think I'm not cut out for a conventional sort of man. I need a wild-eyed artist or a composer or a drag racer."

Antonia chuckled. "I hope you find one."

"If I did, he'd probably have two wives hidden in another country or something. I do have the worst luck with men."

"It's your liberated image," Antonia said in a conspiratorial tone. "You're devil-may-care and outrageous. You scare off the most secure bachelors."

"Bunkum. If they were secure enough, they'd rush to my door," Barrie informed her. "I'm sure there's a man like that somewhere, just waiting for me."

"I'm sure there is, too," her friend said kindly, and didn't for a minute let on that she thought there was already one waiting in Sheridan.

Beneath Barrie's outrageous persona, there was a sad and rather lonely woman. Barrie wasn't at all what she seemed. Barrie basically was afraid of men—especially her stepbrother, Dawson. He was George's blood son. Dear George, the elderly man who'd been another unfortunate victim of Sally Long's lies. The tales hadn't fazed Dawson, though, who not only knew better, but who was one of the coldest and most intimidating men Antonia had ever met where women were concerned. Barrie never mentioned Dawson, never talked about him. And if his name was mentioned, she changed the subject. It was common knowledge that they didn't get along. But secretly, Antonia thought there was something in their past, something that Barrie didn't talk about.

She never had, and now that poor George was dead and Dawson had inherited his estate, there was a bigger rift between them because a large interest in the cattle empire that Dawson inherited had been willed to Barrie.

"I've got to phone Dad and see what his plans are," Antonia murmured, dragging herself back from her memories.

"If he can't come down here, will you go home for Christmas?"

She shook her head. "I don't go home."

"Why not?" She grimaced. "Oh. Yes. I forget from time to time, because you never talk about him. I'm sorry. But it's been nine years. Surely he couldn't hold a grudge for that long? After all, he's the one who called off the wedding and married your best friend less than a month later. And she caused the scandal in the first place!"

"Yes, I know," Antonia replied.

"She must have loved him a lot to take such a risk. But he did eventually find out the truth," she added, tugging absently on a strand of her long, wavy black hair.

Antonia sighed. "Did he? I suppose someone told him, eventually. I don't imagine he believed it, though. Powell likes to see me as a villain."

"He loved you…"

"He wanted me," Antonia said bitterly. "At least that's what he said. I had no illusions about why he was marrying me. My father's name carried some weight in town, even though we were not rich. Powell needed the respectability. The love was all on my side. As it worked out, he got rich and had one child and a wife who was besotted with him. But from what I heard, he didn't love her either. Poor Sally," she added on a cold laugh, "all that plotting and lying, and when she got what she wanted, she was miserable."

"Good enough for her," Barrie said curtly. "She ruined your reputation and your parents'."

"And your stepfather's," she added, sadly. "He was very fond of my mother once."

Barrie smiled gently. "He was very fond of her up until the end. It was a blessing that he liked your father, and that they were friends. He was a good loser when she married your father. But he still cared for her, and that's why he did so much to help you."

"Right down to paying for my college education. That was the thing that led to all the trouble. Powell didn't like George at all. His father lost a lot of land to George—in fact, Dawson is still at odds with Powell over that land, even today, you know. He may live in Sheridan, but his ranch covers hundreds of acres right up against Powell's ranch, and I understand from Dad that he gives him fits at any opportunity."

"Dawson has never forgotten or forgiven the lies that Sally told about George," came the quiet reply. "He spoke to Sally, you know. He cornered her in town and gave her hell, with Powell standing right beside her."

"You never told me that," Antonia said on a quick breath.

"I didn't know how to," Barrie replied. "It hurts you just to have Powell's name mentioned."

"I suppose Powell stood up for her," she said, fishing.

"Even Powell is careful about how he deals with Dawson," Barrie reminded her. "Besides, what could he say? Sally told a lie and she was caught, red-handed. Too late to do you any good, they were already married by then."

"You mean, Powell's known the truth for nine years?" Antonia asked, aghast.

"I didn't say he believed Dawson," the other woman replied gently, averting her eyes.

"Oh. Yes. Well." Antonia fought for composure. How ridiculous, to think Powell would have accepted the word of his enemy. He and Dawson never had gotten along. She said it aloud even as she thought it.

"Is it likely that they would? My stepfather beat Old Man Long out of everything he owned in a poker game when they were both young men. The feud has gone on from there. Dawson's land borders Powell's, and they're both bent on empire building. If a tract comes up for sale, you can bet both men will be standing on the Realtor's doorstep trying to get first dibs on it. In fact, that's what they're butting heads about right now, that strip of land that separates their ranches that the widow Holton owns."

"They own the world between them," Antonia said pointedly.

"And they only want what joins theirs." Barrie chuckled. "Ah, well, it's no concern of ours. Not now. The less I see of my stepbrother, the happier I am."

Antonia, who'd only once seen the two of them together,

had to agree. When Dawson was anywhere nearby, Barrie became another person, withdrawn and tense and almost comically clumsy.

"Well, if you change your mind about the holidays, my door is open," Barrie reminded her.

Antonia smiled warmly. "I'll remember. If Dad can't come down for the holidays, you could come home with me," she added.

Barrie shivered. "No, thanks! Bighorn is too close to Dawson for my taste."

"Dawson lives in Sheridan."

"Not all the time. Occasionally he stays at the ranch in Bighorn. He spends more and more time there these days." Her face went taut. "They say the widow Holton is the big attraction. Her husband had lots of land, and she hasn't decided who she'll sell it to."

A widow with land. Barrie had mentioned that Powell was also in competition with Dawson for the land. Or was it the widow? He was a widower, too, and a long-standing one. The thought made her sad.

"You need to eat more," Barrie remarked, concerned by her friend's appearance. "You're getting so thin, Annie, although it does give you a more fragile appearance. You have lovely bone structure. High cheekbones and good skin."

"I inherited the high cheekbones from a Cheyenne grandmother," she said, remembering sadly that Powell had called her Cheyenne as a nickname—actually meant as a corruption of "shy Ann," which she had been when they first started dating.

"Good blood," Barrie mused. "My ancestry is black Irish—from the Spanish armada that was blown off course to the coast of Ireland. Legend has it that one of my ancestors was a Spanish nobleman, who ended up married to a stepsister of an Irish lord."

"What a story."

"Isn't it, though? I must pursue historical fiction one day—in between stuffing mathematical formulae into the heads of innocents." She glanced at her watch. "Heavens, I'll be late for my date with Bob! Gotta run. See you Monday!"

"Have fun."

"I always have fun. I wish you did, once in a while." She waved from the door, leaving behind a faint scent of perfume.

Antonia loaded her attaché case with papers to grade and her lesson plan for the following week, which badly needed updating. When her desk was cleared, she sent a last look around the classroom and went out the door.

HER SMALL APARTMENT overlooked "A" mountain in Tucson, so-called because of the giant letter A that was painted at its peak and was repainted year after year by University of Arizona students. The city was flat and only a small scattering of tall buildings located downtown made it seem like a city at all. It was widespread, sprawling, sandy and hot. Nothing like Bighorn, Wyoming, where Antonia's family had lived for three generations.

She remembered going back for her mother's funeral less than a year ago. Townspeople had come by the house to bring food for every meal, and to pay their respects. Antonia's mother had been well-loved in the community. Friends sent cartloads of the flowers she'd loved so much.

The day of the funeral had dawned bright and sunny, making silver lights in the light snow covering, and Antonia thought how her mother had loved spring. She wouldn't see another one now. Her heart, always fragile, had finally given out. At least, it had been a quick death. She'd died at the stove, in the very act of putting a cake into the oven.

The service was brief but poignant, and afterward Antonia and her father had gone home. The house was empty. Dawson Rutherford had stopped to offer George's sympathy, because George had been desperately ill, far too ill to fly across the ocean from France for the funeral. In fact, George had died less than two weeks later.

Dawson had volunteered to drive Barrie out to the airport to catch her plane back to Arizona, because Barrie had come to the funeral, of course. Antonia had noted even in her grief how it affected Barrie just to have to ride that short distance with her stepbrother.

Later, Antonia's father had gone to the bank and Antonia had been halfheartedly sorting her mother's unneeded clothes and putting them away when Mrs. Harper, who lived next door and was helping with the household chores, announced that Powell Long was at the door and wished to speak with her.

Having just suffered the three worst days of her life, she was in no condition to face him now.

"Tell Mr. Long that we have nothing to say to each other," Antonia had replied with cold pride.

"Guess he knows how it feels to lose somebody, since he lost Sally a few years back," Mrs. Harper reminded her, and then watched to see how the news would be received.

Antonia had known about Sally's death. She hadn't sent flowers or a card because it had happened only three years after Antonia had fled Bighorn, and the bitterness had still been eating at her.

"I'm sure he understands grief," was all Antonia said, and waited without saying another word until Mrs. Harper got the message and left.

She was back five minutes later with a card. "Said to give you this," she murmured, handing the business card to Antonia, "and said you should call him if you needed any sort of help."

Help. She took the card and, without even looking at it, deliberately tore it into eight equal parts. She handed them back to Mrs. Harper and turned again to her clothes sorting.

Mrs. Harper looked at the pieces of paper in her hand. "Enough said," she murmured, and left.

It was the last contact Antonia had had with Powell Long since her mother's death. She knew that he'd built up his purebred Angus ranch and made a success of it. But she didn't ask for personal information about him after that, despite the fact that he remained a bachelor. The past, as far as she was concerned, was truly dead. Now, she wondered vaguely why Powell had come to see her that day. Guilt, perhaps? Or something more? She'd never know.

SHE FOUND A message on her answering machine and played it. Her father, as she'd feared, was suffering his usual bout of winter bronchitis and his doctor wouldn't let him go on an airplane for fear of what it would do to his sick lungs. And he didn't feel at all like a bus or train trip, so Antonia would have to come home for Christmas, he said, or they'd each have to spend it alone.

She sat down heavily on the floral couch she'd purchased at a local furniture store and sighed. She didn't want to go home. If she could have found a reasonable excuse, she wouldn't have, either. But it would be impossible to leave her father sick and alone on the holidays. With resolution, she picked up the telephone and booked a seat on the next commuter flight to Billings, where the nearest airport to Bighorn was located.

BECAUSE WYOMING WAS so sparsely populated, it was lacking in airports. Powell Long, now wealthy and able to afford all the advantages, had an airstrip on his ranch. But there was nowhere in Bighorn that a commercial aircraft, even a commuter one, could land. She knew that Barrie's stepbrother had a Learjet and that he had a landing strip near Bighorn on his own ranch, but she would never have presumed on Barrie's good nature to ask for that sort of favor. Besides, she admitted to herself, she was as intimidated by Dawson Rutherford as Barrie was. He, like Powell, was high-powered and aggressively masculine. Antonia felt much safer seated on an impersonal commuter plane.

She rented a car at the airport in Billings and, with the easy acceptance of long distances on the road from her time in Arizona, she set out for Bighorn.

The countryside was lovely. There were scattered patches of snow, something she hadn't thought about until it was too late and she'd already rented the car. There was snow on the ground in Billings, quite a lot of it, and although the roads were mostly clear, she was afraid of icy patches. She'd get out, somehow, she told herself. But she did wish that she'd had the forethought to ask her father about the local weather when she'd phoned to say she was leaving Tucson on an early-morning flight. But he was hoarse and she hadn't wanted to stress his voice too much. He knew when she was due to arrive, though, and if she was too long overdue, she was certain that he'd send someone to meet her.

She gazed lovingly at the snow-covered mountains, thinking of how she'd missed this country that was home to her, home to generations of her family. There was so much of her history locked into these sweeping mountain ranges and valleys, where lodgepole pines stood like sentinels over shallow, wide blue streams. The forests were green and majestic, looking much as they must have when mountain men plied their trade here. Arizona had her own forests, too, and mountains. But Wyoming was another world. It was home.

The going got rough the closer to home she went. It was just outside Bighorn that her car slipped on a wide patch of ice and almost went into a ditch. She knew all too well that if she had, there would have been no way she could get the vehicle out, because the slope was too deep.

With a prayer of thanks, she made it into the small town of Bighorn, past the Methodist Church and the post office and the meat locker building to her father's big Victorian house on a wide street off the main thoroughfare. She parked in the driveway under a huge cottonwood tree. How wonderful to be home for Christmas!

There was a decorated tree in the window, all aglow with the lights and ornaments that had been painstakingly purchased over a period of years. She looked at one, a crystal deer, and remembered painfully that Powell had given it to her the Christmas they'd become engaged. She'd thought of smashing it after his desertion, but she couldn't bring herself to do it. The tiny thing was so beautiful, so fragile; like their destroyed relationship. So long ago.

Her father came to the door in a bathrobe and pajamas, sniffling.

He hugged her warmly. "I'm so glad you came, girl," he said hoarsely, and coughed a little. "I'm much better, but the damn doctor wouldn't let me fly!"

"And rightly so," she replied. "You don't need pneumonia!"

He grinned at her. "I reckon not. Can you stay until New Year's?"

She shook her head. "I'm sorry. I have to go back the day after Christmas." She didn't mention her upcoming doctor's appointment. There was no need to worry him.

"Well, you'll be here for a week, anyway. We won't get to go out much, I'm afraid, but we can keep each other company, can't we?"

"Yes, we can."

"Dawson said he might come by one evening," he added surprisingly. "He's just back from Europe, some convention or other he said he couldn't miss."

"At least he never believed the gossip about George and me," she said wistfully.

"Why, he knew his father too well," he replied simply.

"George was a wonderful man. No wonder you and he were friends for so long."

"I miss him. I miss your mother, too, God rest her soul. She was the most important person in my life, next to you."

"You're the most important person in mine," she agreed, smiling. "It's good to be home!"

"Still enjoy teaching?"

"More than ever," she told him warmly.

"There's some good schools here," he remarked. "They're always short of teachers. And two of them are expecting babies any day. They'll have problems getting supply teachers in for that short little period." He eyed her. "You wouldn't consider...?"

"I like Tucson," she said firmly.

"The hell you do," he muttered. "It's Powell, isn't it? Damn fool, listening to that scatterbrained woman in the first place! Well, he paid for it. She made his life hell."

"Would you like some coffee?" she asked, changing the subject.

"Oh, I suppose so. And some soup. There's some canned that Mrs. Harper made for me."

"Does she still live next door?"

"She does," he murmured with a wicked smile, "and she's a widow herself. No need to ask why she brought the soup, is there?"

"I like Mrs. Harper," she said with a grin. "She and Mother were good friends, and she's like family already. Just in case you wondered what I thought," she added.

"It's only been a year, girl," he said, and his eyes were sad.

"Mother loved you too much to want you to go through life alone," she said. "She wouldn't want you to grieve forever."

He shrugged. "I'll grieve as long as I please."

"Suit yourself. I'll change clothes and then I'll see about the soup and coffee."

"How's Barrie?" her father asked when Antonia came out of her bedroom dressed in jeans and a white sweatshirt with golden sequined bells and red ribbon on it.

"She's just fine. Spunky as ever."

"Why didn't you bring her with you?"

"Because she's juggling four boyfriends," she said, chuckling as she went about warming soup.

"Dawson won't wait forever."

She glanced at him. "Is that what you think, too? She won't talk about him."

"He won't talk about her, either."

"What's this rumor about him and the widow Holton?"

He sat down in a chair at the table with a painful breath. "The widow Holton is redheaded and vivacious and a mankiller," he said. "She's after Dawson. And Powell Long. And any other man with money and a passable face."

"I see."

"You don't remember her, do you? Came here before you went off to college, but she and her husband traveled a lot. She was some sort of actress. She's been home more since he died."

"What does she do?"

"For a living, you mean?" He chuckled and had to fight back a cough. "She's living on her inheritance. Doesn't have to do anything, lucky girl."

"I wouldn't want to do nothing," Antonia remarked thoughtfully. "I like teaching. It's more than just a job."

"Some women aren't made for purposeful employment."

"I guess not."

She finished heating the soup and poured the coffee she'd made. They ate in silence.

"I wish your mother was here," he said.

She smiled sadly. "So do I."

"Well, we'll make the most of what we have and thank God for it."

She nodded. "We have more than some people do."

He smiled, seeing her mother's face in her own. "And a lot more than most," he added. "I'm glad you came home for Christmas."

"So am I. Eat your soup." She poured him some more, and thought that she was going to make this Christmas as happy for him as she could.

CHAPTER TWO

DAWSON RUTHERFORD WAS TALL, lean and drop-dead gorgeous with blond, wavy hair and eyes that seemed to pierce skin. Even if he hadn't been so handsome, his physical presence was more than enough to make him attractive, added to a deep voice that had the smoothness of velvet, even in anger. But he was as icy a man as she'd ever known, especially with women. At his father's funeral, she'd actually seen him back away from a beautiful woman to avoid being touched. Odd, that, when she knew for a fact that he'd been quite a rounder with women in his checkered past.

If Antonia hadn't given her heart to Powell Long so many years before, she wouldn't have minded setting her cap at Dawson, intimidating though he was. But he was plainly meant for another type of woman altogether. Barrie, perhaps.

It was Christmas Eve, and he'd stopped by with a pipe for her father. Antonia walked him out a few minutes later.

"Shame on you," she muttered, pausing on the porch.

Dawson's green eyes twinkled. "He'll get over the bronchitis. Besides, you know he won't quit smoking, whether or not I give him a new pipe. You've tried and I've tried for years to break him. The best we can do is make him smoke it outdoors."

"I know that," she agreed, and smiled. "Well, it was a nice gesture."

"Want to see what he gave me?" he asked, and produced a smooth silver lighter with inlaid turquoise.

"I didn't know you smoked," she observed.

"I don't."

Her eyes widened.

"I did, just briefly, smoke cigars." He corrected himself. "I gave it up months ago. He doesn't know, so don't tell him."

"I won't. But good for you!" she said approvingly.

He shrugged. "I don't know any smokers who don't want to quit." His eyes narrowed, and he watched her without blinking. "Except one, maybe."

She knew he was talking about Powell, who always had smoked cigars, and presumably still did. Her face began to close up. "Don't say it."

"I won't. You look tortured."

"It was nine years ago."

"Somebody should have shot him for the way he treated you," he replied. "I've never liked him, but that didn't win him any points with me. I loved my father. It was a low thing, for Sally to make him out a foolish old man with a lust for young girls."

"She wanted Powell."

His eyes narrowed. "She got him. But he made her pay for it, let me tell you. She took to alcohol because he left her alone so much, and from all accounts, he hated their daughter."

"But why?" Antonia asked, shocked. "Powell loved children, surely…!"

"Sally trapped him with the child," he replied. "Except for that, he'd have left her. Don't you think he knew what a stupid thing he'd done? He knew the truth, almost from the day he married Sally."

"But he stayed with her."

"He had to. He was trying to build a ranch out of nothing, and this is a small town. How would it look for a man to walk out on a pregnant woman, or on his own newborn daughter?" He pursed his lips. "He hates you, you know," he added surprisingly. "He hates you for not making him listen, for running. He blames his misery on you."

"He's your worst enemy, so how do you know so much?" she retorted.

"I have spies." He sighed. "He can't admit that the worst mistake was his own, that he wouldn't believe Sally capable of such underhanded lies. It wasn't until he married her that he realized how she'd conned him." He shrugged. "She wasn't a bad woman, really. She was in love and she couldn't bear losing him, even to you. Love does crazy things to people."

"She destroyed my reputation, and your father's, and made it impossible for me to live here," Antonia said without pity. "She was my enemy, and he still is. Don't think I'm harboring any tender feelings for him. I'd cut his throat given the slightest opportunity."

His eyebrows levered up. Antonia was a gentle soul herself for the most part, despite an occasional outburst of temper and a keen wit that surprised people. She hadn't ever seemed vindictive, but she harbored a long-standing grudge against her former best friend, Sally. He couldn't really blame her.

He fingered the lighter her father had given him. "How's Barrie?" he asked with deliberate carelessness.

"Fending off suitors," she said with a grin, her soft gray eyes twinkling. "She was juggling four of them when I left."

He laughed coldly. "Why doesn't that surprise me? One

man was never enough for her, even when she was a teen-ager."

She was curious about his antagonism toward Barrie. It seemed out of place. "Why do you hate her so?" she asked bluntly.

He looked surprised. "I don't...hate her," he said. "I'm disappointed at the way she behaves, that's all."

"She isn't promiscuous," she said, defending her colleague. "She may act that way, but it's only an act. Don't you know that?"

He looked at the lighter, frowning slightly. "Maybe I know more than you think," he said curtly. His eyes came up. "Maybe you're the one wearing blinders."

"Maybe you're seeing what you want to see," she replied gently.

He pocketed the lighter with a curt gesture. "I'd better go. I've got a deal cooking. I don't want the client to get cold feet."

"Thanks for coming to see Dad. You cheered him up."

"He's my friend." He smiled. "So are you, even when you stick your nose in where you shouldn't."

"Barrie's my friend."

"Well, she's not mine," he said flatly. "Merry Christmas, Annie."

"You, too," she replied with a warm smile. He was kind, in his way. She liked him, but she felt sorry for Barrie. He was a heartbreaker. And unless she missed her guess, Barrie was in love with him. His feelings were much less readable.

After he left, she went back to join her father in the kitchen, where he was fixing hot chocolate in a double boiler. He glanced over his shoulder.

"Did he leave?"

"Yes. Can I help?"

He shook his head. He poured hot chocolate into two mugs and nodded for her to take one while he put the boiler in water to soak.

"He gave me a pipe," he told her when they were seated at the small kitchen table, sipping the hot liquid. He grinned. "Didn't have the heart to tell him that I've finally given it up."

"Dad!" She reached across and patted his hand. "Oh, that's great news!"

He chuckled. "Figured you'd like it. Maybe I won't have so much trouble with my lungs from now on."

"Speaking of lungs," she said, "you gave Dawson a lighter. Guess what he's just given up, and didn't have the heart to tell you?"

He burst out laughing. "Well, maybe he can use it to light fires under his beef cattle when he throws barbecues out on the Rutherford spread."

"What a good idea! I'll suggest it to him the next time we see him."

"I wouldn't hold my breath," he replied. "He travels a lot these days. I hardly ever see him." He lifted his eyes to hers. "Powell came by last week."

Her heart fluttered, but her face was very composed. "Did he? Why?"

"Heard I was sick and came to check on me. Wanted to know where you were."

Her frozen expression grew darker. "Did he?"

"I told him you didn't know about the bronchitis and that he should mind his own business."

"I see."

He sipped hot chocolate and put the mug down with a thud. "Had his daughter with him. Quiet, sullen little thing. She never moved a muscle the whole time, just sat and glared. She's her mother all over."

Antonia was dying inside. She stared into her hot chocolate. That woman's child, here, in her home! She could hardly bear the thought. It was like a violation to have Powell come here with that child.

"You're upset," he said ruefully. "I guessed you would be, but I thought you'd better know. He said he'd be back to check on me after Christmas. Wouldn't want him to just show up without my telling you he was expected sooner or later. Not that I invited him," he added curtly. "Surprised me, too, that he'd come to see about me. Of course, he was fond of your mother. It hurt him that the scandal upset her so much and caused her to have that first heart attack. Anyway, he's taken it upon himself to be my guardian angel. Even sent the doctor when I first got sick, conspired with Mrs. Harper next door to look after me." He sounded disgusted, but he smiled, too.

"That was nice of him," she said, although Powell's actions surprised her. "But thanks for warning me." She forced a smile to her lips. "I'll arrange to do something in the kitchen if he turns up."

"It's been nine years," he reminded her.

"And you think I should have forgotten." She nodded. "You forgive people, Dad. I used to, before all this. Perhaps I should be more charitable, but I can't be. He and Sally made my life hell." She stopped, dragging in a long breath.

"No other suitors, in all that time," he remarked. "No social life, no dating. Girl, you're going to die an old maid, with no kids of your own, no husband, no real security."

"I enjoy my own company," she said lightly. "And I don't want a child." That was a lie, but only a partial one. The children she had wanted were Powell's, no one else's.

CHRISTMAS DAY PASSED uneventfully, except for the meager gifts she and her father exchanged and their shared memories of her late mother to keep them company.

The next day, she was packed and dressed for travel in a rose knit suit, her hair carefully coiffed, her long legs in hose and low-heeled shoes on her feet. Her burgundy velvet, full-length coat was slung over one arm, its dark lining gleaming in the overhead light, as she put her suitcase down and went to find her father to say goodbye.

Voices from the living room caught her attention and she moved in that direction. But at the doorway, she froze in place, and in time. That deep, gravelly voice was as familiar as her own, despite the many years since she'd last heard it. And then a tall, lean man turned, and cast narrow black eyes on her face. Powell!

She lifted her face slowly, not allowing a hint of emotion to show either in her posture or her eyes. She simply looked at him, reconciling this man in his thirties with the man who'd wanted to marry her. The memories were unfavorable, because he was definitely showing his age, in the new lines beside his mouth and eyes, in the silver that showed at his temples.

He was doing his share of looking, too. The girl he'd jilted was no longer visible in this quiet, conservatively dressed woman with her hair in a bun. She looked schoolmarmish, and he was surprised that the sight of her was still like a knife through the heart, after all these years. He'd been curious about her. He'd wanted to see her again, God knew why. Maybe because she refused to see him at her mother's funeral. Now here she was, and he wasn't sure he was glad. The sight of her touched something sensitive that he'd buried inside himself.

Antonia was the first to look away. The intensity of

his gaze had left her shaking inside, but that reaction was quickly hidden. It would never do to show any weakness to him. "Sorry," she told her father. "I didn't realize you had company. If you'll come and see me off, I'll be on my way."

Her father looked uncomfortable. "Powell came by to see how I was doing."

"You're leaving so soon?" Powell asked, addressing her directly for the first time in so many long years.

"I have to report back to work earlier than the students," she said, pleased that her voice was steady and cool.

"Oh, yes. You teach, don't you?"

She couldn't quite meet his eyes. Her gaze fell somewhere between his aggressive chin and his thin but sensuous mouth, below that straight, arrogant nose and the high cheekbones of his lean face. He wasn't handsome, but five minutes after they met him, most women were enchanted with him. He had an intangible something, authority perhaps, in the sureness of his movements, even in the way he held his head. He was overwhelming.

"I teach," she agreed. Her eyes hadn't quite met his. She turned to her father. "Dad?"

He excused himself and came forward to hug her. "Be careful. Phone when you get there, to let me know that you made it all right, will you? It's been snowing again."

"I'll be fine. I have a phone in the car, if I get stuck."

"You're driving to Arizona, in this weather?" Powell interrupted.

"I've been driving in this weather most of my adult life," she informed him.

"You were terrified of slick roads whcn you were in your teens," he recalled solemnly.

She smiled coldly at him. "I'm not a teenager now."

The way she looked at him spoke volumes about her feelings. He didn't avert his gaze, but his eyes were dark and quiet, full of secrets and seething accusation.

"Sally left a letter for you," he said unexpectedly. "I never got around to posting it. Over the years, I'd forgotten about it."

Her chest rose in a quick, angry breath. It reminded her of the letter that Sally had sent soon after Antonia had left town, the one she'd returned unopened. "Another one?" she asked in a frozen tone. "Well, I want nothing from your late wife, not even a letter."

He bristled. "She was your friend once," he reminded her curtly.

"She was my enemy." She corrected him. "She ruined my reputation and all but killed my mother! Do you really believe I'd want any reminder of what she did?"

He didn't seem to move for a minute. His face hardened. "She did nothing to hurt you deliberately," he said tersely.

"Really? Will her good intentions bring back George Rutherford or my mother?" she demanded hotly, because George himself had died so soon after her mother had. "Will it erase all the gossip?"

He turned away and bent his head to light a cigar, apparently unconcerned. Antonia fought for control. Her hands were icy cold as she picked up her suitcase and winced at her father's worried expression.

"I'll phone you, Dad. Please take care of yourself," she added.

"You're upset," he said distractedly. "Wait a bit…"

"I won't… I can't…" Her voice choked on the words and she averted her eyes from the long back of the man who was turned away from her. "Bye, Dad!"

She was out the door in a flash, and within two minutes

she'd loaded her cases into the trunk and opened the door. But before she could get in, Powell was towering over her.

"Get a grip on yourself," he said curtly, forcing her to look at him. "You won't do your father any favors by landing in a ditch in the middle of nowhere!"

She shivered at the nearness of him and deliberately backed away, her gray eyes wide, accusing.

"You look so fragile," he said, as if the words were torn from him. "Don't you eat?"

"I eat enough." She steadied herself on the door. "Goodbye."

His big hand settled beside hers on the top of the door. "Why was Dawson Rutherford here a couple of nights ago?"

The question was totally unexpected. "Is that your business?" she asked coldly.

He smiled mockingly. "It could be. Rutherford's father ruined mine, or didn't you remember? I don't intend to let his son ruin me."

"My father and George Rutherford were friends."

"And you and George were lovers."

She didn't say a word. She only looked at him. "You know the truth," she said wearily. "You just don't want to believe it."

"George paid your way through college," he reminded her.

"Yes, he did," she agreed, smiling. "And I rewarded him by graduating with honors, second in my graduating class. He was a philanthropist and the best friend my family ever had. I miss him."

"He was a rich old man with designs on you, whether you'll admit it or not!"

She searched his deep-set black eyes. They never smiled. He was a hard man, and the passing years had only added to his sarcastic, harsh demeanor. He'd grown up dirt poor, looked down on in the community because of his parents. He'd struggled to get where he was, and she knew how difficult it had been. But his hard life had warped his perception of people. He looked for the worst, always. She'd known that, somehow, even when they were first engaged. And now, he was the sum of all the tragedies of his life. She'd loved him so much, she'd tried to make up to him for the love he'd never had, the life his circumstances had denied him. But even while he was courting her, he'd loved Sally most. He'd told Antonia so, when he broke their engagement and called her a streetwalker with a price tag...

"You're staring," he said irritably, ramming his hands into the pockets of his dark slacks.

"I was remembering the way you used to be, Powell," she said simply. "You haven't changed. You're still the loner who never trusted anyone, who always expected people to do their worst."

"I believed in you," he replied solemnly.

She smiled. "No, you didn't. If you had, you wouldn't have swallowed Sally's lies without—"

"Damn you!"

He had her by both shoulders, his cigar suddenly lying in the snow at their feet. He practically shook her, and she winced, because she was willow thin and he had the grip of a horseman, developed after long years of back-breaking ranch work long before he ever made any money at it.

She looked up into blazing eyes and wondered dimly why she wasn't afraid of him. He looked intimidating with his black eyes flashing and his straight black hair falling down over his thick eyebrows.

"Sally didn't lie!" he reiterated. "That's the hell of it, Antonia! She was gentle and kind and she never lied to me. She cried when you had to leave town over what happened. She cried for weeks and weeks, because she hadn't wanted to tell me what she knew about you and George! She couldn't bear to see you two-timing me!"

She pulled away from him with a strength she didn't know she had. "She deserved to cry!" she said through her teeth.

He called her a name that made her flush. She only smiled.

"Sticks and stones, Powell," she said in a steady, if husky, tone. "But if you say that again, you'll get the same thing I gave you the summer after I started college."

He remembered very well the feel of her shoe on his shin. Even through his anger, he had to stifle a mental smile at the memory. Antonia had always had spirit. But he remembered other things, too; like her refusal to talk to him after her mother's death, when he'd offered help. Sally had been long dead by then, but Antonia wouldn't let him close enough to see if she still felt anything for him. She wouldn't even now, and it caused him to lose his temper when he'd never meant to. She wouldn't let go of the past. She wouldn't give him a chance to find out if there was anything left of what they'd felt for each other. She didn't care.

The knowledge infuriated him.

"Now, if you're quite through insulting me, I have to go home," she added firmly.

"I could have helped, when your mother died," he said curtly. "You wouldn't even see me!"

He sounded as if her refusal to speak to him had hurt. What a joke that would be. She didn't look at him again. "I had nothing to say to you, and Dad and I didn't want your help. One way or another, you had enough help from us to build your fortune."

He scowled. "What the hell do you mean by that?"

She did look up then, with a mocking little smile. "Have you forgotten already? Now if you'll excuse me…?"

He didn't move. His big fists clenched by his sides as she just walked around him to get into the car.

She started it, put it into Reverse, and pointedly didn't look at him again, not even when she was driving off down the street toward the main highway. And if her hands shook, he couldn't see them.

HE STOOD WATCHING, his boots absorbing the freezing cold of the snow around them, snowflakes touching the wide brim of his creamy Stetson. He had no idea what she'd meant with that last crack. It made him furious that he couldn't even get her to talk to him. Nine years. He'd smoldered for nine years with seething outrage and anger, and he couldn't get the chance to air it. He wanted a knock-down, drag-out argument with her, he wanted to get everything in the open. He wanted…second chances.

"Do you want some hot chocolate?" Ben Hayes called from the front door.

Powell didn't answer him for a minute. "No," he said in a subdued tone. "Thanks, but I'll pass."

Ben pulled his housecoat closer around him. "You can damn her until you die," he remarked quietly. "But it won't change one thing."

Powell turned and faced him with an expression that wasn't easily read. "Sally didn't lie," he said stubbornly. "I don't care what anyone says about it. Innocent people don't run, and they both did!"

Ben studied the tormented eyes in that lean face for a long moment. "You have to keep believing that, don't you?" he asked coldly. "Because if you don't, you've got nothing at all to show for the past nine years. The hatred you've saved up for Antonia is all that's left of your life!"

Powell didn't say another word. He strode angrily back to his four-wheel-drive vehicle and climbed in under the wheel.

CHAPTER THREE

ANTONIA MADE IT back to Tucson without a hitch, although there had been one or two places along the snow-covered roads that gave her real problems. She was shaken, but it never affected her driving. Powell Long had destroyed enough of her life. She wasn't going to give him possession of one more minute of it, not even through hatred.

She kept busy for the remainder of her vacation and spent New Year's Eve by herself, with only a brief telephone call to her father for company. They didn't mention Powell.

Barrie stopped by on New Year's Day, wearing jeans and a sweatshirt and trying not to look interested in Dawson's visit to Antonia's father's house. It was always the same, though. Whenever Antonia went to Wyoming, Barrie would wait patiently until her friend said something about Dawson. Then she pretended that she wasn't interested and changed the subject.

But this time, she didn't. She searched Antonia's eyes. "Does he…look well?" she asked.

"He's fine," Antonia replied honestly. "He's quit smoking, so that's good news."

"Did he mention the widow?"

Antonia smiled sympathetically and shook her head. "He doesn't have much to do with women, Barrie. In fact, Dad says they call him 'the iceman' around Bighorn. They're still looking for a woman who can thaw him out."

"Dawson?" Barrie burst out. "But he's always had women hanging on him…!"

"Not these days. Apparently all he's interested in is making money."

Barrie looked shocked. "Since when?"

"I don't know. For the past few years at least," Antonia replied, frowning. "He's your stepbrother. You'd know more about that than I would. Wouldn't you?"

Barrie averted her eyes. "I don't see him. I don't go home."

"Yes, I know, but you must hear about him…"

"Only from you," the other woman said stiffly. "I don't… we don't have any mutual friends."

"Doesn't he ever come to see you?"

Barrie went pale. "He wouldn't." She bit off the words and forced a smile to her face. "We're poison to each other, didn't you know?" She looked at her watch. "I'm going to a dance. Want to come?"

Antonia shook her head. "Not me. I'm too tired. I'll see you back at work."

"Sure. You look worse than you did when you left. Did you see Powell?"

Antonia flinched.

"Sorry," came the instant reply. "Listen, don't tell me anything about Dawson even if I beg, and I swear I won't mention Powell again, okay? I'm really sorry. I suppose we both have wounds too raw to expose. See you!"

Barrie left, and Antonia quickly found something to do, so that she wouldn't have to think any more about Powell.

But, oh, it was hard. He'd literally jilted her the day before the wedding. The invitations had been sent out, the church booked, the minister ready to officiate at the ceremony. Antonia had a dress from Neiman Marcus, a heavenly creation that George had helped her buy—which had become part of the fiasco when she admitted it to Powell. And then, out of the blue, Sally had dropped her bombshell. She'd told Powell that George Rutherford was Antonia's sugar daddy and he was paying for her body. Everyone in Bighorn knew it. They probably did, Sally had worked hard enough spreading the rumor. The gossip alone was enough to send Powell crazy. He'd turned on Antonia in a rage and canceled the wedding. She didn't like remembering the things he'd said to her.

Some of the guests didn't get notified in time and came to the church, expecting a wedding. Antonia had had to face them and tell them the sad news. She had been publicly humiliated, and then there was the scandal that involved poor George. He'd had to move back to Sheridan, to the headquarters ranch of the Rutherford chain. It had been a shame, because the Rutherford Bighorn Ranch had been his favorite. He'd escaped a lot of the censure and spared Antonia some of it, especially when he exiled himself to France. But Antonia and her father and mother got the whole measure of local outrage. Denial did no good, because how could she defend herself against knowing glances and haughty treatment? The gossip had hurt her mother most, leaving her virtually isolated from most of the people who knew her. She'd had a mild heart attack from the treatment of her only child as a social outcast. Ironically that had seemed to bring some people to their senses, and the pressure had been eased a bit. But Antonia had left town very quickly, to spare her mother any more torment, taking her broken heart with her.

Perhaps if Powell had thought it through, if the wedding hadn't been so near, the ending might have been different. He'd always been quick-tempered and impulsive.

He hated being talked about. Antonia knew that at least three people had talked to him about the rumors, and one of them was the very minister who was to marry them. Later, Antonia had discovered that they were all friends of Sally and her family.

To be fair to Powell, he'd had more than his share of public scandal. His father had been a hopeless gambler who lost everything his mother slaved at housekeeping jobs to provide. In the end he'd killed himself when he incurred a debt he knew he'd never be able to repay. Powell had watched his mother be torn apart by the gossip, and eventually her heart wore out and she simply didn't wake up one morning.

Antonia had comforted Powell. She'd gone to the funeral home with him and held his hand all through the ordeal of giving up the mother he'd loved. Perhaps grief had challenged his reason, because although he'd hidden it well, the loss had destroyed something in him. He'd never quite recovered from it, and Sally had been behind the scenes, offering even more comfort when Antonia wasn't around. Susceptible to her soft voice, perhaps he'd listened when he shouldn't have. But in the end, he'd believed Sally, and he'd married her. He'd never said he loved Antonia, and it had been just after they'd become engaged that Powell had managed several loans, on the strength of her father's excellent references, to get the property he'd inherited out of hock. He was just beginning to make it pay when he'd called off the wedding.

The pain was like a knife. She'd loved Powell more than her own life. She'd been devastated by his defection. The only consolation she'd had was that she'd put him off physically until after the wedding. Perhaps that had hurt him most, thinking that she was sleeping with poor old George when she wouldn't go to bed with him. Who knew? She couldn't go back and do things differently. She could only go forward. But the future looked much more bleak than the past.

SHE WENT BACK to work in the new year, apparently rested and unworried. But the doctor's appointment was still looming at the end of her first week after she started teaching.

She didn't expect them to find anything. She was rundown and tired all the time, and she'd lost a lot of weight. Probably she needed vitamins or iron tablets or something. When the doctor ordered a blood test, a complete blood count, she went along to the lab and sat patiently while they worked her in and took blood for testing. Then she went home with no particular intuition about what was about to happen.

It was early Monday morning when she had a call at work from the doctor's office. They asked her to come in immediately.

She was too frightened to ask why. She left her class to the sympathetic vice principal and went right over to Dr. Claridge's office.

They didn't make her wait, either. She was hustled right in, no appointment, no nothing.

He got up when she entered his office and shook hands. "Sit down, Antonia. I've got the lab results from your blood test. We have to make some quick decisions."

"Quick...?" Her heart was beating wildly. She could barely breathe. She was aware of her cold hands gripping her purse like a life raft. "What sort of decisions?"

He leaned forward, his forearms on his legs. "Antonia, we've known each other for several years. This isn't an easy thing to tell someone." He grimaced. "My dear, you've got leukemia."

She stared at him without comprehension. Leukemia. Wasn't that cancer? Wasn't it…fatal?

Her breath suspended in midair. "I'm…going to die?" she asked in a hoarse whisper.

"No," he replied. "Your condition is treatable. You can undergo a program of chemotherapy and radiation, which will probably keep it in remission for some years."

Remission. Probably. Radiation. Chemotherapy. Her aunt had died of cancer when Antonia was a little girl. She remembered with terror the therapy's effects on her aunt. Headaches, nausea…

She stood up. "I can't think."

Dr. Claridge stood up, too. He took her hands in his. "Antonia, it isn't necessarily a death sentence. We can start treatment right away. We can buy time for you."

She swallowed, closing her eyes. She'd been worried about her argument with Powell, about the anguish of the past, about Sally's cruelty and her own torment. And now she was going to die, and what did any of that matter?

She was going to die!

"I want…to think about it," she said huskily.

"Of course you do. But don't take too long, Antonia," he said gently. "All right?"

She managed to nod. She thanked him, followed the nurse out to reception, paid her bill, smiled at the girl and walked out. She didn't remember doing any of it. She drove back to her apartment, closed the door and collapsed right there on the floor in tears.

Leukemia. She had a deadly disease. She'd expected a future, and now, instead, there was going to be an ending. There would be no more Christmases with her father. She wouldn't marry and have children. It was all…over.

When the first of the shock passed, and she'd exhausted

herself crying, she got up and made herself a cup of coffee. It was a mundane, ordinary thing to do. But now, even such a simple act had a poignancy. How many more cups would she have time to drink in what was left of her life?

She smiled at her own self-pity. That wasn't going to do her any good. She had to decide what to do. Did she want to prolong the agony, as her aunt had, until every penny of her medical insurance ran out, until she bankrupted herself and her father, put herself and him through the long drawn-out treatments when she might still lose the battle? What quality of life would she have if she suffered as her aunt had?

She had to think not what was best for her, but what was best for her father. She wasn't going to rush into treatment until she was certain that she had a chance of surviving. If she was only going to be able to keep it at bay for a few painful months, then she had some difficult decisions to make. If only she could think clearly! She was too shocked to be rational. She needed time. She needed peace.

Suddenly, she wanted to go home. She wanted to be with her father, at her home. She'd spent her life running away. Now, when things were so dire, it was time to face the past, to reconcile herself with it, and with the community that had unjustly judged her. There would be time left for that, to tie up all the loose ends, to come to grips with her own past.

Her old family doctor, Dr. Harris, was still in Bighorn. She'd get Dr. Claridge to send him her medical files and she'd go from there. Perhaps Dr. Harris might have some different ideas about how she could face the ordeal. If nothing could be done, then at least she could spend her remaining time with the only family she had left.

Once the decision was made, she acted on it at once.

She turned in her resignation and told Barrie that her father needed her at home.

"You didn't say that when you first came back," Barrie said suspiciously.

"Because I was thinking about it," she lied. She smiled. "Barrie, he's so alone. And it's time I went back and faced my dragons. I've been running too long already."

"But what will you do?" Barrie asked.

"I'll get a job as a relief teacher. Dad said that two of the elementary school teachers were expecting and they didn't know what they'd do for replacements. Bighorn isn't exactly Tucson, you know. It's not that easy to get teachers who are willing to live at the end of the world."

Barrie sighed. "You really have thought this out."

"Yes. I'll miss you. But maybe you'll come back one day," she added. "And fight your own dragons."

Barrie shivered. "Mine are too big to fight," she said with an enigmatic smile. "But I'll root for you. What can I help you do?"

"Pack," came the immediate reply.

As FATE WOULD have it, when she contacted her old school system in Bighorn, one of the pregnant teachers had just had to go into the hospital with toxemia and they needed a replacement desperately for a fourth-grade class. It was just what Antonia wanted, and she accepted gratefully. Best of all, there had been no discussion of the reason she'd left town in the first place. Some people would remember, but she had old friends there, too, friends who wouldn't hold grudges. Powell would be there. She refused to even entertain the idea that he had any place in her reasons for wanting to go home.

She arrived in Bighorn with mixed emotions. It made

her feel wonderful to see her father's delighted expression when he was told she was coming back there to live permanently. But she felt guilty, too, because he couldn't know the real reason for her return.

"We'll have plenty of time to visit, now," she said. "Arizona was too hot to suit me, anyway," she added mischievously.

"Well, if you like snow, you've certainly come home at a good time," he replied, grinning at the five feet or so that lay in drifts in the front yard.

ANTONIA SPENT THE weekend unpacking and then went along to work the following Monday. She liked the principal, a young woman with very innovative ideas about education. She remembered two of her fellow teachers, who had been classmates of hers in high school, and neither of them seemed to have any misgivings about her return.

She liked her class, too. She spent the first day getting to know the children's names. But one of them hit her right in the heart. Maggie Long. It could have been a coincidence. But when she called the girl's name and a sullen face with blue eyes and short black hair looked up at her, she knew right away who it was. That was Sally's face, except for the glare. The glare was Powell all over again.

She lifted her chin and stared at the child. She passed over her and went on down the line until she reached Julie Ames. She smiled at Julie, who smiled back sweetly. She remembered Danny Ames from school, too, and his redheaded daughter was just like him. She'd have known Danny's little girl anywhere.

She pulled out her predecessor's lesson plan and looked over it before she took the spelling book and began making assignments.

"One other thing I'd like you to do for Friday is write a one-page essay about yourselves," she added with a smile. "So that I can learn something about you, since I've come in the middle of the year instead of the first."

Julie raised her hand. "Miss Hayes, Mrs. Donalds always assigned one of us to be class monitor when she was out of the room. Whoever she picked got to do it for a week, and then someone else did. Are you going to do that, too?"

"I think that's a good idea, Julie. You can be our monitor for this week," she added pleasantly.

"Thanks, Miss Hayes!" Julie said enthusiastically.

Behind her, Maggie Long glared even more. The child acted as if she hated Antonia, and for a minute, Antonia wondered if she knew about the past. But, then, how could she? She was being fanciful.

She dismissed the class at quitting time. It had been nice to have her mind occupied, not to have to think about herself. But with the end of the day came the terror again. And she still hadn't talked to Dr. Harris.

She made an appointment to see him when she got home, smiling at her father as she told him glibly that it was only because she needed some vitamins.

Dr. Harris, however, was worried when she told him Dr. Claridge's diagnosis.

"You shouldn't wait," he said flatly. "It's always best to catch these things early. Come here, Antonia."

He examined her neck with skilled hands, his eyes on the wall behind her. "Swollen lymph nodes, all right. You've lost weight?" he asked as he took her pulse.

"Yes. I've been working rather hard," she said lamely.

"Sore throat?"

She hesitated and then nodded.

He let out a long sigh. "I'll have him fax me your medical

records," he said. "There's a specialist in Sheridan who's done oncology," he added. "But you should go back to Tucson, Antonia."

"Tell me what to expect," she said instead.

He was reluctant, but when she insisted, he drew in a deep breath and told her.

She sat back in her chair, pale and restless.

"You can fight it," he persisted. "You can hold it at bay."

"For how long?"

"Some people have been in remission for twenty-five years."

She narrowed her eyes as she gazed at him. "But you don't really believe I'll have twenty-five years."

His jaw firmed. "Antonia, medical research is progressing at a good pace. There's always, always, the possibility that a cure will be discovered…"

She held up a hand. "I don't want to have to decide today," she said wearily. "I just need…a little time," she added with a pleading smile. "Just a little time."

He looked as if he were biting his tongue to keep from arguing with her. "All right. A little time," he said emphatically. "I'll look after you. Perhaps when you've considered the options, you'll go ahead with the treatment, and I'll do everything I can. But, Antonia," he added as he stood up to show her out, "there aren't too many miracles in this business where cancer is concerned. If you're going to fight, don't wait too long."

"I won't."

She shook hands and left the office. She felt more at peace with herself now than she could ever remember feeling. Somehow in the course of accepting the diagnosis, she'd accepted something much more. She was stronger now. She could face whatever she had to. She was so glad she'd come home. Fate had dealt her some severe blows, but being home helped her to withstand the worst of them. She had to believe that fate would be kinder to her now that she was home.

BUT IF FATE had kind reasons for bringing her back to Bighorn, Maggie Long wasn't one of them. The girl was unruly, troublesome and refused to do her schoolwork at all.

By the end of the week, Antonia kept her after class and showed her the zero she'd earned for her nonattempt at the spelling test. There was another one looming, because Maggie hadn't done one word of the essay Antonia had assigned the class to write.

"If you want to repeat the fourth grade, Maggie, this is a good start," she said coolly. "If you won't do your schoolwork, you won't pass."

"Mrs. Donalds wasn't mean like you," the girl said snappily. "She never made us write stupid essays, and if there was a test, she always helped me study for it."

"I have thirty-five students in this class," Antonia heard herself saying. "Presumably you were placed in this grade because you were capable of doing the work."

"I could do it if I wanted to," Maggie said. "I just don't want to. And you can't make me, either!"

"I can fail you," came the terse, uncompromising reply. "And I will, if you keep this up. You have one last chance to escape a second zero for the essay you haven't done. You can do it over the weekend and turn it in Monday."

"My daddy's coming home today," she said haughtily. "I'm going to tell him that you're mean to me, and he'll come and cuss you out, you just wait and see!"

"What will he see, Maggie?" she asked flatly. "What does it say about you if you won't do your work?"

"I'm not lazy!"

"Then do your assignment."

"Julie didn't do all of her test, and you didn't give her a zero!"

"Julie doesn't work as fast as some of the other students. I take that into account," Antonia explained.

"You like Julie," she accused. "That's why you never act mean to her! I'll bet you wouldn't give her a zero if she didn't do her homework!"

"This has nothing to do with your ability to do your work," Antonia interrupted. "And I'm not going to argue with you. Either do your homework or don't do it. Now run along."

Maggie gave her a furious glare. She jerked up her books and stomped out of the room, turning at the door. "You wait until I tell my daddy! He'll get you fired!"

Antonia lifted an eyebrow. "It will take more than your father to do that, Maggie."

The girl jerked open the door. "I hate you! I wish you'd never come here!" she yelled.

She ran down the hallway and Antonia sat back and caught her breath. The child was a holy terror. She was a little surprised that she was so unlike her mother in that one way. Sally, for all her lying, had been sweet in the fourth grade, an amiable child, not a horror like Maggie.

Sally. The name hurt. Just the name. Antonia had come home to exorcise her ghosts and she wasn't doing a very good job of it. Maggie was making her life miserable. Perhaps Powell would interfere, at least enough to get his daughter to do her homework. She hated that it had come to this, but she hadn't anticipated the emotions Maggie's presence in her class had unleashed. She was sorry that she couldn't like the child. She wondered if anyone did. She seemed little more than a sullen, resentful brat.

Powell probably adored the child and gave her everything she wanted. But she did ride the bus to and from school and more often than not, she showed up for class in torn jeans and stained sweatshirts. Was that deliberate, and didn't her father notice that some of her things weren't clean? Surely he had a housekeeper or someone to take care of such things.

She knew that Maggie had been staying with Julie this week, because Julie had told her so. The little redheaded Ames girl was the sweetest child Antonia had ever known, and she adored her. She really was the image of her father, who'd been in Antonia's group of friends in school here in Bighorn. She'd told Julie that, and the child had been a minor celebrity for a day. It gave her something to be proud of, that her father and her teacher had been friends.

Maggie hadn't liked that. She'd given Julie the cold shoulder yesterday and they weren't speaking today. Antonia wondered at their friendship, because Julie was outgoing and generous, compassionate and kind…all the things Maggie wasn't. Probably the child saw qualities in Julie that she didn't have and liked her for them. But what in the world did Julie see in Maggie?

CHAPTER FOUR

POWELL LONG CAME home from his cattle-buying trip worn out from the long hours on the plane and the hectic pace of visiting three ranches in three states in less than a week. He could have purchased his stud cattle after watching a video, and he sometimes did if he knew the seller, but he was looking over new territory for his stock additions, and he wanted to inspect the cattle in person before he made the acquisition. It was a good thing he had, because one of the ranches had forwarded a video that must have been of someone else's cattle. When he toured the ranch, he found the stock were underfed, and some were lacking even the basic requirements for good breeding bulls.

Still, it had been a profitable trip. He'd saved several thousand dollars on seed bulls simply by going to visit the ranchers in person. Now he was home again and he didn't want to be. His house, like his life, was full of painful memories. Here was where Sally had lived, where her daughter still lived. He couldn't look at Maggie without seeing her mother. He bought the child expensive toys, whatever her heart desired. But he couldn't give her love. He didn't think he had it in him to love the product of such a painful marriage. Sally had cost him the thing he'd loved most in all the world. She'd cost him Antonia.

Maggie was sitting alone in the living room with a book.

She looked up when he entered the room with eyes that avoided his almost at once.

"Did you bring me something?" she asked dully. He always did. It was just one more way of making her feel that she was important to him, but she knew better. He didn't even know what she liked, or he wouldn't bring her silly stuffed toys and dolls. She liked to read, but he hadn't noticed. She also liked nature films and natural history. He never brought her those sort of things. He didn't even know who she was.

"I brought you a new Barbie," he said. "It's in my suitcase."

"Thanks," she said.

Never a smile. Never laughter. She was a little old woman in a child's body, and looking at her made him feel guilty.

"Where's Mrs. Bates?" he asked uncomfortably.

"In the kitchen cooking," she said.

"How's school?"

She closed the book. "We got a new teacher last week. She doesn't like me," she said. "She's mean to me."

His eyebrows lifted. "Why?"

She shrugged, her thin shoulders rising and falling restlessly. "I don't know. She likes everybody else. She glares at me all the time. She gave me a zero on my test, and she's going to give me another zero on my homework. She says I'm going to fail fourth grade."

He was shocked. Maggie had always made good grades. One thing she did seem to have was a keen intelligence, even if her perpetual frown and introverted nature made her enemies. She had no close friends, except for Julie. He'd left Maggie with Julie's family, in fact, last week. They were always willing to keep while he was out of town.

He glowered at her. "Why are you here instead of at Julie's house?" he demanded suddenly.

"I told them you were coming home and I wanted to be here, because you always bring me something," she said.

"Oh."

She didn't add that Julie's friendship with the detestable Miss Hayes had caused friction, or that they'd had a terrible argument just this morning, precipitating Maggie's return home. Fortunately Mrs. Bates was working in the house, so that it was possible for her to be here.

"The new teacher likes Julie," she said sullenly. "But she hates me. She says I'm lazy and stupid."

"She says what?"

That was the first time her father had ever reacted in such a way, as if it really mattered to him that someone didn't like her. She looked at him fully, seeing that angry flash of his black eyes that always meant trouble for somebody. Her father intimidated her. But, then, he intimidated everyone. He didn't like most people any more than she did. He was introverted himself, and he had a bad temper and a sarcastic manner when people irritated him. Over the years Maggie had discovered that she could threaten people with her father, and it always worked.

Locally he was a legend. Most of her teachers had bent over backward to avoid confrontations with him. Maggie learned quickly that she didn't have to study very hard to make good grades. Not that she wasn't bright; she simply didn't try, because she didn't need to. She smiled. Wouldn't it be nice, she thought, if she could use him against Miss Hayes?

"She says I'm lazy and stupid," she repeated.

"What's this teacher's name?" he asked coldly.

"Miss Hayes."

He was very still. "Antonia Hayes?" he asked curtly.

"I don't know her first name. She came on account of

Mrs. Donalds quit," she said. "Mrs. Donalds was my friend. I miss her."

"When did Miss Hayes get here?" he asked, surprised that he'd heard nothing about her returning to Bighorn. Of course, he'd been out of town for a week, too.

"I told you—last week. They said she used to live here." She studied his hard face. It looked dangerous. "Did she, Daddy?"

"Yes," he said with icy contempt. "Yes, she used to live here. Well, we'll see how Miss Hayes handles herself with another adult," he added.

He went to the telephone and picked it up and dialed the principal of the Bighorn Elementary School.

Mrs. Jameson was surprised to hear Powell Long on the other end of the phone. She'd never known him to interfere in school matters before, even when Maggie was up to her teeth in trouble with another student.

"I want to know why you permit an educator to tell a child that she's lazy and stupid," he demanded.

There was a long pause. "I beg your pardon?" the principal asked, shocked.

"Maggie said that Miss Hayes told her she was lazy and stupid," he said shortly. "I want that teacher talked to, and talked to hard. I don't want to have to come up there myself. Is that clear?"

Mrs. Jameson knew Powell Long. She was intimidated enough to agree that she'd speak to Antonia on Monday.

And she did. Reluctantly.

"I HAD A call from Maggie Long's father Friday afternoon after you left," Mrs. Jameson told Antonia, who was sitting rigidly in front of her in her office. "I don't believe for a minute that you'd deliberately make insulting remarks to that child. Heaven knows, every teacher in this school except Mrs. Donalds has had trouble with her, although Mr. Long has never interfered. It's puzzling that he would intervene, and that Maggie would say such things about you."

"I haven't called her stupid," Antonia said evenly. "I have told her that if she refuses to do her homework and write down the answers on tests, she will be given a failing grade. I've never made a policy of giving undeserved marks, or playing favorites."

"I'm sure you haven't," Mrs. Jameson replied. "Your record in Tucson is spotless. I even spoke to your principal there, who was devastated to have lost you. He speaks very highly of your intelligence and your competence."

"I'm glad. But I don't know what to do about Maggie," she continued. "She doesn't like me. I'm sorry about that, but I don't know what I can do to change her attitude. If she could only be helpful like her friend Julie," she added. "Julie is a first-rate little student."

"Everyone loves Julie," the principal agreed. She folded her hands on her desk. "I have to ask you this, Antonia. Is it possible that unconsciously you might be taking out old hurts on Maggie? I know that you were engaged to her father once... It's a small town," she added apologetically when Antonia stiffened, "and one does hear gossip. I also know that Maggie's mother broke you up and spread some pretty terrible lies about you in the community."

"There are people who still don't think they were lies," Antonia replied tersely. "My mother eventually died because of the pressure and censure the community put on her because of them."

"I'm sorry. I didn't know that."

"She had a bad heart. I left town, to keep the talk to a minimum, but she never got over it." Her head lifted, and she forced a weak smile. "I was innocent of everything I had been accused of, but I paid the price anyway."

Mrs. Jameson looked torn. "I shouldn't have brought it up."

"Yes, you should," Antonia replied. "You had the right to know if I was deliberately persecuting a student. I despised Sally for what she did to me, and I have no more love for Maggie's father than for his late wife. But I hope I'm not such a bad person that I'd try to make a child suffer for something she didn't do."

"Nor do I believe you would, consciously," Mrs. Jameson replied. "It's a touchy situation, though. Mr. Long has enormous influence in the community. He's quite wealthy and his temper is legendary in these parts. He has no compunction about making scenes in public, and he threatened to come up here himself if this situation isn't resolved." She laughed a little unsteadily. "Miss Hayes, I'm forty-five years old. I've worked hard all my life to achieve my present status. It would be very difficult for me to find another job if I lost this one, and I have an invalid husband to support and a son in college. I plead with you not to put my job in jeopardy."

"I never would do that," Antonia promised. "I'd quit before I'd see an innocent person hurt by my actions. But Mr. Long is very wrong about the way his daughter is being treated. In fact, she's causing the problems. She refuses to do her work and she knows that I can't force her to."

"She certainly does. She'll go to her father, and he'll light fires under members of the school board. I believe at least one of them owes him money, in fact, and the other three are afraid of him." She cleared her throat. "I'll tell you flat that I'm afraid of him, myself."

"No freedom of speech in these parts, I gather?"

"If your freedom impinges on his prejudices, no, there isn't," Mrs. Jameson agreed. "He's something of a tyrant in his way. We certainly can't fault him for being concerned about his child, though."

"No," Antonia agreed. She sighed. Her own circumstances were tenuous, to say the least. She had her own problems and fear gnawed at her all the time. She wasn't afraid of Powell Long, though. She was more afraid of what lay ahead for her.

"You will try...about Maggie?" Mrs. Jameson added.

Antonia smiled. "Certainly I will. But may I come to you if the problem doesn't resolve itself and ask for help?"

"If there's any to give, you may." She grimaced. "I have my own doubts about Maggie's cooperation. And we both have a lot to lose if her father isn't happy."

"Do you want me to pass her anyway?" Antonia asked. "To give her grades she hasn't earned, because her father might be upset if she fails?"

Mrs. Jameson flushed. "I can't tell you to do that, Miss Hayes. We're supposed to educate children, not pass them through favoritism."

"I know that," Antonia said.

"But you wondered if I did," came the dry reply. "Yes, I do. But I'm job scared. When you're my age, Miss Hayes," she added gently, "I can guarantee that you will be, too."

Antonia's eyes were steady and sad. She knew that she might never have the problem; she might not live long enough to have it. She thanked Mrs. Jameson and went back to her classroom, morose and dejected.

MAGGIE WATCHED HER as she sat down at her desk and instructed the class to proceed with their English lesson. She didn't look very happy. Her father must have shaken them up, Maggie thought victoriously. Well, she wasn't going to do that homework or do those tests. And when she failed, her father would come storming up here, because he never doubted his little girl's word. He'd have Miss Hayes on the run in no time. Then maybe Mrs. Donalds would have her baby and come back, and everything would be all right again. She glared at Julie, who just ignored her. She was sick of Julie, kissing up to Miss Hayes. Julie was a real sap. Maggie wasn't sure who she disliked more—Julie or Miss Hayes.

There was one nice touch, and that was that Miss Hayes coolly told her that she had until Friday to turn in her essay and the other homework that Antonia had assigned the class.

THE NEXT FOUR days went by, and Antonia asked for homework papers to be turned in that she'd assigned at the beginning of the week. Maggie didn't turn hers in.

"You'll get a zero if you don't have all of it by this afternoon, including the essay you owe me," Antonia told her, dreading the confrontation she knew was coming, despite all her hopes. She'd done her best to treat Maggie just like the other students, but the girl challenged her at every turn.

"No, I won't," Maggie said with a surly smile. "If you give me a zero, I'll tell my daddy, and he'll come up here."

Antonia studied the sullen little face. "And you think that frightens me?"

"Everybody's scared of my dad," she returned proudly.

"Well, I'm not," Antonia said coldly. "Your father can come up here if he likes and I'll tell him the same thing

I've told you. If you don't do the work, you don't pass. And there's nothing he can do about it."

"Oh, really?"

Antonia nodded. "Oh, really. And if you don't turn in your homework by the time the final bell sounds, you'll find out."

"So will you," Maggie replied.

Antonia refused to argue with the child. But when the end of class came and Maggie didn't turn the homework in, she put a zero neatly next to the child's name.

"Take this paper home, please," she told the child, handing her a note with her grade on it.

Maggie took it. She smiled. And she didn't say a word as she went out the door. Miss Hayes didn't know that her daddy was picking her up today. But she was about to find out.

ANTONIA HAD CHORES to finish before she could go home. She didn't doubt that Powell would be along. But she wasn't going to back down. She had nothing to lose now. Even her job wasn't that important if it meant being blackmailed by a nine-year-old.

Sure enough, it was only minutes since class was dismissed and she was clearing her desk when she heard footsteps coming down the hall. Only a handful of teachers would still be in the building, but those particular steps were heavy and forceful, and she knew who they belonged to.

She turned as the door opened and a familiar tall figure came into the room with eyes as dark as death.

He didn't remove his hat, or exchange greetings. In his expensive suit and boots and Stetson, he looked very prosperous. But her eyes were seeing a younger man, a ragged and lonely young man who never fit in anywhere, who dreamed of not being poor. Sometimes she remembered that young man and loved him with a passion that even in dreams was overpowering.

"I've been expecting you," she said, putting the past away in the back drawers of her mind. "She did get a zero, and she deserved it. I gave her all week to produce her homework, and she didn't."

"Oh, hell, you don't have to pretend noble motives. I know why you're picking on the kid. Well, lay off Maggie," he said shortly. "You're here to teach, not to take out old grudges on my daughter."

She was sitting at her desk. She folded her hands together on its worn surface and simply stared at him, unblinking. "Your daughter is going to fail this grade," she said composedly. "She won't participate in class discussions, she won't do any homework, and she refuses to even attempt answers on pop tests. I'm frankly amazed that she's managed to get this far in school at all." She smiled coldly. "I understand from the principal, who is also intimidated by you, that you have the influence to get anyone fired who doesn't pass her."

His face went rigid. "I don't need to use any influence! She's a smart child."

She opened her desk drawer, took out Maggie's last test paper and slid it across the desk to him. "Really?" she asked.

He moved into the classroom, to the desk. His lean, dark hand shot down to retrieve the paper. He looked at it with narrow, deep-set eyes, black eyes that were suddenly piercing on Antonia's face.

"She didn't write anything on this," he said.

She nodded, taking it back. "She sat with her arms

folded, giving me a haughty smile the whole time, and she didn't move a muscle for the full thirty minutes."

"She hasn't acted that way before."

"I wouldn't know. I'm new here."

He stared at her angrily. "And you don't like her."

She searched his cold eyes. "You really think I came all the way back to Wyoming to take out old resentments on Sally's daughter?" she asked, and hated the guilt she felt when she asked the question. She knew she wasn't being fair to Maggie, but the very sight of the child was like torture.

"Sally's and mine," he reminded her, as if he knew how it hurt her to remember.

She felt sick to her stomach. "Excuse me. Sally's and yours," she replied obligingly.

He nodded slowly. "Yes, that's what really bothers you, isn't it?" he said, almost to himself. "It's because she looks just like Sally."

"She's her image," she agreed flatly.

"And you still hate her, after all this time."

Her hands clenched together. She didn't drop her gaze. "We were talking about your daughter."

"Maggie."

"Yes."

"You can't even bring yourself to say her name, can you?" He perched himself on the edge of her desk. "I thought teachers were supposed to be impartial, to teach regardless of personal feelings toward their students."

"We are."

"You aren't doing it," he continued. He smiled, but it wasn't the sort of smile that comforted. "Let me tell you something, Antonia. You came home. But this is my town. I own half of it, and I know everybody on the school board.

If you want to stay here, and teach here, you'd better be damn sure that you maintain an impartial attitude toward all the students."

"Especially toward your daughter?" she asked.

He nodded. "I see you understand."

"I won't treat her unfairly, but I won't play favorites, either," she said icily. "She's going to receive no grades that she doesn't earn in my classroom. If you want to get me fired, go ahead."

"Oh, hell, I don't want your job," he said abruptly. "It doesn't matter to me if you stay here with your father. I don't even care why you suddenly came back. But I won't have my daughter persecuted for something that she didn't do! She has nothing to do with the past."

"Nothing?" Her eyes glittered up into his. "Sally was pregnant with that child when you married her, and she was born seven months later," she said huskily, and the pain was a living, breathing thing. Even the threat of leukemia wasn't that bad. "You were sleeping with Sally while you were swearing eternal devotion to me!"

Antonia didn't have to be a math major to arrive at the difference. He'd married Sally less than a month after he broke up with Antonia, and Maggie was born seven months later. Which meant that Sally was pregnant when they married.

He took a slow, steady breath, but his eyes, his face, were terrible to see. He stared down at her as if he'd like to throw something.

Antonia averted her gaze to the desk, where her hands were so tightly clasped now that the knuckles were white. She relaxed them, so that he wouldn't notice how tense she was.

"I shouldn't have said that," she said after a minute. "I

had no right. Your marriage was your own business, and so is your daughter. I won't be unkind to her. But I will expect her to do the same work I assign to the other students, and if she doesn't, she'll be graded accordingly."

He stood up and shoved his hands into his pockets. The eyes that met hers were unreadable. "Maggie's paid a higher price than you know already," he said enigmatically. "I won't let you hurt her."

"I'm not in the habit of taking out my personal feelings on children, whatever you think of me."

"You're twenty-seven now," he said, surprising her. "Yet you're still unmarried. You have no children of your own."

She smiled evenly. "Yes. I had a lucky escape."

"And no inclination to find someone else? Make a life for yourself?"

"I have a life," she said, and the fear came up into her mouth as she realized that she might not have it for much longer.

"Do you?" he asked. "Your father will die one day. Then you'll be alone."

Her eyes, full of fear, fell to the desk again. "I've been alone for a long time," she said quietly. "It's something… one learns to live with."

He didn't speak. After a minute, she heard his voice, as if from a distance. "Why did you come back?"

"For my father."

"He's getting better day by day. He didn't need you."

She looked up, searching his face, seeing the young man she'd loved in his dark eyes, his sensuous mouth. "Maybe I needed someone," she said. She winced and dropped her eyes.

He laughed. It had an odd sound. "Just don't turn your

attention toward me, Antonia. You may need someone. I don't. Least of all you."

Before she could say a word, he'd gone out the door, as quietly as he'd come in.

MAGGIE WAS WAITING at the door when he walked in. He'd taken her home before he had his talk with Antonia.

"Did you see her? Did you tell her off?" she asked excitedly. "I knew you'd show her who's boss!"

His eyes narrowed. She hadn't shown that much enthusiasm for anything in years. "What about that homework?"

She shrugged. "It was stupid stuff. She wanted us to write an essay about ourselves and do math problems and make up sentences to go with spelling words."

He scowled. "You mean, you didn't do it—any of it?"

"You told her I didn't have to, didn't you?" she countered.

He tossed his hat onto the side table in the hall and his eyes flashed at her. "Did you do any of the homework?"

"Well…no," she muttered. "It was stupid, I told you."

"Damn it! You lied!"

She backed up. She didn't like the way he was looking at her. He frightened her when he looked that way. He made her feel guilty. She didn't lie as a rule, but this was different. Miss Hayes was hurting her, so didn't she have the right to hurt back?

"You'll do that homework, do you hear me?" he demanded. "And the next time you have a test, you won't sit through it with your arms folded. Is that clear?"

She compressed her lips. "Yes, Daddy."

"My God." He bit off the words, staring at her furiously. "You're just like your mother, aren't you? Well, this is going to stop right now. No more lies—ever!"

"But, Daddy, I don't lie…!"

He didn't listen. He just turned and walked away. Maggie stared after him with tears burning her eyes, her small fists clenched at her sides. Just like her mother. That's what Mrs. Bates said when she misbehaved. She knew that her father hadn't cared about her mother. Her mother had cried because of it, when she drank so much. She'd said that she told a lie and Powell had hated her for it. Did this mean that he hated Maggie, too?

She followed him out into the hall. "Daddy!" she cried.

"What?"

He turned, glaring at her.

"She doesn't like me!"

"Have you tried cooperating with her?" he replied coldly.

She shrugged, averting her eyes so that he wouldn't see the tears and the pain in them. She was used to hiding her hurts in this cold house. She went up the staircase to her room without saying anything else.

He watched her walk away with a sense of hopelessness. His daughter had used him to get back at her teacher, and he'd let her. He'd gone flaming over to the school and made all sorts of accusations and charges, and Antonia had been the innocent party. He was furious at having been so gullible. It was because he didn't really know the child, he imagined. He spent as little time with her as possible, because she was a walking, talking reminder of his failed marriage.

Next time, he promised himself, he'd get his facts straight before he started attacking teachers. But he wasn't sorry about what he'd said to Antonia. Let her stew on those charges. Maybe it would intimidate her enough that she wouldn't deliberately hurt Maggie. He knew how she felt about Sally, he couldn't help but know. Her resentments were painfully visible in her thin face.

He wondered why she'd come back to haunt him. He'd almost pushed her to the back of his mind over the years. Almost. He'd gone to see her father finally to get news of her, because the loneliness he felt was eating into him like acid. He'd wondered, for one insane moment, if there was any chance that they might recapture the magic they'd had together when she was eighteen.

But she'd quickly disabused him of any such fancies. Her attitude was cold and hard and uncaring. She seemed to have frozen over in the years she'd been away.

How could he blame her? All of Antonia's misfortunes could be laid at his door, because he was distrustful of people, because he'd jumped to conclusions, because he hadn't believed in Antonia's basic innocence and decency. One impulsive decision had cost him everything he held dear. He wondered sometimes how he could have been so stupid.

Like today when he'd let Maggie stampede him into attacking Antonia for something she hadn't done. It was just like old times. Sally's daughter was already a master manipulator, at age nine. And it seemed that he was just as impulsive and dim as he'd ever been. He hadn't really changed at all. He was just richer.

Meanwhile, there was Antonia's reappearance and her disturbing thinness and paleness. She looked unwell. He wondered absently if she'd had some bout with disease. Perhaps that was why she'd come home, and not because of her father at all. But, wouldn't a warm climate be the prescription for most illnesses that caused problems? Surely no doctor sent her into northern Wyoming in winter.

He had no answers for those questions, and it would do

him well to stop asking them, he thought irritably. It was getting him nowhere. The past was dead. He had to let it go, before it destroyed his life all over again.

CHAPTER FIVE

ANTONIA DIDN'T MOVE for a long time after Powell left the classroom. She stared blindly at her clasped hands. Of course she knew that he didn't want her. Had she been unconsciously hoping for something different? And even if she had, she realized, there was no future at all in that sort of thinking.

She got up, cleared her desk, picked up her things and went home. She didn't have time to sit and groan, even silently. She had to use her time wisely. She had a decision to make.

While she cooked supper for her father and herself, she thought about everything she'd wanted to do that she'd never made time for. She hadn't traveled, which had been a very early dream. She hadn't been involved in church or community, she hadn't planned past the next day except to make up lesson plans for her classes. She'd more or less drifted along, assuming that she had forever. And now the line was drawn and she was close to walking across it.

Her deepest regret was losing Powell. Looking back, she wondered what might have happened if she'd challenged Sally, if she'd dared Powell to prove that she'd been two-timing him with her mother's old suitor. She'd only been eighteen, very much in love and trusting and full of dreams. It would have served her better to have been suspicious and hard-hearted, at least where Sally was concerned. She'd never believed that her best friend would stab her in the back. How silly of her not to realize that strongest friends make the best enemies; they always know where the weaknesses are hidden.

Antonia's weakness had been her own certainty that Powell loved her as much as she loved him, that nothing could separate them. She hadn't counted on Sally's ability as an actress.

Powell had never said that he loved Antonia. How strange, she thought, that she hadn't realized that until they'd gone their separate ways. Powell had been ardent, hungry for her, but never out of control. No wonder, she thought bitterly, since he'd obviously been sleeping with Sally the whole time. Why should he have been wild for any women when he was having one on the side?

He'd asked Antonia to marry him. Her parents had been respected in the community, something his own parents hadn't been. He'd enjoyed being connected to Antonia's parents and enjoyed the overflow of their acceptance by local people in the church and community. He'd spent as much time with them as he had with Antonia. And when he talked about building up his little cattle ranch that he'd inherited from his father, it had been her own father who'd advised him and opened doors for him so that he could get loans, financing. On the strength of his father's weakness for gambling, nobody would have loaned Powell the price of a theater ticket. But Antonia's father was a different proposition; he was an honest man with no visible vices.

Antonia had harbored no suspicions that an ambitious man might take advantage of an untried girl in his quest for wealth. Now, from her vantage point of many years, she could look back and see the calculation that had led to Powell's proposal of marriage. He hadn't wanted Antonia with any deathless passion. He'd wanted her father's influence. With it, he'd built a pitiful little fifty-acre ranch into a multimillion-dollar enterprise of purebred cattle and land. Perhaps breaking the engagement was all part of his master plan, too. Once he'd had what he wanted from the engagement, he could marry the woman he really loved—Sally.

It wouldn't have surprised Antonia to discover that Sally had worked hand in glove with Powell to help him achieve his goals. The only odd thing was that he hadn't been happy with Sally, from all accounts, nor she with him.

She wondered why she hadn't considered that angle all those years ago. Probably the heartbreak of her circumstances had blinded her to any deeper motives. Now it seemed futile and unreal. Powell was ancient history. She had to let go of the past. Somehow, she had to forgive and forget. It would be a pity to carry the hatred and resentment to her grave.

Grave. She stared into the pan that contained the stir-fry she was making for supper. She'd never thought about where she wanted to rest for eternity. She had insurance, still in effect, although it wasn't much. And she'd always thought that she'd rest beside her mother in the small Methodist church cemetery. Now she had to get those details finalized, just in case the treatment wasn't successful—if she decided to have it—and without her father knowing. He wasn't going to be told until the last possible minute.

She finished preparing supper and called her father to the table, careful to talk about mundane things and pretend to be happy at being home again.

But he wasn't fooled. His keen eyes probed her face. "Something's upset you. What is it?"

She grimaced. "Maggie Long," she said, sidestepping the real issue.

"I see. Just like her father when he was a kid, I hear," he added. "Little hellion, isn't she?"

"Only to me," Antonia mused. "She liked Mrs. Donalds."

"No wonder," he replied, finishing his coffee. "Mrs. Donalds was one of Sally's younger cousins. So Maggie was related to her. She petted the kid, gave her special favors, did everything but give her answers to tests. She was teacher's pet. First time any teacher treated her that way, so I guess it went to her head."

"How do you know?"

"It's a small town, girl," he reminded her with a chuckle. "I know everything." He stared at her levelly. "Even that Powell came to see you at school this afternoon. Gave you hell about the kid, didn't he?"

She shifted in her chair. "I won't give her special favors," she muttered. "I don't care if he does get me fired."

"He'll have a hard time doing that," her father said easily. "I have friends on the school board, too."

"Perhaps they could switch the girl to another class," she wondered aloud.

"It would cause gossip," Ben Hayes said. "There's been enough of that already. You just stick to your guns and don't give in. She'll come around eventually."

"I wouldn't bet on it," she said heavily. She ran a hand over her blond hair. "I'm tired," she added with a wan smile. "Do you mind if I go to bed early?"

"Of course not." He looked worried. "I thought you went to see the doctor. Didn't he give you something to perk you up?"

"He said I need vitamins," she lied glibly. "I bought some, but they haven't had time to take effect. I need to eat more, too, he said."

He was still scowling. "Well, if you don't start getting

better soon, you'd better go back and let him do some tests. It isn't natural for a woman your age to be so tired all the time."

Her heart skipped. Of course it wasn't, but she didn't want him to suspect that she was so ill.

"I'll do that," she assured him. She got up and collected the plates. "I'll just do these few dishes and then I'll leave you to your television."

"Oh, I hate that stuff," he said. "I'd much rather read in the evenings. I only keep the thing on for the noise."

She laughed. "I do the same thing in Tucson," she confessed. "It's company, anyway."

"Yes, but I'd much rather have you here," he confessed. "I'm glad you came home, Antonia. It's not so lonely now."

She had a twinge of conscience at the pleasure he betrayed. He'd lost her mother and now he was going to lose her. How would he cope, with no relatives left in the world? Her mother had been an only child, and her father's one sister had died of cancer years ago. Antonia bit her lip. He was in danger of losing his only child, and she was too cowardly to tell him.

He patted her on the shoulder. "Don't you do too much in here. Get an early night. Leave those if you want, and I'll wash them later."

"I don't mind," she protested, grinning. "I'll see you in the morning, then."

"Don't wake me up when you leave," he called over his shoulder. "I'm sleeping late."

"Lucky devil," she called back.

He only laughed, leaving her to the dishes.

She finished them and went to bed. But she didn't sleep. She lay awake, seeing Maggie Long's surly expression and hating eyes, and Powell's unwelcoming scrutiny. They'd both love to see her back in Arizona, and it looked as if they were going to do their combined best to make her life hell if she stayed here. She'd be walking on eggshells for the rest of the school year with Maggie, and if she failed the child for not doing her homework, Powell would be standing in her classroom every day to complain.

She rolled over with a sigh. Things had been so uncomplicated when she was eighteen, she thought wistfully. She'd been in love and looking forward to marriage and children. Her eyes closed on a wave of pain. Maggie would have been her child, her daughter. She'd have had blond hair and gray eyes, perhaps, like Antonia. And if she'd been Antonia's child, she'd have been loved and wanted and cared for. She wouldn't have a surly expression and eyes that hated.

Powell had said something about Maggie…what was it? That Maggie had paid a higher price than any of them. What had he meant? Surely he cared for the child. He certainly fought hard enough when he felt she was attacked.

Well, it wasn't her problem, she decided finally. And she wasn't going to let it turn into her problem. She still hadn't decided what to do about her other problem.

JULIE WAS THE brightest spot in Antonia's days. The little girl was always cheerful, helpful, doing whatever she could to smooth Antonia's path and make it easy for her to teach the class. She remembered where Mrs. Donalds had kept things, she knew what material had been covered and she was always eager to do anything she was asked.

Maggie on the other hand was resentful and ice-cold. She did nothing voluntarily. She was still refusing to turn in her homework. Talking to her did no good. She just glared back.

"I'll give you one more chance to make up this work,"

Antonia told her at the end of her second week teaching the class. "If you don't turn it in Monday, you'll get another zero."

Maggie smiled haughtily. "And my daddy will cuss you out again. I'll tell him you slapped me, too."

Antonia's gray eyes glittered at the child. "You would, wouldn't you?" she asked coldly. "I don't doubt that you can lie, Maggie. Well, go ahead. See how much damage you can do."

Maggie's reaction was unexpected. Tears filled her blue eyes and she shivered.

She whirled and ran out of the classroom, leaving Antonia deflated and feeling badly for the child. She clenched her hands on the desk to keep them from shaking. How could she have been so hateful and cold?

She cleaned up the classroom, waiting for Powell to storm in and give her hell. But hc didn't show up. She went home and spent a nerve-rackingly quiet weekend with her father, waiting for an explosion that didn't come.

The biggest surprisc arrived Monday morning, when Maggie shoved a crumpled, stained piece of paper on the desk and walked back to her seat without looking at Antonia. It was messy, but it was the missing homework. Not only that, it was done correctly.

Antonia didn't say a word. It was a small victory, of sorts. She wouldn't admit to herself that she was pleased. But the paper got an A.

JULIE BEGAN TO sit with her at recess, and shared cupcakes and other tidbits that her mother had sent to school with her.

"Mom says you're doing a really nice job on me, Miss Hayes," Julie said. "Dad remembers you from school, did you know? He said you were a sweet girl, and that you were shy. Were you, really?"

Antonia laughed. "I'm afraid so. I remember your father, too. He was the class clown."

"Dad? Really?"

"Really. Don't tell him I told you, though, okay?" she teased, smiling at the child.

From a short distance away, Maggie glared toward them. She was, as usual, alone. She didn't get along with the other children. The girls hated her, and the boys made fun of her skinny legs that were always bruised and cut from her tom-boyish antics at the ranch. There was one special boy, Jake Weldon. Maggie pretended not to notice him. He was one of the boys who made fun of her, and it hurt really bad. She was alone most of the time these days, because Julie spent her time with the teacher instead of Maggie.

Miss Hayes liked Julie. Everyone knew it, too. Julie had been Maggie's best friend, but now she seemed to be Miss Hayes's. Maggie hated both of them. She hadn't told her father what Miss Hayes had said about her homework. She wanted her teacher to know that she wasn't bad like her mother. She knew what her mother had done, because she'd heard them talking about it once. She remembered her mother crying and accusing him of not loving her, and him saying that she'd ruined his life, she and her prema-ture baby. There had been something else, something about him being drunk and out of his mind or Maggie wouldn't have been born at all.

It hadn't made sense then. But when she was older, she'd heard him say the same thing to the housekeeper, that Mag-gie had been born prematurely.

After that, she'd stopped listening. That was when

she knew her father didn't love her. That was when she'd stopped trying to make him notice her by being good.

Her daddy knew Miss Hayes. She heard him tell the housekeeper that Antonia had come to Bighorn to make his life miserable and that he didn't want her here. If she'd been able to talk to Miss Hayes, she'd have told her that her father hated both of them, and that it made them sort of related.

She wondered if her dad hadn't wanted to marry her mother, and why he had. Maybe it had something to do with why her daddy hated her. People had said that Sally didn't love her little child, that Maggie was just the rope she'd used to tie up Powell Long with. Maybe they were right, because her mother never spent any time doing things with her. She never liked Maggie, either.

She slid down against the tree into the dirt, getting her jeans filthy. Mrs. Bates, the housekeeper, would rage and fuss about that, and she didn't care. Mrs. Bates had thrown away most of her clothes, complaining that they were too dirty to come clean. She hadn't told her dad. When she ran out of clothes, maybe somebody would notice.

She wished Mrs. Bates liked her. Julie did, when she wasn't fawning over teachers to make them give her special privileges. She liked Julie, she did, but Julie was a kiss-up. Sometimes she wondered why she let Julie be her friend at all. She didn't need any friends. She could make it all by herself. She'd show them all that she was somebody special. She'd make them love her one day. She sighed and closed her eyes. Oh, if only she knew Julie's secret; if only she knew how to make people like her.

"There's Maggie," Julie commented, grimacing as she glanced toward her friend. "Nobody likes her except me," she confided to Miss Hayes. "She beats up the boys and she can bat and catch better than any of them, so they don't like her. And the girls think she's too rough to play with. I sort of feel sorry for her. She says her daddy doesn't like her. He's always going away somewhere. She stays with us when he's gone, only she doesn't want to this week because—" She stopped, as if she was afraid she'd already said too much.

"Because?" Antonia prompted curiously.

"Oh, nothing," Julie said. She couldn't tell Miss Hayes that she'd fought with Maggie over their new teacher. "Anyway, Maggie mostly stays with us if her dad's away longer than overnight."

Involuntarily, Antonia glanced toward the child and found her watching them with those cold, sullen eyes. The memories came flooding back—Sally jealous of Antonia's pretty face, jealous of Antonia's grades, jealous of Antonia having any other girlfriends, jealous...of her with Powell.

She shivered faintly and looked away from the child. God forgive her, it was just too much. She wondered if she could possibly get Maggie transferred to another class. If she couldn't then there was no other option. The only teaching job available was the one she had. She couldn't wait for another opening. Her eyes closed. She was running out of time. Why, she asked herself, why was she wasting it like this? She'd told herself she was coming home to cope with her memories, but they were too much for her. She couldn't fight the past. She couldn't even manage to get through the present. She had to consider how she would face the future.

"Miss Hayes?"

Her eyes opened. Julie was looking worried. "Are you all right?" the little girl asked, concerned.

"I'm tired, that's all," Antonia said, smiling. "We'd better go in now."

She called the class and led them back into the building.

MAGGIE WAS WORSE than ever for the rest of the day. She talked back, refused to do a chore assigned to her, ignored Antonia when she was called on in class. And at the end of the day, she waited until everyone else left and came back into the room, to stand glaring at Antonia from the doorway.

"My dad says he wishes you'd go away and never come back," she said loudly. "He says you make his life miserable, and that he can't stand the sight of you! He says you make him sick!"

Antonia's face flushed and she looked stunned.

Maggie turned and ran out the door. Her father had said something like that, to himself, and it made her feel much better that she'd told Miss Hayes about it. That had made her look sick, all right! And it wasn't a lie. Well, not a real lie. It was just something to make her feel as bad as Maggie had felt when Miss Hayes looked at her on the playground and shuddered. She knew the teacher didn't like her. She didn't care. She didn't like Miss Hayes, either.

MAGGIE WAS SMUG the next day. She didn't have any more parting shots for Antonia, and she did her work in class. But she refused to do her homework, again, and dared Antonia to give her a zero. She even dared her to send a note home to her father.

Antonia wanted to call her bluff, but she was feeling sicker by the day and it was increasingly hard for her to get up in the mornings and go to work at all. The illness was progressing much more quickly than she'd foreseen. And Maggie was making her life hell.

For the rest of the week, Antonia thought about the possibility of getting Maggie moved out of her class. Surely she could approach the principal in confidence.

And that was what she did, after school.

Mrs. Jameson smiled ruefully when Antonia sat down beside her desk and hesitated.

"You're here about Maggie Long again," she said at once.

Antonia's eyes widened. "Why...yes."

"I was expecting you," the older woman said with resignation. "Mrs. Donalds got along quite well with her, but she's the only teacher in the past few years who hasn't had trouble with Maggie. She's a rebel, you see. Her father travels a good deal. Maggie is left with Julie's family." She grimaced. "We heard that he was thinking of marrying again, but once that rumor started, Maggie ran away from home. She, uh, isn't keen on the widow Holton."

Antonia was wondering if anyone was keen about the widow Holton, from what she'd already heard from Barrie. It was a surprise to hear that Powell had considered marrying the woman—if it was true and not just gossip.

The principal sighed, her attention returning to the task at hand. "You want Maggie moved, I suppose. I wish I could oblige you, but we only have one fourth-grade class, because this is such a small school, and you're teaching it." She lifted her hands helplessly. "There it is. I'm really sorry. Perhaps if you spoke with her father?"

"I already have," Antonia replied calmly.

"And he said...?"

"That if I pushed him, he'd do his best to have me removed from my position here," she said bluntly.

The older woman pursed her lips. "Well, as we've already discussed, he wouldn't have to work that hard to do it. It's a rather ticklish situation. I'm sorry I can't be more optimistic."

Antonia leaned back in her seat with a long sigh. "I

shouldn't have come back to Bighorn," she said, almost to herself. "I don't know why I did."

"Perhaps you were looking for something."

"Something that no longer exists," Antonia replied absently. "A lost part of my life that I won't find here."

"You are going to stay, aren't you?" Mrs. Jameson asked. "After this school term, I mean. Your students say wonderful things about you. Especially Julie Ames," she added with a grin.

"I went to school with her father," Antonia confessed. "To this school, as a matter of fact. She's just like her dad."

"I've met him, and she is a lot like him. What a pity all our students can't be as energetic and enthusiastic as our Julie."

"Yes, indeed."

"Well, I'll give you all the moral support I can," Mrs. Jameson continued. "We do have a very good school counselor. We've sent Maggie to her several times, but she won't say a word. We've had the counselor talk to Mr. Long, but he won't say a word, either. It's a difficult situation."

"Perhaps it will work itself out," Antonia replied.

"Do think about staying on," the older woman said seriously.

Antonia couldn't promise that. She forced a smile. "I'll certainly think about it," she agreed.

But once out of the principal's office, she was more depressed than ever. Maggie hated her, and obviously would not cooperate. It was only a matter of time before she had to give Maggie a failing grade for her noneffort, and Powell would either come back for some more heated words or get her fired. She didn't know if she could bear another verbal tug-of-war with him, especially after the last one. And as for getting fired, she wondered if that really mattered anymore. At the rate her health was failing, it wasn't going to matter for much longer, anyway.

She wandered back to her schoolroom and found Powell sitting on the edge of her desk, looking prosperous in a dark gray suit and a red tie, with a gray Stetson and handtooled leather boots that complemented his suit. He was wearing the same signet ring on his little finger that he'd worn when they were engaged, a script letter L. The ring was very simple, 10K gold and not very expensive. His mother had given it to him when he graduated from high school, and Antonia knew how hard the woman had had to work to pay for it. The Rolex watch on his left wrist was something he'd earned for himself. The Longs had never had enough money at any time in their lives to pay for a watch like that. She wondered if Powell ever thought back to those hard days of his youth.

He heard her step and turned his head to watch her enter the classroom. In her tailored beige dress, with her blond hair in a bun, she looked thinner than ever and very dignified.

"How you've changed," he remarked involuntarily.

"I was thinking the same thing about you," she said wearily. She sat down behind the desk, because just the walk to the office had made her tired. She looked up at him with the fatigue in her face. "I really need to go home. I know why you're here. She can't be moved to another class, because there isn't one. The only alternative is for me to leave..."

"That isn't why I came," he said, surprised.

"No?"

He picked up a paper clip from the desk and looked at it intently. "I thought you might have something to eat with me," he said. "We could talk about Maggie."

She was nauseated and trying not to let it overwhelm her. She barely heard him. "What?"

"I said, let's get together tonight," he repeated, frowning. "You look green. Put your head down."

She turned sideways and lowered her head to the hands resting on her knees, sucking in air. She felt nauseous more and more these days, and faint. She didn't know how much longer she was going to be mobile. The thought frightened her. She would have to make arrangements to get on with the therapy, while there was still time. It was one thing to say that dying didn't matter, but it was quite another when the prospect of it was staring her in the face.

"You're damn thin." He bit off the words. "Have you seen a doctor?"

"If one more person asks me that...!" She erupted. She took another breath and lifted her head, fighting the dizziness as she pushed back a wisp of hair from her eyes. "Yes, I've seen a doctor. I'm just run-down. It's been a hard year."

"Yes, I know," he said absently, watching her.

She met his concerned eyes. If she'd been less feeble, she might have wondered at the expression in them. As it was, she was too tired to care.

"Maggie's been giving everyone fits," he said unexpectedly. "I know you're having trouble with her. I thought if we put our heads together, we might come up with some answers."

"I thought my opinion didn't matter," she replied dully.

He averted his gaze. "I've had a lot on my mind," he said noncommittally. "Of course your opinion matters. We need to talk."

She wanted to ask what good he thought it would do to talk, when he'd told his daughter that he was sick of Miss Hayes and wanted her out of town because she was making his life miserable. She wasn't going to mention that. It would be like tattling. But it hurt more than anything else had in recent days.

"Well?" he persisted impatiently.

"Very well. What time shall I meet you, and where?"

The question seemed to surprise him. "I'll pick you up at your home, of course," he said. "About six."

She really should refuse. She looked into his dark eyes and knew that she couldn't. One last date, she was thinking sadly. She could have one last date with him before the ordeal began...

She managed a smile. "All right."

He watched her sort out the papers on her desk and put them away methodically. His eyes were on her hands, on the unusual thinness of them. She looked unwell. Her mother's death surely had affected her, but this seemed much more than worry. She was all but skeletal.

"I'll see you at six," she said when she'd put up the classroom and walked out into the hall with him.

He looked down at her, noting her frailty, her slenderness. He still towered over her, as he had years before. She was twenty-seven, but his eyes saw a vivacious, loving girl of eighteen. What had happened to change her whole personality so drastically? She was an old soul in a young body. Had he caused all that?

She glanced up at him curiously. "Was there something else?"

He shrugged. "Maggie showed me an A on her homework paper."

"I didn't give her the grade," she replied. "She earned it. It was good work."

He stuck his hands into his pockets. "She has a bright mind, when she wants to use it." His eyes narrowed. "I said some harsh things the last time I was here. Now's as good a time as any to apologize. I was out of line." He couldn't go further and admit that Maggie had lied to him. He was still raw, as Antonia surely was, about Sally's lies. It was too much to admit that his daughter was a liar as well.

"Most parents who care about their children would have challenged a zero," she said noncommittally.

"I haven't been much of a parent," he said abruptly. "I'll see you at six."

She watched him with sad eyes as he walked away, the sight of his long back reminding her poignantly of the day he'd ended their engagement.

He paused at the door, sensing her eyes, and he turned unexpectedly to stare at her. It was so quick that she didn't have time to disguise her grief. He actually winced, because he knew that she'd looked like that nine years ago. He hadn't looked back, so he hadn't known.

She drew in a steadying breath and composed her features. She didn't say anything. There was nothing to say that he hadn't already read in her face.

He started to speak, but apparently he couldn't find the words, either.

"At six," she repeated.

He nodded, and this time he went through the doorway.

CHAPTER SIX

ANTONIA WENT THROUGH every dress she had in her closet before she settled on a nice but simple black crepe dress with short sleeves and a modest neckline. It reached just below her knees and although it had once fit her very nicely, it now hung on her. She had nothing that looked the right size. But it was cold and she could wear a coat over it, the one good leather one she'd bought last season on sale. It would cover the dress and perhaps when she was seated, it wouldn't look so big on her. She paired the dress with a thin black leather belt, gold stud earrings and a small gold cross that her mother had given her when she graduated from high school. She wore no other jewelry, except for the serviceable watch on her wrist. She saw the engagement ring that Powell had bought for her, a very modest little diamond in a thin gold setting. She'd sent it back to him, but he'd refused to accept it from her father. It had found its way back to her, and she kept it here in her jewelry box, the only keepsake she had except for the small cross she always wore.

She picked the ring up and looked at it with sad gray eyes. How different her life, and Powell's, might have been if he hadn't jumped to conclusions and she hadn't run away.

She put the ring back into the box, into the past, where it belonged, and closed it up. This would be the last time she'd go out with Powell. He only wanted to talk about Maggie.

If he was serious about the widow Holton, of whom she'd heard so much, then this would certainly not be an occasion he'd want to repeat. And even if he asked, Antonia knew that she would have to refuse a second evening out with him. Her heart was still all too vulnerable. But for tonight, she took special care with her makeup and left her blond hair long around her shoulders. Even thin, she looked good. She hoped Powell would think so.

She sat in the living room with her curious but silent father, waiting for the clock to chime six. He had ten minutes left to make it on time. Powell had been very punctual in the old days. She wondered if he still was.

"Nervous?" her father asked gently.

She smiled and nodded. "I don't know why he wanted to take me out to talk about Maggie. We could have talked here, or at school."

He smoothed a hand over his boot, crossed over his other leg. "Maybe he's trying to make things up with you."

"I doubt that," she replied. "I hear he's been spending time with the widow Holton…"

"So has Dawson. But love isn't the reason. They both want her south pasture. It borders on both of theirs."

"Oh. Everybody says she's very pretty."

"So she is. But Dawson won't have anything to do with women in a romantic way, and Powell is playing her along."

"I heard that he was talking marriage."

"Did you?" He frowned. "Well…that's surprising."

"Mrs. Jameson said his daughter ran away when she thought he was going to marry Mrs. Holton."

Her father shook his head. "I'm not surprised. That child doesn't get along with anyone. She'll end up in jail one day if he doesn't keep a better eye on her."

She traced a pattern in the black crepe purse that

matched her dress. "I haven't been quite fair to her," she confessed. "She's so much like Sally." She grimaced. "She must miss her."

"I doubt it. Her mother left her with any available baby-sitter and stayed on the road until the drinking started taking its toll on her. She never was much of a driver. That's probably why she went into the river."

Into the river. Antonia remembered hearing about the accident on the news. Powell had been rich enough that Sally's tragic death made headlines. She'd felt sorry for him, but she hadn't gone to the funeral. There was no point. She and Sally had been enemies for so long. For so long.

The sound of a car in the driveway interrupted her musings. She got up and reached the door just as Powell knocked.

She felt embarrassed when she saw how he was dressed. He was wearing jeans and a flannel shirt with a heavy denim jacket and old boots. If she was surprised, so was he. She looked very elegant in that black dress and the dark leather coat she wore with it.

His face drew in sharply at the sight of her, because even in her depleted condition, she took his breath away.

"I'm running late." She improvised to explain the way she was dressed. "I've just now come back from town," she lied, redfaced. "I'll hurry and change and be ready in a jiffy. Dad can talk to you while I get ready. I'm sorry...!"

She dashed back into the bedroom and closed the door. She could have died of shame. So much for her dreams of the sort of date they'd once shared. He was dressed for a cup of coffee and a sandwich at a fast-food joint, and here she was rigged out for a restaurant. She should have asked him where they were going in the first place, and not tried to second-guess him!

She quickly changed into jeans and a sweatshirt and put her hair up in its usual bun. At least the jeans fit her better than the dress, she thought dryly.

POWELL STARED AFTER her and grimaced. "I had an emergency on the ranch with a calving heifer," he murmured. "I didn't realize she'd be dressed up, so I didn't think about changing…"

"Don't make it worse," her father said curtly. "Spare her pride and go along with what she said."

He sighed heavily. "I never do the right thing, say the right thing." His dark eyes were narrow and sad. "She's the one who was hurt the most, and I just keep right on adding to the pain."

Ben Hayes was surprised at the remark, but he had no love for Powell Long. He couldn't forget the torment the man had caused his daughter, nor what Antonia had said about Powell using his influence to open financial doors for him. All Powell's pretended concern for his health hadn't changed what he thought of the man. And tonight his contempt knew no bounds. He hated seeing Antonia embarrassed like that.

"Don't keep her out long," Ben said coldly. "She isn't well."

Powell's eyes cut around to meet the older man's. "What's wrong with her?" he asked.

"Her mother's barely been dead a year," he reminded him. "Antonia misses her a lot."

"She's lost weight, hasn't she?" he asked Ben.

Ben shifted in the chair. "She'll pick back up, now that she's home." He glared at Powell. "Don't hurt her again, boy," he said evenly. "If you want to talk to her about your daughter, fine. But don't expect anything. She's still raw about the past, and I don't blame her. You were wrong and you wouldn't listen. But she's the one who had to leave town."

Powell's jaw went taut. He stared at the older man with eyes that glittered, and he didn't reply.

It was a tense silence that Antonia walked back into. Her father looked angry, and Powell looked...odd.

"I'm ready," she said, sliding into her leather coat.

Powell nodded. "We'll go to Ted's Truck Stop. It's open all night and he serves good coffee, if that suits you."

She read an insult into the remark, and flushed. "I told you I was dressed up because I'd just come back from town," she began. "Ted's suits me fine."

He was stunned by the way she emphasized that, until he realized what he'd said. He turned on his heel and opened the front door for her. "Let's go," he said.

She told her father goodbye and went through the door. Powell closed it behind them, shutting them in the cold, snowy night. A metallic gold Mercedes-Benz was sitting in the driveway, not the four-wheel-drive vehicle he usually drove. Although it had chains to get through snow and ice, it was a luxury car and a far cry from the battered old pickup truck Powell had driven when they'd been engaged.

Flakes of snow fell heavily on the windshield as he drove the mile down the highway to Ted's, which was a bar and grill, just outside the Bighorn city limits. Ted's sold beer and wine and good food, but Antonia had never been inside the place before. It wasn't considered a socially respectable place, and she wondered if Powell had a reason for taking her there. Perhaps he was trying to emphasize the fact that this wasn't a routine date. It was to be a business discussion, but he didn't want to take her anyplace where they might be recognized. So if that was the case, maybe he really was serious about the widow Holton after all. It made her sad, even though she knew she had no future with him, or with anyone.

"You're quiet," he remarked as he pulled up in the almost deserted parking lot. It was early for Ted's sort of trade, although a couple of tractor trailers were sitting apart in the lot.

"I suppose so," she replied.

He felt the unease about her, the muted sadness. He felt guilty about bringing her here. She'd dressed up for him, and he'd slapped her down unintentionally. He hadn't even considered that she might think of this as a date. She was as sensitive now as she had been at eighteen.

He went around the car to open her door, but she was already out of it and standing in the snow when he got there. She joined him at the fender and walked toward the bar. Her sneakers were getting wet and the snow was deep enough that it leaked in past her socks, but it didn't matter. She was so miserable already that cold feet just seemed to go with her general mood.

Powell noticed, though, and his lips compressed. It was already a bust of an evening, and it was his own damn fault.

They sat down in a booth and the waitress, a big brunette named Darla, smiled and handed them a menu.

"Just coffee for me," Antonia said with a quiet smile.

Powell's eyes flashed. "I brought you here for a meal," he reminded her firmly.

She evaded his angry eyes. "I'll have a bowl of chili, then. And coffee."

He ordered steak and salad and coffee and handed the menu back to the waitress. He couldn't remember a time when he'd felt as helpless, or as ashamed.

"You need more than that," he said softly.

The tone of his voice brought back too many memories. They'd gone out to eat very rarely in the old days, in his old Ford pickup truck with the torn seat and broken dash. A hamburger had been a treat, but it was being together that had made their dates perfect. They'd wolf down their food and then drive out to the pasture near Powell's house. He'd shut off the engine and turn to her, and she'd go into his arms like a homing pigeon.

She could still taste those hot, deep, passionate kisses they'd shared so hungrily. It was amazing that he'd had the restraint to keep their dates innocent. She'd rushed head-long into desire with no self-preservation at all, wanting him so much that nothing else had mattered. But he'd put on the brakes, every time. That hadn't bothered her at the time. She'd thought it meant that he respected her enough to wait for the wedding ceremony. But after he'd called off the wedding and married Sally, and Maggie was born seven months later, his restraint had made a terrible sort of sense. He hadn't really wanted Antonia. He'd wanted her father's influence. She'd been too much in love to realize it.

"I said, you need to eat more than that," he repeated.

She looked up into his dark eyes with the memories slicing through her. She swallowed. "I haven't felt too good today," she said evasively. "I'm not really hungry."

He saw the shadows under her eyes and knew that lack of sleep had certainly added to her depleted health.

"I wanted to talk to you about Maggie," he said suddenly, because it bothered him to be with Antonia and remember their old relationship. "I know she's given you problems. I hope we can work out something."

"There's nothing to work out," Antonia said. "She's done her homework. I think she'll adjust to me eventually."

"She had a lot to say about you last night," he continued, as if she hadn't spoken. "She said that you threatened to hit her."

She looked him right in the eye. "Did she?"

He waited, but she didn't offer any defense. "And she said that you told her that you hated her and that you didn't want her in your class, because she reminded you too much of her mother."

Her eyes didn't fall. It wasn't the truth, but there was enough truth in it to twist. Maggie certainly was perceptive, she thought ruefully. And Powell sat there with his convictions so plain on his lean face that he might as well have shouted them.

She knew then why he'd invited her here, to this bar. He was showing her that he thought too little of her to take her to a decent place. He was putting her down in a cold, subtle way, while he raked her over the coals of his anger for upsetting his little girl.

She managed a smile. "Does the city cab run out this far?" she asked in a tone that was tight enough to sound choked. "Then I won't even have to ask you to take me home." She started to get up, but he rose, too, and blocked her way out of the booth.

"Here it is." The waitress interrupted them, bringing steaming black coffee in two mugs. "Sorry I took so long. Is anything wrong?" she added when Powell didn't move.

"No," he said after a minute, his eyes daring Antonia to move as he sat back down. "Nothing at all. But we'll just have the coffee, if it isn't too late to change the order."

"It's all right, I'll take care of it," the waitress said quickly. She'd seen the glint of tears in Antonia's eyes, and she recognized a kindling argument when she saw one starting. She put down the cream pitcher and wrote out the check. If she was any judge of angry women, there would barely be time for them to drink their one cup each before the explosion.

She thanked them, put down the check and got out of the line of fire.

"Don't cry," Powell said through his teeth as he stared at Antonia's white face. "Don't!"

She took a steadying breath and put both hands around the coffee cup. She stared at it instead of him, but her hands trembled.

He closed his eyes, fighting memories and prejudices and gossip and pain. He'd forgotten nothing. Forgiven nothing. Seeing her alone like this brought it all back.

She was fighting memories of her own. She lifted the coffee to her lips and burned them trying to drink it.

"Go ahead," he invited coldly. "Tell me she's lying."

"I wouldn't tell you the time of day," she said in a voice like warmed-over death. "I never learn. You said we'd discuss the problem, but this isn't a discussion, it's an inquisition. I'll tell you flat-out—I've already asked Mrs. Jameson to move Maggie out of my class. She can't do that, and the only option I have left is to quit my job and go back to Arizona."

He stared at her without speaking. He hadn't expected that.

She met his startled eyes. "Do you think she's a little angel?" she asked. "She's rebellious, haughty and she lies better than her mother ever did."

"Damn you!"

The whip of his voice made her sick inside. She reached for her purse and this time she got up. She pushed past him, and ran out into the snow with tears streaming down her face. She'd walk back to town, she would…!

Her foot slipped on a patch of ice, and she went down

hard. She felt the snow on her hot face and lifted it, to the cooling moisture of fresh snowflakes, just as a pair of steely hands jerked her back to her feet and propelled her toward the car.

She didn't react as he unlocked the door and put her inside. She didn't look at him or say a word, even when he fastened her shoulder harness and sat glaring at her before he finally started the car and headed it back toward town.

When they arrived at her father's house, she reached for the catch that would unfasten the harness, but his hand was there, waiting.

"Why can't you admit the truth?" he demanded. "Why do you keep lying about your relationship with George Rutherford? He bought your wedding dress, he paid your college tuition. The whole damn town knew you were sleeping with him, but you've convinced everyone from your father to George's own son that it was perfectly innocent! Well, you never convinced me and you never will!"

"I know that," she said without looking at him. "Let me go, Powell."

His hand only tightened. "You slept with him!" he accused through his teeth. "I would have died for you…!"

"You were sleeping with my best friend!" she accused hotly. "You got her pregnant while you were engaged to me! Do you think I give a damn about your opinion or your feelings? You weren't jealous of George! You never even loved me! You got engaged to me so that my father's influence could get you a loan that you needed to save your family ranch!"

The accusation startled him so much that he didn't have the presence of mind to retaliate. He stared at her in the dim light from the front porch as if she'd gone mad.

"Sally's people didn't have that kind of clout," she continued, tears of anger and pain running down her cheeks like tiny silver rivers. "But mine did. You used me! The only decent thing you did was to keep from seducing me totally, but then, you didn't need to go that far, because you were already sleeping with Sally!"

He couldn't believe what he was hearing. It was the first time in his life that he'd been at a loss for words, but he was literally speechless.

"And you can accuse me of lying?" she demanded in a choked tone. "Sally lied. But you wanted to believe her because it got you out of our engagement the day before the wedding. And you still believe her, because you can't admit that I was only a means to an end for your ambition. It isn't a broken heart you're nursing, it's broken pride because you couldn't get anywhere without a woman's family name to get you a loan!"

He took a short breath. "I got that loan on my own collateral," he said angrily.

"You got it on my father's name," she countered. "Mr. Sims, the bank president, said so. He even laughed about it, about how you were already making use of your future father-in-law to help you mend your family fortunes!"

He hadn't known that. He'd put the land up for security and he'd always assumed that it had been enough. He should have realized that his father's reputation as a gambler would have made him a dangerous risk as a borrower.

"Antonia," he began hesitantly, reaching out a hand.

She slapped it away immediately. "Don't you touch me," she said hotly. "I've had the Longs to hell and back! You can take this for gospel—if your daughter doesn't study, she won't pass. And if that costs me my job, I don't care!"

She jerked open the door and got out, only to find Powell there waiting for her, dark-eyed and glowering.

"I'm not going to let you take out any sort of vengeance on Maggie," he said shortly. "And if you don't stop giving her hell because of grudges against her mother, you'll be out of a job, I promise you."

"Do your worst," she invited with soft venom, her gray eyes flashing at him. "You can't hurt me more than you already have. Very soon now, I'll be beyond the reach of any vengeance you like to pursue!"

"Think so?" With a lightning-quick movement, he jerked her against his lean, hard body and bent to her mouth.

The kiss was painful, and not just physically. He kissed her without tenderness. His tongue insinuated itself past her lips in a cold, calculating parody of sex, while his hands twisted her body against his lean hips.

She opened her eyes and looked at him, stared at him, until he thought she'd had enough. Just at the last, he relented. His mouth became soft and slow and sensuous, teasing, testing. His hands slid up to her waist and he nibbled at her lower lip with something like tenderness. But she refused him even the semblance of response. She stood like a statue in his grasp, her eyes open, wet with tears, her mouth rigid.

When his eyes opened again, he looked oddly guilty. Her mouth was swollen and her face was very pale.

He winced. "I shouldn't have done that," he said curtly.

She laughed coldly. "No, it wasn't necessary," she agreed. "I'd already gotten the message. You held me in such contempt that you didn't even change out of your working clothes. You took me to a bar…" She pulled away from him, a little shakily. "You couldn't have made your opinion of me any plainer."

He pushed his hat back on his head. "I didn't mean it to turn out like this," he said angrily.

"Didn't you?" She stared up at him with eyes that hated him and loved him, with eyes that would soon lose the ability to see him at all. She took a breath and it ended on a sob.

"Oh, God, don't," he groaned. He pulled her into his arms, but this time without passion, without anger. He held her against his heart with hands that protected, cherished, and she felt his lips in her hair, at her temple. "I'm sorry. I'm sorry, Annie." He bit off the words.

It was the first time he'd used the nickname he'd called her when she was eighteen. The sound of his deep voice calmed her. She let him hold her. It would be the last time. She closed her eyes and it was as if it was yesterday—she was a girl in love, and he was the beginning of her world.

"It was...so long ago," she whispered brokenly.

"A lifetime," he replied in a hushed tone. His arms cradled her and she felt his cheek move tenderly against her blond hair. "Why didn't I wait?" he whispered almost to himself, and his eyes closed. "Another day, just one more day..."

"We can't have the past back," she said. His arms were warm against the cold, and strong, comforting. She savored the glory of them around her for one last time. No matter how he felt about her, she would have this memory to take down into the dark with her.

She fought tears. Once, he would have done anything for her. Or she'd thought that he would. It was cruel to think that he had only used her as a means to an end.

"You're skin and bones," he said after a minute.

"I've had a hard year."

He nuzzled his cheek against her temple. "They've all been hard years, one way or another." He sighed heavily. "I'm sorry about tonight. God, I'm sorry!"

"It doesn't matter. Maybe we needed to clear the air."

"I'm not sure we cleared anything." He drew back and looked down at her sad face. He touched her swollen mouth tenderly, and he looked repentant. "In the old days, I never hurt you deliberately," he said quietly. "I've changed, haven't I, Annie?"

"We've both changed. We've grown older."

"But not wiser, in my case. I'm still leading with my chin." He pushed a few wisps of blond hair away from her mouth. "Why did you come home? Was it because of me?"

She couldn't tell him that. "My father hasn't been well," she said, evading a direct answer. "He needs me. I never realized how much until Christmas."

"I see."

She looked up into his black eyes with grief already building in her face.

"What's wrong?" he asked gently. "Can't you tell me?".

She forced a smile. "I'm tired. That's all, I'm just tired." She reached up and smoothed her hand slowly over his lean cheek. "I have to go inside." On an impulse, she stood on tiptoe. "Powell...would you kiss me, just once...the way you used to?" she asked huskily, her gray eyes pleading with him.

It was an odd request, but the stormy evening had robbed him of the ability to reason properly. He didn't answer. He bent, nuzzling her face, searching for her lips, and he kissed her as he had on their very first date, so long ago. His mouth was warm and searching and cautious, as if he didn't want to frighten her. She reached up to him and held him close. For a few precious seconds, there was no dreaded future, no painful past. She melted into the length of him, moaning softly when she felt the immediate response of his body to hers. He half lifted her against him, and his mouth became demanding, insistent, intimate. She gave what he asked, holding him close. For this moment, he belonged to her and she loved him so...!

An eternity later, she drew gently away without looking at him, pulling her arms from around his neck. The scent of his cologne was in her nostrils, the taste of him was in her mouth. She hoped that she could remember this moment, at the end.

She managed a smile as she stood on shaky legs. "Thanks," she said huskily. She stared up at him as if she wanted to memorize his face. In fact, she did.

He scowled. "I took you out because I wanted to talk to you," he said heavily.

"We talked," she replied, moving back. "Even if nothing got settled. There are too many scars, Powell. We can't go back. But I won't hurt Maggie, even if it means leaving the job, okay?"

"You don't have to go that far," he snapped.

She just smiled. "It will come to that," she replied. "She's got the upper hand, you see, and she knows it. It doesn't matter," she added absently as she stared at him. "In the long run, it doesn't matter at all. Maybe it's even for the best." She took a long, slow breath, drinking in the sight of him. "Goodbye, Powell. I'm glad you've been so successful. You've got everything you ever wanted. Be happy."

She turned and went into the house. She hadn't thanked him for the coffee. But, then, he probably didn't expect it. She was glad that her father was watching a television program intently, because when she called good-night, he didn't ask how it had gone. It saved her the pain of telling him. It spared her his pity when he saw the tears she couldn't stem.

POWELL'S STEP WAS slow and leaden as he went into his house. He was drained of emotion, tired and disheartened. Always he'd hoped that one day he and Antonia would find their way back together again, but he couldn't seem to get past the bitterness, and she'd closed doors tonight. She'd kissed him as if she were saying goodbye. Probably she had been. She didn't like Maggie, and that wouldn't change. Maggie didn't like her, either. Sally was gone, but she'd left a barrier between them in the person of one small belligerent girl. He couldn't get to Antonia because Maggie stood in the way. It was a sad thought, when he'd realized tonight how much Antonia still meant to him.

Surprisingly he found his daughter sitting on the bottom step of the staircase in her school clothes, waiting for him when he walked into his house.

"What are you doing up? Where's Mrs. Bates?" he asked.

She shrugged. "She had to go home. She said I'd be okay since you weren't supposed to be gone long." She studied his face with narrowed, resentful eyes. "Did you tell Miss Hayes that she'd better be nice to me from now on?"

He frowned. "How did you know I took Miss Hayes out?"

"Mrs. Bates said you did." She glared harder. "She said Miss Hayes was sweet, but she's not. She's mean to me. I told her that you hated her. I told her that you wanted her to go away and never come back. You did say that, Daddy, you know you did."

He felt frozen inside. No wonder Antonia had been so hostile, so suspicious! "When did you tell Miss Hayes that?" he demanded.

"Last week." Her lower lip protruded. "I want her to go away, too. I hate her!"

"Why?" he asked.

"She's so stupid," she muttered. "She goes all gooey when Julie brings her flowers and plays up to her. She doesn't even know that Julie's just doing it so she can be teacher's pet. Julie doesn't even come over to play with me anymore, she's too busy drawing pictures for Miss Hayes!"

The resentment in his daughter's face was a revelation. He remembered Sally being that way about Antonia. When they'd first been married, she'd been scathing about Antonia going to college and getting a job as a teacher. Sally hadn't wanted to go away to school. She'd wanted to marry Powell. She'd said that Antonia had laughed about his calling off the wedding and saying that she'd marry George who was richer anyway…lies, all lies!

"I want you to do your homework from now on," Powell told the child. "And stop behaving badly in class."

"I do not behave badly! And I did my homework! I did!"

He wiped a hand over his brow. Maggie was a disagreeable child. He bought her things, but he couldn't bear to spend any time around her. She always made him feel guilty.

"Did she tell you I wasn't behaving?" she demanded.

"Oh, what does it matter what she said?" He glared at her angrily, watching the way she backed up when he looked at her. "You'll toe the line or else."

He stormed off, thoroughly disgusted. He didn't think how the impulsive outburst might hurt a sensitive child who carefully hid her sensitivity from the cold adults around her. All her belligerence was nothing more than a mask she wore to keep people from seeing how much they could hurt her. But now, the mask was down. She stared up after her father with blue eyes brimming with tears, her small fists clenched at her sides.

"Daddy," she whispered to herself, "why don't you love me? Why can't you love me? I'm not bad. I'm not bad, Daddy!"

But he didn't hear her. And when she went to bed, her head was full of wicked Miss Hayes and ways to make her sorry for the way her daddy had just treated her.

CHAPTER SEVEN

THE CLASS HAD a test the following Monday. Maggie didn't answer a single question on it. As usual, she sat with her arms folded and smiled haughtily at Antonia. When Antonia stopped beside her desk and asked if she wasn't going to try to answer any of the questions, things came to a head.

"I don't have to," she told Antonia. "You can't make me, either."

Antonia promptly took Maggie to the principal's office and decided to let Powell carry through with his threat to get her fired. It no longer mattered very much. She was tired of the memories and the future, and she was no closer to an answer about her own dilemma. Part of her wanted to take the chance that drastic therapy might save her. Another part was scared to death of it.

"I'm sorry," she said when Mrs. Jameson came out into the waiting room, "but Maggie refuses to do the test I'm giving the class. I thought perhaps if you explained the seriousness of the situation to her..."

This was Maggie's best chance, and she took it at once. "She hates me!" Maggie cried piteously, pointing at Antonia. "She said I was just like my mommy and that she hated me!" She actually sobbed. Real tears welled in her blue eyes.

Antonia's face went red. "I said no such thing, and you know it!" she said huskily.

"Yes, you did," Maggie lied. "Mrs. Jameson, she said

that she was going to fail me and there was nothing I could do about it. She hates me 'cause my daddy married my mommy instead of her!"

Antonia leaned against the door facing for support, staring at the child with eyes that were full of disbelief. The attack was so unexpected that she had no defense for it. Had Powell been merciless enough to tell the child that? Had he been that angry?

"Antonia, surely this isn't true," Mrs. Jameson began hesitantly.

"No, it's not true," Antonia said in a stilted tone. "I don't know who's been saying such things to her, but it wasn't me."

"My daddy told me," Maggie lied. Actually she'd overheard Mrs. Bates telling that to one of her friends last night on the telephone. It had given Maggie a trump card that she was playing for all it was worth.

Antonia felt the blow all the way to her heart. She'd known that Powell was angry, but she hadn't realized that he was heartless enough to tell Maggie such a painful truth, knowing that she'd use it as a weapon against her despised teacher. And it was a devastating remark to make in the school office. One of the mothers was in there to pick up a sick child, and the two secretaries were watching with wide, eager eyes. What Maggie had just said would be all over town by nightfall. Another scandal. Another humiliation.

"She's awful to me," Maggie continued, letting tears fall from her eyes. It wasn't hard to cry; all she had to do was think about how her father hated her. Choking, she pointed at Antonia. "She says she can be as mean to me as she wants to, because nobody will believe me when I tell on her! I'm scared of her! You won't let her hit me, will you, Mrs. Jameson?" she added, going close to the older woman to look up at her helplessly. "She said she was going to hit me!" she wailed.

Mrs. Jameson had been wavering. But Maggie's eyes were overflowing with tears and she wasn't a hard enough woman to ignore them. She opened her office door. "Go inside and sit down, please, dear," she said. "Don't cry, now, it will be all right. No one will hurt you."

The little girl sniffed back more tears and wiped her eyes on the back of her hand. "Yes, ma'am," she said, keeping her eyes down so that Antonia wouldn't see the triumph in them. *Now you'll have to go away*, she thought gleefully, *and Mrs. Donalds will come back.*

She closed the door behind her. Antonia just stared at Mrs. Jameson.

"Antonia, she's never been that upset," Mrs. Jameson said reluctantly. "I've never seen her cry. I think she's really afraid of you."

Hearing the indecision in the other woman's voice, Antonia knew what she was thinking. She'd heard all the old gossip, and she didn't know Antonia well. She was afraid of Powell's influence. And Maggie had cried. It didn't take a mind reader to figure the outcome. Antonia knew she was beaten. It was as if fate had taken a hand here, forcing her to go back to Arizona. Perhaps it was for the best, anyway. She couldn't have told her father the truth. It would have been too cruel, and very soon now her health was going to break. She couldn't be a burden on the man she loved most.

She met the older woman's eyes tiredly. "It's just as well," she said gently. "I wouldn't have been able to work much longer, anyway."

"I don't understand," Mrs. Jameson said, frowning.

She only smiled. She would understand one day. "I'll save you the trouble of firing me. I quit. I hope you'll release me without proper notice, and I'll forfeit my pay in lieu of it," she said. "Maybe she was right," she said, nodding toward the office. "Maybe I could have been kinder to her. I'll clear out my desk and leave at once, if you can have someone take over my class."

She turned and walked out of the office, leaving a sad principal staring after her.

WHEN MAGGIE CAME back to the classroom, after a long talk with Mrs. Jameson and then lunch, Miss Hayes was no longer there. Julie was crying quietly while the assistant principal put the homework assignment on the board.

Julie glared at Maggie for the rest of the day, and she even refused to speak to her until they left the building to catch the bus home.

"Miss Hayes left," Julie accused. "It was because of you, wasn't it? I heard Mr. Tarleton say they fired her!"

Maggie's face flushed. "Well, of course you liked her, teacher's pet! But she was mean to me!" Maggie snapped. "I hated her. I'm glad she's gone!"

"She was so kind," Julie sobbed. "You lied!"

Maggie went even redder. "She deserved it! She would have failed me!"

"She should have!" Julie said angrily. "You lazy, hateful girl!"

"Well, I don't like you, either," Maggie yelled at her. "You're a kiss-up, that's all you are! Mrs. Donalds doesn't like you, she likes me, and she's coming back!"

"She's having a baby, and she isn't coming back!" Julie raged at her.

"Why did Miss Hayes have to leave?" one of the boys muttered as he and his two friends joined them at the bus queue.

"Because Maggie told lies about her and she got fired!" Julie said.

"Miss Hayes got fired? You little brat!" the boy, Jake, said to Maggie, and pushed her roughly when the bus started loading. "She was the best teacher we ever had!"

"She wasn't, either!" Maggie said defensively. She hadn't realized that people were going to know that she got Miss Hayes fired, or that the teacher had been so well liked by her class.

"You got her fired because she didn't like you," Jake persisted, holding up the line. "Well, they ought to fire the whole school, then, because nobody likes you! You're ugly and stupid and you look like a boy!"

Maggie didn't say a word. She ignored him and the others and got on the bus, but she sat alone. Nobody spoke to her. Everybody glared and whispered. She huddled in her seat, trying not to look at Jake. She was crazy about him, and he hated her, too. It was a good thing that nobody knew how she felt.

At least, Miss Hayes was gone, she thought victoriously. That was one good thing that had come out of the horrible day.

ANTONIA HAD TO tell her father that she'd lost her job and she was leaving town again. It was the hardest thing she'd ever had to do.

"That brat!" he raged. He went to the telephone. "Well, she's not getting away with those lies. I'll call Powell and we'll make her tell the truth!"

Antonia put her hand over his on the receiver and held it in place. She coaxed him back into his easy chair and she sat on the very edge of the sofa with her hands clenched together.

"Powell believes her," she said firmly. "He has no reason not to. Apparently she doesn't tell lies as a rule. He won't believe you any more than he believed me. He'll side with Maggie and nothing will change. Nothing at all."

"Oh, that child," Ben Hayes said through his teeth.

She smoothed down her skirt. "I disliked her and it showed. That wasn't her fault. Anyway, Dad, it doesn't matter. I'll still come back and visit and you can come and see me. It won't be so bad. Really."

"I'd only just got you home again," he said heavily.

"And maybe I'll come back one day," she replied, smiling. She'd spared him the truth, at least. She hugged him. "I'll leave in the morning. It's best if I don't drag it out."

"What will they do about a teacher?" he demanded.

"They'll hire the next person on their list," she said simply. "It isn't as if I'm not expendable."

"You are to me."

She kissed him. "And you are to me. Now, I'd better go pack."

SHE PHONED BARRIE that night and was invited to share her apartment for the time being. She didn't tell Barrie what was wrong. That could wait.

She said goodbye to her father, climbed into her car and drove off toward Arizona. He'd wanted her to take the bus, but she wanted to be alone. She had plenty of thinking to do. She had to cope with her fears. It was time for that hard decision that she might already have put off for too long.

BACK IN ARIZONA, Barrie fed her cake and coffee and then waited patiently for the reason behind her best friend's return.

When Antonia told her about Powell's daughter's lies, she was livid.

Barrie bit her lower lip, a nervous habit that sometimes left them raw. "I could shake them both," she said curtly. "You're so thin, Annie, so worn. Maybe it's for the best that you came back here. You look worse than ever."

"I'll perk up now that I'm back. I need to see about my job, if they've got something open."

"Your replacement, Miss Garland, was offered a job in industry at three times the pay and she left without notice," Barrie told her. "I expect they'd love you to replace her. There aren't many people who'll work as hard as we do for the pay."

That made Antonia smile. "Absolutely. That's a bit of luck at last! I'll phone first thing tomorrow."

"It's good to have you back," Barrie said. "I've really missed you."

"I've missed you, too. Have you heard from Dawson… Barrie!"

Barrie had bitten right through her lip.

Antonia handed her a tissue. "You have to stop doing that," she said, glad to be talking about something less somber than her sudden departure from Bighorn.

"I do try, you know." She dabbed at the spot of blood and then stared miserably at her friend. "Dawson came to see me. We had an argument."

"About what?"

Barrie clammed up.

"All right, I won't pry. You don't mind if I stay here? Really?"

"Idiot," Barrie muttered, hugging her. "You're family. You belong here."

Antonia fought tears. "You're family, too."

She patted the other woman's back. "I know. Now let's eat something before we start wailing, and I'll tell you about the expansion plans they've just announced for the math department. I may be offered the head teaching position in the department!"

"I'm so happy for you!"

"So am I. Oh, I'm so lucky!" Her enthusiasm was catching. Antonia closed her eyes and leaned silently on Barrie's strength. She had to keep going, she told herself. There must be a reason why she was here, now, instead of happily teaching for what was left of her life in Bighorn. There had to be some purpose to the chain of events that had brought her back to Arizona. The thought of the treatments still frightened her, but not as much as they had only three weeks before. She would go back and see the doctor, and discuss those options.

MAGGIE WAS SPENDING the weekend without any company. Julie wouldn't speak to her, and she had no other friends. Mrs. Bates, having heard all about why Miss Hayes had to leave, was avoiding the child as well. She'd moved into the house just to take care of Maggie, because she refused to stay with Julie. But it was a very tense arrangement, and Mrs. Bates muttered while she kept house.

Powell had gone to a business meeting in Denver on Thursday. He'd been out of town when the trouble started. He arrived back without knowing about Antonia's sudden departure. He'd thought about nothing except his disastrous date with Antonia and the things she'd said to him. He'd finally admitted to himself that she really was innocent of any affair with George Rutherford. Her accusations that he'd only used her for financial gain had clinched it.

Of course that wasn't true; he'd never thought of doing

such a thing. But if she believed it, it would explain why she hadn't tried to defend herself. She'd never thought he cared one way or the other about her. Presumably she thought he'd been in love with Sally all along, and the fact that Maggie had been premature had helped convince her that he was sleeping with Sally during their engagement. It wasn't true. In fact, he'd only ever slept with Sally once, the night after Antonia left town. He'd been heartbroken, betrayed and so drunk he hardly knew what he was doing.

When he woke the next morning beside Sally, the horror of what he'd done had killed something inside him. He'd known that there was no going back. He'd seduced Sally, and he'd had to marry her, to prevent another scandal. He'd been trapped, especially when she missed her regular period only two weeks later and turned to him to protect her from scandal. Ironically, he had.

Antonia didn't know that. She didn't know he'd loved her, because he'd never told her so. He hadn't been able to bring himself to say the words. Only when it was too late did he realize what he'd lost. The years between had been empty and cold and he'd grown hard. Sally, knowing he didn't love her at all, knowing he hated her for breaking up his engagement to Antonia, had paid the price, along with her daughter.

Sally had turned to alcohol to numb her pain, and once she'd started, she'd become an alcoholic. Powell had sent her to one doctor after another, to treatment centers. But nothing had worked. His total rejection had devastated her, and even after she'd died he hadn't been able to mourn her.

Neither had Maggie. The child had no love for either of her parents, and she was as cold a human being as Powell had ever known. Sometimes he wondered if she was his child, because there seemed to be nothing of him in her.

Sally had hinted once that Powell hadn't been her first lover. She'd even hinted that Powell wasn't Maggie's father. He'd wondered ever since, and it had colored his relationship with the gloomy child who lived in his house.

He tossed his suitcase onto the floor in the hall and looked around. The house was empty, or seemed to be. He looked up the staircase and Maggie was sitting there, by herself, in torn jeans and a stained sweatshirt. As usual, she was glowering.

"Where's Mrs. Bates?" he asked.

She shrugged. "She went to the store."

"Don't you have anything to do?"

She lowered her eyes to her legs. "No."

"Well, go watch television or something," he said irritably when she didn't look up. A thought struck him. "You didn't get in trouble at school again, did you?" he asked.

Her shoulder moved again. "Yes."

He moved to the bottom step and stared at her. "Well?"

She shifted restlessly. "Miss Hayes got fired."

He didn't feel his heart beating. His eyes didn't move, didn't blink. "Why did she get fired?" he asked in a soft, dangerous tone.

Maggie's lower lip trembled. She clenched her hands around her thin knees. "Because I lied," she said under her breath. "I wanted her…to go away, because she didn't like me. I lied. And they fired her. Everybody hates me now. Julie especially." She swallowed. "I don't care!" She looked up at him belligerently. "I don't care! She didn't like me!"

"Well, whose fault is that?" he asked harshly.

She hid the pain, as she always did. Her stubborn little chin came up. "I want to go live somewhere else," she said with a pathetic kind of pride.

He fought down guilt. "Where would you go?" he asked,

thinking of Antonia. "Sally's parents live in California and they're too old to take care of you, and there isn't anybody else."

She averted her wounded eyes. He sounded as if he wanted her to leave, too. She was sick all over.

"You'll go to school with me in the morning, and you'll tell the principal the truth, do you understand?" he asked flatly. "And then you'll apologize to Miss Hayes."

She clenched her teeth. "She's not here," she said.

"What?"

"She left. She went to Arizona." She winced at the look in his dark eyes.

He took an unsteady breath. The expression in his eyes was like a whiplash to Maggie.

"You don't like her," she accused in a broken voice. "You said so! You said you wished she'd go away!"

"You had no right to cost her that job," he said coldly. "Not liking people doesn't give you the right to hurt them!"

"Mrs. Bates said I was bad like my mama," she blurted out. "She said I was a liar like my mama." Tears filled her eyes. "And she said you hate me like you hated my mama."

He didn't speak. He didn't know what to say, how to deal with this child, his daughter. He hesitated, and in that split second, she got up and ran up the stairs with a heart that broke in two, right inside her. Mrs. Bates was right. Everybody hated her! She ran into her room and closed the door and locked it.

"I'm bad," she whispered to herself, choking on the words. "I'm bad! That's why everybody hates me so."

It had to be true. Her mother had gotten drunk and told her how much she hated her for trapping her in a loveless marriage, for not looking like her father, for being a burden. Her father didn't know that. She couldn't talk to him, she couldn't tell him things. He didn't want to spend any time with her. She was unlovable and unwanted. And she had no place at all to go. Even if she ran away, everybody knew her and they'd just bring her back. Only it would make things worse, because her dad would be even madder at her if she did something like that.

She sat down on the carpeted floor and looked around at the pretty, expensive things that lined the spacious room. All those pretty things, and not one of them was purchased with love, was given with love. They were substitutes for affectionate hugs and kisses, for trips to amusement parks and zoos and carnivals. They were guilt offerings from a parent who didn't love her or want her. She stared at them with anguish in her eyes, and wondered why she'd ever been born.

POWELL GOT INTO his car and drove over to Antonia's father's house. He didn't expect to be let in, but Ben opened the door wide.

"I won't come in," Powell said curtly. "Maggie told me what she did. She and I will go to Mrs. Jameson in the morning and she'll tell the truth and apologize. I'm sure they'll offer Antonia her job back."

"She won't come," Ben replied in a lackluster tone. "She said it was just as well that things worked out that way, because she didn't want to live here."

Powell took off his hat and smoothed back his black hair. "I can only say I'm sorry," he said. "I don't know why Maggie dislikes her so much."

"Yes, you do," Ben said unexpectedly. "And you know why she dislikes Maggie, too."

His chest rose and fell in a soundless breath. "Maybe I do. I've made a hell of a lot of mistakes. She said I wouldn't believe the truth because I couldn't admit that." His shoulders shifted. "I suppose she was right. I knew it wasn't true about her and George. But admitting it meant admitting that I had ruined not only her life, but mine and Sally's as well. My pride wouldn't let me do that."

"We pay a high price for some mistakes," Ben said. "Antonia's still paying. After all these years, she's never looked at another man."

His heart jumped. He searched Ben's eyes. "Is it too late?"

Ben knew what the other man was asking. "I don't know," he said honestly.

"Something's worrying her," Powell said. "Something more than Maggie, or the past. She looks ill."

"I made her go see Dr. Harris. She said he prescribed vitamins."

Powell stared at him. He recognized the suspicion in the other man's eyes, because he'd felt it himself. "You don't buy that, Ben. Neither do I." He took a long breath. "Look, why don't you call Dr. Harris and ask him what's going on?"

"It's Sunday."

"If you don't, I will," the younger man said.

Ben hesitated only for a minute. "Maybe you're right. Come in."

He phoned Dr. Harris. After a few polite words, he asked him point-blank about Antonia.

"That's confidential, Ben," the doctor said gently. "You know that."

"Well, she's gone back to Arizona," Ben said hotly. "And she looks bad. She said you told her all she needed was vitamins. I want the truth."

There was a hesitation. "She asked me not to tell anyone. Not even you."

Ben glanced at Powell. "I'm her father."

There was a longer hesitation. "She's under the care of a doctor in Tucson," Dr. Harris said after a minute. "Dr. Harry Claridge. I'll give you his number."

"Ted, tell me," Ben pleaded.

There was a heavy sigh. "Ben, she's taking too long to make up her mind about having treatment. If she doesn't hurry, it...may be too late."

Ben sat down heavily on the sofa, his face pale and drawn. "She needs treatment...for what?" he asked, while Powell stood very still, listening, waiting.

"God, I hate having to tell you this!" the doctor said heavily. "I'm violating every oath I ever took, but it's in her best interest..."

"She's dragging her feet over treatment for what?" Ben burst out, glancing at Powell, whose face was rigid with fear.

"For cancer, Ben. The blood work indicates leukemia. I'm sorry. You'd better speak with Dr. Claridge. And see if you can talk some sense into her. She could stay in remission for years, Ben, years, if she gets treatment in time! They're constantly coming up with new medicines, they're finding cures for different sorts of cancer every day! You can't let her give up now!"

Ben felt tears stinging his eyes. "Yes. Of course. Give me...that number, will you, Ted?"

The phone number of the doctor in Arizona was passed along.

"I won't forget you for this. Thank you," Ben said, and hung up.

Powell was staring at him with dawning horror. "She refused treatment. For what?"

"Leukemia," Ben said heavily. "She didn't come home to be with me. She came home to die." He looked up into Powell's white, drawn face, furiously angry. "And now she's gone, alone, to face that terror by herself!"

CHAPTER EIGHT

POWELL DIDN'T SAY a word. He just stared at Ben while all
the hurtful things he'd said to Antonia came rushing back
to haunt him. He remembered how brutally he'd kissed her,
the insulting things he'd said. And then, to make it worse,
he remembered the way she'd kissed him, just at the last,
the way she'd looked up at him, as if she were memoriz-
ing his face.

"She was saying goodbye," he said, almost choking on
the words.

"What?"

Powell drew in a short breath. There was no time for
grief now. He couldn't think of himself. He had to think of
Antonia, of what he could do for her. Number one on the
list was to get her to accept help. "I'm going to Arizona."
He put his hat back on and turned.

"You hold on there a minute," Ben said harshly. "She's
my daughter…!"

"And she doesn't want you to know what's wrong with
her," Powell retorted, glaring over his shoulder at the man.
"I'll be damned if I'm going to stand around and let her
do nothing! She can go to the Mayo Clinic. I'll take care
of the financial arrangements. But I'm not going to let her
die without a fight!"

Ben felt a glimmer of hope even as he struggled with his
own needs, torn between agreeing that it was better not to

let her know that he was aware of her condition and wanting to rush to her to offer comfort. He knew that Powell would do his best to make her get treatment; probably he could do more with her than Ben could. But Powell had hurt her so badly in the past...

Powell saw the hesitation and relented. He could only imagine how Ben felt about his only child. He wasn't close enough to his own daughter to know how he might react to similar news. It was a sobering, depressing thought. "I'll take care of her. I'll phone you the minute I can tell you something," he told Ben quietly. "If she thinks you know, it will tear her up. Obviously she kept it quiet to protect you."

Ben grimaced. "I figured that out for myself. But I hate secrets."

"So do I. But keep this one for her. Give her peace of mind. She won't care if I know," he said with a bitter laugh. "She thinks I hate her."

Ben was realizing that whatever Powell felt, it wasn't hate. He nodded, a curt jerk of his head. "I'll stay here, then. But the minute you know something...!"

"I'll be in touch."

POWELL DROVE HOME with his heart in his throat. Antonia wouldn't have told anyone. She'd have died from her stubborn refusal to go ahead and have treatment, alone, thinking herself unwanted.

He went upstairs and packed a suitcase with memories haunting him. He'd have given anything to be able to take back his harsh accusations.

He was vaguely aware of eyes on his back. He turned. Maggie was standing there, glowering again.

"What do you want?" he asked coldly.

She averted her eyes. "You going away again?"

"Yes. To Arizona."

"Oh. Why are you going there?" she asked belligerently.

He straightened and looked at the child, unblinking. "To see Antonia. To apologize on your behalf for costing her her job. She came back here because she's sick," he added curtly. "She wanted to be with her father." He averted his eyes. The shock was wearing off. He felt real fear. He couldn't imagine a world without Antonia.

Maggie was an intelligent child. She knew from the way her father was reacting that Miss Hayes meant something to him. Her eyes flickered. "Will she die?" she asked.

He took a breath before he answered. "I don't know."

She folded her thin arms over her chest. She felt worse than ever. Miss Hayes was dying and she had to leave town because of Maggie. She lowered her eyes to the floor. "I didn't know she was sick. I'm sorry I lied."

"You should be. Furthermore, you're going to go with me to see Mrs. Jameson when I get back, and tell her the truth."

"Yes, sir," she said in a subdued tone.

He finished packing and shouldered into his coat.

Her wounded blue eyes searched over the tall man who didn't like her. She'd hoped all her young life that he'd come home just once laughing, happy to see her, that he'd catch her up in his arms and swing her around and tell her he loved her. That had never happened. Julie had that sort of father. Maggie's dad didn't want her.

"You going to bring Miss Hayes back?" she asked.

"Yes," he said flatly. "And if you don't like it, that's too bad."

She didn't answer him. He seemed to dislike her all over again now, because she'd lied. She turned and went back into her room, closing the door quietly. Miss Hayes would hate her. She'd come back, but she wouldn't forget what

Maggie had done. There'd be one more person to make her life miserable, to make her feel unloved and unwanted. She sat down on her bed, too sad even to cry. Her life had never seemed so hopeless before. She wondered suddenly if this was how Miss Hayes felt, knowing she was going to die and then losing the only job she could get in town, so she had to go live in a place where she didn't have any family.

"I'm really sorry, Miss Hayes," Maggie said under her breath. The tears started and she couldn't stop them. But there was no one to comfort her in the big, elegant empty house where she lived.

POWELL FOUND MRS. BATES and told her that he was going to Arizona, but not why. He left at once, without seeing Maggie again. He was afraid that he wouldn't be able to hide his disappointment at what she'd done to Antonia.

He made it to Tucson by late afternoon and checked into a hotel downtown. He found Antonia's number in the telephone directory and called it, but the number had been disconnected. Of course, surely she'd had to give up her apartment when she went back to Bighorn. Where could she be?

He thought about it for a minute, and knew. She'd be staying with Dawson Rutherford's stepsister. He looked up Barrie Bell in the directory. There was only one B. Bell listed. He called that number. It was Sunday evening, so he expected the women to be home.

Antonia answered the phone, her voice sounding very tired and listless.

Powell hesitated. Now that he had her on the phone, he didn't know what to say. And while he hesitated, she assumed it was a crank call and hung up on him. He put the receiver down. Perhaps talking to her over the phone was a bad idea, anyway. He noted the address of the apartment, and decided that he'd just go over there in the morning. The element of surprise couldn't be discounted. It would give him an edge, and he badly needed one. He got himself a small bottle of whiskey from the refrigerator in the room and poured it into a glass with some water. He didn't drink as a rule, but he needed this. It had occurred to him that he could lose Antonia now to something other than his own pride. He was afraid, for the first time in his life.

He figured that Antonia wouldn't be going immediately back to work, and he was right. When he rang the doorbell at midmorning the next day after a sleepless night, she came to answer it, Barrie having long since gone to work.

When she saw Powell standing there, her shock gave him the opportunity to ease her back into the apartment and close the door behind him.

"What are you doing here?" she demanded, recovering.

He looked at her, really seeing her, with eyes dark with pain and worry. She was wearing a sweatshirt and jeans and socks, and she looked pitifully thin and drawn. He hated the pain he and Maggie had caused her.

"I talked to Dr. Harris," he said shortly, bypassing her father so that she wouldn't suspect that Ben knew about her condition.

She went even paler. He knew everything. She could see it in his face. "He had no right...!"

"You have no right," he snapped back, "to sit down and die!"

She took a sharp breath. "I can do what I like with my life!" she replied.

"No."

"Go away!"

"I won't do that, either. You're going to the doctor. And

you'll start whatever damn treatment he tells you to get," he said shortly. "I'm through asking. I'm telling!"

"You aren't telling me anything! You have no control over me!"

"I have the right of a fellow human being to stop someone from committing suicide," he said quietly, searching her eyes. "I'm going to take care of you. I'll start today. Get dressed. We're going to see Dr. Claridge. I made an appointment for you before I came here."

Her mind was spinning. The shock was too sudden, too extreme. She simply stared at him.

His hands went to her shoulders and he searched her eyes slowly. "I'm going to take Maggie to see Mrs. Jameson. I know what happened. You'll get your job back. You can come home."

She pulled away from him. "I don't have a home anymore," she said, averting her face. "I can't go back. My father would find out that I have leukemia. I can't do that to him. Losing Mother almost killed him, and his sister died of cancer. It was terrible, and it took a long time for her to die." She shuddered, remembering. "I can't put him through any more. I must have been crazy to try to go back there in the first place. I don't want him to know."

He couldn't tell her that her father already knew. He shoved his hands into his pockets and stared at her straight back.

"You need to be with people who care about you," he said.

"I am. Barrie is like family."

He didn't know what else to say, how to approach her. He jingled the loose change in his pocket while he tried to find ways to convince her.

She noticed his indecision and turned back to him. "If

you'd made this decision, if it was your life, you wouldn't thank anyone for interfering."

"I'd fight," he said, angry with her for giving up. "And you know it."

"Of course you would," she said heavily. "You have things to fight for—your daughter, your wealth, your businesses."

He frowned.

She saw the look and laughed bitterly. "Don't you understand? I've run out of things to fight for," she told him. "I have nothing! Nothing! My father loves me, but he's all I have. I get up in the morning, I go to work, I try to educate children who'd rather play than do homework. I come home and eat supper and read a book and go to bed. That's my life. Except for Barrie, I don't have a friend in the world." She sounded as weary as she felt. She sat down on the edge of an easy chair with her face propped in her hands. It was almost a relief that someone knew, that she could finally admit how she felt. Powell wouldn't mind talking about her condition because it didn't matter to him. "I'm tired, Powell. It's gaining on me. I've been so sick lately that I'm barely able to get around at all. I don't care anymore. The treatment scares me more than the thought of dying does. Besides, there's nothing left that I care enough about to want to live. I just want it to be over."

The terror was working its way into his heart as he stared at her. He'd never heard anyone sound so defeated. With that attitude, all the treatment in the world wouldn't do any good. She'd given up.

He stood there, staring down at her bent head, breathing erratically while he searched for something to say that would inspire her, that would give her the will to fight. What could he do?

"Isn't there anything you want, Antonia?" he asked slowly. "Isn't there something that would give you a reason to hold on?"

She shook her head. "I'm grateful to you for coming all this way. But you could have saved yourself the trip. My mind is made up. Leave me alone, Powell."

"Leave you alone...!" He choked on the words. He wanted to rage. He wanted to throw things. She sounded so calm, so unmoved. And he was churning inside with the force of his emotions. "What else have I done for nine long, empty damn years?" he demanded.

She leaned forward, letting her long, loose blond hair drape over her face. "Don't lose your temper. I can't fight anymore. I'm too tired."

She looked it. His eyes lingered on her stooped posture. She looked beaten. It was so out of character for her that it devastated him.

He knelt in front of her, taking her by the wrists and pulling her toward him so that she had to look up.

His black eyes bit into her gray ones from point-blank range. "I've known people who had leukemia. With treatment, you could keep going for years. They could find a cure in the meantime. It's crazy to just let go, not to even take the chance of being able to live!"

She searched his black eyes quietly, with an ache deep inside her that had seemed to have been there forever. Daringly, her hand tugged free of his grasp and found his face. Such a beloved face, she thought brokenly. So dear to her. She traced over the thick hair that lay unruly against his broad forehead, down to the thick black eyebrows, down his nose to the crook where it had been broken, over one high cheekbone and down the indented space to his jutting chin. Beloved. She felt the muscles clench and saw the faint glitter in his eyes.

He was barely breathing now, watching her watch him. He caught her hand roughly and held it against his cheek. What he saw in her unguarded face tormented him.

"You still love me," he accused gruffly. "Do you think I don't know?"

She started to deny it, but there was really no reason to. Not anymore. She smiled sadly. "Oh, yes," she said miserably. Her fingers touched his chiseled, thin mouth and felt it move warmly beneath them as he reacted with faint surprise to her easy admission. "I love you. I never stopped. I never could have." She drew her fingers away. "But everything ends, Powell. Even life."

He caught her hand, pulling it back to his face. "This doesn't have to," he said quietly. "I can get a license today. We can be married in three days."

She had to fight the temptation to say yes. Her eyes fell to his collar, where a pulse hammered relentlessly. "Thank you," she said with genuine feeling. "That means more to me than you can know, under the circumstances. But I won't marry you. I have nothing to give you."

"You have the rest of your life," he said shortly. "However long that is!"

"No." Her voice was weaker. She was fighting tears. She turned her head away and tried to get up, but he held her there.

"You can live with me. I'll take care of you," he said heavily. "Whatever you need, you'll get. The best doctors, the best treatment."

"Money still can't buy life," she told him. "Cancer is… pretty final."

"Stop saying that!" He gripped her arms, hard. "Stop

being a defeatist! You can beat anything if you're willing to try!"

"Oh, that sounds familiar," she said, her eyes misting over with memory. "Remember when you were first starting to build your pedigree herd up? And they told you you'd never manage it with one young bull and five heifers. Remember what you said? You said that anything was possible." Her eyes grew warm. "I believed you'd do it. I never doubted it for a minute. You were so proud, Powell, even when you had nothing, and you fought on when so many others would have dropped by the wayside. It was one of the things I admired most about you."

He winced. His face clenched; his heart clenched. He felt as if he was being torn apart. He let her go and got to his feet, moving away with his hands tight in his pockets.

"I gave up on you, though, didn't I?" he asked with his back to her. "A little gossip, a few lies and I destroyed your life."

She studied her thin hands. It was good that they were finally discussing this, that he'd finally admitted that he knew the truth. Perhaps it would make it easier for him, and for her, to let go of the past.

"Sally loved you," she said, making excuses for her friend for the first time. "Perhaps love makes people act out of character."

His fists clenched in his pockets. "I hated her, God forgive me," he said huskily. "I hated her every day we were together, even more when she announced that she was pregnant with Maggie." He sighed wearily. "God, Annie, I resent my own child because I'm not even sure she's mine. I'll never be sure. Even if she is, every time I look at her, I remember what her mother did."

"You did very well without me," she said without malice. "You built up the ranch and made a fortune doing it. You have respect and influence…"

"And all it cost me was you." His head bowed. He laughed dully. "What a price to pay."

"Maggie is a bright child," she said uncertainly. "She can't be so bad. Julie likes her."

"Not recently. Everybody's mad at her for making you leave," he said surprisingly. "Julie won't speak to her."

"That's a shame," she said. "She's a child who needs love, so much." Antonia had been thinking of what had happened the past few weeks, and Maggie's role in it.

He turned, scowling. "What do you mean?"

She smiled. The reasons for Maggie's bad behavior were beginning to be so clear. "Can't you see it in her? She's so alone, Powell, just like you used to be. She doesn't mix with the other children. She's always apart, separate. She's belligerent because she's lonely."

His face hardened. "I'm a busy man…"

"Blame me. Blame Sally. But don't blame Maggie for the past," she pleaded. "If nothing else comes out of this, there should be something for Maggie."

"Oh, God, St. Antonia speaks!" he said sarcastically, because her defense of his daughter made him ashamed of his lack of feeling for the child. "She got you fired, and you think she deserves kindness?"

"She does," she replied simply. "I could have been kinder to her. She reminded me of Sally, too. I was holding grudges of my own. I wasn't deliberately unkind, but I made no overtures toward her at all. A child like Julie is easy to love, because she gives love so generously. A child like Maggie is secretive and distrustful. She can't give love because she doesn't know how. She has to learn."

He thought about that for a minute. "All right. If she

needs it, you come home with me and teach me how to give it."

She searched over his rigid expression with eyes that held equal parts of love and grief. "I'm already going down-hill," she said slowly. "I can't do that to her, or to you and my father." Her eyes skimmed over his broad shoulders lovingly. "I'll stay with Barrie until I become a liability, then I'll go into a hospice... Powell!"

He had her up in his arms, clear off the floor, his hot face buried in her throat. He didn't speak, but his arms had a fine tremor and his breathing was ragged. He held her so close that she felt vaguely bruised, and he paced the floor with her while he tried to cope with the most incredible emotional pain he'd ever felt.

"I won't let you die," he said roughly. "Do you hear me? I won't!"

She slid her arms around his neck and let him hold her. He did care, in his own way, and she was sorry for him. She'd had weeks to come to grips with her condition, but he'd only had a day or so. Denial was a very real part of it, as Dr. Claridge had already told her.

"It's because of the night you took me to the bar, isn't it?" she asked quietly. "There's no need to feel guilty about what you said. I know it hasn't been an easy nine years for you, either. I don't hold any more grudges. I don't have time for them now. I've put things into perspective in the past few weeks. Hatred, guilt, anger, revenge...they all become so insignificant when you realize your time is limited."

His arms contracted. He stopped pacing and stood hold-ing her, cold with fear.

"If you take the treatments, you have a chance," he re-peated.

"Yes. I can live, from day to day, with the fear of it coming back. I can have radiation sickness, my hair will fall out, the very quality of my life will be impaired. What there is left of it, that is."

He drew in a sharp breath, rocking her against him. His eyes, if she could have seen them, were wide and bleak in a face gone rigid with grief.

"I'll be there. I'll help you through it! Life is too precious to throw away." His mouth searched against her throat hungrily. "Marry me, Annie. If it's only for a few weeks, we'll make enough memories to carry us both into eternity!"

His voice was husky as he spoke. It was the most beautiful thing he'd ever said to her. She clung, giving way to tears at last.

"Yes?" he whispered.

She didn't speak. It was too much of a temptation to resist. She didn't have the willpower to say no, despite her suspicion of his motives.

"I want you," he said harshly. "I want you more than I've ever wanted anything in my life, sick or well. Say yes," he repeated insistently. "Say yes!"

If it was only physical, if he didn't love her, was she doing the right thing to agree? She didn't know. But it was more than she could do to walk away from him a second time. Her arms tightened around his neck. "If you're sure... if you're really sure."

"I'm sure, all right." His cheek slid against hers. He searched her wet eyes. His mouth closed them and then slid down to cover her soft, trembling, tear-wet mouth. He kissed her tenderly, slowly, feeling her immediate response.

The kisses quickly became passionate, intense, and he drew back, because this was a time for tenderness, not desire. "If you'll have the treatments," he said carefully, "if it's even remotely possible afterward, I'll give you a child."

As bribery went, it was a master stroke. She looked as if she thought he was going insane. Her pale eyes searched his dark ones warily.

"Don't you want a child, Antonia?" he asked curtly. "You used to. It was all you talked about while we were engaged. Surely you didn't give up those dreams."

She felt the heat rush into her cheeks. It was an intimate thing to be talking about. Her eyes escaped his, darting down to the white of his shirt.

"Don't," she said weakly.

"We'll be married," he said firmly. "It will all be legal and aboveboard."

She sighed miserably. "Your daughter won't like having me in the house, for however long I have."

"My daughter had better like it. Having you around her may be the best thing that ever happened to her. But you keep harping on my daughter—I told you before, I don't even think Maggie's mine!"

Her eyes came up sharply.

"Oh, you think you're the only one who paid the price, is that it?" he asked bluntly. "I was married to an alcoholic, who hated me because I couldn't bear to touch her. She told me that Maggie wasn't mine, that she'd been with other men."

She tried to pull away, but he wouldn't let her. He put her back on her feet, but he held her there in front of him. His eyes were relentless, like his hold on her. "I told you that I believed Sally about George, but I didn't. After that one, she told so many lies…so many…!" He let go of her abruptly and turned his back, ramming his hands into the pockets of his slacks as he went to look out the window that overlooked the city of Tucson with "A" Mountain in the distance. "I've lived in hell. Until she died, and afterward. You said you couldn't bear Maggie in your class because of the memories, and I accused you of cruelty. But it's that way with me, too."

The child's behavior made a terrible kind of sense. Her mother hadn't wanted her, and neither did her father. She was unloved, unwanted. No wonder she was a behavioral problem.

"She looks like Sally," she said.

"Oh, yes. Indeed she does. But she doesn't look like me, does she?"

She couldn't argue that point, as much as she might have liked to reassure him.

She joined him at the window. Her eyes searched his. The pain and the anguish of his life were carved into his lean face, in deep lines and an absence of happiness. He looked older than he was.

"What stupid mistakes we make, Antonia, when we're young. I didn't believe you, and that hurt you so much that you ran away. Then I spent years pretending that it wasn't a lie, because I couldn't bear to see the waste and know that I caused it. It's hard to admit guilt, fault. I fought it tooth and nail. But in the end, there was no one else to blame."

She lowered her eyes to his chest. "We were both much younger."

"I never used you to get loans on your father's name," he said bluntly. "That was the furthest thing from my mind."

She didn't answer him.

He moved closer, so that as she stared at the floor, his legs filled her line of vision. They were long legs, muscular and powerful from hours working in the saddle.

He took her cold hands in his. "I was a loner and a misfit. I grew up in poverty, with a father who'd gamble the food out of a baby's mouth and a mother who was too afraid of him to leave. It was a rough childhood. The only thing I ever wanted was to get out of the cycle of poverty, to never have to go hungry again. I wanted to make people notice me."

"You did," she said. "You have everything you ever wanted—money and power and prestige."

"There was one other thing I wanted," he said, correcting her. "I wanted you."

She couldn't meet his eyes. "That didn't last."

"Yes, it did. I still want you more than any woman I've ever known."

"In bed," she scoffed.

"Don't knock it," he replied. "Surely by now you've learned how passion can take you over."

She looked up. Her eyes were guileless, curious, totally innocent.

He caught his breath. "No?"

She lowered her gaze again. "I stopped taking risks after you. Nobody got close enough to hurt me again. In any way."

He caught her small hand in his and rubbed his thumb slowly over its delicate back. He watched the veins in it, traced their blue paths to her fingers. "I can't say the same," he replied quietly. "It would have been more than I could bear to go without a woman for years."

"I suppose it's different for men."

"For some of us," he agreed. He clasped her fingers tight. "They were all you," he added on a cold laugh. "Every one was you. They numbed the pain for a few minutes, and then it came back full force and brought guilt with it."

She reached out hesitantly and touched his dark hair. It was cool under her fingers, clean and smelling of some masculine shampoo.

"Hold me," he said quietly, sliding his arms around her waist. "I'm as frightened as you are."

The words startled her. By the time she reacted to them, he had her close, and his face was buried in her throat.

Her hands hovered above his head and then finally gave in and slid into his hair, holding his cheek against hers.

"I can't let you die, Antonia," he said in a rough whisper.

Her fingers smoothed over his hair protectively. "The treatments are scary," she confessed.

He lifted his head and searched her eyes. "If I went with you, would it be so bad?" he asked softly. "Because I will."

She was weakening. "No. It wouldn't be…so bad, then."

He smiled gently. "Leukemia isn't necessarily fatal," he continued. "Remission can last for years." He traced her mouth. "Years and years."

Tears leaked out of her eyes and down into the corners of her mouth.

"You'll get better," he said, his voice a little rough with the control he was exercising. "And we'll have a baby together."

Her lips compressed. "If I have to have radiation, I don't think I can ever have children."

He hadn't wanted to think about that. He took her hand and brought it hungrily to his mouth. "We'll talk to the doctor. We'll find out for certain."

It was like being caught in a dream. She stopped thinking and worrying altogether. Her eyes searched his and she smiled for the first time.

"All right?" he prompted.

She nodded. "All right."

DR. CLARIDGE WAS less than optimistic about pregnancy, and he said so. "You can't carry a child while you're undergoing the treatment," he explained patiently, and watched their faces fall. He hated telling them that.

"And afterward?" she asked, clinging to Powell's strong hand.

"I can't make any promises." He looked at her file, frowning. "You have a rare blood type, which makes it even more dangerous..."

"Rare blood type?" she echoed. "I thought Type O positive was garden variety."

He stared at her. "Yours is not O positive—it's much more rare."

"It is not!" she argued, surprised. "Dr. Claridge, I certainly do know my own blood type. I had an accident when I was in my teens and they had to give me blood. You remember," she told Powell. "I wrecked my bike and cut a gash in my thigh on some tin beside the house."

"I remember," he said.

She looked back at Dr. Claridge. "You can check with Dr. Harris. He'll tell you I'm Type O."

He was frowning as he read the test results again. "But, this is your file," he said to himself. "This is the report that came back from the lab. The names match." He buzzed his nurse and had her come in and verify the file.

"Have we ever done a complete blood profile on Antonia in the past?" he asked. "There's no record of one here."

"No, we haven't," the nurse agreed.

"Well, do one now. Something is wrong here."

"Yes, sir."

The nurse went out and came back a minute later with the equipment to draw blood. She drew two vials.

"Get a rush on that. Get a local lab to do it. I want to know something by morning," he told her.

"Yes, sir."

The doctor turned back to Antonia. "Don't get your hopes up too high," he said. "It might be a misprint on the blood type and everything else could still be correct. But we'll double-check it. Meanwhile," he added, "I think it would be wise to wait until tomorrow to make any more decisions. You can call me about ten. I should know something then."

"I'll do that. Thank you."

"Remember. Don't expect too much."

She smiled. "I won't."

"But, just on the off chance, has anyone you've been in contact with had infectious mononucleosis lately?"

She blinked. "Why, yes. One of my female students had it a few weeks ago," she said. "I remember that her mother was very concerned because the girl had played spin the bottle at a party. Ten years old, can you imagine...?" She laughed nervously.

He went very still. "Did you come into contact with any of her saliva?"

She chuckled weakly. "I don't go around kissing my girls."

"Antonia!"

"We shared a soda," she recalled.

He began to smile. "Well, well. Of course, there's still the possibility that we're no better off, but mono and leukemia are very similar in the way they show up in blood work. A lab technician could have mixed them up."

"It might have been a mistake?" she asked hopefully.

"Maybe. But only maybe. We can't discount the other symptoms you've had."

"A maybe is pretty good," she said. "What are the symptoms of mononucleosis?"

"Same as leukemia," he confirmed. "Weakness, sore

throat, fatigue, fever..." He glanced at Powell and cleared his throat. "And highly contagious."

Powell smiled crookedly. "I wouldn't care."

The doctor chuckled. "I know how you feel. Well, go home, Antonia. We'll know something in the morning. The labs are careful, but mistakes can happen."

"If only this is one," she said huskily. "Oh, if only!"

When they were outside, Powell held her hand tight in his, and paused to bend and kiss her very gently on her mouth.

"I can't think of anything I'd rather have than mononucleosis," he remarked.

She smiled tearfully. "Neither can I!"

"You're sure about that blood type."

"Positive."

"Well, we'll cross our fingers and pray. Right now, let's get some lunch. Then we might go for a drive."

"Okay."

He took her back to his hotel for lunch and then they drove out of town, through the Saguaro National Monument and looked at the giant cacti. The air was cold, but the sun was out and Antonia felt a little more hopeful than she had before.

They didn't talk. Powell simply held her hand tight in his and the radio played country and western music.

BARRIE WAS HOME when they drove up to her apartment building. She was surprised to see Powell, but the expression on his face and on Antonia's made her smile.

"Good news, I hope?" she asked.

"I hope so," Antonia said.

Barrie frowned, and then Antonia realized that she didn't know what was going on.

"We're getting married," Powell said, covering for her.

"We are?" Antonia asked, shocked.

"You said yes, remember? What else did you think I meant when I started talking about children?" he asked haughtily. "I won't live in sin with you."

"I didn't ask you to!"

"Good. Because I won't. I'm not that kind of man," he added, and he smiled at her with a new and exciting tenderness.

Antonia caught her breath at the warmth in the look he gave her, tingling from head to toe with new hope. *Please God*, she thought, *let this be a new beginning.*

Barrie was smiling from ear to ear. "Do I say congratulations?"

"Does she?" Powell asked Antonia.

Antonia hesitated. She knew that Powell only wanted her; maybe he felt sorry for her, too. He hadn't really had time to get used to the possibility that she might die. His motives disturbed her. But she'd never stopped loving him. Would it be so bad to marry him? He might learn to love her, if there was enough time.

"I'll tell you tomorrow," she promised.

He searched her eyes quietly. "It will be all right," he promised. "I know it."

She didn't. She was afraid to hope. But she didn't argue.

"There's a nice film on television tonight, if you're staying," Barrie told Powell. "I thought I'd make popcorn."

"That's up to Antonia," he said.

Antonia smiled at him. "I'd like you to stay."

He took off his hat. "I like butter on my popcorn," he said with a grin.

CHAPTER NINE

IT WAS THE longest night of Antonia's life. Powell went to his hotel at midnight, and she went to bed, still without having told Barrie what she had to face in the morning.

After Barrie went to work, Antonia got dressed. When Powell came for her at nine, she was more than ready to sit in the doctor's waiting room. She wasn't about to trust the telephone about anything that important. And apparently, neither was he.

They drove around until ten, when they went to Dr. Claridge's office for their appointment. They sat in his waiting room and waited patiently through an emergency until he invited Antonia into his office, with Powell right behind her.

They didn't need to ask what he'd found. He was grinning from ear to ear.

"You're garden variety Type O," he told her without preamble, smiling even wider at her delight as she hugged an equally jubilant Powell. "Furthermore, I called the lab that did the blood work before, and they'd just fired a technician who kept mixing up test results. Yours was one he did. The other assistants turned him in, apparently. They're very professional. They don't tolerate sloppy work."

"Oh, thank God!" Antonia burst out.

"I'm very sorry for the ordeal you've had because of this," he added.

"I hid my head in the sand," she said. "If I'd come right in for treatment, and you'd done more blood work, you'd have discovered it sooner."

"Well, there is some bad news," he added with a rueful smile. "You really do have mononucleosis."

Dr. Claridge explained the course of the disease, and then warned them again about how contagious mono was.

"I've seen this run through an entire school in the cafeteria in the old days," he recalled. "And sometimes people spend weeks in bed with it. But I don't believe that'll be necessary in your case. I don't think you will lose a lot of work time."

"She won't have to worry about that," Powell said. "She's marrying me. She won't have to work. And I don't think she'll mind a few days in bed, getting rid of the infection."

She looked up at his suddenly grim face and realized that he was going through with the marriage regardless of her new diagnosis. It didn't make sense for a minute, and then it made terrible sense. He'd given his word. He wouldn't go back on it, no matter what. His pride and honor were as much a part of his makeup as his stubbornness.

"We'll talk about that later," she said evasively. "Dr. Claridge, I can't thank you enough."

"I'm just happy to be able to give a cheerful prognosis on your condition now," he said with genuine feeling. "These things happen, but they can have tragic consequences. There was such a lab work mix-up in a big eastern city many years ago…it caused a man to take his own life out of fear. Generally I encourage people to have a second blood test to make sure. Which I would have certainly done in your case, had you come back to see me sooner," he added deliberately.

She flushed. "Yes. Well, I'll try to show a little more fortitude in the future. I was scared to death and I panicked."

"That's a very human reaction," Dr. Claridge assured her. "Take care. If you have any further problems, let me know."

"We'll be going back to Bighorn," Powell said. "But Dr. Harris will be in touch if he needs to."

"Good man, Harris," Dr. Claridge said. "He was very concerned about you when he contacted me. He'll be happy with the new diagnosis."

"I'm sure he will. I'll phone him the minute I get home and tell him," Antonia added.

They left the doctor's office and Antonia paused on the sidewalk to look around her with new eyes. "I thought I'd lost everything," she said aloud, staring with unabashed delight at trees and people and the distant mountains. "I'd given up. And now, it's all new, it's all beautiful."

He caught her hand in his and held it tight. "I wish I'd known sooner," he said.

She smiled faintly. "It was my problem, not yours."

He didn't answer that. He could tell from her attitude that she was going to try to back out of their wedding. Well, he thought, she was going to find that it was more difficult than she imagined. He had her. He wasn't letting go now.

"If you're hungry, we can have something to eat. Late breakfast or early lunch, whichever you like. But first, we'll get these filled," he added, putting the prescriptions into his pocket.

THEY FILLED THE prescriptions and then went straight to Powell's hotel, and up in the elevator to his luxurious suite overlooking the Sonoran Desert.

"We can eat up here, and we can talk in private," he

said, "without prying eyes. But first, I want to phone your father."

"My father? Why?"

He picked up the telephone, got an outside line and dialed. "Because he knew," he said.

"How?"

He glanced at her. "I made him phone Dr. Harris. We both felt that something was wrong. He wanted to rush down here, but I didn't want you to know... Hello, Ben? There was a mix-up at the lab. She has mononucleosis, not cancer, and she'll be back on her feet in no time." He smiled at the excitement on the other end of the line. "He wants to talk to you," he said, holding out the receiver.

"Hi, Dad," Antonia said softly, glaring at Powell. "I didn't know you knew."

"Powell wouldn't rest until he had the truth. It is the truth, this time?" Ben asked sharply. "It really was a mistake?"

"It really was, thank God," she said with genuine relief. "I was scared to death."

"You weren't the only one. This is wonderful news, girl. Really wonderful news! When are you coming back? Powell tell you Maggie was going to tell the truth? You can get your old job back."

She glanced at Powell warily. He was listening, watching, intently. "Nothing's definite yet. I'll phone you in a day or two and let you know what I decide to do. Okay?"

"Okay. Thank God you're all right," he said heavily. "It's been a hell of a couple of days, Antonia."

"For me, too. I'll talk to you soon. Love you, Dad."

"Love you."

She hung up, turning to glare at Powell. "You had to interfere!"

"Yes, I did," he agreed. "I agree with your father—I don't like secrets, either."

He took off his hat, holding her gaze the whole time. He looked incredibly grim. He slipped off his jacket and his tie, and loosened the top buttons of his shirt, exposing a dark, muscular chest thick with black hair.

The sight of him like that brought back long-buried needs and hungers.

"What are you doing?" she asked when his belt followed the rest and he'd dropped into a chair to shed his boots.

"Undressing," he said. He got back up again and moved toward her.

She started to sidestep, but she was seconds too late. He picked her up and carried her into the bedroom. He threw her onto the bed, following her down with a minimum of exertion.

With his arms on either side of her supporting his weight, she was trapped.

"Powell..."

His black eyes were faintly apologetic. "I'm sorry," he murmured as his mouth eased down against hers.

In the old days, their lovemaking had been passionate, but he'd always been the one to draw back. His reserve was what had convinced her later that he hadn't loved her.

Now, there was no reserve at all, and he was kissing her in a way he never had. His lips didn't cherish, they aroused, and aroused violently. He made her tremble with longings she'd never felt, even with him. His hands were as reckless as his mouth, touching, invading, probing against her naked skin while the only sounds in the room were his quick, sharp breaths and the thunder of his heart beating against her bare breasts.

She didn't even realize he'd half undressed her. She was

too involved in the pleasure he was giving her to care about anything except that she wanted him to have access to her soft, warm skin. She needed the feel of his mouth on her, ached for it, hurt to have it. She arched up against him, moaning when the pleasure became more than she could bear.

Vaguely she was aware that a lot of skin was touching other skin. She felt the warm strength of his body against hers and there didn't seem to be any fabric separating them anymore. The hair on his long legs brushed her bare ones as he separated them and moved so that he was lying completely against her in an intimacy they'd never shared.

She panicked then, freezing when she felt his aroused body in intimate contact with her own.

His mouth softened on hers, gentled, so tender that she couldn't resist him. His hands smoothed up and down her body, and he smiled against her lips.

"Easy," he whispered, lifting his head so that he could see her wet, dazed eyes. His hips moved and she stiffened. "Does that hurt?" he asked softly.

She bit her lower lip. Her hands clenched against his hard arms. "It...yes."

"You're embarrassed. Shocked, too." He brushed his lips against hers as he moved again, tenderly, but even so, the pain was there again and she flinched. His eyes searched hers and the look on his face became strained, passionate, almost grim. "I guess it has to hurt this time," he said unsteadily, "but it won't for long."

She swallowed. "It's...wrong."

He shook his head. "We're going to be married. This is my insurance."

"In...surance?" She gasped, because he was filling her...

"Yes." He moved again, and this time she gasped because it was so sweet, and her hips lifted to prolong it. "I'm giving you a baby, Antonia," he breathed reverently, and even as the words entered her ear, his mouth crushed down over hers and his body moved urgently, and the whole world dissolved in a sweet, hot fire that lifted her like a bird in his arms and slung her headlong up into the sky...

HE DIDN'T LOOK GUILTY. That was her first thought when his face came into vivid focus above her. He was smiling, and the expression in his black eyes made her want to hit him. She flushed to the very roots of her hair, as much from the intimacy of their position as from her memories of the past few hectic, unbelievably passionate minutes.

"That settles all the arguments you might have against marriage, I trust?" he asked outrageously. He drew a strand of damp blond hair over her nose playfully. "If we'd done this nine years ago, nothing could have come between us. It was sweeter than I dreamed it would be, and believe me, I dreamed a lot in nine years."

She sighed heavily, searching his black eyes. They were warm and soft now and she waited for the shame and guilt to come, but it didn't. It was very natural to lie naked in his arms and let him look at her and draw his fingers against her in lazy, intimate caresses.

"No arguments at all?" he asked at her lips, and kissed her gently. "You look worried."

"I am," she said honestly. Her wide eyes met his. "I'm midway between periods."

He smiled slowly. "The best time," he mused.

"But a baby so soon...!"

His fingers covered her lips and stopped the words. "So late," he replied. "You're already twenty-seven."

"I know, but there's Maggie," she said miserably. "She

doesn't like me. She won't want me there at all…and a baby, Powell! It will be so hard on her."

"We'll cross bridges when we come to them," he said. His eyes slid down her body and back up and desire kindled in their black depths again. His face began to tauten, his caresses became arousing. When she shivered and a soft moan passed between her parted lips, he bent to kiss them with renewed hunger.

"Can you take me again?" he whispered provocatively. "Will it hurt?"

She slid closer to him, feeling the instant response of his body, feeling him shiver as she positioned her body to accept his. She looked into his eyes and caught her breath when he moved down.

He stilled, watching her, his heartbeat shaking them both. He lifted and pushed, watched. Her eyes dilated and he eased down again, harder this time, into complete possession.

She gasped. But her hands were pulling at him, not pushing. He smiled slowly and bent to cover her mouth with his. There had never been a time in his life when he felt more masculine than now, with her soft cries in his ear and her body begging for his. He closed his eyes and gave in to the glory of loving her.

EVENTUALLY THEY HAD lunch and went to Barrie's apartment when she was due home. One look at them told the story, and she hugged Antonia warmly.

"Congratulations. I told you it would work out one day."

"It worked out, all right," Antonia said, and then told her friend the real reason why she'd come back to Arizona.

Barrie had to sit down. Her green eyes were wide, her

face drawn as she realized the agony her friend had suffered.

"Why didn't you tell me?" she burst out.

"For the same reason she didn't tell me," Powell murmured dryly, holding Antonia's hand tight in his. "She didn't want to worry anyone."

"You idiot!" Barrie muttered. "I'd have made you go back to the doctor."

"That's why I didn't tell you," Antonia said. "I would have told you eventually, though."

"Thanks a lot!"

"You'd have done exactly the same thing, maybe worse," Antonia said, unperturbed, as she grinned at Barrie. "You have to come to the wedding."

"When is it?"

"Ten in the morning, day after tomorrow, at the county courthouse here," Powell said with a chuckle. "I have the license, Dr. Claridge did the blood work this morning and we're going back to Bighorn wearing our rings."

"I have a spare room," Barrie offered.

Powell shook his head. "Thanks, but she's mine now," he said possessively, searching Antonia's face with quick, hungry eyes. "I'm not letting her out of my sight."

"I can understand that," Barrie agreed. "Well, do you have plans for the evening, or do you want to take in a movie with me? That new period piece is on at the shopping center."

"That might be fun," Antonia said, looking up at Powell.

"I like costume dramas," he seconded. "Suits me."

Besides, he told Antonia later, when they were briefly alone, she wasn't going to be in any shape for what he really wanted for another day or so. That being the case, a movie was as good as anything to pass the time. As long as they were together, he added quietly. If she felt like it. He worried about not keeping her still. She ignored that. She could rest when they got back to Bighorn, she informed him.

Antonia clung to his hand during the movie, and that night, she slept in his arms. It was as if the past nine years had never happened. He still hadn't said anything about love, but she knew that he wanted her. Perhaps in time, love would come. Her real concern was how they were going to cope with Maggie's resentment, especially if their passion for each other bore fruit. It was too soon for a baby, but Powell's ardor had been too headlong to allow for precautions, and his hunger for a child with her was all too obvious. He wasn't thinking about Maggie. He was thinking about all those wasted years and how quickly he could make up for them. But Antonia worried.

THE WEDDING SERVICE was very small and sedate and dignified. Antonia wore a cream-colored wool suit to be married in, and a hat with a small veil that covered her face until the justice of the peace pronounced them man and wife. Powell lifted the veil and looked at her face for a long moment before he bent and kissed her. It was like no kiss he'd ever given her before. She looked into his eyes and felt her legs melt under her. She'd never loved him so much.

Barrie had been one of their witnesses and a sheriff's deputy who was prevailed upon by the justice of the peace was the other. The paperwork was completed, the marriage license handed back with the date and time of the wedding on it. They were married.

THE NEXT DAY they were on the way to Bighorn in Powell's Mercedes-Benz. He was more tense than he'd been for three days and she knew it was probably because her body was still reeling from its introduction to intimacy. She was better, but any intimacy, even the smallest, brought discomfort. She hated that. Powell had assured her that it was perfectly natural, and that time would take care of the problem, but his hunger for her was in his eyes every time he looked at her. At this stage of their new relationship, she hated denying him what he craved. After all, it was the only thing they did have right now.

"Stop looking so morose," he taunted when they neared the Wyoming border hours later. "The world won't end because we can't enjoy each other in bed again just yet."

"I was thinking of you, not me," she said absently.

He didn't reply. His eyes were straight ahead. "I thought you enjoyed it."

She glanced at him and realized that she'd unintentionally hurt his ego. "Of course I did," she said. "But I think it must be more of a need for a man. I mean…"

"Never mind," he mused, glancing at her. "You remembered what I said, didn't you—that I can't go for a long time without a woman? I was talking about years, Antonia, not days."

"Oh."

He chuckled softly. "You little green girl. You're just as you were at eighteen."

"Not anymore."

"Well, not quite." He reached out his hand and she put hers into it, feeling its comforting strength. "We're on our way, honey," he said gently, and it was the first time that he'd used an endearment to address her. "It will be all right. Don't worry."

"What about Maggie?" she asked.

His face hardened. "Let me worry about Maggie."

Antonia didn't say anything else. But she had a bad feeling that they were going to have trouble in that quarter.

THEY STOPPED BY her father's house first, for a tearful reunion. Then they dropped the bombshell.

"Married?" Ben burst out. "Without even telling me, or asking if I wanted to be there?"

"It was my idea," Powell confessed, drawing Antonia close to his side. "I didn't give her much choice."

Ben glared at him, but only for a minute. He couldn't forget that Powell had been more than willing to take on responsibility for Antonia when he thought she was dying. That took courage, and something more.

"Well, you're both old enough to know what you're doing," he said grudgingly, and he smiled at his daughter, who was looking insecure. "And if I get grandkids out of this, I'll shut up."

"You'll have grandchildren," she promised shyly. "Including a ready-made one to start with."

Powell frowned slightly. She meant Maggie.

Antonia looked up at him with a quiet smile. "Speaking of whom, we'd better go, hadn't we?"

He nodded. He shook hands with Ben. "I'll take care of her," he promised.

Ben didn't say anything for a minute. But then he smiled. "Yes. I know you will."

Powell drove them to his home, palatial and elegant, sitting on a rise overlooking the distant mountains. There were several trees around the house and long, rolling hills beyond where purebred cattle grazed. In the old days, the house had been a little shack with a leaking roof and a porch that sagged.

"What a long way you've come, Powell," she said.

He didn't look at her as he swung the car around to the side of the house and pressed the button that opened the garage.

The door went up. He drove in and closed the door behind them. Even the garage was spacious and clean.

He helped Antonia out. "I'll come back for your bags in a few minutes. You remember Ida Bates, don't you? She keeps house for me."

"Ida?" She smiled. "She was one of my mother's friends. They sang together in the choir at church."

"Ida still does."

They went in through the kitchen. Ida Bates, heavyset and harassed, turned to stare at Antonia with a question in her eyes.

"We were married in Tucson," Powell announced. "Meet the new lady of the house."

Ida dropped the spoon in the peas she was stirring and rushed to embrace Antonia with genuine affection. "I can't tell you how happy I am for you! What a surprise!"

"It was to us, too," Antonia murmured with a shy glance at her new husband, who smiled back warmly.

Ida let her go and cast a worried look at Powell. "She's up in her room," she said slowly. "Hasn't come out all day. Won't eat a bite."

Antonia felt somehow responsible for the child's torment. Powell noticed that, and his jaw tautened. He took Antonia's hand.

"We'll go up and give her the news."

"Don't expect much," Ida muttered.

The door to Maggie's room was closed. Powell didn't even knock. He opened it and drew Antonia in with him.

Maggie was sitting on the floor looking at a book. Her

hair was dirty and straggly and the clothes she was wearing looked as if they'd been slept in.

She looked at Antonia with real fear and scrambled to her feet, backing until she could hold on to the bedpost.

"What's the matter with you?" Powell demanded coldly.

"Is she...real?" she asked, wide-eyed.

"Of course I'm real," Antonia said quietly.

"Oh." Maggie relaxed her grip on the bedpost. "Are you...real sick?"

"She doesn't have what we thought," Powell said without preamble. "It was a mistake. She has something else, but she's going to be all right."

Maggie relaxed a little, but not much.

"We're married," Powell added bluntly.

Maggie didn't react at all. Her blue eyes lifted to Antonia and she didn't smile.

"Antonia is going to live with us," Powell continued. "I'll expect you to make her feel welcome here."

Maggie knew that. Antonia would certainly be welcome, as Maggie never had been. She looked at her father with an expression that made Antonia want to cry. Powell never even noticed the anguish in it.

Pick her up, she wanted to tell him. Hold her. Tell her you still love her, that it won't make any difference that you've remarried. But he didn't do that. He stared at the child with an austerity that made terrible sense of what he'd said to Antonia. He didn't know if Maggie was his, and he resented her. The child certainly knew it. His attitude all but shouted it.

"I'll have to stay in bed for a while, Maggie," Antonia said. "It would be nice if you'd read to me sometimes," she added, nodding toward the book on the floor.

"You going to be my teacher, too?" Maggie asked.

"No," Powell said firmly, looking straight at Antonia. "She's going to have enough to do getting well."

Antonia smiled ruefully. It looked as if she was going to have a war on her hands if she tried to take that teaching job back.

"But you and I are still going to see Mrs. Jameson," he told his daughter. "Don't think you're going to slide out of that."

Maggie lifted her chin and looked at him. "I already done it."

"What?" he demanded.

"I told Mrs. Jameson," she said, glaring up at him. "I told her I lied about Miss Hayes. I told her I was sorry."

Powell was impressed. "You went to see her all by yourself?" he asked.

She nodded, a curt little jerk of her head. "I'm sorry," she said gruffly to Antonia.

"It was a brave thing to do," Antonia remarked. "Were you scared?"

Maggie didn't answer. She just shrugged.

"Don't leave that book lying there," Powell instructed, nodding toward it on the carpet. "And take a bath and change those clothes."

"Yes, Daddy," she said dully.

Antonia watched her put the book away, and wished that she could do something, say something, interfere enough that she could wipe that look from Maggie's little face.

Powell tugged her out of the room before she could say anything else. She went, but she was determined that she was going to do something about this situation.

Antonia and Maggie had not started out on the right foot, because of what had happened in the past. But now Antonia wanted to try with this child. Now that she saw the truth in Powell's early words—that Maggie had paid a high price. That price had been love.

Maggie might not like her, but the child needed a champion in this household, and Antonia was going to be her champion.

CHAPTER TEN

WHEN THEY WERE in the master bedroom where Powell slept, Antonia went close to him.

"Don't you ever hug her?" she asked softly. "Or kiss her, and tell her you're glad to see her?"

He stiffened. "Maggie isn't the sort of child who wants affection from adults."

His attitude shocked Antonia. "Powell, you don't really believe that, do you?" she asked, aghast.

The way she was looking at him made him uncomfortable. "I don't know if she's mine." He bit off the words defensively.

"Would it matter so much?" she persisted. "Powell, she's lived in your house since she was born. You've been responsible for her. You've watched her grow. Surely you feel something for her!"

He caught her by the waist and pulled her to him. "I want a child with you," he said quietly. "I promise you, it will be loved and wanted. It will never lack for affection."

She touched his lean cheek. "I know that. I'll love it, too. But Maggie needs us as well. You can't turn your back on her."

His eyebrows went up. "I've always fulfilled my responsibilities as far as Maggie is concerned. I've never wanted to see her hurt. But we've never had a good relationship.

And she isn't going to accept you. She's probably already plotting ways to get rid of you."

"Maybe I know her better than you think," she replied. She smiled. "I'm going to love you until you're sick of it," she whispered, going close to him. "Love will spill out of every nook and cranny, it will fill you up. You'll love Maggie because I'll make you love her." She drew his head down and nibbled at his firm mouth until it parted, until he groaned and dragged her into his arms, to kiss her hungrily, like a man demented.

She returned his kisses until sheer exhaustion drained her of strength and she lay against his chest, holding on for support.

"You're still very weak," he remarked. He lifted her gently and carried her to the bed. "I'll have Ida bring lunch up here. Dr. Claridge said you'd need time in bed and you're going to get it now that we're home."

"Bully," she teased softly.

He chuckled, bending over her. "Only when I need to be." He kissed her softly.

Maggie, passing the door, heard him laugh, saw the happiness he was sharing with Antonia, and felt more alone than she ever had in her young life. She walked on, going down the stairs and into the kitchen.

"Mind you don't track mud in here," Ida Bates muttered. "I just mopped."

Maggie didn't speak. She walked out the door and closed it behind her.

ANTONIA HAD HER lunch on a tray with Powell. It was so different now, being with him, loving him openly, watching the coldness leave him. He was like a different man.

But she worried about Maggie. That evening when Ida

brought another tray, this time a single one because Powell had to go out, she asked about Maggie.

"I don't know where she is," Ida said, surprised. "She went out before lunch and never came back."

"But aren't you concerned?" Antonia asked sharply. "She's only nine!"

"Little monkey goes where she pleases, always has. She's probably out in the barn. New calf out there. She likes little things. She won't go far. She's got no place to go."

That sounded so heartless. She winced.

"You eat all that up, now. Do you good to have some hot food inside you." Ida smiled and went out, leaving the door open. "Call if you need me!"

Antonia couldn't enjoy her meal. She was worried, even if nobody else was.

She got up and searched in her suitcases for a pair of jeans, socks, sneakers and a sweatshirt. She put them on and eased down the stairs, through the living room and out the front door. The barn was to the side of the house, a good little walk down a dirt road. She didn't think about how tired she was. She was worried about Maggie. It was late afternoon, and growing dark. The child had been out all day.

The barn door was ajar. She eased inside it and looked around the spacious, shadowy confines until her eyes became accustomed to the dimness. The aisle was wide and covered in wheat straw. She walked past one stall and another until she found a calf and a small child together in the very last one.

"You didn't have anything to eat," she said.

Maggie was shocked. She stared up at the woman she'd caused so much trouble for and felt sick to her stomach. Nobody else cared if she starved. It was ironic that her worst enemy was concerned about her.

Her big blue eyes stared helplessly up at Antonia.

"Aren't you hungry?" Antonia persisted.

Maggie shrugged. "I had a candy bar," she said, avoiding those soft gray eyes.

Antonia came into the stall and settled down beside the calf in the soft, clean hay. She touched the calf's soft nose and smiled. "Their noses are so soft, aren't they?" she asked. "When I was a little girl, I used to wish I had a pet, but my mother was allergic to fur, so we couldn't have a dog or cat."

Maggie fidgeted. "We don't have dogs and cats. Mrs. Bates says animals are dirty."

"Not if they're groomed."

Maggie shrugged again.

Antonia smoothed the calf's forehead. "Do you like cattle?"

Maggie watched her warily. Then she nodded. "I know all about Herefords and black Angus. That's what my daddy raises. I know about birth weights and weight gain ratios and stuff."

Antonia's eyebrows arched. "Really? Does he know?"

Maggie's eyes fell. "It wouldn't matter. He hates me on account of I'm like my mother."

Antonia was surprised that the child was that perceptive. "But your mother did have wonderful qualities," Antonia said. "When we were in school, she was my best friend."

Maggie stared at her. "She married my daddy instead of you."

Antonia's hand stilled on the calf. "Yes. She told a lie, Maggie," she explained. "Because she loved your daddy very much."

"She didn't like me," Maggie said dully. "She used to

hit me when he wasn't home and say it was my fault that she was unhappy."

"Maggie, it wasn't your fault," Antonia said firmly.

Maggie's blue eyes met hers. "Nobody wants me here," she said stiffly. "Now that you're here, Daddy will make me go away!"

"Over my dead body," Antonia said shortly.

The child sat there like a little statue, as if she didn't believe what she'd heard. "You don't like me."

"You're Powell's little girl," she replied. "I love him very much. How could I possibly hate someone who's part of him?"

For the first time, the fear in the child's eyes was visible. "You don't want to make me go away?"

"Certainly not," Antonia said.

She nibbled on her lower lip. "They don't want me here," she muttered, nodding her head curtly toward the house. "Daddy goes off and leaves me all the time, and she," she added in a wounded tone, "hates having to stay with me. It was better when I could stay with Julie, but she hates me, too, on account of I got you fired."

Antonia's heart went out to the child. She wondered if in all her life any adult had taken the time to sit down and really talk to her. Perhaps Mrs. Donalds had, and that was why Maggie missed her so much.

"You're very young to try to understand this," she told Maggie slowly. "But inadvertently it was because I lost my job that I went back to the doctor and discovered that I didn't have cancer. Your dad made me go to the doctor," she added with a reflective smile. "He came after me when I left. If he hadn't, I don't know what might have happened to me. Things seem fated sometimes, to me," she added thoughtfully. "You know, as if they're meant to happen.

We blame people for playing their part in the scheme of things, and we shouldn't. Life is a test, Maggie. We have obstacles to overcome, to make us stronger." She hesitated. "Is any of this making sense to you?"

"You mean God tests us," the child said softly.

Antonia smiled. "Yes. Does your dad take you to church?"

She shrugged and looked away. "He doesn't take me anywhere."

And it hurt, Antonia thought, because she was beginning to understand just how much this child was enduring. "I like going to church," she said. "My grandparents helped build the Methodist Church where I went when I was little. Would you..." She hesitated, not wanting to lose ground by rushing the child.

Maggie turned her head and looked at her. "Would I...?" she prompted softly.

"Would you like to go to church with me sometimes?"

The change the question made in that sullen face was remarkable. It softened, brightened, with interest. "Just you and me?" she asked.

"At first. Your dad might come with us, eventually."

She hesitated, toying with a piece of wheat straw. "You aren't mad at me anymore?" she asked.

Antonia shook her head.

"He won't mind?"

She smiled. "No."

"Well..." She shifted and then she frowned, glancing up at the woman with sad eyes. "Well, I would like to," she said. "But I can't."

"Can't? Why not?"

Maggie's shoulders hunched forward. "I don't got a dress."

Tears stung Antonia's gray eyes. Hadn't Powell noticed? Hadn't anybody noticed?

"Oh, my dear," she said huskily, grimacing.

The note in her voice got the child's attention. She saw the glitter of tears in the woman's eyes and felt terrible.

"Antonia!"

The deep voice echoed through the barn. Powell saw them together and strode forward.

"What the hell are you doing out of bed?" he demanded, lifting her to her feet with firm hands. He saw the tears and his face hardened as he turned to the child on her knees by the calf. "She's crying. What did you say to her?" he demanded.

"Powell, no!" She put her hand across his lips. "No! She didn't make me cry!"

"You're defending her!"

"Maggie," Antonia said gently, "you tell your dad what you just told me. Don't be afraid," she added firmly. "Tell him."

Maggie gave him a belligerent glare. "I don't got a dress," she said accusingly.

"Don't have a dress," Antonia corrected her belatedly.

"I don't have a dress," Maggie said obligingly.

"So?" he asked.

"I want to take her to church with me. She doesn't have anything to wear," Antonia told him.

He looked down at his daughter with dawning realization. "You haven't got a dress?"

"No, I don't!" Maggie returned.

He let out a heavy breath. "My God."

"Tomorrow after school you and I are going shopping," Antonia told the child.

"You and me?" Maggie asked.

"Yes."

Powell stared from one of them to the other with open

curiosity. Maggie got to her feet and brushed herself off. She looked up at Antonia warily. "I read this fairy tale about a woman who married a man with two little kids and she took them off and lost them in the forest."

Antonia chuckled. "I couldn't lose you, Maggie," she told the child. "Julie told me that you could track like a hunter."

"She did?"

"Who taught you how to track?" Powell demanded.

Maggie glared at him. "Nobody. I read it in a Boy Scout manual. Jake loaned me his."

"Why didn't you ask your dad to buy you one of your own?" she asked the child.

Maggie glared at him again. "He wouldn't," she said. "He brings me dolls."

Antonia's eyebrows lifted. She looked at Powell curiously. "Dolls?"

"She's a girl, isn't she?" he demanded belligerently.

"I hate dolls," Maggie muttered. "I like books."

"Yes, I noticed," Antonia said.

Powell felt like an idiot. "You never said," he muttered at his daughter.

She moved a little closer to Antonia. "You never asked," she replied. She brushed at the filthy sweatshirt where wheat straw was sticking to it.

"You look like a rag doll," Powell said. "You need a bath and a change of clothes."

"I don't got no more clothes," she said miserably. "Mrs. Bates said she wouldn't wash them because I got them too dirty to get clean."

"What?"

"She threw away my last pair of blue jeans," Maggie continued, "and this is the only sweatshirt I got left."

"Oh, Maggie," Antonia said heavily. "Maggie, why didn't you tell her you didn't have any other clothes?"

"Because she won't listen," the child said. "Nobody listens!" She looked at her father with his own scowl. "When I grow up, I'm going to leave home and never come back! And when I have little kids, I'm going to love them!"

Powell was at a complete loss for words. He couldn't even manage to speak.

"Go and have a bath," Antonia told the child gently. "Have you a gown and robe?"

"I got pajamas. I hid them or she'd have throwed them away, too," she added mutinously.

"Then put them on. I'll bring up your supper."

Powell started to speak, but she put her hand over his mouth again.

"Go ahead, Maggie," she urged the child.

Maggie nodded and with another majestic glare at her father, she stalked off down the aisle.

"Oh, she's yours, all right," Antonia mused when she'd gone out of the barn and they were alone. "Same scowl, same impatient attitude, same temper, same glare..."

He felt uncomfortable. "I didn't know she didn't have any damned clothes," he said.

"Now you do. I'm going to take her shopping to buy new ones."

"You aren't in any shape to go shopping or to carry trays of food," he muttered. "I'll do it."

"You'll take her shopping?" she asked with mischief twinkling in her gray eyes.

"I can take a kid to a dress shop," he said belligerently.

"I'm sure you can," she agreed. "It's just the shock of having you volunteer to do it, that's all."

"I'm not volunteering," he said. "I'm protecting you."

She brightened. "Was that why? You sweet man, you."

She reached up and kissed him softly, lingeringly, on his hard mouth. He only resisted for a split second. Then he lifted her clear off the ground, and kissed her with muted hunger, careful not to make any more demands on her than she was ready for. He turned and carried her down the aisle, smiling at her warmly between kisses.

MRS. BATES WAS STANDING in the middle of the floor looking perplexed when they walked in, although she smiled at the sight of the boss with his wife in his arms.

"Carrying her over the threshold?" she teased Powell.

"Sparing her tired legs," he corrected. "Did Maggie go through here?"

"Indeed she did," Mrs. Bates said with a rueful smile. "I'm a wicked witch because I threw away the only clothes she had and now she has to go shopping for more."

"That's about the size of it," he agreed, smiling at Antonia.

"I didn't know," Mrs. Bates said.

"Neither did I," replied Powell.

They both looked at Antonia.

"I'm a schoolteacher," she reminded them. "I'm used to children."

"I guess I don't know anything," Powell said with a heavy sigh.

"You'll learn."

"How about taking a tray up to Maggie?" Powell asked Mrs. Bates.

"It's the least I can do," the older woman said sheepishly. "I'll never live that down. But you can't imagine the shape those jeans were in. And the sweatshirts!"

"I'm taking her shopping tomorrow after school," Powell said. "We'll get some new stuff for her to wear out."

Mrs. Bates was fascinated. In all the years she'd worked here, Powell Long hadn't taken his daughter anywhere if she wasn't in trouble.

"I know," he said, reading the look accurately. "But there has to be a first step."

Mrs. Bates nodded. "I guess so. For both of us."

Antonia just smiled. Progress at last!

POWELL FELT OUT of place in the children's boutique. The saleslady was very helpful, but Maggie didn't know what to get and neither did he.

They looked at each other helplessly.

"Well, what do you want to buy?" he demanded.

She glared at him. "I don't know!"

"If I could suggest some things," the saleslady intervened diplomatically.

Powell left her to it. He couldn't imagine that clothes were going to do much for his sullen child, but Antonia had insisted that it would make a difference if he went with her. So far, he didn't see any difference.

But when the child went into the dressing room with the saleslady and reappeared five minutes later, he stared at her as if he didn't recognize her.

She was wearing a ruffled pink dress with lace at the throat, a short-skirted little thing with white leggings and patent leather shoes. Her hair was neatly brushed and a frilly ribbon sat at a jaunty angle in it beside her ear.

"Maggie?" he asked, just to be sure.

The look on her dad's face was like a miracle. He seemed surprised by the way she looked. In fact, he smiled. She smiled back. And the change the expression made in her little face was staggering.

For the first time, he saw himself in the child. The eyes were the wrong color, but they were the same shape as his own. Her nose was going to be straight like his—well, like his used to be before he got it broken in a fight. Her mouth was thin and wide like his, her cheekbones high.

Sally had lied about this, too, about Maggie not being his. He'd never been so certain of anything.

He lifted an ironic eyebrow. "Well, well, from ugly duckling to swan," he mused. "You look pretty."

Maggie's heart swelled. Her blue eyes sparkled. Her lips drew up and all at once she laughed, a gurgle of sound that hit Powell right in the heart. He had never heard her laugh. The impact of it went right through him and he seemed to see down the years with eyes full of sorrow and regret. This child had never had a chance at happiness. He'd subconsciously blamed her for Sally's betrayal, for the loss of Antonia. He'd never been a proper father to her in all her life. He wondered if it was going to be too late to start now.

The laughter had changed Maggie's whole appearance. He laughed at the difference.

"Hell," he said under his breath. "How about something blue, to match her eyes?" he asked the saleslady. "And some colorful jeans, not those old dark blue things she's been wearing."

"Yes, sir," the saleslady said enthusiastically.

Maggie pirouetted in front of the full-length mirror, surprised to see that she didn't look the way she usually did. The dress made her almost pretty. She wondered if Jake would ever get to see her in it, and her eyes brightened even more. Now that Antonia was back, maybe everyone would stop hating her.

But Antonia was sick, and she wouldn't be teaching. And that was still Maggie's fault.

"What's the matter?" Powell asked gently. He went down on one knee in front of the child, frowning. "What's wrong?"

Maggie was surprised that he was concerned, that he'd even noticed her sudden sadness. He didn't, usually.

She lifted her eyes to his. "Miss Hayes won't be teaching. It's still my fault."

"Antonia." He corrected her. "She isn't Miss Hayes anymore."

A thought occurred to her. "Is she...my mom, now?"

"Your stepmother," he said tersely.

She moved closer. Hesitantly she reached out and put her hand on his shoulder. It barely touched and then rested, like a butterfly looking for a place to light. "Now that she's back, you don't...hate me anymore, do you?" she asked softly.

His face contorted. With a rough sound, deep in his throat, he swept her close and held her, standing with her in his arms. He hugged her and rocked her, and she clung to him with a sound like a muffled sob.

"Please don't...hate me...anymore!" She wept. "I love you, Daddy!"

"Oh, dear God," Powell whispered huskily, his eyes closed as he weighed his sins. His arms contracted. "I don't hate you," he said curtly. "God knows, I never hated you, Maggie!"

She laid her head on his shoulder and closed her own eyes, savoring the newness of a father's arms, a father's comfort. This was something she'd never known. It was so nice, being hugged. She smiled through her tears.

"Say," he said after a minute, "this is nice."

She gurgled.

He put her down and looked into her uplifted face. Tears were streaming down it, but she was smiling.

He dug in his pocket and cursed under his breath. "Hell. I never carry handkerchiefs," he said apologetically.

She wiped her eyes on the back of her hands. "Me, neither," she said.

The saleslady came back with an armload of dresses. "I found a blue suit," she said gaily, "and another skirt and top in blue."

"They're very pretty!" Maggie said enthusiastically.

"Indeed they are. Why don't you try them on?" he said invitingly.

"Okay!"

She danced off with the saleslady and he watched, astonished. That was his child. He had a very pretty daughter, and she loved him in spite of all the mistakes he'd made. He smiled reflectively. Well, well, and they said miracles didn't happen. He felt in the middle of one right now. And somehow, it all went back to Antonia, a cycle that had begun and ended with her in his life. He smiled as he thought about the process that had brought them, finally, together and made such a vital change in the way things had been. He glanced at himself in the mirror and wondered where the bitter, hard man he'd been only weeks before, had gone.

CHAPTER ELEVEN

MAGGIE RAN INTO Antonia's bedroom ahead of her father, wearing the blue dress and leggings and new shoes.

She came to a sudden stop at the side of the bed and seemed to become suddenly shy as she looked at the pink-clad woman in the bed. Antonia's blond hair was around her shoulders and she was wearing a pink lacy gown with an equally lacy bed jacket. She looked fragile, but she also looked welcoming, because she smiled.

"Oh, how nice," Antonia said at once, wondering at the change in the child. "How very nice! You look like a different girl, Maggie!"

Maggie felt breathless. "Daddy got me five new outfits and jeans and shirts and sweatshirts and shoes," she sputtered. "And he hugged me!"

Antonia's face lit up. "He did?"

Maggie smiled shyly. "Yeah, he did!" She laughed. "I think he likes me!"

"I think he does, too," Antonia said in a loud whisper.

Maggie had something in her hand. She hesitated, glancing warily at Antonia. "Me and Daddy got you something," she said shyly.

"You did?" she asked, too surprised to correct the child's grammar.

Maggie moved forward and put it into Antonia's hands. "It plays a song."

It was a small box. Antonia unwrapped it and opened it. Inside was a music box, a fragile, porcelain-topped miniature brass piano that, when wound and opened, played "Clair de Lune."

"Oh," she exclaimed. "I've never had anything so lovely!"

Maggie smiled crookedly.

"Did your dad pick it out?" she asked, entranced by the music.

Maggie's face fell.

Antonia saw the expression and could have hit herself for what she'd asked. "You picked it out, didn't you?" she asked immediately, and watched the child's face brighten again. She would have to be careful not to do any more damage to that fragile self-esteem. "What wonderful taste you have, Maggie. Thank you!"

Maggie smiled. "You're welcome."

Powell came in the door, grinning when he saw Antonia with the music box. "Like it?" he asked.

"I love it," she replied. "I'll treasure it, always," she added with a warm glance at Maggie.

Maggie actually blushed.

"You'd better put your clothes away," Powell said.

Maggie winced at the authority in his tone, but when she looked up at him, he wasn't angry or impatient. He was smiling.

Her eyes widened. She smiled back. "Okay, Dad!"

She glanced again at Antonia and darted out the door.

"I hear we're handing out hugs today," Antonia murmured dryly.

He chuckled. "Yes, we are. I could get to like that."

"She could, too."

"How about you?" he asked with a speculative glance,

She held out her arms. "Why don't you come down here and find out?"

He laughed softly as he tossed his hat into the chair and eased down on the bed beside her, his arms on either side of her to balance him. She reached up to draw him down, smiling under the warm, slow crush of his mouth.

He kissed her hungrily, but with a tenderness she remembered from their early days together. She loved the warmth of his kisses, the feel of his body against her. She writhed under his weight suggestively and felt him tense.

"No," he whispered, easing to one side.

She sighed wistfully. "Heartless man."

"It's for your own good," he said, teasing her lips with his forefinger. "I want you to get well."

"I'm trying."

He smiled and bent to nuzzle her nose against his. "Maggie looks pretty in blue," he murmured.

"Yes, she does." She searched his black eyes. "You noticed, didn't you?"

"Noticed what?"

"How much she favors you. I saw it when she smiled. She has the same wrinkles in her face that you have in yours when you smile. Of course, she has your nasty temper, too."

"Curses with the blessings." He chuckled. His eyes searched hers and he drew in a heavy breath. "I never dreamed when I went off to Arizona to find you that it would end up like this."

"Is that a complaint?"

"What do you think?" he murmured and kissed her again.

HE CARRIED HER down to the table, and for the first time, he and Antonia and Maggie had a meal together. Maggie was nervous, fidgeting with the utensils because she didn't know which one to use.

"There's plenty of time to learn that," Powell said when he saw her unease. "You aren't under the microscope, you know. I thought it might be nice to have a meal together for a change."

Maggie looked from one adult to the other. "You aren't going to send me away, are you?" she asked her father.

"Idiot," he muttered, glaring at her.

She glared right back. "Well, you didn't like me," she reminded him.

"I didn't know you," he replied. "I still don't. That's my fault, but it's going to change. You and I need to spend more time together. So suppose instead of riding the bus, I take you to and from school all the time?"

She was elated and then disappointed. Jake rode the bus. If she didn't, she wouldn't get to see him.

Powell didn't know about Jake. He scowled even more at her hesitation.

"I'd like to," Maggie said. She blushed. "But..."

Antonia remembered what Julie had told her. "Is there someone who rides the bus that you don't want to miss seeing?" she asked gently, and the blush went nuclear.

Powell pursed his lips. "So that's it," he said, and chuckled. "Do I know this lucky young man who's caught my daughter's eye?"

"Oh, Daddy!" Maggie groaned.

"Never mind. You can go on riding the bus," he said, with a wicked glance at Antonia. "But you might like to come out with me some Saturdays when I'm checking up on my cattle operation."

"I'd like to do that," Maggie said. "I want to know about your weight gain ratios and heritability factors."

Powell's fork fell from his fingers and made a clanging noise against his plate. To hear those terms coming from a nine-year-old floored him.

Maggie saw that, and grinned. "I like to read about cattle, too. He's got these herd books," she explained to Antonia, "and they have all the statistics on proper genetic breeding. Do you breed genetically, Daddy?"

"Good God," he said on a heavy breath. "She's a cattleman."

"Yes, she is," Antonia agreed. "Surprise, surprise. Speaking of genetics, I wonder who she inherited that from?"

He looked sheepish, but he grinned from ear to ear. "Yes, I do breed genetically," he told his daughter. "If you're that interested, I'll take you around the operation and show you the traits I'm breeding for."

"Like easy calving and low birth weight?" Maggie asked.

Powell let out another breath, staring at his daughter with pure admiration. "And here I was worried that I wouldn't have anyone to leave the ranch to."

Antonia burst out laughing. "It looks as if you're going to leave it in the right hands," she agreed, glancing warmly at Maggie.

Maggie blushed and beamed, all at once. She was still in shell shock from the sudden change of her life. She owed that to Antonia. It was like coming out of the darkness into the sunshine.

Antonia felt the same when she looked at her ready-made family.

"That reminds me," she said. "Your granddad would like to take you with him on an antique-buying binge next weekend. He's going to drive over to an auction in Sheridan."

"But I don't got a granddad," Maggie said, perplexed.

"Don't have," Antonia corrected her. She smiled. "And yes, you do have one. My father."

"A real granddaddy of my own?" Maggie asked, putting down her fork. "Does he know me?"

"You went to see him with your dad. Don't you remember?"

"He lived in a big white house. Oh, yes." Her face brightened, and then it fell. "I was scared and I didn't speak to him. He won't like me."

"He likes you very much," Antonia said. "And he'll enjoy teaching you about antiques, if you'd like to learn. It's his hobby."

"That would be fun!"

"I can see that you're going to be much in demand from now on, Maggie," Antonia said, smiling. "Will you mind?"

Maggie shook her head. She smiled a little unsteadily. "Oh, no, I won't mind at all!"

ANTONIA WAS HALF asleep when Powell slid into bed beside her with a long sigh and stretched.

"She beat me," he said.

Antonia rolled over, pillowing her head on his bare, hair-roughened chest. "At what?" she murmured drowsily.

"Checkers. I still don't see how she set me up." He yawned. "God, I'm sleepy!"

"So am I." She curved closer. "Good night."

"Good night."

She smiled as she slipped back into oblivion, thinking as she did how lucky they were to have each other. Powell had changed so much. He might not love her as she loved him, but he seemed very content. And Maggie was friendly enough. It would take time, but she felt very much at home here already. Things looked bright.

THE NEXT MORNING, she was afraid she'd spoken too soon. Maggie went off to school, and Powell went to a cattle sale, leaving Antonia at home by herself on what was Mrs. Bates's day off. The persistent ringing of the doorbell got her out of bed, and she went downstairs in a long white robe, still half asleep, to answer it.

The woman standing on the other side of the door came as a total shock.

If Antonia was taken aback, so was the gorgeous redhead gaping at her with dark green eyes.

"Who are you?" she demanded haughtily.

Antonia looked her over. Elegant gray suit, pink camisole a little too low-cut, short skirt and long legs. Nice legs. Nice figure. But a little ripe, she thought wickedly. The woman was at least five years older than she was; perhaps more.

"I'm Mrs. Powell Long," Antonia replied with equal hauteur. "What can I do for you?"

The woman just stared at her. "You're joking!"

"I'm not joking." Antonia straightened. "What do you want?"

"I came to see Powell. On a private matter," she added with a cold smile.

"My husband and I don't have secrets," Antonia said daringly.

"Really? Then you know that he's been at my house every night working out the details of a merger, don't you?"

Antonia didn't know how to answer that. Powell had been working late each night, but she'd never thought it was anything other than business. Now, she didn't know. She was insecure, despite Powell's hunger for her. Desire wasn't love, and this woman was more beautiful than any that Antonia had ever seen.

"Powell won't be home until late," Antonia said evasively.

"Well, in that case, I won't wait," the redhead murmured.

"Can I take a message?"

"Yes. Tell him Leslie Holton called to see him," she replied. "I'll, uh, be in touch, if he asks. And I'm sure he will." Her cold eyes traveled down Antonia's thin body and back up again with faint contempt. "There's really no understanding the male mind, is there?" she mused aloud and with a nod, turned and walked back to her late-model Cadillac.

Antonia watched her get in it and drive away. The woman even drove with an attitude, haughty and efficient. She wished and wished that the car would run over four big nails and have all four tires go flat at once. But to her disappointment, the car glided out of sight without a single wobble.

So that was the widow Holton, who was trying to get her claws into Dawson Rutherford and Powell. Had she succeeded with Powell? She seemed very confident. And she was certainly lovely. Obviously he hadn't been serious about marrying the widow, but had there been something between them?

Antonia found herself feeling uncertain and insecure. She didn't have the beauty or sophistication to compete with a woman like that. Powell did want her, certainly, but that woman would know all the tricks of seduction. What if she and Powell had been lovers? What if they still were? Antonia hadn't been up to bouts of lovemaking, since that one long night she'd spent with Powell. Was abstinence making him desperate? He'd teased her about not being able to go without a woman for long periods of time, and he'd said years, not weeks. But was he telling the truth or just sparing Antonia's feelings? She had to find out.

LATE THAT AFTERNOON, another complication presented itself. Julie Ames came home with Maggie and proceeded to make herself useful, tidying up Antonia's bedroom and fluffing up her pillows. She'd come in with a bouquet of flowers, too, and she'd rushed up to hug Antonia at once, all loving concern and friendliness.

Maggie reacted to this as she always had, by withdrawing, and Antonia wanted so badly to tell her that Julie didn't mean to hurt her.

"I'll go get a vase," Maggie said miserably, turning.

"I'll bet Julie wouldn't mind doing that," Antonia said, surprising both girls. "Would you?" she asked Julie. "You could ask Mrs. Bates to find you one and put water in it."

"I'd be happy to, Mrs. Long!" Julie said enthusiastically, and rushed out to do as she was asked.

Antonia smiled at Maggie, who was still staring at her in a puzzled way.

"Whose idea was it to pick the flowers?" she asked knowingly.

Maggie flushed. "Well, it was mine, sort of."

"Yes, I thought so. And Julie got the credit, and it hurt."

Maggie was surprised. "Yes," she admitted absently.

"I'm not as dim as you think I am," she told Maggie. "Just try to remember one thing, will you? You're my daughter. You belong here."

Maggie's heart leaped. She smiled hesitantly.

"Or I'm your stepmother, if you'd rather…"

She moved closer to the bed. "I'd rather call you Mom," she said slowly. "If…you don't mind."

Antonia smiled gently. "No, Maggie. I don't mind. I'd be very, very flattered."

Maggie sighed. "My mother didn't want me," she said in a world-weary way. "I thought it was my fault, that there was something wrong with me."

"There's nothing wrong with you, darling," Antonia said gently. "You're fine just the way you are."

Maggie fought back tears. "Thanks."

"Something's still wrong, isn't it?" she asked softly. "Can you tell me?"

Maggie looked at her feet. "Julie hugged you."

"I like being hugged."

She looked up. "You do?"

She smiled, nodding.

Maggie hesitated, but Antonia opened her arms, and the child went into them like a homing pigeon. It was incredible, this warm feeling she got from being close to people. First her own dad had hugged her, and now Antonia had. She couldn't remember a time when anyone had wanted to hug her.

She smiled against Antonia's warm shoulder and sighed.

Antonia's arms contracted. "I do like being hugged."

Maggie chortled. "So do I."

Antonia let her go with a smile. "Well, we'll both have to put in some practice, and your dad will, too. You're very pretty when you smile," she observed.

"Here's the vase!" Julie said, smiling as she came in with it. She glanced at Maggie, who was beaming. "Gosh, you look different lately."

"I got new clothes," Maggie said pointedly.

"No. You smile a lot." Julie chuckled. "Jake said you looked like that actress on his favorite TV show, and he was sort of shocked. Didn't you see him staring at you in class today?"

"He never!" Maggie exclaimed, embarrassed. "Did he?" she added hopefully.

"He sure did! The other boys teased him. He didn't even get mad. He just sort of grinned."

Maggie's heart leaped. She looked at Antonia with eyes brimming with joy and discovery.

Antonia felt that same wonder. She couldn't ever regret marrying Powell, regardless of how it all ended up. She thought of the widow Holton and grew cold inside. But she didn't let the girls see it. She only smiled, listening to their friendly discussion with half an ear, while she wondered what Powell was going to say when she told him about their early-morning visitor.

HE SAID NOTHING at all, as it turned out. And that made it worse. He only watched her through narrowed black eyes when she mentioned it, oh, so carelessly, as they prepared for bed that night.

"She didn't tell me what she wanted to discuss with you. She said that it was personal. I told her I'd give you the message. She did say that she'd be in touch." She peered up at him.

His hard face didn't soften. He searched her eyes, looking for signs of jealousy, but none were there. She'd given him the bare bones of Leslie's visit with no emotion at all. Surely if he meant anything to her, it would have mattered that he was carrying on private, personal discussions with another woman. And Leslie's name had been linked with his in past years. She must have known that, too.

"Was that all?" he asked.

She shrugged. "All that I remember." She smiled. "She's

a knockout, isn't she?" she added generously. "Her hair is long and thick and wavy. I've never seen a human being with hair like that…it's almost alive. Does she model?"

"She was a motion picture actress until the death of her husband. She was tired of the pace so when she inherited his fortune, she gave it up."

"Isn't it boring for her here, in such a small community?"

"She spends a lot of time chasing Dawson Rutherford."

That was discouraging, for Barrie, anyway. Antonia wondered if Barrie knew about her stepbrother's contact with the woman. Then she remembered what her father had said about Dawson.

"Does he like her?" she asked curiously.

"He likes her land," he replied. "We're both trying to get her to sell a tract that separates his border from mine. Her property has a river running right through it. If he gets his hands on it, I'll have an ongoing court battle over water rights, and vice versa."

"So it really is business," she blurted out.

He cocked an eyebrow. "I didn't say that was all it was," he replied softly, mockingly. "Rutherford is a cold fish with women, and Leslie is, how can I put it, overstimulated."

Her breath caught in her throat. "How overstimulated is she?" she demanded suddenly. "And by whom?"

He pursed his lips and toyed with his sleeve. "My past is none of your concern."

She glared at him and sat upright in the bed. "Are you sleeping with her?"

His eyebrows jumped up. "What?"

"You heard me!" she snapped. "I asked if you were so determined to get that land that you'd forsake your marriage vows to accomplish it!"

"Is that what you think?" he asked, and he looked vaguely threatening.

"Why else would she come here to the house to see you?" she asked. "And at a time when she knew you were usually home and Maggie was in school?"

"You're really unsettled about this, aren't you? What did she say to you?"

"She said you'd been at her house every evening when you were supposedly working late," she muttered sharply. "And she acted as if I were the interloper, not her."

"She wanted to marry me," he remarked, digging the knife in deeper.

"Well, you married me," she said angrily. "And I'm not going to be cuckolded!"

"Antonia! What a word!"

"You know what I mean!"

"I hope I do," he said quietly, searching her furious eyes. "Why don't you explain it to me?"

"I wish I had a bottle, I'd explain it," she raged at him, "right over your hard head!"

His dark eyes widened with humor. "You're so jealous you can't see straight," he said, chuckling.

"Of that skinny redheaded cat?" she retorted.

He moved closer to the bed, still grinning. "Meow."

She glared at him, her fists clenched on the covers. "I'm twice the woman she is!"

He cocked one eyebrow. "Are you up to proving it?" he challenged softly.

Her breath came in sharp little whispers. "You go lock that door. I'll show you a few things."

He laughed with sheer delight. He locked the door and turned out the top light, turning back toward the bed.

She was standing beside it by then, and while he

watched, she slid her negligee and gown down her arms to the floor.

"Well?" she asked huskily. "I may be a little thinner than I like, but I..."

He was against her before she could finish, his arms encircling her, his mouth hungry and insistent on her lips. She yielded at once, no argument, no protest.

He laid her down and quickly divested himself of everything he was wearing.

"Wait a minute," she protested weakly, "I'm supposed to be...proving something."

"Go ahead," he said invitingly as his mouth opened on her soft breast and his hands found new territory to explore.

She tried to speak, but it ended on a wild little cry. She arched up to him and her nails bit into his lean hips. By the time his mouth shifted back to hers and she felt the hungry pressure of his body over her, she couldn't even manage a sound.

Later, storm-tossed and damp all over from the exertion, she lay panting and trembling in his arms, so drained by pleasure that she couldn't even coordinate her body.

"You were too weak," he accused lazily, tracing her mouth with a lazy finger as he arched over her. "I shouldn't have done that."

"Yes, you should," she whispered huskily, drawing his mouth down over hers. "It was beautiful."

"Indeed it was." He smiled against her lips. "I hope you were serious about wanting children. I meant to stop by the drugstore, but I forgot."

She laughed. "I love children, and we've only got one so far."

He lifted his head and searched her eyes. "You've changed her."

"She's changed me. And you." Her arms tightened

around his neck. "We're a family. I've never been so happy. And from now on, it will only get better."

He nodded. "She's very forgiving," he replied. "I've got to earn back the trust I lost along the way. I'm ashamed for what I've put her through."

"Life is all lessons," she said. "She's got you now. She'll have sisters and brothers to spoil, too." Her eyes warmed him. "I love you."

He traced the soft line of her cheek. "I've loved you for most of my life," he said simply, shocking her, because he'd never said the words before. "I couldn't manage to tell you. Funny, isn't it? I didn't realize what I had until I lost it." His eyes darkened. "I wouldn't have wanted to live, if you hadn't."

"Powell," she whispered brokenly.

He kissed away the tears. "And you thought I wanted the widow Holton!"

"Well, she's skinny, but she is pretty."

"Only on the outside. You're beautiful clean through, especially when you're being Maggie's mom."

She smiled. "That's because I love Maggie's dad so much," she whispered.

"And he loves you," he whispered back, bending. "Outrageously."

"Is that so?" she teased. "Prove it."

He groaned. "The spirit is willing, but you've worn out the flesh. Besides," he added softly, "you aren't up to long sessions just yet. I promise when you're completely well, I'll take you to the Bahamas and we'll see if we can make the world record book."

"Fair enough," she said. She held him close and closed her eyes, aglow with the glory of loving and being loved.

CHAPTER TWELVE

THE NEW TEACHER for Maggie's class found a cooperative, happy little girl as ready to help as Julie Ames was. And Maggie came home each day with a new outlook and joy in being with her parents. There were long evenings with new movies in front of the fire, and books to look at, and parties, because Antonia arranged them and invited all the kids Maggie liked—especially Jake.

Powell had done some slowing down, although he was still an arch rival of Dawson Rutherford's over that strip of land the widow Holton was dangling between them.

"She's courting him," Powell muttered one evening. "That's the joke of the century. The man's ice clean through. He avoids women like the plague, but she's angling for a weekend with him."

"Yes, I know. I spoke to Barrie last week. She said he's tried to get her to come home and chaperone him, but they had a terrible fight over it and now they're not speaking at all. Barrie's jealous of her, I think."

"Poor kid," he replied, drawing Antonia closer. "There's nothing to be jealous of. Rutherford doesn't like women."

"He doesn't like men, either."

He chuckled. "Me, especially. I know. What I meant was that he's not interested in sexual escapades, even with lovely widows. He just wants land and cattle."

"Women are much more fun," she teased, snuggling close.

"Barrie might try showing him that."

"She'd never have the nerve."

"Barrie? Are we talking about the same woman who entertained three admirers at once at dinner?"

"Dawson is different," she replied. "He matters."

"I begin to see the light."

She closed her eyes with a sigh. "He's a nice man," she said. "You don't like him because of his father, but he's not as ruthless as George was."

He stiffened. "Let's not talk about George."

She lifted away and looked at him. "You don't still believe...!"

"Of course not," he said immediately. "I meant that the Rutherfords have been a thorn in my side for years, in a business sense. Dawson and I will never be friends."

"Never is a long time. Barrie is my friend."

"And a good one," he agreed.

"Yes, well, I think she might end up with Dawson one day."

"They're related," he said shortly.

"They are not. His father married her mother."

"He hates her, and vice versa."

"I wonder," Antonia said quietly. "That sort of dislike is suspicious, isn't it? I mean, you avoid people you really dislike. He's always making some excuse to see Barrie and give her hell."

"She gives it right back," he reminded her.

"She has to. A man like that will run right over a woman unless she stands up to him." She curled her fingers into his. "You're like that, too," she added, searching his black eyes quietly. "A gentle woman could never cope with you."

"As Sally found out," he agreed. His fingers contracted. "There's something about our marriage that I never told you. I think it's time I did. Maggie was born two months premature. I didn't sleep with Sally until after I broke our engagement. And I was so drunk that I thought you'd come back to me," he added quietly. "You can't imagine how sick I felt when I woke up with her the next morning and realized what I'd done. And it was too late to put it right."

She didn't say anything. She swallowed down the pain. "I see."

"I was cruel, Antonia," he said heavily. "Cruel and thoughtless. But I paid for it. Sadly, Sally and Maggie paid with me, and so did you." He searched her eyes. "From now on, baby, if you tell me green is orange, I'll believe it. I wanted to tell you that from the day you came back to your father's house and I saw you there."

"You made cutting remarks instead."

He smiled ruefully. "It hurts to see what you've lost," he replied. "I loved you to the soles of your feet, and I couldn't tell you. I thought you hated me."

"Part of me did."

"And then I found out why you'd really come here to teach," he said. "I wanted to die."

She went into his arms and nuzzled closer to him. "You mustn't look back," she said. "It's over now. I'm safe, and so are you, and so is Maggie."

"My Maggie," he sighed, smiling. "She's a hell of a cattlewoman already."

"She's your daughter."

"Mmm. Yes, she is. I'm glad I finally realized that Sally had lied about that. There are too many similarities."

"Far too many." She smiled against his chest. "It's been

six weeks since that night I offered to prove I was more of a woman than the widow Holton," she reminded him.

"So it has."

She drew away a little, her eyes searching his while a secret smile touched her lips. But he wasn't waiting for surprises. His lean hand pressed softly against her flat stomach and he smiled back, all of heaven in his dark eyes.

"You know?" she whispered softly.

"I sleep with you every night," he replied. "And I make love to you most every one. I'm not numb. And," he added, "you've lost your breakfast for the past week."

"I wanted to surprise you."

"Go ahead," he suggested.

She glared at him. "I'm pregnant," she said.

He jumped up, clasped his hands over his heart and gave her such a look of wonder that she burst out laughing.

"Are you, truly?" he exclaimed. "My God!"

She was all but rolling on the floor from his exaggerated glee. Mrs. Bates stuck her head in the door to see what the commotion was all about.

"She's pregnant!" he told her.

"Well!" Mrs. Bates exclaimed. "Really?"

"The home test I took says I am," she replied. "I still have to go to the doctor to have it confirmed."

"Yes," Powell said. "And the results from this test won't be frightening."

She agreed wholeheartedly.

THEY TOLD MAGGIE that afternoon. She was apprehensive when they called her into the living room. Things had been so wonderful lately. Perhaps they'd changed their minds about her, and she was going to be sent off to school…

"Antonia is pregnant," Powell said softly.

Maggie's eyes lit up. "Oh, is that it!" she said, relieved. "I thought it was going to be something awful. You mean we're going to have a real baby of our own?" She hugged Antonia warmly and snuggled close to her on the sofa. "Julie will be just green, just green with envy!" she said, laughing. "Can I hold him when he's born, and help you take care of him? I can get books about babies…"

Antonia was laughing with pure delight. "Yes, you can help," she said. "I thought it might be too soon, that you'd be unhappy about it."

"Silly old Mom," Maggie said with a frown. "I'd love a baby brother. It's going to be a boy, isn't it?"

Powell chuckled. "I like girls, too," he said.

Maggie grinned at him. "You only like me on account of I know one end of a cow from another," she said pointedly.

"Well, you're pretty, too," he added.

She beamed. "Now, I'll have something really important to share at show and tell." She looked up. "I miss you at school. So does everybody else. Miss Tyler is nice, but you were special."

"I'll go back to teaching one day," Antonia promised. "It's like riding a bike. You never forget how."

"Shall we go over and tell your granddad?" Powell asked.

"Yes," Maggie said enthusiastically. "Right now!"

BEN WAS OVERWHELMED by the news. He sat down heavily in his easy chair and just stared at the three of them sitting smugly on his couch.

"A baby," he exclaimed. His face began to light up. "Well!"

"It's going to be a boy, Granddad," Maggie assured him. "Then you'll have somebody who'll appreciate those old electric trains you collect. I'm sorry I don't, but I like cattle."

Ben chuckled. "That's okay, imp," he told her. "Maybe someday you can help teach the baby about Queen Anne furniture."

"He likes that a lot," Maggie told the other adults. "We spend ever so much time looking at furniture."

"Well, it's fun," Ben said.

"Yes, it is," Maggie agreed, "but cattle are so much more interesting, Granddad, and it's scientific, too, isn't it, Dad?"

Powell had to agree. "She's my kid. You can tell."

"Oh, yes." Ben nodded. He smiled at the girl warmly. Since she'd come into his life, whole new worlds had opened up for him. She came over sometimes just to help him organize his books. He had plenty, and it was another love they shared. "That reminds me. Found you something at that last sale."

He got up and produced a very rare nineteenth-century breed book. He handed it to Maggie with great care. "You look after that," he told her. "It's valuable."

"Oh, Granddad!" She went into raptures of enthusiasm.

Powell whistled through his teeth. "That's expensive, Ben."

"Maggie knows that. She'll take care of it, too," he added. "Never saw anyone take the care with books that she does. Never slams them around or leaves them lying about. She puts every one right back in its place. I'd even lend her my first editions. She's a little jewel."

Maggie heard that last remark and looked up at her grandfather with an affectionate smile. "He's teaching me how to take care of books properly," she announced.

"And she's an excellent pupil." He looked at Antonia

with pure love in his eyes. "I wish your mother was here," he told her. "She'd be so happy and proud."

"I know she would. But, I think she knows, Dad," Antonia said gently. And she smiled.

THAT NIGHT, ANTONIA phoned Barrie to tell her the news. Her best friend was overjoyed.

"You have to let me know when he's born, so that I can fly up and see him."

"Him?"

"Boys are nice. You should have at least one. Then you'll have a matched set. Maggie and a boy."

"Well, I'll do my best." There was a pause. "Heard from Dawson?"

There was a cold silence. "No."

"I met the widow Holton not so long ago," Antonia remarked.

Barrie cleared her throat. "Is she old?"

"About six years older than I am," Antonia said. "Slender, redheaded, green-eyed and very glamorous."

"Dawson should be ecstatic to have her visiting every weekend."

"Barrie, Dawson really could use a little support where that woman is concerned," she said slowly. "She's hard and cold and very devious, from what I hear. You never know what she might do."

"He invited her up there," Barrie muttered. "And then had the audacity to try and get me to come play chaperone, so that people wouldn't think there was anything going on between them. As if I want to watch her paw him and fawn all over him and help him pretend it's all innocent!"

"Maybe it is innocent. Dawson doesn't like women, Barrie," she added. "They say he's, well, sexually cold."

"Dawson?"

"Dawson."

Barrie hesitated. She couldn't very well say what she was thinking, or what she was remembering.

"Are you still there?" Antonia asked.

"Yes." Barrie sighed. "It's his own fault, he wants that land so badly that he'll do anything to get it."

"I don't think he'd go this far. I think he just invited Mrs. Holton up there to talk to her, and now she thinks he had amorous intentions instead of business ones and he can't get rid of her. She strikes me as the sort who'd be hard to dissuade. She's a very pushy woman, and Dawson's very rich. It may be that she's chasing him, instead of the reverse."

"He never said that."

"Did you give him a chance to say anything?" Antonia asked.

"It's safer if I don't," Barrie muttered. "I don't know if I want to risk giving Dawson a whole weekend to spend giving me hell."

"You could try. He might have had a change of heart."

"Not likely." There was a harsh laugh. "Well, I'll call him, and if he asks me again, I'll go, but only if there are plenty of people around, not just the widow."

"Call him up and tell him that."

"I don't know…"

"He's not an ogre. He's just a man."

"Sure." She sounded unconvinced.

"Barrie, you're not a coward. Save him."

"Imagine, the iceman needing saving." She hesitated. "Who told you they called him that?"

"Just about everybody I know. He doesn't date. The widow is the first woman he's been seen with in years." Antonia's voice softened. "Curious, isn't it?"

It was, but Barrie didn't dare mention why. She had some ideas about it, and she wondered if she had enough courage to go to Sheridan and find out the truth.

"Maybe I'll go," Barrie said.

"Maybe you should," Antonia agreed, and shortly afterward, she hung up, giving Barrie plenty to think about.

Powell came to find her after she'd gotten off the phone, smiling at her warmly. "You look pretty in pink," he remarked.

She smiled back. "Thanks."

He sat down beside her on the sofa and pulled her close. "What's wrong?"

"The widow Holton is giving Dawson a hard time."

"Good," Powell said.

She glared at him. "You might have the decency to feel sorry for the poor man. You were her target once, I believe."

"Until you stepped in and saved me, you sweet woman," he replied, and bent to kiss her warmly.

"There isn't anybody to save Dawson unless Barrie will."

"He can fight his own dragons. Or should I say dragonettes?" he mused thoughtfully.

"Aren't you still after that strip of land, too?"

"Oh, I gave up on it when we got married," he said easily. "I had an idea that she wanted more than money for it, and you were jealous enough of her already."

"I like that!" she muttered.

"You never had anything to worry about," he said. "She wasn't my type. But, I had an idea she'd make mischief if I kept trying to get those few acres, so I let the idea go. And I'll tell you something else," he added with a chuckle. "I don't think Dawson Rutherford's going to get that strip, either. She may string him along to see if she can get him interested in a more permanent arrangement, but unless he wants to propose..."

"Maybe he does," she said.

He shook his head. "I don't like him," he said, "but he's not a fool. She isn't his type of woman. She likes to give orders, not take them. He's too strong willed to suit her for long. More than likely, it's because she can't get him that she wants him."

"I hope so," she replied. "I'd hate to see him trapped into marriage. I think Barrie cares a lot more for him than she'll admit."

He drew her close. "They'll work out their own problems. Do you realize how this household has changed since you married me?"

She smiled. "Yes. Maggie is a whole new person."

"So am I. So are you. So is your father and Mrs. Bates," he added. "And now we've got a baby on the way as well, and Maggie's actually looking forward to it. I tell you, we've got the world."

She nestled close to him and closed her eyes. "The whole world," she agreed huskily.

SEVEN MONTHS LATER, Nelson Charles Long was born in the Bighorn community hospital. It had been a quick, easy birth, and Powell had been with Antonia every step of the way. Maggie was allowed in with her dad to see the baby while Antonia fed him.

"He looks like you, Dad," Maggie said.

"He looks like Antonia," he protested. "You look like me," he added.

Maggie beamed. There was a whole new relationship between Maggie and her father. She wasn't threatened by the baby at all, not when she was so well loved by both parents. The cold, empty past was truly behind her now, just as it had finally been laid to rest by her parents.

Antonia had asked Powell finally what Sally had written in the letter she'd sent back, so many years ago. Sally had told him very little about it, he recalled, except he recalled one line she'd quoted from some author he couldn't quite remember: Take what you want, says God, and pay for it. The letter was to the effect that Sally had discovered the painful truth of that old proverb, and she was sorry.

Too late, of course. Much too late.

Sally had been forgiven, and the joy Antonia felt with Powell and Maggie grew by the day. She, too, had learned a hard lesson from the experience, that one had to stand and fight sometimes. She would teach that lesson to Maggie, she thought as she looked adoringly up at her proud husband, and to the child she held in her arms.

* * * * *

CHAMPAGNE GIRL

For Melinda, Aurora and Pat of Texas

CHAPTER ONE

COMANCHE FLATS WAS one of the biggest ranches around, and Catherine Blake always felt a sense of small-town friendliness in the town that had grown up around the ranch. Friendliness and peace. Not that Matt gave her much peace, but she did enjoy the company of her mother and her other stepcousins.

She grinned as she wheeled her small rebuilt white Volkswagen convertible between neat white fences to the big Spanish stucco house beyond, her pale-green eyes on the distant line of oaks visible across the prairie. There were twenty-two square miles of land on this ranch, an hour or so out of Fort Worth, Texas, that her great-uncle had built into an empire. It was always described as lying between the Eastern and Western Cross Timbers, long bands of oaks, once formidable, but now reduced in numbers by encroaching civilization. The bands ran from north to south, and in the days of the great cattle drives they had been a point of reference for cattlemen.

Her slender hand brushed back her dark-chestnut hair from her oval, olive-complexioned face, and she felt again a wild thrill of excitement at having graduated from college with a degree in journalism. While at college in Fort Worth, she'd lived in a dorm during the week and come home on weekends. Often Matt had flown over to get her. The ranch was far enough away from the sprawling Dallas-

Fort Worth airport that Matt preferred flying in his private plane, which had a hangar at the tiny airport in Comanche Flats. Catherine smiled, thinking about that, proud of her graduation with honors and her promise of a good job in New York. Matthew Dane Kincaid might pull everybody else's strings, but he was through pulling Catherine's as of now. She was almost twenty-two and feeling feverish with independence.

She was just returning from a four-day trip to San Antonio, where she'd tried to find work at a small public relations firm. That hadn't panned out, but through a contact she'd obtained a job at a bigger firm in New York. The job wasn't open immediately; it would take several weeks for her office to be readied. But she must have impressed the executive vice-president, because he'd flown all the way down to San Antonio to check out her credentials and had hired her on the spot. She felt excited about that. And about having the opportunity to escape her family. And, especially, Matt.

Odd, she thought, how possessive he'd gotten since her graduation from college. He owned the ranch where she and her mother lived, of course, and the feedlot, and he even had a controlling interest in the local real estate companies. But he was only a stepcousin, and Catherine deeply resented his domination. The loss of her father—he had died during the Vietnam War, when she was a baby—had made her independent-minded at an early age, and she'd fought Matt tooth and nail for years for every inch of freedom she had. When she wasn't dying of unrequited love for him, she admitted bitterly. Hal and Jerry were never so overbearing. Of course, Matt's brothers lacked his fiery temper and shrewd business mind. And his inborn arrogance. Matt made arrogance an art.

Betty Blake, all silvery hair and bright eyes and laughter, came rushing down the steps to meet her daughter.

"Darling, you're home!" she enthused. "How lovely to have you back!"

"It was only for four days," Catherine reminded her as she returned her mother's hug. "How did Matt take it?"

"He's barely spoken to me," Betty confessed. "Oh, Kit, you've landed me in the fire this time!"

"I have to be independent," Catherine said, her green eyes wide and pleading. "Matt just wants his own way again, as usual, but this time he isn't winning. I'll go if I have to wait on tables. But I won't need to," she said stubbornly. "I still have my income from the stock. I'll live on that!"

Betty started to speak but nibbled on her lower lip instead. "Come in and get settled," she said eventually. "Did you get the job?"

"Not the one in San Antonio," Catherine said with a sigh. She glowered. "Imagine, having to sneak off and make up stories about holidays with a nonexistent girlfriend just to go and apply! Honestly, Matt is such a tyrant..." She grinned at her mother's worried face. "I won't start again, I promise. Anyway, I did get a job. But it's in New York."

"New York!" Betty looked shocked.

"It pays well, and I don't start for a month. Plenty of time to get ready."

"Matt won't like it," Betty said grimly.

"Matt doesn't matter!"

"You know better than that," Betty replied. "Without Matt, you and I would be living in low-income housing right now. You know your father got us up to our ears in debt just before he was killed in Vietnam. I've told you often enough."

"And Great-Uncle Henry got us out of trouble and brought us to live with him. Yes, I know," she said broodingly. She followed her mother into the enormous house where the beauty of the Spanish styling of the hall and staircase staggered her as much now as it had in her childhood. Betty had been raised in this house, too, by Uncle Henry. "Oh, I love this house," Catherine murmured.

"Your great-uncle was quite a man," Betty said with a laugh. "He had style and taste."

"Except in wives," Catherine muttered darkly.

"Just because Matt's mother was young is no excuse for a remark like that. You know very well she adored Henry. And she gave him three strong stepsons, too."

Catherine didn't reply. She and her mother went up the winding staircase leading to Catherine's bedroom. Matt and Hal, who were both bachelors, lived at the other side of the enormous, sprawling house. Jerry and his wife, Barrie, lived in a house farther down the ranch road.

"The family are all coming for dinner tomorrow night," Betty remarked. "Matt flew to Houston this afternoon, but he'll be back late tonight, I expect. The rains have been horrible. We're expecting more tonight, and there are flash-flood warnings out. I do hope he'll fly carefully."

"At least he's not driving, thank God. Matt has never driven carefully," Catherine said dryly. "How many cars did he wreck before he got out of college?"

Betty laughed. "Not as many as Hal did."

Catherine stopped on the way down the hall to stare at the huge portrait of Great-Uncle Henry that hung on the wall between a pair of sconces. "I don't like him up here," she said as she studied the face that was so much like her late grandfather's—dark hair and green eyes and an olive complexion, the features Catherine had inherited from her mother's people. "He belongs downstairs in the living room," she added absently.

"I can't watch television with him glaring at me," Betty said reasonably. "Besides, I always feel safe going down the hall in the dark, knowing he's here."

Catherine laughed softly. "Oh, Mama."

"He was my idol when I was growing up." The older woman smiled, staring at the portrait. "I adored him. I still do."

"Even though he provided you with a stepaunt half your age?"

"I like Evelyn quite well, in fact," Betty answered softly. "She took great care of all of us. My parents died when I was so young, I barely remember them." She sighed. "I miss your father so much sometimes…"

"So do I, Mama." Catherine hugged her gently and gave her a sound kiss on the cheek. "I'm glad I've got you," she said warmly, then quickly changed the subject. "Now, come and tell me all the news! I'm terribly out of touch."

BETTY AND CATHERINE sat down to dinner alone, listening to Annie's mutterings as she waddled around the table putting food on it.

"Never can get the family together all at one time," Annie grumbled, glaring at the food as if it were responsible for her dilemma. "Mr. Hal never shows up until Mr. Matt yells at him, and Mr. Jerry and Miss Barrie gone off again, and—"

"We'll eat twice as much," Catherine promised the buxom, white-haired woman who'd come there with Matt's mother.

Annie relented. "Well, I made enough. We can freeze some, I guess."

She went back into the kitchen, and Catherine and Betty exchanged knowing glances.

"Where is Hal, anyway?" Catherine asked.

"I don't know. Before Matt left, he told him to help the boys move some cattle off the flats, and Hal went out into the rain in a huff. He hates getting wet, you know."

"He hates taking orders more," the younger woman replied.

"A trait he shares with you, my darling." Betty sighed as she lifted her fork. "I do hope you won't start right in on Matt. He's been in a terrible temper since you left."

"I'll wait a day or two, all right?"

Betty looked faintly apprehensive. "All right."

CATHERINE HAD GONE to bed when Hal came in. She heard him talking to Betty as he went past her door. Good old Hal, she thought with a smile. He was her only ally in Matt's family. She and Hal were a lot alike, both renegades, both refugees from Matt's authority.

She closed her eyes and slept, feeling safe and comfortable in her warm bed, hearing the rain come down in torrents. She wondered if Matt would be able to fly back tonight.

A few hours later the sound of a motor awakened her, and she lifted the window curtain beside the bed to peek out. The outside lights were ablaze, and a tall, lean man in a distinctive tan trench coat and a silverbelly Stetson was getting out of a car. He lifted an attaché case and plowed toward the house in the drenching rain. Matt!

With faint misgivings she stared down at his hard, formidable face. It was a shock to catch Matt unawares; he was almost always lighthearted and smiling when he was around Catherine. He smiled more with her than with anyone else. But when he didn't know she was looking, he became a stranger. Matt was a puzzle she'd never solved.

Most of his men were afraid of him, although he was never unfair or overly demanding. It was that air of authority he wore, the remnants of his strict upbringing.

Matt was the oldest of Evelyn's sons from her first marriage, and from all accounts, his childhood hadn't been an easy one. Matt's real father had been a military man, and Matt's early life had been spent at military academies. When his father died and Evelyn married Great-Uncle Henry, he'd stayed in the academy for another year. Then he went on to boarding school, then college, and then service in the Marine Corps, with little chance for parental love in between. Henry was a formidable man himself, and Evelyn was more businesswoman than mother.

But Matt seemed to have gotten enough love from other sources, she thought wryly, remembering the occasional woman she'd seen him with and the adoring glances that came his way. When she was in college, Catherine's girlfriends had begged to come to the ranch, just for a glimpse of Matt.

Catherine pursed her lips and studied Matt's tall, muscular body as he started through the gate. He was devastating physically, all right. And he had Spanish eyes, very dark and sparkling, and a deeply tanned face that was sharp-featured and aristocratic. He was something else. She tingled with pride, just looking at him, although she was ready for a fight if it was going to take one to get out from under his thumb. Part of her knew that Matt would never be able to return her tempestuous feelings for him. And it was because of that, more than anything else, that she had to escape. It was devastating to be around Matt and watch him go out with other women all the time. He seemed to have a different one every month. All of them were experienced, sensual women. Nothing like poor little Kit, who had to hide her tears from him. It would have killed her if he'd known how she really felt—that all her outbursts of anger were just defensive tactics.

"Tomorrow," she whispered, and smiled. "Tomorrow we'll have it out, big cousin."

She lay back and closed her eyes.

THE NEXT MORNING when Catherine came down for breakfast Hal was at the breakfast table with Betty, but Matt was already out the door and gone. Hal looked up, his brown eyes sparkling in a mischievous face. At twenty-three he was the youngest of the three brothers. He was shorter than Matt and not as muscular. Hal had a good brain, when he used it, and was a whiz with machinery. But he preferred the nightspots to the ranch and slipped away at every opportunity. He played at life, and Matt had threatened to throw him off the property because of his penchant for playing practical jokes. But he was loveable, for all his wicked ways, and Catherine had a soft spot for him. In her younger days, he'd been her staunchest ally in dodging Matt's temper.

"Hi, cousin!" he grinned. "How was the big city?"

"Great!" She sat down and filled her plate. "I got a job!" She told him all about it, enjoying his amazed look as she talked.

"Have you told Matt?" he asked after a minute, his gaze quietly curious.

"I haven't seen him yet."

Hal pursed his lips. "She doesn't know?" he asked Betty.

Catherine cocked her head at him. "Know what?" she asked hesitantly.

"Matt found out where you really were. He's stopped your allowance."

"Oh, Hal, why did you do that!" Betty groaned.

Catherine's eyes sparkled with passion as she threw down her napkin. "Stopped my allowance? He can't! Those shares are mine!"

"He can do what he likes until you're twenty-five," Hal said.

"Where is he?" Catherine demanded.

"Down on the flats, checking to make sure the cattle were all moved before the rains came," Betty said reluctantly. "He told Hal to get them moved before he left for Houston."

Hal didn't reply. He looked disturbed and reached for his coffee cup.

Catherine didn't notice. She was fuming. She needed that allowance to set herself up in New York. She wouldn't have any money until her first paycheck. And Matt knew it!

"I'll shoot him," she muttered.

"Now, darling, don't be hasty," Betty said, trying to soothe her.

But Catherine was already on her way upstairs to change into jodhpurs and boots.

CHAPTER TWO

THE SUNLIGHT WAS wonderful after the thundering flood of late-summer rain the night before, but Catherine wasn't paying the least attention to the beauty of the wide-open land and grazing cattle or the distant enormity of the feedlot. Her narrowed green eyes were flashing, and the set of her slender body in the saddle was as rigid as her perfect mouth.

She shivered a little in the early-morning chill. Autumn was coming on. Already the hardwoods were beginning to get crisp leaves on them. She searched the horizon for Matt, but he was nowhere to be seen. She could have screamed. There were times when being part of the Kincaid clan was an absolute torment, and this was one of them. She had a great future in New York in public relations. Why couldn't Matt let her go after it? Of course, he didn't know about the New York job offer, but what he'd done would prevent her from going anywhere without his approval. It was always like that. She made plans and Matt fouled them up. He'd done it for years, and nobody had ever stood up to him. Except Catherine, of course.

This time he wasn't having it all his own way. The fact that he was the chief stockholder in the Kincaid Corporation was irrelevant. Even the fact that she was madly in love with him was irrelevant. He wasn't going to get away with telling her how to live her life.

She spotted movement down on the soggy river flats, where a few red-coated, white-faced Herefords were mired in mud, and she smiled coldly. She saw only a couple of his men, and that was just as well; she didn't really want an audience.

Her heartbeats quickened as she coaxed the little mare into a canter and felt the breeze tossing her straight thick dark hair in the wind. She looked good in her jodhpurs and in her neat little blue-checked shirt that left her brown arms bare, but it hadn't been for Matthew's sake that she'd dressed so neatly. Matthew wouldn't notice if she did a Lady Godiva unless she scared his precious cattle. He was immune to women, she thought. Freedom was an obsession with Matt. He'd said often enough that the woman hadn't been born who could get him in front of a minister.

Catherine had thought about that. She'd thought about making love to Matt, about feeling his hard sensuous mouth on her own. She'd daydreamed for years about it, about marrying him and living on Comanche Flats forever. But she'd learned over the years to keep her deeper longings to herself. Matt helped by ignoring her occasional stray glance that lingered too long and the quickening of her breath when he came close. She'd dated at college and had brought some of the boys home. To Betty's frank astonishment, Matt had given them a thorough grilling, every one, and he'd set the rules about when Catherine had to be in. It was another of the domineering traits she'd once taken for granted and now resented bitterly. Matt would never want her the way a man wanted a woman. But he had control of her life, and he liked that.

At last she saw him. He was kneeling to examine a hoof of one of the cows. His dark hair was concealed by the wide brim of his hat, and he looked almost like one of the cowboys in his faded denims and chambray shirt and worn boots. But when he stood up, all comparison ended. Matt had the kind of physique that turned up once in a blue moon outside motion pictures. His broad shoulders rippled with muscle, and his lithe body had a sensual rhythm that held women's eyes when he moved. He was long and lean and darkly tanned, and he had eyes so black that they looked like coal. His nose had been broken once or twice and looked it, and his mouth had a perpetual mocking twist that could put Catherine's back up in seconds. His cheekbones were high, a legacy of a Comanche ancestor, and he looked as if he needed a shave even when he didn't because the shadow of his beard was so dark. But he was immaculate for a cattleman. His nails were always trimmed and clean, and he had an arrogant, regal carriage that made Catherine think of the highlander who had come to Texas so many years ago to found the Kincaid line.

The Kincaids had been a political power in this part of the state at one time. Catherine had learned that from listening to Matt's mother talk about Jackson Kincaid, her first husband. She was proud of Matt's lineage and never let him forget it. The Kincaid Corporation, the remnant of a small empire, was Matt's legacy. Evelyn had given shares in it to Great-Uncle Henry, combining both families' interests. But it was Matt who held the power, and nobody forgot it.

Matt's sharp ears caught the sound of her mount's hooves, and he whirled gracefully. His grim face and dark eyes brightened at the look on her face. He tilted his hat back and propped a boot against the oak tree behind him. He leaned back, watching her with an expression that made her want to hit him.

"So there you are," she muttered, fumbling her way out of the saddle.

"Honey, you'll never learn to be a good rider if you don't listen when I try to teach you things. That's no way to come down off a horse," he said good-naturedly.

"Don't 'honey' me," she said. She went right up to him, glaring at him, hating him, her small hands clenched at her back. "Mama told me what you've done. Now you listen to me, Matthew Kincaid. I just grew up, and you can stop trying to put me back in your hip pocket. I won't fit! You gave me those shares when I turned eighteen, and you can't take them away."

His narrow eyebrows arched. "Who, me?" he asked innocently. Still watching her with amusement, he pulled a cigarette from his pocket and lit it with maddening carelessness. "I didn't take them away, I just had the interest you were drawing reinvested." He grinned wider. "Look in the small print, Kit. I retained that right when I signed over the shares to you."

Her eyes lanced into him. "What am I going to do to pay my rent in New York, beg on street corners?"

"I don't remember any discussion about New York," he returned at once.

She hated that smile. She knew it all too well from years past. It meant he'd dug in his heels and there wouldn't be any moving him. Well, she'd just see about that.

"I've been offered a job with a very prestigious New York public relations firm," she told him. "It wasn't easy to get, and it was only because the father of one of my college friends works there that I was even considered. It's a plum of a job, Matt. The salary—"

"You're only twenty-one," he said, pursing his lips. "And New York is a wild place for a little country girl."

"I'm not little!"

His eyes went pointedly to her small breasts, and he grinned. "No?"

She let out a furious cry and aimed a kick at his shins with one hard-booted toe. He sidestepped with lightning grace, and she went down flat on her back in the wet grass and mud.

He grinned at the shock on her face, then flashed a look at two of his men who were riding by with curious looks on their faces.

"Better get up quick, honey, or Ben and Charlie there will think you're trying to entice me into making love to you," he said outrageously.

"Matthew... Dane Kincaid... I hate you...!" she sputtered as she tried to get to her feet.

He was trying to stop laughing, but without much success. His white teeth flashed and black eyes were alive in his swarthy face. He reached down to grab her wrist and jerked her to her feet. His strength was a little frightening. He looked lithe and limber, but he could have forced her to her knees if he'd flexed his hand, and she knew it. Her angry eyes scanned his hard face, her fury kindling all over again at the traces of humor she saw lingering there. She drew back a hand, but it hovered in midair.

"Hold it right there, honey," he said, chuckling. "I don't mind a little dirt, but if you connect with that muddy hand, I'll hit you where it hurts most."

"I'll tell Mama!" she threatened.

"Betty would hold you still for me."

He loosed her wrist, and she rubbed it, surprised at the tingling sensation that lingered after his hard fingers had withdrawn.

She tugged her long-tailed shirt out of her jodhpurs and used the hem of it to wipe off the mud. He stuck his hands on his lean hips and watched her with the infuriating superiority that clung to him like the faint mud stains on his shirt.

She sighed. "I hate you, you know."

"No you don't, Kit." He grinned. "You just want your own way. And this time, you're not getting it. I'd never forgive myself if I turned you loose in that big city all alone, fresh out of college in Forth Worth."

"And that's another sore spot," she threw back at him, shivering a little in the cool air. "You hardly even let me go off to college. Not me, oh, no, I had to commute on weekends! It's a wonder you didn't come with me and hold my hand as I crossed streets!"

"I did think about it," he murmured dryly.

"I'm grown up!"

"Not yet," he corrected. His eyes went down to her breasts and lingered there, where the hard tips were visible through her thin shirt, and he smiled slowly. "But you're getting there."

She stared at him unblinkingly, surprised at the remark, at the way he was studying her breasts. Boys had looked at her that way when she wore swimsuits or low-cut blouses, but Matt never had. It shocked her that he'd even bothered to look. Perhaps it was just another way of getting back at her. She folded her arms over her breasts as a scarlet flush covered her cheeks. She avoided meeting his eyes.

"Hey," he commanded softly.

"What?"

"Look at me."

She forced her embarrassed eyes up, but he wasn't teasing her. He looked faintly kind, for Matt.

"If you want to practice public relations, I'll put you to work," he said. "You can publicize my foundation sale month after next."

"Matt, that's not a job!"

"It's a job," he said firmly. "A lot of work goes into that annual sale, and a lot depends on its being a success. I usually hire an outside agency to handle it, but since you're here, you can do it. I'll even let you design the brochure." He eyed her closely. "That's a challenge, honey. Show me how capable you are, and I'll make you a present of an apartment in New York and find you another job to boot. I've got some contacts of my own."

She wavered. It was tempting. Very tempting. And if he hadn't been trying to bend her to his will, she might have accepted his offer. But he was calling the shots, and if she made a success of the job, he'd probably find some way to make her keep working for him. She'd never get away.

So, he wanted his sale publicized, did he? She smiled faintly. Okay. She'd do it. And in such a way that he'd be more than delighted to send her on her way.

"Okay," she agreed after a minute, her green eyes sparkling. "I'll just take that dare."

"I'll start you off tomorrow morning. Be at the office eight-thirty sharp," he replied. "Now you'd better get home and change into something a little more decent, or Betty will come after me with a shotgun."

"I can just see you now, running for the border," she returned dryly.

He smiled wickedly. "This far away?" he said with a chuckle. "Hell, no, I'd drive." He pulled his hat low over his eyes. "Hadn't you better go home and change?"

She knew when she was defeated. Green eyes glared up at him. "You're just stifling me," she ground out. "Smothering me! My gosh, you tie me to the house. You grill every man I date. You won't let me go to New York and find my own way in life—Matt, I'm a grown woman," she said, trying to reason with him. "You're an old bachelor…!"

His eyebrows lifted as he lit another cigarette. "Honey, I'm just thirty-one."

"And someday you'll be fifty-one and all alone, and what will you do then?" she asked haughtily.

He smiled slowly. "I guess I'll start seducing kids your age."

She opened her mouth, started to speak, thought better of it and closed her mouth with a snap.

"My, my, the fish aren't biting today," he said conversationally. Boldly, his dark eyes wandered slowly down the length of her slender body, assessing her; then suddenly they shot up to catch her eyes. She stared back, and the world narrowed to Matt's face. Cows bellowed all around and cowboys whistled and called, moving them along, but she no longer noticed them. A wild tingling feeling raced through her body as she studied Matt. Never before had she looked at him so intently.

He touched the cigarette to his chiseled mouth, breaking the spell. "No comeback, Kit?" he murmured dryly.

She sighed. "I can't fight you," she muttered. "You just laugh at me."

"It's less dangerous than doing what I'd like," he returned, his dark eyes sparkling.

"Try slinging me over your knee, cattle baron, and I'll make you a legend in your own time with that brochure you want drawn up," she threatened.

"No you won't." He threw down the cigarette and ground it out. "We're buddies, remember?"

"We used to be. Then you started being so horrible to me," she reminded him. She dusted off her stained jodhpurs. "God knows what I'll tell Mama about the way I look," she added, giving him a mischievous glance.

"Tell her you tried to seduce me," he suggested with a wicked grin.

"That'll be the day," she said darkly, turning back toward her horse.

"Don't you think you could?" he teased.

She mounted, feeling odd at the suggestion, and glanced down at him. "Actually," she told him, "I don't know how."

"No experience?" he asked mockingly, but there was a serious note in his deep, drawling voice.

"I've been saving myself for you, didn't you know?"

He laughed softly. "Have you?"

It was new and heady to flirt openly with Matt. She'd never done it before. She wrapped the reins gently around one hand and stilled the nervous little mare, patting her neck as she talked softly to her. Her amused eyes met Matt's. "Better lock your door at night."

His dark eyes twinkled with new lights. "I do. I've been terrified of you since you graduated from high school."

"Have you really?" She grinned. "I did notice all the women you gathered around you to protect yourself from me."

He didn't smile. His eyes narrowed thoughtfully. "Your suitors have been conspicuous by their absence the past few months," he remarked.

She lifted her shoulders. "Jack gave me up in the early summer," she said. "He was afraid you'd kill him if he tried anything with me. He even said so."

He looked toward the cowboys, who were starting to drive cattle through a nearby opening in the fence. "I've got work to do, honey."

"Conference over." She sighed. "You never talk to me."

He looked up, and something in his black eyes made her nervous. "I may do that—sooner than you think, little Kit." His gaze grew piercing, searching. "After all, you're straining at the bonds for the first time. You'll fly away if I'm not careful."

"I'm not a bird, you know," she said pleasantly.

"More of a tadpole," he murmured.

"You call me a frog again, and I'll tell Hal and Jerry," she threatened.

"Tadpole, not frog. Go ahead and tell them," he challenged, smiling. "Remember me, Kit? I'm the black sheep."

"Some black sheep. You're the one with the brains and the strong back," she had to admit, softening as she looked down at him. His face was creased with harsh lines that neither of his brothers had. It was always Matt who'd had the lion's share of the responsibility. Hal did what he pleased, and Jerry did what he could, but he didn't have Matt's business sense and was intelligent enough to admit it.

"Was I asking for a vote of confidence?" he asked with mock astonishment.

"You never would. But you've got mine," she said with a soft smile.

He seemed to tauten at the softness in her voice. "Risky, Kit, looking at me that way," he said with a faint smile. "I might go crazy right here."

"You, go crazy over a woman?" she asked with a laugh. "That'll be the day. Anyway, it would take someone with experience and pizzazz. I'm just your pesky stepcousin."

"You're a beauty, young Catherine," he returned, and seemed to really mean it. She colored gently at the masculine appreciation in the look he gave her. "Quality, all the way."

"You're not bad yourself, cowboy," she murmured demurely. "I have to go home and change. I thought I'd go see a movie later."

"Did you? What kind of movie?"

"There's one of those very adult shows at the drive-in," she confided. "I thought I'd take Hal and educate him."

His face went hard all at once, and the sudden eclipse of humor surprised her. "No," he said quietly. "Not Hal. If you go to any drive-ins, I'll take you. And not tonight. I've got a date already. I'll take you Friday."

It was like sticking her finger in an electric socket. She simply stared at him. "What?"

"I said I'll take you to the movies Friday, Kit," he replied, and grinned at her. "I'm not letting you corrupt Hal. Besides, he's too young for you."

She burst out laughing. She must have imagined his sudden anger, she told herself. Matt had only been teasing all along.

"I suppose he is," she had to admit. "Are you?"

His mouth curled. "What do you think, honey?" he asked in a tone he'd never used with her before. It was like velvet. Soft. Honey smooth. Seductive.

She stared down at him curiously. "You're too old for drive-ins," she said slowly.

He shook his head. "We'll take the pickup and I'll buy you a pizza. It will rejuvenate me," he added with a grin.

"I can just see you at a drive-in," she murmured. Her green eyes flirted with his dark ones. "Okay. But I won't kiss you if you drink beer."

His eyebrows lifted and something flashed in his eyes. He laughed gently. "Okay."

She'd shocked herself with her impulsive remark, and now she felt embarrassed. As if Matt would want to kiss her! But her eyes fell to his hard mouth as if of their own accord, and she stared at his lips with unexpected curiosity. She looked up in time to see a wildness in his eyes. A shock of electric current linked them, making her want to dive down into his arms and kiss his hard, sexy mouth until the aching of her young body stopped. And that shocked her enough that she dragged her eyes away.

"You did mean what you said, about letting me go to New York if I do a good job on your sale?" she persisted.

He turned back toward his men. "I meant it."

"Matt—"

"Hey, Charlie, bring the truck for this one!" he called to an old cowboy and he gestured toward a downed cow farther along the trail.

She sighed in irritation. Well, that was that, he'd just forgotten that she was alive. That was his response to discussions he didn't want. He just walked away from them. She glared at his back for a long moment before she suddenly wheeled her mount and started toward the ranch.

Well, at least she had a chance to escape now. Her face burned as she remembered what she'd said to him about the drive-in. She'd probably shocked him with that silly remark about kissing him.

She shifted in the saddle, thinking about going to a drive-in with Matt. Her body tingled with delight at the prospect. He'd never taken her anywhere alone. And probably he wasn't going to now, either. He'd invite one of the family to go with them. And why would he take the pickup?

Matt bothered her. He puzzled her. He was a cutup, a wild man—except when he was being Mr. Kincaid. She'd seen him do that. She'd watched him put down men who thought they could walk all over him because he seemed easygoing. There was a white-hot temper and a will like iron underneath his good humor.

Worrying about things wasn't going to help, she told herself. She'd do better to concentrate on how to promote the cattle sale. It was her only chance of escape from her family. And from Matt. She couldn't spend the rest of her life waiting for him. She couldn't live near him and watch him marry someone else—and he would eventually. The corporation would have to have an heir, and he was in control. Probably it would be some sophisticated socialite with holdings of her own. A merger more than a marriage.

She leaned forward over the little mare's mane and gave her her head as they went toward the barn.

CHAPTER THREE

JERRY AND BARRIE were at supper that night. Jerry, like Hal and Matt, had dark eyes, but he alone of the three had sandy-blond hair and a receding hairline. He was taller than Hal, but not as tall as Matt. Barrie was redheaded and blue eyed and very petite and mischievous. Catherine had always adored her.

As Annie waddled in with the salads, Catherine allowed Hal to seat her, and she noted his thoughtful glances. Matt hadn't made an appearance yet, and Catherine found herself watching the doorway, waiting. She knew he was going out, that he wouldn't be joining them for the evening meal, but she couldn't help watching for him. Habits were hard to break. She looked down at her blue shirtwaist dress and imagined I Adore Matt written all over it with a felt-tip marker. That was vaguely amusing and she laughed.

"That's better," Hal murmured. "You were looking solemn, little cousin."

"Who, me?" She gaped. "I'm never solemn."

"I know," he returned.

"Betty said you were trying to go to New York to work," Jerry said, glancing at her. He smiled absently. "I knew you'd only come to grief."

"How?"

"I know my brother. Matt keeps you on a short leash, doesn't he?"

Catherine glared at him. "I can do what I please. As it happens," she said to save face, "Matt's offered me a job. I'm organizing the foundation sale."

"Darling, how lovely!" Barrie exclaimed. "You'll do a grand job."

"You and your cattle hang-up," Jerry growled at her. "I can see you now, leading that prize bull of yours around, with the baby under one arm—when you ever decide to have a baby."

"Don't be silly, my love," Barrie murmured, peering up at him. "I'll have the baby in one of those carry things they wear these days. He'll learn the business from the ground up." She elbowed her husband. "Anyway, what do you mean, 'when I decide to have a baby'? How can I? You're never at home. It takes two," she added with a poisonous smile.

Jerry cleared his throat and offered Betty the rolls.

Catherine and Hal exchanged amused glances just as Matt walked in. It was obvious he'd changed for his date, because he was wearing a dark dinner jacket with a red tie. He looked so devastating that Catherine had to drop her eyes.

"Hal, I'd like a word with you," he said without preamble.

Hal looked uncomfortable and made a face, but he got up and went with his stern older brother out into the hall. The door closed and everyone exchanged puzzled glances.

"He didn't move those cattle like Matt told him," Barrie volunteered with a grimace. "At least four of them drowned."

So that was what Matt had been doing on the flats, Catherine thought suddenly, amazed that she hadn't connected the mired cattle with Hal's disobedience. Poor old Hal, she thought. Matt would eat him alive.

"Will he ever grow up?" Jerry grumbled. "He plays at life."

"He's very young, dear," Betty intervened.

Catherine was just about to rush to his defense, too, just as a loud voice broke the silence in the hall, followed by a thump and a hard thud. Catherine jumped to her feet and opened the door to find Hal just picking himself up from the floor. Matt was standing over him, unruffled, his face like stone, his eyes blazing with anger. He glanced at Catherine, and he was a stranger again, all authority and bristling masculinity. He laughed curtly.

"Florence Nightingale to the rescue," he chided. "Pick him up and pet him, if you like, but do it damned fast. He's leaving for Houston. And if he doesn't straighten out his priorities while he's there," he added with a cold glare at Hal, who was gingerly touching his jaw, "he can damned well stay in Houston."

"My God, it was only four head—" Hal began.

"One head would have been one too many," Matt replied.

"Jerry and I have a stake in the corporation, too," Hal shot back. "You're not the whole show!"

"I am until you can carry your share of the load," Matt returned. "Grow up!"

Hal got to his feet and glared at the taller man. "The iron man, aren't you?" He laughed mirthlessly. "No chinks in your armor, no human weaknesses. Not even a weakness for a special woman."

"You'd better phone and see if you can get a flight out of here tonight," Matt said, ignoring the little speech.

Hal inclined his head. "Whatever you say, boss." He fingered his jaw and glanced ruefully at Catherine. "Be sure to duck, cousin."

Catherine watched him turn toward the stairs. She started back toward the dining room, but Matt caught her arm.

The light touch was indescribable. He came up behind her and was so close that she could hear his heavy breath as it sighed out over her hair. His fingers were steely through the soft jersey of her dress sleeve, and she couldn't seem to get her breath.

Someone had closed the door to the dining room after she'd gone through it. Probably Jerry, she thought dazedly; he wasn't one to eavesdrop.

"Afraid of me?" he asked at her back.

She turned and looked up at him with soft green eyes. "No. Not really. It's just that you seem like a stranger sometimes, Matt."

"Hal has to learn responsibility," he said.

"I won't argue that," she replied. "But he won't ever be you."

He sighed half-angrily. His dark eyes searched hers in the sudden stillness of the hall.

"Don't you have a date to rush off to?" she asked pointedly.

"I have a social engagement," he replied. He pulled out a gold cigarette case—the one she'd given him for Christmas last year—and casually lit a cigarette, as if he had all the time in the world.

"Same difference," she said.

He shook his head, then lifted the cigarette to his smiling mouth. "It's a formal dinner. And women weren't included, except for the wives of the organizers."

"You don't owe me any explanations, Matt." She started toward the dining room, but he drew her back with the lightest pressure of his fingers.

"No, I don't," he agreed. She stared at his red tie.

His fingers moved to her throat and stroked its soft elegant line, and her mouth trembled. She looked up at him with her breath sticking in her throat.

"Don't," she pleaded breathlessly. It was the first time he'd ever touched her like that, and it frightened her. All her wild dreams went into hiding at the reality. The uncontrolled pleasure she felt was unexpected.

"Why not?" he murmured. "Bachelors are entitled to play a little, honey," he said with a slow smile, and his fingers stroked over a larger area, edging under the neck of her dress and onto her shoulder.

"Not with me, you don't," she said. She reached up to catch his fingers. "It's not fair, Matt. Shooting fish in a barrel."

"Why not, when it's the only way you can get the fish at all?"

"Matt…"

He looked down at her soft, full mouth, outlined carefully with a delicate lipstick. He moved closer, the hand that held the cigarette sliding around her waist to draw her body to the length of his.

She couldn't breathe at all now. She looked up into dark, secretive eyes and felt her body begin to throb. He'd held her before, of course, to comfort her when she cried and once to carry her over a rising stream bed. He'd even carried her to bed once when she was sick. But it had never been like this before, with his dark eyes hungry as they looked into hers and a nameless awareness between them that grew by the second.

"Have you ever been kissed properly?" he asked in a deep, gruff whisper.

Her lips parted under a rush of breath. "Of…course."

"I like it hard," he whispered, bending his head. "I may be rough with you at first. Don't be frightened."

"Matt!" Her voice sounded wild.

His fingers tilted her chin, and there was a sensuality in his face that she'd never seen before. "What are you so nervous about?" he breathed against her lips.

Her mouth felt the threat of his, and her hands clenched on his lapels as the images in her mind overwhelmed her. Her body was trembling, and he was so close to her that he had to feel it.

"So hungry," he whispered, threatening her mouth with his without ever coming close enough to take it. "Aching for me. And all it would take is another fraction of an inch, like this," he whispered, moving his head down so that she could breathe the minty scent of him, "and I could have you, Kit…"

"Please," she whimpered, stiffening as the words and his cologne and the warmth of his whipcord body all weakened her. "Matt, please, please…" She didn't realize that she was reaching up, her cold and trembling hands at the nape of his neck, her body at fever pitch with wanting.

"Oh, no." He laughed softly. Both hands caught her by the waist. "Not yet."

Her eyes widened. She was shaking. Shaking! And he was smiling at her with such worldly amusement…

"Damn you," she said under her breath, tears threatening.

"I'm late already," he said. "Go eat your dinner, honey. We'll put everything on hold until tomorrow night. The movie," he reminded her in a low whisper. "And I won't drink beer."

"I won't go!" She stared at him, eyes enormous in her

face, her body shaking with what he'd aroused and not satisfied.

"Yes you will." He brushed back a strand of chestnut hair from her shoulder. His eyes held hers.

She moved away from him, fighting for composure. "I won't be just one in a line," she said. "I won't let you seduce me. You're just after a new thrill. And I'm not going to be it," she said firmly.

He laughed deep in his throat, and his eyes were bright with amusement. "Coward," he murmured dryly.

She flushed, and almost ran back into the dining room. Catching herself, she slowly opened the door and left him standing in the hall.

CATHERINE DIDN'T HEAR another word that was said to her for the rest of the night. She smiled and talked automatically, and all the while she felt Matt's hands, the sigh of his breath on her mouth. She ached all over with strange new hungers, feeling oddly restless and irritable. And in the morning she was going to have to pretend she felt nothing because Matt was astute and it would be humiliating to let him see how she felt. If only she knew what kind of game he was playing! Would he really go that far? Would he tease her just to keep her under his thumb? She lay awake until the early hours, worrying about it, more determined than ever to break free before she fell victim to his dark, sensuous charm.

Hal flew out sometime in the night and wasn't at the breakfast table the next morning. Betty was, though. And Matt.

He watched Catherine over his second cup of coffee, his eyes mocking as she fumbled her way through bacon and eggs.

"Such a lovely day, after all that rain," Betty was saying. "I think I'll drive into Fort Worth and do some shopping. Catherine, can I pick up anything for you?"

"No, thank you, Mama," Catherine replied, trying to stop her renegade heart from running wild every time Matt looked in her direction. He was wearing a three-piece gray suit, and he looked debonair and worldly.

She had on a simple short-sleeved green knit top and a skirt, and was worried that she might be overdressed for her first day on the job. "I didn't know what to wear this morning," she began hesitantly.

"Angel and the other girls usually wear dresses or skirts," Matt told her. "Jack, our sales manager, wears a suit. I alternate between suits and jeans, depending on my schedule. Today I have to fly down to San Antonio, so I'm a bit more formal. But we don't have a dress code. You can wear jeans if you like."

"I'll remember tomorrow. Do I get my own office?" she asked with a smile.

"You can share mine, honey. I've got an extra desk." He finished his coffee. "Ready?"

"Yes. See you later, Mama," she murmured, rising as Matt held her chair. She couldn't help but be puzzled by his new polite behavior. Even Betty seemed to notice, but she only smiled.

It felt strange riding beside Matt in his Lincoln. He glanced at her curiously; it wasn't like her to be so silent, so subdued.

"What's wrong?" he asked gently as he pulled up in front of the ranch office.

"Nothing," she said quickly and gave him a flashing smile. "I was just thinking up ideas for the sale."

Fortunately, he took that at face value. He got out and

opened her door, but he paused when she expected him to move, so that she cannoned into him.

His hands, firm and strong, caught her shoulders and he was so close that she felt his breath in her hair. He smelled of spice and tobacco, and the muscular warmth of his body enveloped her from head to toe. She couldn't quite breathe, and she didn't dare look up. Her heart was beating like mad.

"You've avoided looking at me all morning," he said quietly. "Is it because I tried to kiss you...or because I stopped too soon?"

Her face burned in reaction. And still she couldn't look up. Her lips parted on a rush of breath. "It's...new."

"Yes."

"Matt..."

"What?"

"Just... Matt." She lifted her face then, and her misty green eyes sought his. He seemed to stop breathing and just stared at her. He didn't smile. His eyes searched, probed.

"Don't be afraid of me, Kit," he said, his voice deep and slow and soft.

"You're a stranger..."

He shook his head. "No. You're just looking at me in a different way."

"Why?" she asked, needing to know.

His hands tightened on her shoulders. "One day at a time, honey," he said then. "Don't ask questions until you want the answers. Let's get to work."

He turned her and prodded her toward the big one-story building that housed an impressive computer set-up. He had four young women working for him and two salesmen. Hal, when he was in town, had his own office, as well. It was a smoothly run operation. Thousands of dollars' worth of cattle were bought and sold without a single head being moved physically. Matt even had cattle on videocassettes so he could show them to prospective buyers out of town. It was a wildly progressive kind of business, and Matt ran it with ease.

He showed her into his private, carpeted office. The room looked like it belonged to Matt, all tough leather and earth colors and hardwood. There were two desks: his and a smaller one, where a computer and printer sat.

"You know how to use this, don't you?" he asked, smiling amusedly.

She glared up at him. "Yes. I had one just like it at school."

His eyes dropped to her mouth, and she was glad there were other girls working here. It kept him from doing what she really wanted him to do.

"If you have any problems with the computer, Angel can help you. She's the brunette at the desk outside my office. She has the preliminary information on the sale, as well. Until I volunteered you, it was her job to get it together for the public relations people. Okay?"

"Okay." She sat down and stared at the keyboard, a hundred conflicting emotions making her restless, disturbing her. She was hot despite the air-conditioning. It was already late September, but the weather was getting hotter instead of colder, if today was any indication.

"Don't wear your hair like that tonight," he said suddenly.

She glanced up, remembering that she had her chestnut waves in a bun on top of her head. "What?"

"Leave it loose. I hate hairpins."

"Do you ever stop giving orders?" she asked.

"Sure. In bed."

Her face flushed, and he smiled—a sensual, confident

smile that frightened her a little. He was a predator, and she was the quarry. That was what she'd always thought she wanted, but now that it was happening, she was afraid.

"Anyway," she continued nervously, "I'm not sure I want to go to a drive-in with you."

"Yes, you do," he returned. He leaned over her, surrounding her, one hand on her chair, the other on the edge of the desk. His dark face was close to hers, and she could see the hard lines in it, the twist of his firm lips, the silver sprinkled in the darkness of his straight, thick hair. His cheek was very close, and she wanted to touch its hardness.

Her eyes lifted to his and got lost there. She saw the muscles in his jaw go taut as they stared at each other, and his breathing began to get ragged.

"I want your mouth, Catherine," he said unexpectedly. "So I think I'd better get out of here before I shock a few people."

He stood up, and she fumbled with the papers on the desk, feeling all thumbs and inexperienced while she tried to decide if she'd just been hearing things or if he'd really said what she thought she'd heard.

"I'll, uh, get started," she said in a husky voice.

"You do that." He stuck his hands in his pockets, reading the flash of uncertainty on her face. "Catherine, I won't hurt you," he said under his breath.

She really crimsoned then, and he sauntered out of the office, catching other pairs of eyes as he walked. He really was the most devastating man!

What was she going to do? She wanted him so much. There had never really been anyone in her heart except Matt though the only interest he'd ever shown in her before was to check out the competition. He seemed to accept it as a necessity, but he made it as uncomfortable as he could for her few dates.

She wondered at the extent of his possessiveness. He'd worked his way into her life so slowly that, before she'd realized it, he'd become her life. And he knew it. That was what hurt most, that he had her in the palm of his hand while he was still going out with a string of women. He didn't even make a secret of it. Because, she told herself, he never got serious. He wouldn't get serious about her, either. She'd have to keep that in mind in case she got stupid and started begging him to kiss her at the drive-in.

For the time being, she decided to concentrate all her energy on preparing the publicity she would get out for Matt's foundation sale. And that meant she needed a list of the lots of cattle he was going to sell. She pulled them out of the computer, complete with herd numbers, lineage, weights and gaining ratios. It was a complicated business, cattle raising, but Catherine knew enough about it to get by.

She worked out a set of dates for releasing information and got together a list of potential out-of-state buyers to contact, all her tumultuous feelings forgotten in her fascination with her new job. Then she went to find Matt.

"If you're looking for Matt, he's already gone." Angel sighed, chin in her hands as she stared wistfully at the door. "He's flying down to San Antonio with his lunch date. I'll bet it's that Laredo real estate agent again," she murmured. "She's been hanging around for a month. Well, at least she's better than the oil company executive lady from New Orleans," she added with a bright smile.

"I didn't know there was a current lady," Catherine said, trying to sound lighthearted. "We never see them at the house."

"I don't imagine so!" Angel said meaningfully. "We only

know because they call him here. This last one has been around for about three months. But I think he's getting tired of her. He's been dodging her calls all week."

It was a horrible reminder of what would happen to her if she let Matt get too close, of what would happen when he tired of her innocence. He wasn't a marrying man; he'd said so. That only left one thing he could want, and after last night, she knew she was on the endangered-species list. That almost-kiss had knocked her to her knees. She could barely imagine what it would be like if he started making love to her.

And tonight he was going to take her to a drive-in, and she was going to go under in a haze if he touched her. She had to find an excuse not to go. The real estate agent from Laredo could have him, she thought venomously. She didn't care!

Catherine returned to her desk and turned the computer back on. She entered more information onto the disk, then hit the wrong keys. The program disk crashed before her startled eyes and she felt herself caving in. What a beautiful way to start a new job!

"Angel," she called sweetly.

The older girl stuck her head around the doorway with a grin. "Problems?"

"Uh, do you happen to have a spare program disk?" Catherine asked.

Angel grinned. "I did that my first day. Now I don't feel so alone. Back in a jiffy."

Catherine started all over again, furious with Matt for his attitude toward her when all the time he was seeing another woman. She glared at the screen and smiled slowly. Well, she did want to go to New York, didn't she? And if she failed at this, she was sure to get there even quicker. Matt's anger would be a minor obstacle, but she'd face it when she had to. With a wicked smile, she began to alter the names of the cattle. Only a little, of course. Names like "Comanche Flats Mile High #42" To "Comanche Flats Mule High #42." And then there was "Black Gold #20" To "Black Mold #20." When she got to the part about each bull's sire and dam, it got better. "This young bull's mother was the lovely Comanche Flats debutante heifer Miss Standish #10, who early in life married the dashing Comanche Flats bull Mr. Struts."

She had to close the door to Matt's office to keep Angel from overhearing her wild giggles as she entered the information for the brochure. Well, Matt wanted something catchy, didn't he? What a surprise this would be!

CHAPTER FOUR

CATHERINE SPENT THE rest of the day hiding in laughter. But she kept thinking ahead to the night and tingled all over. Waves of feeling like nothing she'd ever experienced in her life were buffeting her. She wanted Matt with a fever. She wanted Matt so much that even remembering the Laredo real estate agent didn't faze her. She wasn't a shrinking violet, after all. She had a few things going for her, too. And if last night was any indication, Matt wasn't exactly immune to her. That gave her an edge.

He hadn't come back when it was quitting time, so Catherine hitched a ride back up to the house with Angel. There was a note from Betty saying she'd gone into town to visit Mrs. Guthrie, one of her friends, and would be late. Annie always visited her sister on Friday night, so she wasn't there. Hal was in Houston. With a sigh, Catherine wondered if Matt would be back tonight, and since she hadn't heard otherwise, she assumed he would.

Since he'd said they were going to a movie, she dressed casually in a soft lavender silk blouse that buttoned and a striped lavender, burgundy and gray wraparound skirt. She left her hair long, brushing it until it fell softly and silkily around her face and shoulders. She stared at herself, liking what she saw. Now, if only Matt liked what he saw...

It was after six when he came home. He looked tired

for once, but his eyes darkened and twinkled when he saw Catherine.

"Nice," he murmured deeply.

She curtsied. "I had my body designed just to please you," she said with a laugh.

A smile crossed his tired face. "Butterfly," he said. "You color the world, Kit."

"Flowery speeches? Why, Mr. Kincaid, I didn't know you had it in you."

"Let me shower and change," he murmured as he came closer, "and I'll show you what else I've got."

"Promises, promises," she said coquettishly.

He smiled and turned toward the stairs. "I'll hurry so we don't miss the first show," he said. "Any particular thing you want to *not* see? If I don't drink beer, that is?" he added mischievously.

She flushed to her hairline, hating the ease with which he disconcerted her. "I like science fiction," she mumbled.

"So do I. Okay, we'll see that new picture at the Grand that they're raving about."

IT WAS A chilly night, and she was glad she'd worn a sweater, but Matt turned on the heater in the big new pickup truck, and it was toasty warm. He looked nice, she thought as he pulled into a parking space at the drive-in. He was wearing new jeans with a patterned blue shirt and shiny tan boots and a cream Stetson, and he looked so sexy that her hands itched to touch him.

He seemed to know that, and the sideways look he gave her as he reached out for the speaker said it all. She quickly averted her eyes to the screen. Previews were showing.

He turned up the sound, and she made a pretense of listening, but all the while all she could hear was the sound of her own wild heartbeat. Why was he taking her to a movie, when he'd spent years keeping her at arm's length? Was it because she was trying to get out from under his thumb, and this was some new way he'd thought up to keep her at Comanche Flats?

"How about some pizza?" he asked.

"Can I have that and coffee, too?" she asked.

"Whatever you want, Kit," he murmured, watching her with eyes that promised heaven.

She blushed helplessly as she looked back at him, a pirate sitting there with his sensuous mouth smiling at her, his dark eyes mischievous, teasing.

"Greenhorn," he chuckled. "Are you afraid of me?"

"I'd like that coffee," she sidestepped.

"Come on, then." He slid toward her so they could get out on her side and not have to put the speaker up again.

She got out, and he followed, taking her hand in his as they walked down the lot to the concession stand. Her fingers tingled as they locked with his big ones, and she felt very feminine and smug as they walked into the roomy snack bar. Especially when she saw other young women coveting him.

One particular woman, a striking blonde, was really giving him the eye. And, incredibly, he ignored her.

Catherine stared up at him uncomprehendingly as he ordered coffee and pizza.

He glanced down and tugged her closer with an arm around her waist. "Why so puzzled, Kit?" he murmured.

She shifted, her gaze going helplessly to the blonde, who'd given up and moved away with her date, a tall lanky youth who couldn't hold a candle to Matt's rough sensuality.

Matt's hand squeezed her waist. "Do I really strike you

as the kind of man who flirts with other women when he's out on a date?" he asked curiously.

She stared at his broad chest. "No. I'm sorry. But she was so lovely," she added, smiling.

"Not half as lovely as you are. Is that what you wanted to hear?"

"You don't have to flatter me."

He studied her averted face as the waitress brought their pizza. "Later, young Kit, you're going to eat those words. I promise."

Her body tingled with the threat of a revenge sweeter than her wildest dreams. She couldn't meet his eyes as they went back to the truck.

"Why the truck?" she asked when they were safely inside eating pizza.

"It's got vinyl seats," he said with a grin. "You don't think I'm going to eat pizza in that velour-covered dream of a Lincoln I drive on business?"

"Silly old me," she mumbled with a wicked smile.

"Besides," he added, sipping coffee to wash down the last of his pizza, "the Lincoln's front seat is smaller than this cab."

She frowned up at him. "What difference does that make?"

He lifted an eyebrow and chuckled softly. "I couldn't stretch out in it."

"Oh." She still didn't understand, and he was laughing more uproariously by the minute.

"It has something to do with not drinking beer...?" he prodded.

Her face burned, but she didn't drop her indignant eyes. "Now see here, Matthew Dane Kincaid!"

"Well, honey, you were the one who started it," he reminded her. He swept off his Stetson and looped it into a hat carrier above the rearview mirror. "I didn't have a thought in my mind until you told me you wouldn't kiss me if I drank beer. And I've gone dry all day in the heat, just thinking about it."

"I never know when to take you seriously," she said, defeated by his wide grin.

"Yes. I like it that way." He slid his arm across the back of the seat and stared at her as the feature film's opening credits flashed across the big screen. The light spilling from the screen accentuated the planes and curves of Matt's handsome face and the odd look in his narrowed eyes. "Come here, Kit."

Her heart stopped as she stared back at him, her face soft and hesitant, showing just a little fear of the stranger beside her.

"Come on," he coaxed. "I won't kiss you until you want me to."

"You're the most dreadful tease," she muttered to disguise the throbbing hunger of her body. She slid across the seat, stiffening a little as his arm went around her shoulders with lazy carelessness. Seconds later, when his arm remained still and warm, and the clean spicy scent of his body settled around her, she relaxed and let her cheek rest against his broad shoulder.

She watched the screen and saw nothing. Matt's lean, strong fingers kept brushing her neck and her cheek and her hair, and she tingled from the contact while she tried to decide if it was accidental or deliberate. Whatever it was, her pulse was going wild.

She turned her face so that she could see his, and he looked down at her in the semidarkness. His fingers brushed the side of her neck again, then suddenly pressed lightly against the visible throb of her pulse.

Her breath stopped. She was hungry for him, and now he knew how hungry. His other hand went under her chin and gently cupped it, and his head bent toward hers.

She stopped breathing altogether. The people on the big screen were suddenly screaming as a creature emerged from part of a spaceship, but Catherine didn't even hear them. All she heard was the soft sigh of Matt's smoky breath as his mouth brushed lightly against hers.

His fingers closed about her cheeks, parting her lips, and slowly he took them under his for the first time. Her breath caught as she felt the texture of his hard, warm mouth, the slight bristly pressure where his shaven cheek touched her skin. She savored the expert firmness of his lips as he began to deepen the kiss.

Her hands went hesitantly to his shirtfront and stopped there as she tried to decide what to do with them.

Matt lifted his mouth and held it poised over hers like a heady threat. "I'm not wearing an undershirt," he whispered outrageously. "If you want to touch me, go ahead."

It was too much too soon, and she stiffened. He laughed softly, as if her uncertainty delighted him.

"Virgin," he whispered, brushing his mouth lightly against hers. "Virgin. I feel as if I've never made love before, never tasted a woman's mouth or wanted her hands on me. You make it new for me, Kit."

"You know a lot," she whispered as his teeth nipped her earlobe and made her pulse jump.

"Of course I know a lot. I'm thirty-one." His fingers slid up and down her throat caressingly. "Hold me, Kit."

He helped her, sliding her arms up and around his neck, bringing her close so that her breasts slid softly against his hard chest. Her blouse was thin, and there was no bra under it—sheer idiocy on her part, she knew, because his own shirt was thin and he had to be able to feel her.

He did. He stiffened. His hands stilled on her back and his mouth opened against her forehead.

"My God, you're soft," he whispered roughly.

She wasn't experienced enough to handle a remark like that. She nuzzled her face into his throat and clung, while his hands slid to her rib cage and ran up and down it, his thumbs edging out to find that softness and explore it in the hot, pulsating silence.

His breath was audible as his mouth went down on hers. He held the kiss a long moment, dragging his lips roughly against hers when she began to respond to him with shy abandon.

"If you'll move away a little, I can touch you," he whispered into her mouth. "I want that. I want to take you in my hands and see just how soft you are."

She trembled and he felt it. His hands moved slowly to her back and smoothed up and down it in long, aching sweeps, while his mouth found her cheek and then her ear.

"Okay," he murmured gently, "I'll slow down." He drew back to look at her, his eyes soft and amused. "Just how green are you?"

She shifted in his loose embrace. "Well…"

"Come on."

Her mutinous mouth pouted as she looked up at him. "It's your fault. Mama never would let me go out with the experienced boys, and you always took her side against me."

"Of course I did," he said. "Do I look stupid?"

"What I got left with were boys who didn't know any

more than I did," she said, then sighed. "That is no way to get educated," she added, glaring.

"I'll do the educating," he said, and he didn't sound as if he were teasing at all. He tilted her chin up and searched her eyes for a long time. "No experience at all?"

"Not really," she confessed. "A French kiss is about as intimate as it ever got, and I think I must be frigid anyway, because I hated it."

He smiled. He chuckled. He caught her hand when she tried to hit him.

"No fair," he murmured. "You'll hurt my feelings."

"You don't have feelings," she shot back. "You're laughing at me, that's all you ever do is...oh!"

His mouth had stopped the snowballing tirade. She started to hit him, then felt his tongue enter her mouth and she froze. Her eyes opened to find his open, too. He was watching her reaction. His eyes were dark and smoldering, and his tongue was doing the wildest things to her mouth. She gasped. Her hands caught his shoulders and clung bruisingly; her heart seemed to stop beating.

She couldn't help it: she went under. Her eyes closed on a wild little moan and her nails stabbed into him rhythmically like the paws of a kitten in a pleasured daze.

He moved her so that she was lying across him with her head in the crook of his arm. And while the kiss made her crazy, his fingers began a slow, tender progression up her rib cage. They moved up just to a soft curve of her breast and then down again, in a lazy teasing pattern that managed eventually to make her arch and cry out in frustration.

Her eyes opened as he finally released her mouth to look into her flushed, surrendered face.

"I thought you didn't like French kisses," he mused.

"It's different when you do it," she whispered back, wonder in the look she gave him.

"I know how," he said simply. His fingers went back up her body again. "I know how to do this, too. And when you're half out of your mind wanting it, I'll touch you."

"I already am half out of my mind," she said shakily. Her whole body trembled this time when his fingers started back down to her waist again. "Are you trying…to make me beg?"

He shook his head. "I'm not into ego trips. This," he whispered, emphasizing his words with another achingly slow trailing of his fingertips against the blouse, "makes the pleasure so much sweeter when it happens. There's nothing sensuous about being grabbed."

"I've never been…grabbed."

"I know." He bent and kissed the very tip of her nose. "Why didn't you wear a bra, Catherine?" he asked softly. "Were you afraid it might discourage me?"

Her lips parted as she looked up at him, helpless, hungry. "I didn't think at all." Her eyes searched his slowly, her breath ragged as he delicately began to increase the area his fingers were tantalizing. "Matt, I'm going to faint when you touch me…"

"Yes, so am I," he whispered. He held her eyes. "Look at me."

His fingers moved, and this time they didn't stop. She felt them against the delicate rise of her body, coming down, cupping her in their warmth so that his palm rested gently against the hard tip. And she shuddered, her hands clinging to him, her teeth biting into her lower lip so that she wouldn't cry out.

His hand caressed her tenderly as he held her eyes, and the sound of his fingers against the silky fabric seemed almost as loud as the speaker. "You watched a movie with me when you were about sixteen," he said softly, holding her eyes, "and there was a very adult scene in it where a woman was being seduced. She cried out, and you were concerned that the man was hurting her. Do you remember?"

"You said...that she was crazy with pleasure," she whispered. "And I didn't understand."

"And now you do."

"Yes."

His head bent. "I could live forever on your mouth, Kit..." He kissed her gently and then not gently. And she clung to him, turning so that her body pressed against his and the whole world disappeared as his hand suddenly went under her blouse and against her soft, bare skin.

"It drives me wild when you cry out like that," he whispered roughly in her ear, his hand contracting as her body arched. "God, touching you like this is so sweet. So sweet." He kissed her trembling lips softly, tenderly, and his fingers stroked her lightly as a breath, lingering at the tiny hardness that told him everything she was feeling.

A sound outside the car brought Matt's head up. He was breathing as unsteadily as she was, and his mouth looked a little swollen, sensuous. He glanced in the rearview mirror and slowly moved his hand to her shoulder with an uneven sigh.

"You'd better sit up, honey," he said quietly. "We're about to have company."

He reached into his pocket for a cigarette and lit it, then slid his arm around a shaking Catherine as he pretended an avid interest in the movie. A strolling policeman with a flashlight wandered by, glancing into the truck and then going on along the row.

Catherine watched as a young couple under a blanket

struggled furiously to get separated as the flashlight aimed itself into their car. The policeman stopped there, and she turned her attention back to the screen, thinking how embarrassed she'd have been if he'd come along just a little sooner.

"He's the safety valve," Matt said quietly, smiling down at her. He leaned closer. "Strolling birth control."

She burst out laughing and buried her face in his chest. "You're horrible!"

"You didn't seem to think so a few minutes ago."

She nuzzled closer. "Didn't I?"

His fingers stroked her cheek and he pressed a slow, tender kiss into her disheveled hair. "I guess we'd better watch the movie. I can imagine how the family would react if they had to bail us out of jail for indecent exposure."

"They wouldn't believe it," she said simply.

He looked down at her. "They'd believe it, all right," he said, studying her face. "You look as if you've been made love to."

"So do you," she returned.

He smiled slowly. "I'll have to teach you how," he murmured. "You don't quite know how to give it back yet, do you?"

"I'm just a beginner," she reminded him, trying to keep her head.

"You'll stay that way, too, in the important way," he said, his voice deep and serious as he met her gaze. "Do you understand me, Kit? Seduction is not part of the plan."

"You won't take me to bed?" she asked with mock incredulity. "What's wrong with me?"

"Not one damned thing," he returned. "Except that Betty trusts me." He drew her close and kissed her forehead lightly. "I have to take excellent care of you, Kit. The last thing I want is a shotgun wedding."

That brought it all back. "The last thing you want is a wedding, period," she said, forcing herself to be light about it though she was dying because he didn't want to marry her. "Join the club. I have a career to look forward to, once I convince you that I'm capable of it."

He frowned, as if he hadn't expected her reply. "Are you serious?"

"Of course! You did promise me, Matt," she reminded him, and quickly put her day's work to the back of her mind. She knew he wouldn't keep that promise, and so did he. But when she failed miserably, he'd let her go. He'd probably buy the ticket. And that was a little depressing, especially after what they'd just shared. She cocked her head at him. "You promised," she repeated.

He sighed, turning his eyes back to the screen. "So I did."

She laid her head back against his broad chest, loving him so much that she hurt all over. But she couldn't let him see that. "Sorry."

"About what?"

"That your strategy didn't work," she murmured. "I like kissing you, Matt, but it won't keep me on Comanche Flats."

His face, if she'd seen it, would have been a revelation. His arm tightened around her roughly for a minute before he relaxed and brought his cigarette back to his lips. "Well then, little Kit, I guess I'll have to find another tack."

That was an admission, she told herself. He'd brought her here trying to give her another incentive to stay home. He knew she wanted him, although he didn't know how much. Well, it wouldn't work. She was going to New York, where she wouldn't be vulnerable, and she was going to find a man who'd love her, not dominate her.

"But meanwhile," he murmured, tipping her head back, "I'm going to see to it that you get a little educating in the things that matter. Just so that you can protect yourself." And his mouth went down against hers roughly, hungrily and for so long that she was dazed when he finally lifted it again. He searched her shocked eyes. "Just don't get addicted to me, honey," he added in a cutting tone, "because nobody gets me for keeps. Not even you."

She could hardly believe what she'd heard. Matt had never been cynical with her before. "I won't," she promised curtly.

He laughed mirthlessly. "We'll see."

Her fingers touched his mouth as he started to bend again. "You might warn the real estate agent from Laredo, too," she said, smiling as the shock touched his face. "She might need the warning even more than I do." She turned her attention back to the screen, and he slowly crushed out his cigarette in the ashtray.

"Who told you about Layne?" he asked quietly.

She gave him a haughty stare. "Do you think the family doesn't know about your women, just because you don't bring them home?"

His eyes returned to hers, quiet, watchful. "Layne is working on a project with me," he said after a minute. "I'm expanding a feedlot, and she has a client with land that adjoins mine."

"What does she look like?" she asked, hating herself for wanting to know.

He didn't seem to mind telling her, oddly enough. He even smiled. "She's twenty-nine, tall, dark-eyed and dark-haired."

"And experienced?" she asked.

"And experienced. Most of my women are, if you're curious about that part of my life. You've never expressed any interest in it until now."

"I'm not interested," she hedged.

"No?" He stretched lazily, and her eyes went uncontrollably to the lean, hard-muscled length of his body, down his broad chest to his narrow hips and powerful long legs and big booted feet. "I like your body, too, Kit," he murmured, catching her out. "I especially like the way it feels."

"What an interesting movie!" she enthused, crossing her arms as she curled up on the seat to watch the space creature devour a human.

"Is it? If you won't sit on my lap, then give me your hand." He reached out his lean fingers and laced hers with them. Then he leaned back to smoke another cigarette and watch the movie while Catherine ground her teeth in frustration.

They went home at midnight in a silence unbroken except for the radio. She walked into the house beside Matt, conflicting emotions tearing at her self-control. She didn't know what he wanted, and she was afraid, now that he'd seen how vulnerable she was to him.

Once he'd closed and locked the outside door, she turned, wanting to ask him what the game was. But he turned back and, holding her eyes with his dark ones, he tossed his Stetson onto the hall table. He started toward her with a steady, measured stride.

"Matt..." she began.

He caught her by the waist and drew her to him. "It's a hell of a lot more exciting to kiss standing up," he murmured. "Come closer, Kit. Your legs won't melt if they touch mine."

"I don't—" She caught her breath as his hands slid to her hips and brought her thighs into total contact with his.

"That's better," he whispered, smiling wickedly.

"Mama told me not to ever—" she tried again.

"Shut up." He bent and caught the back of her head with both hands, holding her face where he wanted it while his mouth made mincemeat of her protests. He forced her set lips to part, and his tongue penetrated the soft line of them delicately, sensually. His hips moved slowly against hers in a rhythm that made her blush, and still the kiss went on and on until it had the effect he meant it to have. With a tiny moan, she stood on tiptoe to get closer to him and linked her arms around his neck to lift herself in an even more intimate embrace.

"Yes," he breathed into her hungry mouth. "Yes!" His arms lifted her clear of the floor, and the world spun away in a blaze of open mouths and wildly beating hearts.

She couldn't get enough of him. It was so sweet to kiss him like this, to feel his heart slamming at the walls of his chest, to feel his teeth cutting into her lip as he deepened and lengthened the hard, devouring kiss.

All at once his body went rigid. Quickly, he put her back on her feet and held her away from him. He looked down at her with dark, smoldering eyes.

"Go upstairs, honey," he said huskily. "Go fast."

"But, Matt," she protested, her voice a mere whisper, her body trembling.

"I want you like hell," he ground out, and his desire showed in his eyes, his shaking chest. "Get out of here while you can."

She didn't argue. She wanted to, and for one wild instant she was tempted, but then the logical part of her mind started thinking about consequences, and that sent her up the stairs. She slid her hand along the banister, still tasting Matt on her mouth, her breasts throbbing from the hard pressure of his chest against them. She stopped at the very top of the stairway and looked down.

Matt was standing there, bareheaded, a cigarette in one hand, his eyes intent on her, his stance rigid.

She lifted her fingers to her lips and impulsively blew him a kiss. And he smiled.

It took all her strength to go on to bed. She knew suddenly and deliciously that Matt was as vulnerable as she was. He wanted her. That gave her a weapon to fight back with, and she was going to use it. Matt wasn't going to win this time. She was. At last she could escape his domination. But did she really want to?

CHAPTER FIVE

IT WAS HARD to sleep and in the morning it was even harder for Catherine to get on her clothes and go down to breakfast. Everything seemed different. Matt had changed from a wickedly teasing stepcousin into a sensuous stranger. She didn't know how to handle the side of him she'd glimpsed last night, and she couldn't begin to guess at the reason for his behavior. He wasn't looking for permanent ties; he'd made that very plain. Why, then? Just to keep her at home? That didn't seem likely. He wouldn't like her hanging around mooning over him all the time. Maybe he'd had a fight with the real estate agent from Laredo and was just biding his time, playing with her until his ladylove got over her anger.

She still hadn't worked it out when she went downstairs, half excited and half apprehensive about seeing Matt again. She was wearing a green shirtwaist dress with high heels, her hair in a neat French twist, and Matt's eyes came up immediately when he saw her at the doorway of the dining room. She almost jumped at the impact of the level, probing stare, but she didn't look away.

Betty was just finishing her own breakfast. "Good morning, darling," she called gaily. "I'm just off to Jane's for a coffee. That Barnes girl is getting married, you know, and we're all taking turns with the fetes. I'll be back about noon. We can have lunch in town if Matt can spare you."

"I'll do my best," Matt said with a meaningful smile at Catherine. He was looking smart in denim jeans with a chambray shirt open at his chest, and Catherine had to force her eyes away.

"That would be lovely," she told her mother with a bright smile.

Betty kissed her cheek as she passed, neat in her oyster-colored suit. "See you later. Bye, Matt. Don't the two of you overdo it."

"We won't," he promised, chuckling at Catherine's blush.

She filled her plate, then sat opposite him, ignoring him, vaguely aware of the sound of Betty's car as she drove away.

"I won't go away," he said dryly.

She glanced up as he sipped black coffee. "I should hope not," she said nonchalantly. "You'd break the Laredo real estate agent's heart!"

"How safe is your own, Catherine Melinda?" he asked gently.

Her green eyes searched his. "Safe enough."

"I wonder." He put down his coffee cup. "I want you."

Her eyes widened.

"That's right," he said, reading the shock in her face, "I want you."

"Well, I'm not up for grabs," she began hesitantly.

"I'm going to get you, too," he continued quietly, the threat in his eyes, in his mocking smile. "Run, if you like, and I'll be two steps behind. Until I catch you."

"I'll get pregnant!" she burst out.

His eyebrows shot up. "Not damned likely," he returned. "Not with strolling birth control on patrol."

"I will not go to any more movies with you!" she flashed.

He sighed wearily. "Well, in that case, we're in a lot of

trouble. Because if we stay alone together for longer than two minutes, you know as well as I do where it will end."

"Not in your bed," she said firmly.

"It's better on the carpet," he returned outrageously. "More adventurous."

The familiar line made her choke on her coffee. Her wet eyes accused him, but he only grinned.

"I'm going to New York to be a public relations person," she told him.

"Not until you finish my sale, you aren't," he replied easily. He leaned back in his chair, watching her, and slowly flicked open yet another button on his shirt.

Her eyes widened as that broad expanse of deeply tanned skin and thick, curling hair peeked out. She swallowed, dragging her gaze to her plate.

"Do I disturb you, Kit?" he murmured. "I can't imagine why. You've seen me without a shirt before."

Sure she had, and she'd gone wobbling off on weak knees every single time; Matt without a shirt on was enough to have that effect on an eighty-year-old manhater. He was perfect.

"We'll be late getting to the office," she said in a choked tone, then finished her bacon and sipped her coffee.

"I'm the boss, remember?"

She dabbed her lips and got up. "I'll just freshen my makeup—"

"Not yet." He cocked his head and looked her up and down with an expression in his dark eyes that made rubber out of her knees. "Come here."

"Matt…"

"Come here, Kit," he said in a tone that would have tamed a charging elephant.

Her legs rebelled. They took her to him, unresisting.

He reached up and drew her down across his lap, turning her, cradling her. "Put this...here." He took her free hand, the one that wasn't curled around his neck, and slid it into the opening of his shirt, watching her expression as she felt his warm hair-roughened skin.

"Yes, I like that," he whispered, bending to her mouth. "I like it a lot. Stroke me, Kit."

"I hate you," she managed with a shaky breath.

"Sure you do. Open your mouth and kiss me."

She did, her neck arching at the wild, warm hunger of his open lips as they moved hungrily against hers. Her fingers caught in the thick hair over his chest and tugged at it, spearing into its thickness, feeling the hardness of muscle beneath it, the hard pulse of his heartbeat.

"Oh, God," he breathed unsteadily. He moved one hand to rip open the remaining shirt buttons and took her fingers on a journey of discovery right down to the taut, rippling muscles of his stomach.

"Matt." His name sounded like a moan, and her eyes opened, looking up helplessly into his.

"I could make a meal of you, right here," he whispered roughly. His hand pressed hers against his chest. "You make the blood rush to my head when you touch me."

She pressed closer, wondering where along the way she'd lost her resolutions. All that seemed to matter now was getting as close to him as she could. His arms wrapped around her, riveting her torso to his, and his face pressed into the curve of her throat and shoulder. He curled her into his lap, rocking her gently against him, while she drowned in his warm strength and the spicy scent of his body.

Where it might have gone from there was anyone's guess, but there was a sudden commotion in the yard as two of the ranch pickups arrived together, apparently in a race. That and their loud voices broke the spell, giving Catherine a chance to collect herself and push out of Matt's enveloping arms.

She got a little distance away and made an effort to reorganize her wild hair and mind, her breath coming all too quickly. She had to stop letting him do that. It was her own fault. The problem was that he was playing and she wasn't.

With her pride carefully in hand, she shot a glance at him as she pushed back the loosened strands of hair. "What's the matter, aren't you getting what you need from the lady in Laredo, Matt?" she asked as carefully as she could, when inside her blood was rippling like white water. "Or am I just a novelty?"

That seemed to take him by surprise. He cocked his head at her, his dark Spanish eyes piercing and level. "Why don't you work on that for a few days, honey, and tell me what you come up with?" He actually grinned at her as he buttoned his shirt and smoothed his own hair. "You'd better do something about your hair," he added. "And a little lipstick might help that pretty, swollen mouth. God, it's sweet to kiss!"

She didn't know whether to laugh or cry or scream. She stared at him with her mind whirling, her body throbbing.

He stood up. "Don't look so worried, Kit, it's all pretty simple. But I keep forgetting how young you are."

"I'm old enough to know that you're one of those men Mama's spent the past six years telling me about," she returned.

He lifted a cigarette to his curving lips and lit it. "Am I?"

"I won't have an affair with you," she told him bluntly, her green eyes throwing off sparks.

His eyebrows jackknifed. "My God, how would we manage that around here?" he asked. "This place is worse than

Grand Central Station! Hal's forever playing tricks, sticking his nose in. Annie's as bad. And your mother, God love her, is as curious as she is the image of you! We'd have to conduct it under the house and even then, Hal would drill holes in the floor to get a better view!"

She tried not to laugh, but her eyes gave her away.

"An affair," he scoffed. His eyes went up and down her. He pursed his lips in mock thoughtfulness. "Although, maybe if we got in the truck and painted the windows black and locked it from the inside—"

"Matt!" she said sharply, her eyes glowering.

"Oh, well, I'll work on it, Kit. You just give me some time." He chuckled, ignoring the fury in her eyes. "Go fix your face. I've got a cattleman coming to look over some culls."

With a sigh, she turned and went toward the stairs. Trying to talk to Matt was like trying to talk to a wall, and about as satisfying. She didn't know any more about his intentions now than she had last night. The only thing she knew for sure was how vulnerable she was. She'd have to keep out of his way from now on or grow a shell. Matt, in pursuit, was formidable.

He seemed to sense her unease, her wariness, because when she came back downstairs, he slipped back into the old, familiar camaraderie and kept it up all the way to the office. She was visibly relaxed by the time they started work.

"Having any trouble with that?" he asked, gesturing toward the computer.

She remembered the crashed program disk and hoped Angel wouldn't give her away. "No," she said airily. "Of course not."

"Then why are you using a backup program disk?" he asked casually, lifting the backup diskette in a lean, tanned hand.

She swallowed. "Why not?"

He chuckled and handed it back. "Everybody crashes a disk now and again. Don't sweat it. How's the listing coming? Got a printout yet?"

How would he react, she wondered, if she showed him her listing of his award-winning cattle? Debutante heifers... She cleared her throat. "Actually," she began, "I'd really rather not worry you with it just yet. I have some more work to do before it's ready."

"Okay," he said easily. "Just don't take too long, honey. It needs to be at the printer's next Monday morning."

"Oh, I'll have it by then, don't worry."

"Angel has last year's booklet. That might help."

"I've already asked her for it," she replied, one jump ahead of him. Her eyes involuntarily dropped to his hard mouth, and she couldn't help the way she stared at it with remembered pleasure.

"Not now," he murmured softly, wickedly. "I have to keep my mind on my work."

He sauntered off before she could manage a sharp comeback.

While he was with his visiting cattleman, she drew out the file of cattle he was selling off and quietly changed it so that it read as it should. She was going to give up the idea of sabotaging his sale. After all, if she wanted to get to New York, her best bet, she decided, was to prove her worth as a public relations expert and then make Matt keep his promise. Fouling up things would only prolong the agony. And if he was going to start pursuing her, she'd have to work fast. She knew she'd never be able to hold out against him.

Angel poked her head around the door just before noon.

"Want to come out with Gail and Dorothy and me for a sandwich?" she asked with a smile.

"I'd love to, but I promised to have lunch with my mother," Catherine said apologetically. "Another time?"

"Fine! If you want to run along now, I'll lock up. Matt went out with Mr. Landers for a business lunch, so he won't be back until afternoon."

"Okay, I'll just close down here." Catherine took out the disk and turned off the machine.

It wasn't until she was on her way to town with Betty that she remembered she hadn't stored the changed information on the disk. She'd cut off the machine with all the changes still in limbo.

"Oh, no," she groaned. "Now I'll have to do it all over again!"

"Do what, darling?" Betty asked.

"Never mind." Catherine sighed, shaking her head. "Just something else I've fouled up. Oh, well, it will all come right in the end, I guess."

The rest of the way into town Betty kept the conversation going all alone. And after they sat down to eat she noticed that Catherine sat and played with her food and did little more than nibble.

Catherine's mind was awash with new images of Matt, with feelings she didn't know how to handle, with longings that made her young body burn. She hadn't felt these sensations before. They were alien and sweet and heady. And she was sure that Matt was only playing, that he wasn't serious. How could he be, when everyone knew he was a confirmed bachelor? Besides, there was the real estate agent from Laredo. Layne. Catherine grimaced at the picture Matt had conjured by talking about the woman. "Experienced," he'd said. Sure. And probably even more experienced by now, after sleeping with Matt. Her eyes closed. She couldn't bear to think of him with another woman. It had hurt for years when he went on dates, but having experienced his ardor for herself, it was so much worse. From now on, she'd be able to picture exactly what he was doing, and it would pierce her heart every time. How would she bear it? She had to get away. And what if the mysterious Layne got through his defenses and he married her? Tears stung her eyes, shocking her.

"I said, how is it going at the office, Catherine?" Betty prodded. Then she saw the distress on her daughter's face and she frowned. "Darling, what's wrong?"

"I crashed a system disk," she blurted out.

"Oh. Well, I don't suppose Matt will yell too much," she comforted her daughter, patting her hand gently. "Don't worry about it."

It wasn't that, but even as she stared hopefully at her mother, she knew she couldn't share her problem. Betty was a loving mother, but she couldn't keep secrets. She'd blurt it out to someone, probably Annie, who'd tell everyone else. That would make it much worse. The only person Catherine had ever been able to tell secrets to was Matt, who was a clam. But she couldn't very well tell Matt she was in love with him.

Catherine finished her coffee and gave a wistful sigh. Well, she'd get through somehow.

THE OTHER GIRLS were already hard at work when Catherine arrived back at the office. Angel gestured toward Matt's closed office door and looked toward the ceiling, a warning if ever there was one. Catherine nodded conspiratorially and eased his door open, then sneaked to her own desk just as a tight, very controlled burst of blue language colored the air around Matt.

He glanced at Catherine, the pencil between his fingers bouncing up and down against the desk as he listened and nodded.

"All right. Meet me at the airport in an hour. I'll talk to him. Sure. Bye, honey."

He hung up, and Catherine made a production of booting up her computer and inserting the program disk.

"I have to fly to Dallas," he said abruptly, rising. "There's been a hitch in the deal for that ranch property I'm trying to buy. Layne said the landowner is trying to jack up the price."

Her pulse leaped as he came to stand beside her. "I thought your real estate agent was from Laredo," she said, trying to sound calm though her pulse was all over the place.

"She was born there, but she lives in Dallas," he said, clearing up the mystery. He stared down at her. "Hal's due back today."

"Is he? How nice."

"I don't want you going out with him."

That brought her head up. She stared at him uncomprehendingly. "What?"

"You heard me." He wasn't teasing now. His gaze was dark and unblinking, his face hard. He was the stranger again, not the familiar jovial man she thought she knew.

"But—"

He reached down, caught her by the upper arms and drew her slowly but relentlessly to her feet so that she was all too close to his powerful, hard-muscled body. His breath was warm and spicy just above her mouth, his eyes watchful, strange.

"Hal competes with me. He always has. If he thinks I want something, he'll do his damndest to beat me out of it."

"But, I don't even feel that way about Hal," she began hesitantly. He was making her feel the wildest hungers. Her hands pressed against his shirt and felt the hard beat of his heart. "And anyway, what…what business is it of yours if I…?" Suddenly her voice faltered.

"You're trembling, Kit," he whispered, his mouth against her lips. His fingers trailed along her throat, inciting, wildly sensuous as he bent his head. "And I can make it even worse."

He did. His mouth covered hers, exploring every soft inch of it with his tongue, biting tenderly at the curve of her upper lip, and all the while his hands smoothed her body to his, so that she could feel the warm muscle, the strength of him. Her hands clutched at his shirt as if she were drowning.

His hands slid down to her hips as he brought her close enough to feel how aroused he was. She protested, but he held her there and lifted his head to stare into her turbulent eyes.

"It's all right," he whispered. "Think of it as nonverbal communication."

Her breath was coming in soft gasps; it disturbed her to know how hungry he was for her. It was new, just as everything with him seemed to be.

"Such big eyes," he murmured, smiling.

"I've never…been like this with a man before," she confessed.

His hands came up to smooth back loose wisps of her hair, but she didn't try to move away. She felt a sudden tremor in his powerful, jeans-clad legs, and her eyes asked a question.

"I'd like to lie with you, Kit," he whispered, then searched her eyes in the hot silence that followed. His eyes slid sideways to the sofa and back again, and his jaw clenched as his breath came roughly. "I'd like to strip you down to the waist and put my mouth…here." One lean hand moved between them. His knuckles drew lightly up and down over the very tip of her breast. He felt it harden, and heard the shocked surge of her breath as it caught.

"Matt," she moaned. Her eyes held his; she was beyond thought, beyond reason. Her body tingled, and she wanted him to see her, to pull off her blouse and look at her as no other man ever had.

"Yes, you'd let me, wouldn't you?" he breathed, looking down at her yielding body, where his fingers now gently searched one perfect, high breast. His thumb rubbed slowly over the throbbing tip and she bit her lip to keep from crying out, her body stiffening, shuddering with unexpected pleasure.

His eyes searched her face, seeing and appreciating the helpless reaction there. "Oh, Kit," he breathed. "What a hell of a time to go all-woman on me. Here I am with a plane to catch and all I want to do is back you up against the wall and crush your body with mine and make your mouth swell with my kisses."

Her lips parted spontaneously at the imagery. "The… wall?" she whispered shakily.

She saw the flash of his eyes, felt herself shudder. He moved, backing her past the sofa, holding her eyes, until they reached the bare wall beside the door.

"Yes. The wall." His body arched down, and he held her eyes as his hips and thighs flattened hers in an intimacy that widened her eyes, opened her mouth, that made her body burn and throb and shudder with frank desire.

The pleasure was almost pain. She made a wild little sound under her breath and felt it go into his open mouth as he bent to her trembling lips and took them. It was an incredible kind of kiss, without pressure, without tangible hunger. It was so tender that she tasted the moist brush of his lips and could feel their very texture, could feel them tremble with the most terrible longing. His eyes were open, and so were hers, and they watched each other in a burning silence as his hips moved suggestively, tenderly, against hers. She felt the wildest kind of ache, and in the throes of it, her hips began to rotate sharply against his, and she moaned, pleading with her eyes as her nails bit into him. She felt him go rigid, heard the rough groan, and she stopped the hungry motion abruptly, apparently just in time.

"What sweet agony that was, Kit," he whispered shakily near her mouth. "And if you move that way again, I'll take you standing up."

She stood quite still, reading the truth in his dark, hot eyes, in the sudden bruising grip of his fingers as they found her hips. And she knew that the slightest movement on her part would cost him his self-control.

He took slow, harsh breaths until he got back the control he'd lost, until he finally collapsed against her, his face at her throat, his body shuddering with the effort.

"Matt," she whispered at his ear. Her arms were around his neck, though she had no idea how they'd got there. She could hear the thunder of his pulse, the rasp of his painful breathing. She didn't move a muscle because Betty had once told her how it was for a man. And this was her fault because she'd forgotten. "Matt, I'm sorry."

"Oh, baby, you burn me up," he whispered roughly. "You make me so damned hungry. Kit, that was a near thing."

She blushed and clung closer, nuzzling against his warm throat. "Are you all right?"

"I'd be a hell of a lot better if we didn't have so many clothes on," he said, nibbling at her ear. "I'd like to feel your skin touching mine, all the way up and down, little virgin."

Her nails bit into him, and she pressed her face closer in an agony of longing.

"Don't," he whispered. His hands bit into her back, pulling her away from the wall even as he put some little distance between her legs and his.

"Then stop making me feel this way," she whispered back. "You do it with words."

"Verbal lovemaking," he breathed into her ear. "I could make you give yourself to me without ever touching you. I could describe it to you…every single detail…"

"No," she moaned. She pulled back, and he bent, catching her mouth with his.

He lifted her in a bruising embrace, and she gave him back the kiss without the slightest protest, her arms clinging, her mouth opening sweetly to the probing demand of his. Somewhere in the distance a phone was ringing, voices murmured, the wind blew. And all she knew was the scent and feel of Matt.

A long minute later, he let her slide back to her feet and lifted his dark head. The look in his eyes surprised her a little because it was so blatantly possessive.

"You're going to be my woman," he said under his breath, staring into her dazed eyes. "Remember that when Hal comes home."

He let her go abruptly and watched her grab the back of a chair for support.

He laughed mockingly, dragging a cigarette from his pocket with fingers that were slightly unsteady. "Can't you stand, Kit? I feel trembly myself. My Lord, you're sweet to make love to!"

She could hardly find enough breath to answer him. "What do you want from me?"

"Lots of things," he murmured, letting his eyes wander down her soft, slender body.

"Things you can't get from Layne?" she asked angrily.

He pursed his lips and studied her. "Layne isn't a virgin," he said.

Her face flamed with anger and embarrassment. She glared at him over the back of the chair. "How sad for you," she burst out. "Just don't think I'm going to take her place."

"That would be difficult," he agreed. He grinned at her. "Speaking of Layne, I'd better get moving. She's expecting me."

"By all means, don't let me hold you up."

"You look as if someone needs to," he observed, moving toward the door. "Want me to pour you a brandy before I go, honey?" he added wickedly.

"You were the one who needed fortifying a minute ago," she returned with an odd sense of pride.

"So I was." He lifted the cigarette to his mouth and watched her through slitted eyes. "We'd have to make love on asbestos sheets, Kit, or we'd set fires."

She picked up a book from his desk and prepared to heave it at him, but he was out the door, laughing, before she could lift it over her head.

CHAPTER SIX

HAL SHOWED UP about supper time, all smiles. Matt had phoned the office just before quitting time to have Angel relay the message that he was going to be in Dallas for several days. That information had made Catherine see red; she was sure he was spending more time with the mysterious Layne than he was on business.

She'd come home in a flap and hadn't come out of it until Hal breezed in the door, bearing a bouquet of exquisite daisies and mums and baby's breath.

"For you," he said with a grin. "There's a flower shop at the airport. I couldn't resist them."

"Oh, Hal, how beautiful!" She lifted the bouquet to her nose, inhaling its beautiful fragrance. "You're a nice man."

He grinned at her with a smile that was too much like Matt's. "My pleasure. Where's old steely eyes?"

"If you mean Matt, dear, he's in Dallas," Betty volunteered as she gestured them into the dining room, where Annie was putting dishes of food on the set table. "He won't be back for several days, didn't he say, Catherine?"

"That's right," she agreed tightly, letting Hal seat her across from Betty. "Several days."

"Aha." Hal glanced speculatively at Catherine before he turned and sat down. "The lovely Layne again, no doubt," he added with soft malice, pinning Catherine with his eyes as he said it, seeing the flicker of her eyelids. "Have you heard about her?"

"Angel said she calls him a lot."

"That isn't all she does," Hal murmured. "From what I hear, she has a way with men."

"Have you met her?" Catherine had to know.

"You know how possessive Matt is about his women, sweet," he said nonchalantly. "He doesn't like competition, so I've never been introduced."

"As if you could compete with Matt, darling," Betty teased.

Hal's face hardened, but he didn't fire back. He helped himself to smothered steak and held out his cup for Annie to fill with freshly brewed black coffee.

"They don't usually last long," Catherine pointed out. She toyed with her carrots. "Matt's women," she emphasized.

"Layne's been around for some time," Hal told her. He savored a piece of steak. "She has staying power, I suppose. You know how determined those successful real estate agents are. They keep going until they get what they want." He lifted his coffee cup and pointedly glanced over the rim at Catherine. "He sent her a barrel of roses on her birthday. I saw the bill. I could have lived on that amount for a month, even the way I spend money."

Catherine felt her body going taut. So she'd been right about Layne and right about Matt's lack of commitment. He'd only been playing with her. She was something to fill in the time when he wasn't with Layne. Well, two could play that game.

"How about riding over to Fort Worth with me tomorrow?" Hal asked her. "I have to see a man about a sports car I'm thinking of buying."

"I'd love to," Catherine said shortly.

"But, darling, don't you have to work on Matt's sale?" Betty asked, her voice hesitant.

"I'm entitled to a few hours off," Catherine replied. "I'll get it done in time, don't worry. What time do you want to leave?" she asked Hal.

He smiled coolly. "About nine. We'll make a day of it."

"I'll look forward to it," Catherine assured him.

Betty lingered over her dessert, shooting worried glances at Catherine until Catherine couldn't take it any longer and went up to bed.

FORT WORTH WAS big and sprawling, and Catherine loved the variety of shops it offered, but Hal was far more interested in seeing his sports car than in watching his cousin shop for clothes.

"We'll stop by one of the malls on the way back if we have time," he said, placating her.

She didn't argue. After all, it was his trip, not hers. She leaned back with a sigh in the seat of his Ferrari. "Why do you want a new one?" she asked curiously, savoring the leather luxury of the year-old automobile.

"Are you kidding? It's last year's," he said, as if she were asking why he wanted to trade in a moth-eaten suit. "I travel first class, kid."

She studied him quietly as he drove, comparing him with Matt. Matt never minded driving one of the pickup trucks. He kept the Lincoln for business, but she'd seen him borrow a friend's Volkswagen and rave about it to the owner. Matt didn't have his head in the clouds. He was a down-to-earth man with no illusions about being better because he had money. Of course, there was this problem he had with women...

She shifted restlessly. "Are you going to get another Ferrari?" she asked conversationally.

"Sure. Why not?" He grinned.

She sighed. "Well, it's sure beyond my pocket," she said with a smile. "I'm lucky to be able to afford a VW, especially since Matt's cut off my allowance." She'd so allowed herself to be charmed by Matt that she'd forgotten that villainous action, but she wasn't admitting that to Hal. How desperately she'd been charmed was something she wanted only to forget!

Hal glanced at her as he took a corner on two wheels. "It's beyond my pocket, too, honey, but as long as I've got brother Matt to cosign, I can buy anything I like."

"Matt's cosigning with you?" she gasped.

"Not exactly," he admitted. "But what he doesn't know won't hurt him." His face darkened and he scowled. "God knows, I never get anything unless I fight him. I get tired of begging for what's mine."

She could feel his bitterness, but she kept thinking about how hard Matt had worked to build up the family's holdings to make it possible for Hal to buy expensive sports cars. Matt hardly ever took any time off, and Hal never did anything except spend. It seemed a little one-sided to her.

She almost said so, but she curbed her temper. After all, Matt wasn't in her good graces at the moment, either. He was off with his Layne, probably having a ball.

"Why don't you take a job with the company, Hal?" she asked gently. "It's what Matt really wants. That's why he makes it so hard for you."

"I don't want a job with the company, Catherine," Hal muttered. He pushed the accelerator a little harder as they sped out onto the highway. "I want to race cars. It's all I've ever wanted, but I can't make Matt understand that I'm not cut out to be a minor executive."

"Have you tried talking to him?" she persisted.

"Talk to Matt?" he burst out, taking his eyes off the road to fix her with an astonished stare. "When did he ever listen? He just turns around and walks off. You know how he is."

"Why don't you turn around and follow him?"

"Because the last time I did that, he hauled back and slugged me," he grumbled. "Nobody could ever accuse big brother of being a wimp, that's for sure."

"You could leave home, Hal, and do it on your own," she reminded him.

"That's a laugh," he told her flatly, and pushed the sports car even harder. "How could I get a job driving without the money to buy my way in?"

"Other people manage."

"I'm not other people," he replied. He took a sharp curve without slowing at all, the tires screeching wildly. "And I'm not giving up my inheritance, not even to get one-up on Matt."

"Hal, hadn't you better slow down?" she asked, apprehension in her voice as she tried to hang on to the dash. And as she spoke, from behind them came the sound of a siren. She turned in the seat to find a state patrol car in hot pursuit. "Oh, Lord!" she cried. "Now we're in for it."

Hal let out a word she rarely heard, and glared in the rearview mirror. "Just my luck," he muttered. "I might just be able to outrun them…"

Before she could react, he'd stomped down on the accelerator. "Hal, no!" she cried, but he wasn't listening.

"If they catch me speeding and Matt hears about it, I'll

never get my new car," he said sharply. "So they aren't catching me. Hold on, honey!"

Hal was hopeless. Like the other members of the family, she wondered sometimes if he would ever grow up. She grabbed the dash and held on for dear life as Hal turned the car in the middle of the superhighway and sped back the other way, passing the state patrol car.

Catherine had never before been so afraid. She knew Hal had a wild streak, and she'd voluntarily gone with him. Matt would kill them both, starting with his brother. Inevitably, the police would get him. Hadn't Hal learned that much?

The car careened wildly as Hal crossed center lines, passed on blind curves and took corners on two wheels. There were two patrol cars in pursuit now, and Catherine knew there would be others farther down the road. Hal had to be crazy! The patrol car was so close behind that they'd have the tag number by now. With a quick check they'd know Hal owned it. They'd have his name and address, and would only have to come to the house and arrest him.

She half turned in the seat to tell Hal so, just as his face froze, and his eyes widened.

"Oh, damn!" he burst out.

A trouble light had suddenly popped into view and Hal hit the wheel to avoid the hole in the road under the light. The car barreled across the shoulder and down an embankment, then came to a sudden, sickening stop against a telephone pole, the sound of shattering glass and ripping metal loud in Catherine's ears.

If they hadn't been wearing seat belts, something Catherine had been angrily persistent about, they'd have been killed. As it was, Hal's nose had hit the steering wheel and was bleeding profusely.

Catherine was all right, except for a wrist that had been

wrenched when she'd frantically braced herself against the dash.

"You okay?" Hal asked her quickly as he reached for a handkerchief to hold against his nose.

"I think so," she said falteringly.

Suddenly sirens were everywhere. Tires screeched. A door opened and closed angrily, and then a uniformed state trooper looked in through the open top and sighed as he surveyed the two occupants.

"You're both damned lucky," he told Hal. "If you'd rolled it, no power on earth would have saved you. Can you walk?"

"Sure," Hal said, dabbing at his nose with the handkerchief.

"Are you all right, miss?" the officer asked, studying Catherine, whose face was as white as cornmeal.

"I think so," she said in a ghostly tone. She grimaced as she moved her hand. "Except for my wrist. I must have... have wrenched it."

"Sit tight," the officer advised gently. "There'll be an ambulance along in a minute or two. The E.M.T.s will know what to do."

She nodded and leaned back in the seat, grateful to be alive. And while Hal went along with the uniformed officer to answer some pointed questions, Catherine wondered how Hal was going to explain his way out of this one. Matt would be a wild man when he found out. Especially when he found out that she had been with Hal, because Matt had told her not to go off with his brother.

Well, she excused herself, he'd gone off with Layne, hadn't he? What right did he have to dictate to her? And then she looked at the mess she was in and decided that maybe, just maybe, he'd been right to forbid her Hal's company. Hal was definitely not the ideal driving companion.

They were taken to the nearest hospital, where Catherine's wrist was bandaged. Only bruised, they told her, and fortunately the soreness would soon be gone.

Hal was scratched, and his nose had taken a beating, but he was fine. At least, he was fine until he had to call Betty to ask her to find a bail bondsman. He'd been arrested on five counts of reckless driving and faced several days in jail unless someone posted bail.

Catherine didn't even feel sorry for him. As they were driven to police headquarters, he was still raving about his monumental bad luck and wasn't showing a shred of guilt for what he'd done. Through her anger, Catherine wondered vaguely why Matt didn't let Hal do what he really wanted to—race cars. That had been the dream of Hal's life, but Matt never listened. He talked only about the company. That was to be Hal's future.

Betty arrived an hour later, nervous and uneasy. She turned over documents and spoke to the police sergeant at the desk while Catherine sat nervously and quietly on a bench in the waiting area along with a scattering of drunks and prostitutes who were waiting to be booked. Minutes later, Catherine and Hal were released, and Betty took them home.

"Those people." Betty shuddered as she drove. "How terrible to have to wait alone in a place like that," she murmured, glancing at Catherine in the front seat beside her. "Darling, I'm so sorry!"

"It was all right. I was too numb to notice," Catherine replied. She glanced in the backseat. Hal was sound asleep!

"Is he awake?" Betty asked softly.

"He's snoring." Catherine laughed mirthlessly. "Oh, Lord, Matt will kill us both!"

"No doubt. And I'm afraid he'll be at the house by the time I get back with you two," Betty added grimly. "He called seconds after you hung up. I had to tell him."

Catherine felt her face going bloodless. "He was coming home?"

"He said he'd meet us at the house." Betty peered ahead into the darkness. "Why did Hal do it?" she moaned.

"He was afraid of a speeding ticket," Catherine answered.

"So he tried for a few reckless-driving charges instead."

"That's about the size of it." It was getting dark quickly. Feeling limp with relief that it was finally over, Catherine closed her eyes. "I hope his life insurance is paid up." The thought of facing Matt didn't relax her one bit. She could picture his face in her mind.

And when they got home, his face looked exactly as she'd imagined it. He was pacing the porch with a lit cigarette in his hand, waiting.

Matt whirled as they came slowly up the steps, his black eyes riveted on Catherine as if she were a ghost.

"Are you all right?" he asked immediately, his gaze missing nothing as it flashed over her. He was frozen in place now, motionless. Catherine noticed he was still wearing his suit slacks and dress shirt, although he'd long since removed the tie and jacket.

"Just a sore wrist," she told him. She stood beside Hal, feeling dragged out, and wondered at the emotion in Matt's hard face as he faced his brother.

"And you?" he asked Hal curtly.

"I'll live," Hal said coldly. "Just my damned luck to get busted when I was on my way to trade cars."

"You could have killed Catherine and yourself," Matt said; the look in his eyes would have melted steel.

Hal shrugged. "I guess so. I didn't expect them to catch us."

"How many times do I have to tell you that the highway isn't a racetrack?" Matt shot at him, his voice deepening in anger.

"Then why the hell won't you let me get off the highways and onto a racetrack?" Hal returned. "I have every right in the world to do what I want with my own life!"

"And when you inherit the trust, you can," Matt agreed. "But until then, I'll do what I promised Mother, and that means you're going to learn the real estate business. Whether or not it kills us both."

"Mother's dead, Matt!"

For an instant, he only stared at Hal. Then, dismissing him, he turned to Catherine, letting his dark eyes reveal his concern. "What about that wrist?"

Hal muttered something and went inside, slamming the door furiously behind him.

"My wrist is all right," Catherine said. She looked up at Matt, and found him closer than she'd expected. "Why won't you let him go?" she added gently. "He's right, you know. He'll never be a company man."

"You, too?" he growled. "For God's sake, this is none of your business!"

That wasn't the familiar Matt. It was the stranger again, the cold, hard man who seemed to turn up at the most unexpected times. She stared at him quietly, trying to comprehend the change.

"You're like your father, aren't you?" she asked absently. "There's the wrong way and your way and no in-between. Can't you see what you're doing to Hal?"

"I'm trying to make a man of him," he replied, lifting the cigarette to his mouth. "Despite interference from you."

"Hal's my friend," she said. "And your brother. If you wouldn't push him so hard, Matt…"

"I was pushed hard," he reminded her. "It didn't hurt me."

"Didn't it?" She studied his hard features, his dark eyes. "You were raised in a military fashion, with rules and regulations instead of pampering. You never knew tenderness because your mother, in her way, was as hard as your father. But it was different for Hal."

"Yes." He laughed coldly. "He had an adoring stepfather, didn't he?" He finished the cigarette and tossed it off the porch. "He and Jerry."

"You were almost a grown man when your mother remarried," she began gently.

"Thank God. I didn't have to endure watching her fawn over him."

She'd never realized how it must have been for Matt, who worshipped his father. She stared up at him with understanding shining like a beacon in her green eyes. No, Matt had never been loved. But she could love him, if only he'd let her. If he'd just forget Layne…

The memory moved her eyes down to his unbuttoned shirt, to hair-roughened olive skin that looked even darker against the white cotton fabric. Layne.

"I thought you had to spend several days in Dallas," she said then.

"I did. I do. But after I spoke to Betty, I flew straight here. I wanted to make sure Hal hadn't killed you."

Bitterness in his voice, and anger. Her eyes glanced off his. "Well, he hasn't. Won't Layne be lonely?" she added sharply.

"Maybe I'm lonely, too," he said deeply, and smiled mockingly as her head came up and her wide eyes were caught and held by his. "That shocks you, does it, Catherine?" he continued, watching her.

"You aren't my idea of a lonely man," she countered.

"I have the occasional woman," he agreed blatantly. "But I don't spend my life in bed, Kit. There's more to a relationship than just sex."

Of all the things she might have expected him to say, that was the very last. "What with the variety you keep around you, I could be forgiven for doubting you," she replied.

"You don't sleep around," he murmured softly.

"Maybe I do, and I'm just putting on an act for you," she returned hotly, hating the vulnerability he was making her feel.

His chiseled lips drew up in a mocking smile. "Are you?" He moved a step closer. "There's an easy way to find out, Kit," he said in a voice like velvet. "Suppose I asked you to prove it to me?"

"I won't sleep with you!" She backed away, glaring.

"I haven't asked you," he reminded her. "Nervous, Kit? All shaky with anticipation? I could make you go down on your knees and beg, and you know it."

"I am not fair game for your misplaced hunting instincts," she shot at him. "Kindly save your amorous exhibitions for the real estate agent from Laredo!"

"Amorous exhibitions?" he mimicked, his eyebrows arching. "My, my, aren't we verbose tonight. Are you sure it was your wrist you sprained and not your tongue, honey?"

"There is nothing wrong with my tongue," she returned.

"Not when you put it in the right place," he agreed in a voice that melted her knees and brought back vivid memories of his own tongue tangling with hers.

"I want to go to bed," she blurted out.

"So do I, baby," he murmured, his dark eyes wandering hungrily over her body. "Eager little thing, aren't you, Kit?"

"Damn it, Matt!"

"There, there, you'll blow a fuse," he teased. She started to turn, but catching her by the waist, he moved her right up against his warm, muscular body. He smelled of cologne and soap, and the smell drugged her, making her vulnerable. His steely fingers bit into her waist, holding her. "How's it going at work?" he asked, his lips close to her forehead.

"Everything's...fine."

"Good. I have to fly back to Dallas tonight, and I won't be home again for three days or so. Stay out of Hal's way until I come back," he added firmly. "No more adventures."

She wasn't going off with Hal again anyway, but she didn't like his commanding tone. "I'm an adult now. I can do what I please."

"Now, where have I heard that before?" he asked dryly.

"Matt...!"

His hand tangled in her hair and held her face up to his. "When I get back," he whispered with his mouth poised over hers, "I'm going to make wild, passionate love to you, Kit. I'm going to throw you down on a bed and strip you to the waist and teach you how to make soft, sweet little noises in my ear."

Her heart went crazy. She stared up at him, heart lodged in her throat, eyes hungry, body feverish.

Suddenly he bent her backward—her hair reached toward the floor—and with a wicked, mischievous laugh, made her wait for the slow, lazy descent of his mouth. Held in that off-balance position, she was all too aware of his strength, of his masculinity. His mouth opened her lips, felt them tremble and part; he felt her body go soft, her arms go around him. And he laughed deep in his throat and teased her lips until she moaned.

Then he straightened, bringing her with him, and let her try to reach him, let her stand on tiptoe, trying to find his mouth.

"Oh, no," he whispered with a soft laugh. "Not tonight." He held her arms down by her sides and brushed a lazy kiss against her cheek. "Go to bed, Kit, and dream of me."

"I won't!" she whispered huskily, her eyes accusing as she drew away from him, frustrated and embarrassed.

"You will." He pulled another cigarette from his pocket. "Maybe I'll dream about you, too."

"With Layne in tow? Fat chance!" She whirled and started inside.

"Kit."

She turned and glared at him, her face red. "What?"

"I might be as vulnerable as you are—did you ever consider that?" he asked quietly.

She tried to speak, failed, and quickly went into the house before she could be frightened by the implications of what he was saying. He was just playing, she reminded herself. Just killing time, amusing himself. And afterward he'd go running back to Layne, who was older and sophisticated and fit into his world. And if she had any sense at all, she'd remember that.

CHAPTER SEVEN

MATT LEFT LATER that evening. Hal didn't say another word to his brother. He went to bed early and didn't show his face the whole of the next day.

"He worries me." Betty sighed the following day as she finished her lunch and poured a second cup of coffee for Catherine, who was taking her lunch hour at home instead of going out with the office girls.

"Who?"

"Hal," her mother replied. "He isn't himself lately."

"He's just miserable, that's all," Catherine told her. "He isn't happy with what Matt's making him do."

"Poor Hal. I'm sorry for him, but nobody wins against Matt. I just hope Hal doesn't go back to his old ways and start trying to get back at Matt. He used to pull some of the most horrible tricks. Oh, well, maybe I'm worrying for nothing." She smiled at Catherine. "How's it going at the office?"

"Very well," the younger woman replied, smiling back. "I've just gotten the programs compiled. I let Angel check them to make sure I hadn't done anything unforgivable. Now I'm going to get some ads ready for the newspapers, and some radio spots, and I'm going to compose a letter to send to selected buyers. Then I have to organize a barbecue..."

"It sounds so complicated!" Betty said.

"It is. But it will prove to Matt that I'm capable of making my own way," she replied. "That's something Hal and I have in common, I suppose. We're both trapped here by Matt."

"For vastly different reasons, I imagine," Betty said enigmatically.

"I doubt that." Catherine put down her coffee cup. "I hate to, but I have to get back to work. I want to take a minute and call the public realations agency in New York to see if they'll wait another month for me. It will take at least that long to get this show on the road."

"Do you think they'll wait to fill the vacancy?" Betty asked.

Catherine shrugged. "I don't know. I hope so," she said wistfully. "But you know how Matt is when he digs in his heels. I have to prove myself to him."

"Maybe he's just trying to make sure you know what you're doing. He doesn't think you'd be happy in New York."

"Well, I'll never find out from here, will I?" came the exasperated reply. "Honestly, sometimes I think Matt just has an overdeveloped sense of responsibility. But he's got to let go sometime!"

"Yes. I suppose so." But Betty didn't sound enthusiastic herself.

"I'll write you," her daughter coaxed. "And phone you. I'll come home on holidays."

"It won't be the same. And who'll make Matt smile? He never does except for you. When you're away, he's a different man."

That puzzled Catherine. She'd wondered for a long time about the stranger who appeared from time to time, the hard-faced man with the cold eyes. That wasn't her Matt.

"Have to run, darling," she told her mother. "My computer awaits without."

"Without what?" Hal asked from the doorway, all eyes.

"Without a program, that's without what," Catherine teased. "Feeling better?"

"Not really, but it's stifling up there alone. What's to eat?"

"Egg salad, dear," Betty said, offering him the plate of sandwiches.

"My favorite." He glanced at Catherine in her neat blue suit. "Who are you dressed up for?"

"The other girls," she offered. "They all dress this way. Sort of office custom."

"Yes, I've seen Angel." He sighed. "Nice-looking lady."

Her eyes sharpened. "Do you think so?"

"Don't get ideas," he said curtly. "I just like the way she looks, that's all."

"I didn't say a word!"

Betty excused herself to get some coffee, and Hal put his sandwich on his plate and looked at Catherine.

"Does Matt make a habit of kissing you like he did night before last?" he asked abruptly, then nodded at her shocked expression. "Yes, I saw. I was on my way back out to make a stand and got the wind knocked out of my sails. Is he trying to put the make on you, Catherine?"

She had to fight for the right words. "He was only teasing."

"It didn't look like teasing to me."

"Well, it was. So don't start any duels on my behalf. And don't worry Mama with it, either!" she continued, nervous now because of the way he was watching her.

"Oh, I wouldn't do that," he agreed.

He looked smug all at once, and she stared at him curiously.

"Isn't it a beautiful day?" he asked merrily. "I feel much better already. Hadn't you better get to work?"

"Yes, I suppose so," she said absently. "Goodbye, Mama!" she called.

"Goodbye, dear," Betty said with a smile as she rejoined Hal. "Have a nice day."

"Of course," Catherine answered, but there was something about Hal's attitude that made the words into a lie. She didn't like having Hal know that Matt had kissed her. He might find a way to turn the knowledge into a weapon in his unending war with his older brother. She wasn't sure what he might do or say, and she went back to the office with butterflies in her stomach.

She called the Bryant Agency in New York to check on the job, and found that she didn't have to worry. There wasn't really a job to lose. They were creating one just for her on the basis of her degree, her résumé and the glowing description given them by her college friend, whose father was one of the agency executives. She came away feeling much better. Except that she knew for a fact that Matt was going to be stubborn about it; she knew, and she wasn't looking forward to the battle.

There was a chance that Matt would relent when he saw how capable she was. But she had to get through the next month, and she was expecting that Matt would use every weapon he had to get his own way—including the teasing, ardent manner he'd adopted with her lately. That was the most frightening of all because she had no resistance. And how could she survive living with him, watching him with women like Layne, always aware of the fact that she herself was only a passing fancy?

She'd have given anything for Matt's love, to have him care about her as she cared about him. But he was too much older, too sophisticated to give his wary heart to a little country mouse like Catherine. That hurt most of all— knowing that she hadn't a chance. It made her even more determined to get away from him.

MATT WAS BACK the next day, and Hal had been disturbingly attentive to Catherine during Matt's absence. She didn't like the look in Matt's eyes. It spelled trouble.

They were watching a recently released movie on the VCR when Matt came home that evening, wearing a khaki leisure suit with cream-colored boots and Stetson. He had the jacket slung over a shoulder, and he was smiling as he stood at the doorway and surveyed the three of them, Catherine, Betty and Hal.

"How cozy," he remarked dryly. "Just like the old days. No date, Hal?"

"Who needs a date?" Hal returned, glancing at Catherine. "The scenery's just great right here."

Catherine was watching Matt's face, and she saw it go hard when he heard the innuendo. Even Betty's enthusiastic greeting didn't bring a smile to his rigid features.

"Did you get your property?" Betty asked.

"I got it," he returned. He tossed his jacket onto a nearby chair and sat down between Hal and Catherine on the sofa, then crossed his long legs as he carelessly lit a cigarette. "How's my sale going?" he asked Catherine, sliding a casual arm behind her head.

"Very well," she said in a subdued tone, aware of Hal's probing stare beyond Matt's broad chest. She was jittery, and her voice showed it. "I, uh, just took the program to the printer's today."

"Without my approval?"

"Angel looked it over to make sure it was all right," she said. "We didn't dare wait, or we'd never get them out on time."

"Let's go over to the office," he said. "I want to check it before it goes to press."

"All right."

"How about some company?" Hal asked pointedly, rising.

Matt glared at him. "How about watching your damned movie?" he returned. "This is business."

"Oh, for sure," Hal replied mockingly.

Matt scowled, and Betty was openly staring at the three of them, her eyes as puzzled as Matt's. Only Hal and Catherine understood what was going on, and Catherine was afraid of what Matt's young brother might say next.

Hal relented all at once, laughing softly as he dropped back down on the sofa. "Okay, but don't be gone long," he joked. "I want Catherine home by midnight."

Matt's eyes darkened, narrowed, and his very stance spelled trouble. "Are you trying to say something, little brother?" he asked curtly.

"Who, me?" Hal asked innocently. "Heavens, no."

Betty had turned back to her movie with a sigh, too confused to listen anymore. Catherine felt pale, and her knees were weak, both from Hal's odd behavior and from the thought of being alone at the office with Matt. Any stolen minute with him was gold, and she'd dreaded the thought that Hal might rob her of those precious seconds.

"Then let's go," Matt told Catherine, standing aside to let her leave the room ahead of him.

She didn't look back, although she heard Hal's amused laughter as they went out of the room and into the hall. She felt chilly despite her jeans and long-sleeved white T-shirt, and she folded her arms over her breasts as they went out into the cool night air.

"Hal's in a strange mood," Matt remarked. He caught her hand as they walked, and locked her fingers into his.

She felt herself melt at the warm, rough pressure of his big hand over her small one, and involuntarily moved closer to his side. "Yes."

"Do you know why?"

She did, but she was too embarrassed to tell him what Hal had seen. "He's just being himself," she hedged.

"He'll do it once too often," came the curt reply. He looked down at her, watching her loosened hair catch the night air and blow around her face. "You look very young, Kit."

"Do I scare you off, old man?" she asked with a laugh, glancing up at him as they reached his Lincoln.

"If you come down to the office with me, it might be the other way around," he murmured seductively, jerking her by the hand so that she came right up against his warm, hard-muscled body. "I might scare you off, honey."

Wary of Hal's keen eyes, perhaps watching, she edged away from him. "Might you?"

Her sudden withdrawal seemed to puzzle him. Anger him. He dropped her hand and opened the door of the Lincoln for her. Without another word or a second glance, he walked around to his side, got in, started the car and headed down to the office.

The building was dark when they arrived. She followed him inside as he turned on the lights and strode into his office. He was ominously silent, until he suddenly whirled on his heel and pierced her with his dark, cool eyes.

"Let's have it," he said curtly. "Why the sudden ice-maiden act back there?"

She might have told him the truth if he hadn't slung his question at her, but his possessive tone, as well as his arrogance, stung. He'd been in Dallas for three days with his precious Layne, and now he was scolding Catherine for not being grateful enough for the crumbs he threw her.

"What did you expect me to do, throw myself into your arms?" she replied, glaring at him. "Isn't Layne enough, or are you just hell-bent on new conquests?"

He didn't move. Seconds later, his hands went to light a cigarette. His eyes went from it to Catherine. "I thought you were learning to trust me," he said then.

"Trust doesn't have anything to do with it," she shot back. She folded her arms across her chest. "You expect too much, Matt. I'm not part of your estate."

"Pity," he said softly, taking a draw on the cigarette. "You'd be the crowning glory, even in jeans and a T-shirt."

She flushed. He had charm all right, but she'd be crazy to take him seriously. So she laughed. "Think so?"

He smiled, too, but it didn't reach his eyes. They seemed dull, lackluster. "Let's see what you've come up with on my cattle."

She went to the computer, fumbling a little as she fed in the program disk and then her work disk. And as luck and bad nerves would have it, what came up was the copy she didn't take to the printer—the interesting bit about the lovely young debutante heifers.

"What the hell are you trying to do to me?" Matt burst out, glaring from the white-on-black computer screen to Catherine's flushed face. "My God, Kit, I trusted you not to play at it like a schoolgirl! Do you have any idea how much work goes into cattle breeding? I'm asking one hell of a price for those cattle. Who's going to take me seriously with this kind of—"

"This isn't what I took to the printer," she interrupted, standing to plead with him. "Matt, please, this was just doodling. I never meant to sabotage you." Well, she had, but that was a long time ago.

He didn't seem much calmer after her confession. His dark eyes accused, probed. "I gave you credit for being an adult," he said quietly. "But you've done everything you could lately to change my mind, haven't you, honey? I guess I've jumped the gun in more ways than just one."

She knew exactly what he meant, and she felt a sinking regret that she hadn't taken him seriously. Going out with Hal had started him doubting her, drawing away from him at the house had complicated it, and finding this foolishness in the computer had cinched it. How was she going to explain herself now? She couldn't tell him that Hal had seen them kissing the night of the wreck and had mentioned it to Catherine. God knew what he'd do to Hal if he found out. What frightened her most was a confrontation; Hal would make sure the rest of the family knew about it, and what then? It would destroy the family and make Matt look like a seducer.

"All right," he said, crushing out his cigarette. "Let's see what you showed Angel."

She fumbled around again until she got the right disk, then scrolled the records up the screen. He leaned over her shoulder to see them. His proximity bothered her, but she steeled herself not to show it. Odd how heavy his breathing sounded—but a man like Matt surely wouldn't be that disturbed by her, not when he had the sophisticated Layne on his string.

"This is what went to the printer?" he asked.

She turned her eyes to meet his, trembling inwardly at the sheer pleasure of looking at him from such a sweet distance. "Yes," she said in a husky tone.

His eyes searched hers and then went down to her mouth, studying it for a long, aching moment before he abruptly stood erect and turned away. "Okay. That's all I wanted to see. We'd better get back to the house."

She removed the disks and cut off the computer, then carefully covered it back up. She turned to him, nervous. "Matt, I'm sorry," she said hesitantly.

"It's not your fault. It's mine," he returned stonily. He glanced at her. "Maybe if I hadn't rushed you, frightened you..."

"I meant about the cattle," she began, thinking he'd misunderstood her.

"Sure. Come on, honey. I'll lock up."

But just as they started out the door, the phone rang. Matt picked it up, frowning.

"Yes!" His face froze. He glanced at Catherine with an unreadable expression as he listened, and she went taut with nerves because there was only one person who knew Matt was there. He listened, muttered something, and listened again with a face like a thunderhead. "Is that so?" he ground out finally, and the look he gave Catherine would have taken rust off a used car. "She is? Well, baby brother, you can just sit and wait!"

He slammed the phone down and glared at Catherine.

"What was that all about?" she asked, her voice weak because she had a horrible suspicion.

"That was Hal," he returned, jerking the door open. "We'd better go back to the house before he has a heart attack worrying about you. What did you tell him, Kit? That

I was trying to seduce you?" he demanded with barely controlled anger.

"Matt, I wanted to tell you—"

"Forget it," he cut her off. "Hal's just made things crystal clear for me. Let's go home."

She went out to the car and waited for him to turn out the office lights and lock the door. She'd never felt so miserable in all her life. Hal had said something to him that had set him off, and how could she defend herself without knowing what? She knew it was only Hal's revenge for all he'd taken from Matt, but that didn't make it hurt less. He'd just killed whatever tiny chance she had with Matt, and now she wanted to kill Hal. Matt would never touch her again, never kiss the breath out of her...

She forced herself not to cry. This wouldn't do. She had to get things in perspective. Matt never wanted to marry her anyway. She'd only been a diversion, someone to play with when Layne wasn't around. She had to remember that; it would make it easier. And letting him make love to her would only have made it worse when she had to let him go. She closed her eyes, shutting out the doubts. A moment later he was beside her, starting the engine. "You're going to have your work cut out for you," he remarked quietly as they drove back to the house.

She turned in the seat. "I don't understand."

"Don't you?" He laughed softly, glancing at her as he pulled up in front of the steps. "He needs someone strong, Kit. Someone to keep him in line. You'll find that out too late, if you aren't careful."

"Hal?" she muttered.

"Hal," he said. "I'm not blind, you know," he added when her eyes widened. "The way he fought me about you tonight, the way you froze me out...it all adds up. I should have real-

ized when you went to Fort Worth with him that you were
trying to tell me how things stood. Why in heaven's name
didn't you tell me at the beginning how you felt about him?"
he demanded.

"But, Matt!" she protested.

"Let it be," he said. "I hate like hell to rake over dead
ashes. Almost as much as I hate being used as a substitute,"
he added coldly.

"But I didn't…!" she burst out.

"It doesn't matter anymore. It's over." He finished his
cigarette and put it out, and when he turned back to her, he
was the stepcousin of years past. "Out, sweet cousin," he
said with a grin. "I've got to call Layne. Get out of my hair."

She hadn't used him as a substitute. She loved him. But
she knew that grin. It meant he was through listening. Her
heart felt like two pounds of lead. He thought she loved Hal;
and Hal had led her right into it. Matt didn't even seem to
care—beyond a little wounded vanity. He was in too much
of a hurry to hear Layne's voice. Incredible, after spending
three days with her!

"All right," she replied. She studied his hard face one
last time, her eyes soft and quiet and hurt. "Good night."

"Goodbye, Kit," he said in a tone like velvet.

She turned away quickly so that he wouldn't see the tears
and went back into the house, alone.

Hal met her in the hall. "So there you are," he said, grinning. "Have fun?"

Without a second thought, without a whisper of remorse,
she drew back her hand and slapped him across the face
with the whole strength of her arm behind it.

"Damn you," she whispered shakily. "Damn you, Hal!"

He held his red cheek, his dark eyes strange as he saw

the wounded fury in her flushed features, her biting eyes.
"Catherine...?"

"I hope you get a dose of your own medicine," she threw
at him. "I hope someday you're on the receiving end. You
spend your life finding ways to hurt people, to shake them
up, to get your own selfish way. You're nothing but a spoiled
little boy, Hal!"

His eyes popped. Catherine had always been on his side,
defending him. She didn't even look like Catherine; she
was all claws and teeth and flying fur.

"But, Catherine..." he protested.

"Leave me alone!" She brushed by him and ran up the
stairs to her room. Thank goodness her mother was nowhere in sight; she didn't think she could answer another
question.

She cursed Hal until she ran out of breath, hating him
for what he'd done. She even hated Matt. He'd refused to
listen when she'd tried to tell him the truth.

Okay. If he wanted a war, he would have one. But he
wasn't going to find it that easy to ignore her. She was going
to show him what he'd missed out on, and she was going to
get even with Hal if it killed her. With that thought firmly
in mind, she finally slept.

CHAPTER EIGHT

IT WAS THE longest night Catherine could ever remember. Her dreams were full of the night Matt had taken her to the movies, of the sweet anguish of being in his arms, feeling his hard mouth move so expertly on her own. It seemed like a lifetime ago, now, and he'd as good as told her that their fragile new relationship was over. It was all Hal's fault, she thought, and then realized that she'd contributed to it as well, with her childish behavior, her refusal to take Matt seriously. And perhaps he had been serious. He'd looked bleak enough last night when Hal made that horrible phone call. What if he'd felt something for her? And now she'd killed it!

The thought tormented her. If he had felt something, was it possible that she could resurrect it? Fight Layne for him and win? She got up and gave herself a pep talk as she fixed her face and dressed carefully in a white peasant dress with layers of ruffles. Perhaps it wasn't too late. But even if it was, she was going to turn over a new leaf. No more little-girl tantrums, no more stammering embarrassment. The old Catherine was going into the closet in mothballs, and the new one was going to be a force to behold. She was going to have her hair fixed, buy some new clothes. But first, she was going to stand Hal on his ear. She would see to it that he understood what he'd done to her last night.

It was late morning when she got downstairs, but oddly

enough the family was still at the breakfast table. Once, Hal would have whistled blatantly when she walked in. But it was a serious, quiet Hal who looked up when she joined them.

"Morning, cousin," he said, searching her face.

"Good morning, Halbert," she returned, using his full name for the first time in memory. She smiled at him dreamily and sighed theatrically. He frowned curiously as her cool glance went to Matt. "Morning."

"Morning, sweet cousin." He grinned, not a trace of ill humor or regret in him as he leaned back in his denims to study her with the old mocking smile. "Head-hunting today, are we?"

"She did that last night," Hal murmured, touching his cheek, and he smiled tentatively. "Knocked some sense into me."

"Did it hurt?" she said with mock sorrow. "Poor darling."

Hal actually flushed, digging into his eggs with renewed vigor. He seemed to have a lot on his mind, and he kept shooting nervous glances toward Matt, who was as impassive as ever. Betty stared around her uncomprehendingly, shaking her head. She didn't understand anything they said these days. Perhaps it was the generation gap at work, cutting her off from the younger people.

"Did what hurt?" Matt asked amiably, then sipped at his second cup of coffee as he leaned back precariously in his chair, Spanish eyes dark and amused, his shirt unbuttoned at the throat and straining against the hard muscle of his chest.

"Oh, I seduced him last night, that's all," Catherine said outrageously. "Did you know he was still a virgin?"

Matt actually choked on his coffee. Hal buried his face

in his hands, and Betty sat like stone, staring blankly at her daughter.

"Poor old dear," Catherine clucked as Matt coughed into his napkin. "It's your age, Matt. You just can't hold your coffee anymore."

He stopped coughing and glared at her. "What the hell's gotten into you this morning?"

"Love." She sighed, staring at Hal with a dreamy expression. "Hal, darling, when are we getting married?"

Hal's face was fascinating. It went white, then red, then purple as he gaped at her. "Married?"

"Well, I can't leave you in the lurch. I still respect you, darling," she added wickedly. "Do marry me."

"I can't," Hal burst out. "And for God's sake, stop talking about seduction!"

"Don't you like being hassled, darling?" she persisted, eyes flashing. "Doesn't it feel good to be on the receiving end?"

"Aha!" Hal burst out, sitting erect, pointing at her. "Aha, that's your game! It's revenge!"

"Darling, what have you ever done to me?" She pouted, blinking her lashes at him. "Except refuse to marry me, that is."

He threw down his napkin. "I'm leaving. I have to get to work," he said, glancing at Matt to see how the older man reacted to that bombshell. Hal grinned at his brother's puzzled expression as he stood up. "I called an old friend early this morning and begged for a job. Matt, you can scream if you like, but I'm going to work for Dan Keogh. He has a racing team, and he's letting me work my way up as a mechanic. I'm starting for minimum wage."

Matt scowled. "You? Working for minimum wage?"

Hal straightened proudly. "I'm not afraid of hard work as

long as it's something I enjoy. I've always loved tinkering with cars, but I'm not cut out for real estate, despite what you promised Mother. She's dead, but I have my own life to live, and I'm going to do it my way. Cut me off without a dime if you like—I don't give a damn." He glanced at Catherine, who was listening intently. "You were right, Catherine," he added gently. "I was a selfish spoiled brat. But people can change. Just stand back and watch me. If I'm needed, I'll be at the garage. Ciao, all."

He threw up his hand in farewell and went out the door. Matt stared after him, aghast. "I'll be damned," he said under his breath, fumbling for a cigarette. "A miracle!"

"Hal, working," Betty echoed. She lifted her napkin to her eyes. "Oh, dear, I think I'm going to cry."

"It won't save him," Catherine said. "I'm still going to marry him to save his good name."

"Darling, you didn't really…?" Betty probed gently, all eyes.

Matt was watching, too, warily.

"I do not kiss and tell," Catherine said smugly. She got up, too. "I'm going to get the advertisements ready this morning, and I've got to arrange a caterer for the barbecue." She looked over at Matt. "Is the caterer you used last year capable?"

"Yes," he said.

"Then I'll get him again. And I need to be off for an hour at lunch," she added. "I have some shopping to do."

"Help yourself," Matt murmured, studying her curiously.

She smiled. Good. Let him guess. She was about to organize a frontal campaign, and he was the objective; but it wouldn't do to let him know it. "See you later."

"She wouldn't seduce Hal, would she?" Betty asked worriedly.

"Of course not," Matt agreed. But his eyes were narrow and thoughtful and a little worried as he watched her flounce out of the room.

CATHERINE WAS HUMMING softly at the computer when Matt came in. Hold on to your heart, girl, she told herself, and steeled herself not to jump or blush when he stood over her.

"Almost through," she told him with a sunny smile. "Angel said the printer would like you to look over the layout before he prints your programs."

"I'll go now," he said. He stared down at her, his hands in the pockets of his tight jeans, his dark eyes shaded by his straw hat, his face impassive. "You haven't slept with Hal, have you?"

She looked up at him sensuously. "Darling, haven't I?" she returned huskily, smiling slowly at the darkness growing in his eyes.

He started to say something, clammed up and slammed out of the office. Catherine only smiled.

She went into town at lunch hour and wandered into a hairdressing salon that specialized in walk-in customers. Twenty minutes later she walked back out into the sun with a wavy short haircut that added years of sophistication to her face, emphasizing her big green eyes and pretty, pouting mouth. She laughed, feeling new and excited. She went to a large department store next and smothered her very traditional instincts. She bought gauzy blouses, low-cut in front, and flaring skirts. She bought slinky dresses and an off-the-shoulder evening gown in a wild jungle-green print. She bought open-toed high heels and sandals and some trendy earrings. And before she went back to work, she donned one of the new outfits—a swirling blue gauze skirt and a deeply cut, puffy-sleeved white blouse. With a touch of red lipstick and some eye makeup she'd never used and big, flashy blue earrings, she looked like something out of *Vogue*. She laughed at her reflection, wondering at the change. And then she went back to work.

The expression on Matt's dark face when he came back from lunch was comical. He stopped in the doorway and stared, just as Angel and the other girls had, but he took longer to recover.

"Well?" she asked huskily, smiling provocatively at him. "Do you like it?"

"My God, you can't come to work dressed like that," he said curtly. He closed the door and jerked out a cigarette.

"You smoke too much, darling," she murmured. She got up and went close to him, winding veils of seductive perfume around him as she gently took the cigarette from his fingers. She was awed by the way he reacted.

"Kit," he said under his breath. His eyes went to the bodice of the blouse, to the deep V that left her smooth breasts revealed.

"What's wrong, cowboy?" she asked, staring up into his darkened eyes. "Do I bother you?"

"Of course you bother me!" he growled. His hands caught her waist and squeezed, pulling her against him. "Why?"

"Why what?" she asked, parting her lips and watching his eyes rivet to them.

"The haircut. The new clothes," he said. "Is this for Hal's benefit? If it is, you'd better lock your door at night, or you may catch the wrong fly, little spider."

"I couldn't catch you," she whispered. "You've got Layne, haven't you?"

He couldn't seem to get his breath. His hands moved up

her sides to her rib cage, feeling the softness of her skin through the flimsy blouse. "Kit..."

She arched her throat, her eyes half closed, lazy. She linked her hands around his neck and swayed back against his arms. "Like it?"

"Fire," he whispered roughly. "Fire, Kit, and you're more flammable than you might think."

"Then burn me," she whispered back, going up on tiptoe to tempt his hard mouth. Her heart throbbed in her chest; her knees felt weak as she experienced the hardness of his lean body against hers. "Burn me, Matthew."

"Oh, God...!" he ground out. His mouth opened as it took hers in a kiss that should have been violent and wasn't. It was a tender taking, a shivery seduction of lips against tender lips, and his mouth trembled with the hunger it aroused in him.

She caught her breath, feeling sensations she'd never experienced before, not even with Matt. Her fingers tangled in the fabric of his denim shirt, holding on as her body began to shudder where it felt the hot imprint of his muscles.

"Open your mouth, baby," he whispered shakily as he moved her closer.

She did, feeling his tongue enter her, her eyes closing as the magic worked and the fires burned. Vaguely, she felt his arms contracting hungrily, grinding her against his aroused body, but her mind was in flames. She reached up and clung to him, her teeth nibbling at his hard mouth, her tongue fencing with his in an intimacy that defied restraint. She moaned, a sound like a whispered scream, and he lifted his head to look at her.

"I've never heard that before," he whispered as he brushed her mouth again with his. "Haven't I aroused you before this?"

"Wh-what?" She tried to think, but it was all she could do to speak.

"That sweet little sound you made," he murmured against her searching lips. "Women make it in passion, when they make love with men and the feeling breaks through. And sometimes, when men do this to them…" His hand moved, his fingers seeking out the hard tip of her breast and teasing around it in a tender searching that brought the sound again.

She looked up at him in a fever. There were too many clothes between them. She wanted to lie down with him and touch his skin. Feel him touching hers. Kissing it. His mouth on her bareness…

"Oh, no," he whispered, laughing softly as he read the thought in her eyes. "No, not here. I don't want an audience."

"Audience?" she echoed, arching to the subtle magic his fingers were working on her body. "Matt…" she moaned, straining to hold that exquisite touch.

He brushed soft kisses against her nose. "Is this what you're trying so hard to make me do?" he asked tenderly, and eased her head gently against his shoulder. His hand lifted, and he turned his eyes downward and watched as his fingers slid inside her blouse, into the deep V neck, and traced patterns on her bare skin.

"Low…lower," she whispered shamelessly, on fire for him.

His breath came as quickly as her own. He held her eyes. "Here?" he breathed, as she felt his fingers searching for the hardness.

She trembled and gasped as he found it, and he watched her face go hot with the tiny consummation. His hand flattened against her breast, taking the hard nipple into his moist palm, molding her while she clung to him and bit her lip to keep from crying out.

"Kit," he whispered achingly. He bent and put his mouth slowly on hers and, teasing her lips apart, tasted the heady mint of her breath. His hand squeezed and she made a sound that stiffened his taut body, that sent his free hand low on her spine to grind her hips into his.

Her mouth opened under the hunger of his, and she reached up and clung to him, glorying in the blatant message his body was relaying to her as he bruised her body into his in a slow, hungry rhythm.

She felt him shudder and pressed closer, trembling the length of her body, aching in places she'd never realized were so sensitive, moaning as she longed for something to end the anguished pleasure that was so new and unbearable...

"No!" He caught her arms and thrust her roughly away from him. "No!" he said hoarsely. He shuddered again, his face unrecognizable in passion, dark and black-eyed and rigid with unsatisfied hunger.

"Matt?" she whispered, staring up at him with her red, swollen mouth parted, tempting, her arms half lifted, her eyes yielding already.

With a harsh groan, he turned away, pressing his hands against the desk, leaning on them for support, his body in a stiff arch. "Get me a whiskey, Kit," he said in a voice thick with pain.

She stood there for a second, trying to get her mind back. She could hardly wobble over to the bar to do as he asked, her legs were trembling so. She poured a measure of whiskey into a shot glass, spilling some of it, and impulsively took a sip. It was hot in her throat, but she got it down and felt it steadying her.

She carried the glass to Matt, and when he didn't take it, she set it on the desk between his outstretched hands.

He took deep, ragged breaths, and Kit began to realize what was wrong with him. Her face went beet red as she remembered what they'd been doing, remembered the effect she could have on his body.

"I'm sorry," she whispered.

He straightened and picked up the whiskey, draining it in a single swallow. His face was pale and strained, and he looked violent. It was a full minute before he turned toward her.

"I won't die," he said when he saw the concern in her eyes. "You threw me off balance, that's all. You've seen it happen before," he reminded her.

"Yes. But not like that." Her gaze lowered to his shuddering chest.

"Not even with Hal?" he asked with a harsh laugh. "Poor boy."

"I don't feel like this with Hal," she blurted out, compounding the problem.

"Love without lust? How puritan," he scoffed. He jerked out a cigarette and lit it. "From now on, keep your attempts at seduction for your victim, Kit, and keep away from me, will you? As you've just seen, I'm pretty vulnerable."

She knew he hated admitting that. Her eyes searched his. "I'm just as vulnerable," she reminded him. "It wasn't just you."

"I realize that. But I'm no more inclined toward marriage than Hal seems to be," he added coldly. "On the other hand, I'm old-fashioned enough that I'd marry you if we made love, so save us both a lot of heartache and practice your wiles elsewhere."

"I thought you believed I'd already succeeded," she probed.

He searched her blushing face. "Kit, I'm not a virgin. I can recognize experience. You don't have it. Not in the way I mean."

"Ah, one of those experts who can recognize innocence with a look?" she teased.

"People who've had sex can control their hungers a little easier," he said tautly.

Her eyebrows arched. "Are you a virgin, too? You didn't seem that much in control to me."

He took a sharp breath. "Catherine…!"

She smiled at him, more confident now than she'd ever been before. Layne evidently wasn't giving him all he needed, or why would he have been so hungry? That gave her hope.

"Next time, I'll be more careful with you, darling," she whispered. "But right now, I have to get back to work."

He didn't seem to have a reply. He puffed on his cigarette while she went back to her computer and picked up where she'd left off.

She glanced up at him with an impish grin. "Feeling better?" she murmured.

"Not a lot, no," he returned. His chest rose and fell heavily as he smoked, and his eyes went over her. "You've grown up with a vengeance, haven't you?"

"It happens to the best of us." She glanced at him meaningfully. "Convinced now that I can handle myself in New York? If you aren't, I'll prove it to you by the time we have the barbecue."

His face clouded over. "How? By seducing Hal and me?"

"Hal won't let me seduce him." She sighed, darting a look up at him. "But you might."

His eyes flashed at her, and despite himself, he smiled. "Think so?"

"Look out," she warned softly. "I'm dangerous."

He held up the empty whiskey glass. "So I've seen. But there's something you'd better remember."

"Oh? What?"

He put the glass down and leaned over her, enveloping her in his spicy cologne. "I'm dangerous, too." He broke her mouth open under his, but before she could drown in the sweet pleasure, he lifted his head and, with a wink, went out the door.

CHAPTER NINE

BETTY WAS DELIGHTED with her daughter's new look. She raved about it when Catherine came home that night.

"You look so different, darling," she exclaimed, smiling at her only child.

"I grew up," Catherine replied, bending to kiss her mother's soft cheek.

"Not quite," Matt murmured as he strode past them toward the study.

"Matthew!" Catherine grumbled, glaring after him.

"And I remember the last time you called me that," he returned, grinning at her. "Do you?"

She did, and her mother's eyebrows arched at the red blush in Catherine's cheeks.

"I do wish I understood what's going on around here." Betty sighed.

The front door opened and Hal came in, grimy and grease stained and smiling from ear to ear. "I'm home!" he called.

"Wonderful!" Catherine greeted him. "Shall I call the minister now, or do you want to wash up first?"

Hal stared at her. "Now, Catherine…"

"I owe it to you to make an honest man of you," she told him. "Now, let's see, it can't be until after the barbecue, or Matt would never forgive us."

"Damned straight," Matt shouted from the den.

"But it will have to be before I leave for New York," she continued, frowning thoughtfully.

"You can forget New York," Matt called. "There are enough professional troublemakers up there without Texas imports."

"I will not forget it," she returned. "The whole point of my going to work for you was to prove that I can take care of myself."

"You haven't yet," he said.

She glared toward his study. "Will you please stop interrupting. I'm trying to set a wedding date in here."

"Sure, honey. I'll be your flower girl," Matt promised.

Betty burst out laughing and winked at Hal, who still wasn't sure whether to laugh or cry.

"Will you wear a pink taffeta dress, Matt, dear?" Catherine baited.

"If you marry Hal, I will."

Hal tried unsuccessfully to smother a grin. "Oh, Catherine," he chuckled. "It would almost be worth my freedom to see Matt in pink taffeta."

"Hal, I'm delighted to hear you say that," Catherine said with a smile. "Now, when do we set the date?"

"On your fifty-sixth birthday. I promise." He held his hand over his heart.

"Well," she said, pretending to consider his offer.

Hal came closer, and brushed a brotherly kiss against her forehead. "Forgive me," he said gently. "I've learned my lesson. And for what it's worth, I'm sorry."

She searched his dark eyes consideringly. "It's a little late for that."

"Do you think so?" he murmured, glancing deliberately toward the den. "I'm not so sure."

"Anyway," she said changing the subject and turning

away, "I don't have time to marry you now, Hal. I'm going to be too busy. Matt, I called the caterer, and I've got the invitations ready to address. Angel and I will start on them tomorrow."

"Okay, honey," he replied.

"I'd better get cleaned up for dinner."

"Annie's waiting to bring in the first course," Betty told everyone, "so let's hurry."

The doorbell rang as Hal went upstairs, and Betty opened the door to let Jerry and Barrie come in.

"Hello, everyone, I hope we're not intruding," Barrie said, flashing a blue-eyed smile at them, "but we have news."

"Big news," Jerry agreed with a grin at his redheaded wife.

"This sounds serious," Catherine said, staring at them. She glanced at Barrie. "Are you expecting?"

"Yes!" Barrie answered, clasping her hands in front of her. "Oh, I'm so excited, I don't know what to do. I've waited so long, and Jerry finally agreed— Catherine, how different you look! I love your hair!"

"Thank you," came the demure reply. "But tell us about you. When is it due?"

"Tomorrow," Barrie said dreamily.

Catherine looked at her flat stomach with wide, unblinking eyes. "Tomorrow?"

"Tomorrow?" Betty echoed with the same astonished look.

Barrie grimaced when she saw where all the eyes were staring. "Not that!" she burst out. "My goodness, not a baby! My herd of cattle!"

Catherine turned away, shaking her head. "I don't believe this. She comes in talking about exciting big news—we think it's a baby, and it's cattle!"

"She wouldn't get that excited over a baby." Jerry sighed, putting an arm around his petite wife. "But Lord, she does love cattle, and I made this great deal on a small herd of purebred Santa Gertrudis."

"Santa Gertrudis!" Matt came storming out of his office. "Like hell you're running Santa Gertrudis next to my purebred Herefords!"

"Now, Matt," Barrie said quickly, "I've got good fences."

"I've seen bulls that can get through a six-foot fence," he returned. "I don't want my purebred cows mixing with other strains—you'll ruin my breeding program!"

"I told you," Jerry groaned.

Barrie smiled at Matt, blinking her big blue eyes. "Now, Matt, I won't put them anywhere near your stock. Why, I've rented some land six miles away, just to keep my cattle on."

"You have?" Jerry asked.

"I have," Barrie said smugly. She grinned at her husband. "I told you I'd have all my bases covered. Jack Halston is renting me his bottoms."

"Bottoms." Matt sighed. "Honey, the first flash flood will take out your whole investment."

"There's some high ground nearby," she said. "I checked. It will work out just fine. I'm so excited! My own herd!"

"Some herd." Jerry chuckled. "Six cows and a bull."

"It's a start," she returned. She lifted her head and sniffed. "Steak! Country-fried steak and mashed potatoes. Oh, my, are we in time for supper? Is there enough? I'm just starved!"

"As usual," Annie observed, bustling to the table with platters of food. "Yes, there's enough. Come on before I chuck it out the back door."

Conversation for the rest of the evening centered on Barrie's cattle. Even Hal seemed to be excited for her. He took time to share his own news about his first day on the job.

"I'm doing fine, Keogh says. He's going to let me run a lap on Saturday on the track. I can hardly wait," he said fervently.

"Just make sure there aren't any embankments nearby," Matt murmured with a wink, leaning back with a brandy in his lean hand.

"Oh, I'll watch myself from now on, for sure," Hal promised. He glanced at Catherine with a smile.

"Stop leering at me, if you please," Catherine said huffily. "Just because I seduced you once is no reason to expect it from now on."

"Will you stop telling people you've seduced me!" Hal burst out as Barrie and Jerry gaped at him. "It isn't true!"

"You told Matt I did," she said, taking a shot in the dark as she remembered the telephone call at the office the night Matt came back from Dallas.

"I lied," Hal grumbled, glancing at Matt. "It was a practical joke, and I'll be the first to admit it backfired. I was out for revenge, but I'm the one who got kicked. I surrender, Catherine."

"It's no use," she said wistfully. "I'm just not in the mood tonight. I have a headache."

"Will you quit that!" Hal moaned.

Matt was watching with curious dark eyes. He studied Catherine quietly, intently, as he sipped his brandy.

She glanced at him, then turned away. Well, he needn't think that anything had really changed just because she'd made Hal admit the truth. She knew Matt wanted her, but there were still Layne and Matt's obsession with freedom. She'd only wanted to clear the slate, she told herself. But deep inside, she wondered what Matt would do now—if he'd do anything.

Matt didn't say another word until Barrie and Jerry had gone home and Hal had gone up to bed. Betty was doing embroidery, and Matt got up and announced that he was going to sit on the porch swing, and asked wouldn't Catherine like some air?

She would, she agreed, but as she said good-night to Betty and followed him outside, it was with apprehension.

As it turned out, she didn't have any reason to worry. Because he seemed to have more important things on his mind than romance under the stars.

"Sit down, honey. I won't bite," he said wickedly when she hesitated.

She plopped down beside him and felt his long legs rock the swing into a rhythmic, creaking motion. Nearby, crickets sang, and from far in the distance came the sound of cars going along the highway. With a sigh, Catherine leaned her head back against Matt's muscular arm and closed her eyes.

"How did you know what Hal said to me that night?" he asked after a while.

"I didn't. I took a lucky shot."

"He has a vindictive streak a mile wide," he remarked.

"Yes, but it's just as well," she said lazily, opening her eyes to smile up at his shadowed face. "You'd only have seduced me and hated yourself."

"Think so?" he murmured, glancing down at her.

"I know so. Sex isn't a good basis for a relationship. I may be green, but I know that much."

His fingers toyed with her hair. "I'm not sure I like it this short," he remarked.

"They'll like it in New York," she assured him.

"You're still determined that you want to go?"

"Yes," she lied, suddenly unsure about her answer.

He lit a cigarette and took a long draw from it. "Don't you like working with Angel and the other girls?"

"I like it very well. But I don't plan to spend the rest of my life here, Matt. I'm not like Barrie. Cattle don't mean the world to me."

"It's all been a game with you, has it?"

"What has?"

He stared out into the darkness. "Playing me off against Hal."

"I wasn't," she protested. She shifted her head against his arm to stare up at him. "You're the one who likes to play around, big cousin, you with your harem. You draw women like flies."

"A certain type of woman," he corrected. He drew on the cigarette, and she could see his hard, even profile in the red glow. "And for all you know, they could have been window dressing, young Catherine. I might have lived like a monk for the past two years."

"Elephants might fly," she replied. "You aren't the monkish type."

His eyes sought hers in the dim light coming from the windows. "Maybe I only want one woman."

"Yes," she said quietly. "The oh-so-sophisticated Layne, of course."

He paused for an instant before he spoke. "You've never been curious about my women before, Kit."

That was true enough. "I've never been an adult before," she replied gradually.

"You aren't yet, either," he murmured deeply. "What you know about men and sex could be written on the head of a straight pin."

"Getting experience wasn't easy with you and Mother bulldogging me," she replied.

"The only experience you've got, I've given you," he said under his breath. He looked down at her, his dark, warm eyes searching over her flushed face. "And it's only beginning."

"No, it isn't," she shot at him. "I won't be a plaything!" She jerked away from him and got to her feet.

"So nervous," he said gently. "So frightened. And if you'd open your eyes, Kit, you'd realize there's nothing to be afraid of."

"That's what you think!"

"It won't hurt that much," he said in a tone that sent chills down her spine. "Maybe not at all. I can be gentle."

She went red and, choking on the attempt to fire back at him, she whirled and stormed back inside to the sound of his predatory laughter.

WHETHER IT WAS a blessing in disguise or a curse, Catherine was much too busy in the following days to fence with Matt. Organizing the public relations end of the sale was the hardest work she'd ever done. There was one detail after another to see to, and getting out the invitations took the better part of two days. Ads had to be worked out for newspapers and trade magazines; there were the logistics of seating the crowds, name tags to buy, all the thousand and one tiny headaches that accompanied fitting out the ranch for the large number of guests.

"We'll never get through addressing envelopes," Angel wailed at the end of a particularly long day, "and I thought we were all finished!"

"I know," Catherine said wearily. "Well, maybe now we are."

The office door opened and Hal came in, looking flashy in slacks and a patterned blue shirt. "Hi," he said. "Thought I'd look in on my way to Fort Worth for the races. Care to go with me, Kit?"

She was tempted, but there were still bits and pieces to coordinate. "Thanks anyway," she said with a smile, "but I'm too far behind."

"How dreadful." Hal sighed. "Here I am, in my first trial, and there's nobody to cheer me on." He stuck his hands in his pockets and shot a curious glance at Angel, who seemed unusually intent on her typewriter. "Say, Angel, do you like auto racing?"

Angel's eyes came up, big and black and nervous. "Why, yes," she answered hesitantly. "My uncle used to race."

Hal grinned. "Want to come to Fort Worth with me?" he asked softly. "We could go out to dinner afterward."

"Well…"

"Go!" Catherine coaxed. "Matt won't say anything. After all, it's Saturday. We've both been working overtime, you know."

Angel smiled shyly at Hal. "In that case, I'd love to go with you. Should I change?"

Hal studied the pretty floral dress she was wearing and slowly shook his head. "No way, honey. You look terrific."

Angel actually blushed, not at all the cool, competent young woman Catherine had come to know. She had to hide a smile as they left, already deep in conversation.

Matt sauntered in minutes later, a puzzled frown crossing his face when he saw Catherine working alone.

"Did your help desert you?" he asked.

"She went off with Hal to cheer him to victory," Catherine answered. "I told her I was sure you wouldn't mind."

"I do mind," he said shortly. "You know Hal. I don't want to lose the best secretary I've ever had. He's a lady-killer."

"Just look who's talking," Catherine chided, glaring up at him.

His dark eyes traveled slowly over the low-cut white blouse and gray slacks she was wearing, the perky gray dotted scarf at her throat. "I don't kill them, honey. I seduce them," he said in a wicked undertone.

"Hal won't seduce Angel," she promised him. "She knows karate."

"Fat lot of good it will do her," he murmured, "if Hal turns on the heat."

"Men are a conceited lot," she remarked as she finished the last envelope and put it beside the printer. "Boy, am I tired!"

"Suppose you come out to supper with me."

She stared up at him uncertainly. "I don't know."

"I'll buy you fried oysters, Kit," he coaxed.

"For fried oysters, I'll come," she said, getting up and covering the printer. "But where are we going to find them around here?"

Two hours later, dining in an exclusive restaurant in Galveston, she didn't have to repeat the question. Matt had hustled her off to the airport and they'd flown there in his private plane.

"I'm not really dressed for this," she murmured, glancing around at all the elegantly dressed women.

"You look fine to me, honey," he replied. He leaned back with a glass of Chablis in his lean hand, studying her across the white tablecloth. He was wearing slacks, a white turtleneck shirt and a blue blazer. He'd added the blazer in the plane; apparently he kept it there for just such emergencies.

"The barbecue's set," she told him.

"No business talk," he said. "Tonight, we're just a man and a woman."

"How exciting," she said with a smile. "What are we going to do?"

"That's a leading question." He sipped his wine. "What would you like to do, Catherine?"

"I think I'd like to be one of your women, just for a night," she said, but it was pure bravado; she'd had two glasses of wine and she shouldn't have.

"How do you think my evenings end, when I take out that kind of woman?"

She finished her second glass of wine. "I have a pretty good idea, and that's not what I meant."

He toyed with his glass, pursing his chiseled lips as he stared across at her. "We could start with some slow dancing," he suggested.

"That sounds safe enough."

It did, until Matt took her in his arms on the small dance floor while a live band played lazy blues tunes. He held her with both arms, while she linked hers around his neck. Although she'd gone to plenty of college parties, Catherine had never danced so close to a man she wanted. And she learned quickly that it was an intoxicating experience. It made her knees weak, made her body throb where it brushed so intimately against his. She looked up with all her uncertainties plain in her wide green eyes.

"Don't be nervous," he said gently, leaning down to brush his mouth over her forehead. "Think of it as making love to music."

"That's what it feels like, Matt," she whispered, inhaling the clean, spicy scent of his skin, feeling the warm strength of his body.

"Yes, I know." He made a sharp turn, and she felt his

thigh against her own and trembled. "Do you like that?" he asked at her ear and did it again.

"Oh, Matt," she whispered shakily, clinging closer. She couldn't seem to help herself; she wanted to be as near him as she could get. Her body ached with needs she was only now discovering.

His teeth found her ear and nibbled it gently. "I've got an apartment here," he whispered.

"H-have you?"

"We could go there."

Give me strength, she prayed. Her eyes shut tight. "No."

"I wouldn't hurt you," he breathed.

Her legs trembled against his. "Don't ask me."

"I want you."

"I know. But I can't."

He laughed softly. "Can't you? I thought you were a modern girl, Kit. Or didn't you know that this is how it's going to be in New York? People hand out sex like a party favor in the circles you'll be traveling in."

She drew a little away from him and searched his mocking eyes. "Is that why you asked me? Is this an object lesson?"

"I think you need one, little innocent," he said quietly.

"Then suppose you take me to your apartment, Matt, and teach me how to survive in the big city?" she challenged.

He held her at arm's length a moment, and his dark eyes cut into hers, then ran down her slender body. Suddenly he pressed her close again, his hands clutching at her back. "I could teach you plenty," he breathed. "But nothing would be the same afterward. Not between us, or with the family. And I could get you pregnant."

She felt her cheeks go hot. "I thought men knew how to prevent it."

"There are only two ways a man has," he said gently, searching her eyes. "One is reliable but uncomfortable, and the other is uncertain at best. The best prevention I know of is strolling birth control," he added with a wicked grin. "But you won't go to movies with me these days."

She hid her face against his broad chest, nuzzling him, feeling his strength as they circled the dance floor. She was throbbing with forbidden hungers, wanting nothing more than to lie with him in a big, cool bed and learn all the secrets, solve the mystery.

His lean hand smoothed over her back, warm and strong through the silky blouse, his fingers wandering from her neck to her waist. "Kit, are you wearing a bra?" he asked in a sultry whisper.

She felt her breasts going taut. "No," she replied.

He tensed as they moved slowly to the music. "That's too bad. Because when we get back to the plane, I'm going to take off this blouse and look at you."

Her eyes came up, wide and shocked, and he held them ruthlessly, his body hard against hers, his hands seductively caressing her back.

"You don't want to stay here any more than I do," he said huskily. "Let's go."

She didn't remember leaving the restaurant or the slow cab ride back to the plane. She was burning as if with a fever and was totally beyond rational thought.

Matt paid the cabdriver and let her go into the plane while he walked around the craft, checking it out. But when he finally got in and closed up the plane, it wasn't to taxi out onto the runway.

He bent and lifted Catherine in his strong arms and sank into one of the wide, comfortable seats with her on his lap.

"Now," he whispered, "we can have dessert."

And as he finished speaking, his mouth crushed gently against hers, opening it to a slow, probing kiss. His free hand moved to her silky blouse, easing each button delicately from its buttonhole while she watched his face in a silence thick with desire.

He slowly peeled the blouse away from her taut, swollen breasts, and she lay quietly in his arms and let him look at her.

"My God, you're lovely," he whispered with something like reverence in his tone. "I'm almost afraid to touch you, Catherine."

His fingers went down to her collarbone and traced patterns there. Her lips parted on a held breath as his fingers moved down slowly, lazily.

"You feel like silk, baby," he breathed, letting his eyes follow the seductive movement of his fingers. "Except for these…so hard to the touch."

He touched her nipples and watched her arch at the exquisite pleasure.

"Kit, I thought I had so much patience," he whispered ruefully. He moved, lifting her up to his mouth. "But I'm hungry, too."

He took one small, perfect breast right into his mouth, creating a warm, moist suction that made her cry out in a voice she didn't recognize.

It was a maelstrom of feeling, of shocked pleasure, of anguished desire. She clung and cried while he devoured her from the waist up, letting her feel his tongue, his teeth. And it was the most beautiful experience of her entire life.

"Matt," she whispered, her trembling hands in his dark hair, holding his mouth against her. "Oh, Matt, I never dreamed, never thought…!"

"I love the taste of you, baby," he whispered against her

body. "I love the smell of you, the sweet softness of you. Kit, I want you so!"

His mouth slid up her chin to cover her mouth, and he drew her against him, feeling her searching hands frantically lifting the bottom of his shirt so that her skin could merge with his hair-roughened chest. He shuddered as he felt her sinking against him, the warm, hard-tipped softness crushing so exquisitely into his hard muscles.

"I could die and I wouldn't mind now," she whispered huskily, clinging to him. "Oh, Matt, it feels so sweet…!"

"I know." His arms tightened, and he ground her against him, rocking her gently, his mouth over hers, shuddering with the tenderness of a kiss that shook them both with its soft intensity.

"You don't know how dangerous this is," he whispered unsteadily.

"You said you wanted me," she reminded him, glorying in the pleasure they were creating.

"I did. I do. And you want me. But we can't make love for the first time in a parked airplane, Kit."

"Why not?" she asked mindlessly, looking up at him with pleading eyes.

He caught his breath, letting her slide down into the crook of his arm so that he could feast his eyes on her sweet nudity. "God, you're so exquisite, Kit!" he whispered, touching her delicately so that she shuddered with pleasure.

"I want you," she whispered.

"Yes. But not like this," he whispered back. He bent and kissed her eyelids closed, and then he buttoned her blouse, slowly, reluctantly. "When it happens, I want it in bed, in private, so that we have all night to enjoy each other."

"When?" she whispered.

"Soon." He bent and brushed his mouth over hers. "But

right now, we have to get home. And I can't fly with you in my arms, honey. I'd crash the plane."

He eased her into a sitting position. "Come sit with me in the cockpit."

She followed him, and let him strap her into the seat before he got into his own and put on the headphones. He flashed her a smile, and minutes later they were airborne.

It didn't take long to get back to the ranch. The lights were all out except for one in the living room and one on the front porch, and when they got inside, it was to find Hal sitting up alone.

"Betty's gone to play bridge with friends," he told them. "And I've just taken Angel home," he added with a strangely shy grin. "You two have fun?"

"We had oysters in Galveston," Catherine volunteered.

"How interesting," he commented with a grin.

"Stop that or I'll make you marry me," Catherine threatened.

"Okay, I'll behave." He sighed.

"Good night. Thanks for the dinner," Catherine told Matt, a little disappointed that they didn't have the house to themselves—and her eyes told him so.

"Good night, little cousin," he said with a smile full of tenderness and memories.

She climbed the stairs reluctantly and got ready for bed. Minutes later, there was a light tap on the door. She opened it to find Hal outside.

"Matt says, will you trade rooms with him for tonight?" Hal said softly. "He says he wants to keep an eye on those new cattle of Barrie's, and he can look out your window and see them."

What an odd request, she thought, but she was so full of

wine that it never registered just how strange the request was. "Okay," she said, yawning, and pulled on her robe.

She climbed into Matt's huge bed in the dark and was almost instantly asleep. So it came as a shock the next morning when she opened her eyes and found Matt sound asleep beside her—apparently without a stitch of clothing on, if his broad chest and flat stomach showing above the precarious sheet were any indication.

She sat up in bed, feeling woolly-headed from the night before, and stared down at him with her gown half off one shoulder. And just as she touched his chest to wake him, the door opened and there stood Betty, a cup of coffee in her hand and disbelief on her face.

CHAPTER TEN

BETTY STOOD FOR long moments like a statue in the doorway. Then she leaned forward, blinking, the cup of coffee hanging precariously in her fingers. She frowned, shook her head and went back out, leaving the door open.

"Matt, wake up!" Catherine squealed in a whisper. She shook him, feeling warm, hard muscle and rough skin and wanting to touch so much more than his broad shoulders.

His eyes opened slowly, looking up into hers. He smiled lazily. "Well, hello, angel. Did I die in my sleep?"

"What are you doing in here?" she burst out.

"It's my bedroom. I think." He sat up, disrupting the cover, and Catherine had a brief, shocking glimpse of what was under the sheet. "Yep, this is my bedroom, all right. What are you doing in it?" he added blankly, staring at her.

"Will you cover yourself up!" she groaned, averting her eyes and her feverish cheeks while he chuckled and dashed the sheet back over his hips.

Outside in the hall there were voices. Matt's eyebrows arched as Betty came back with Hal in tow.

"You see?" Betty murmured, indicating the two still figures in bed. "I told you so."

Hal peered at them, too. "I'm not sure. Maybe it's an illusion. I drank last night. So did Matt."

"That is not an illusion," Betty grumbled. She glanced at Matt and Catherine. "I'll get the others."

"My God, are you selling tickets?" Matt growled at their retreating backs. He turned to Catherine. "What are you doing in my bed?"

"Hal said you wanted to swap rooms with me, so you could watch over Barrie's cattle," she said, then cleared her throat when, cold sober, she realized how stupid that sounded. "I've been had."

"It looks that way, and guess who they'll think has had you?" Matt returned sharply, his dark eyes going over her breasts, which were visible through the nearly transparent blue gown she was wearing. "My, my, Kit, do you always sleep like that?" he added in a seductive tone.

"Stop gaping at me," she muttered.

"You like it, you little coward," he returned. He reached up and brushed his fingers lightly over her breasts, watching her breath catch, her face mirror the shock of pleasure. He reached up and slid his fingers into her short hair. "Come down here."

"Matt—" she started to protest just as voices came closer again.

"Oh, hell," he growled, throwing himself flat on his back. "I feel like a museum exhibit."

Catherine's eyes went over his long, hard-muscled body with smiling awe. "You look better than any painting I've ever seen," she confessed, "even without a fig leaf."

"Kit!"

She averted her face, stunned at her own remark. "Sorry."

The doorway suddenly filled with faces. "See?" Betty was telling the others. Barrie and Jerry stared. So did Hal. They all murmured and pointed and frowned.

Matt groaned and pulled the cover over his face.

"Stop that!" Catherine grumbled at him. "It's all your fault, anyway. Why did you have to come sleep in here?"

"It's my damned bed!" Matt said gruffly from under the sheet.

"That's no excuse," Catherine returned curtly. She glanced at the onlookers. "Hal did it!" she accused, pointing at him. "He told me Matt wanted to trade rooms."

"Me?" Hal burst out, gaping. "I never!"

Catherine's jaw fell. "You did, you liar! You came and knocked on my door and told me Matt wanted me to sleep in his room!"

"I," Hal replied, "am an innocent bystander, being falsely accused."

"I never thought I'd live to see Matt and Catherine in bed together," Jerry remarked.

"Same here," Barrie replied.

"Shocking." Angel clicked her tongue, grinning wickedly. Angel!

"How many people did you bring in with you, Mother!" Catherine asked in what she hoped was a calm tone, although her voice sounded two octaves higher than normal.

"Well, just family, darling," Betty defended herself. "And Angel, and Mr. Bealy, here—he's come to see Matt about a bull."

"Pleased to meet you, ma'am." Mr. Bealy, a middle-aged man, grinned, doffing his hat.

"And Miss Harley, of course," Betty added, introducing a lovely little old lady who occasionally visited Betty.

"Nice to see you again, Catherine," Miss Harley said with a smile.

Catherine glanced from them to the mumbling lump beside her in bed. With a weary sigh, she lay down and pulled the cover over her head, too.

"Nobody will believe the truth in this house," she wailed.

"What did I tell you?" Matt agreed, grinning at her under the sheet.

"I'll have breakfast when you two are hungry, dear," Betty called gaily as the crowd went out. "No hurry." The door closed.

"My reputation is ruined," Catherine wailed. "Hal lied!"

Matt threw off the sheet. "Well, Kit, so much for New York."

"No! Now is the best time for me to go there!" she protested.

He moved, arching over her, resting his weight on his arms. "No it isn't, honey," he murmured with a soft laugh. "Now is the best time for us to announce our engagement—before this sordid story gets spread all over southern Oklahoma and northern Texas."

"Engagement?" Her heart leaped wildly. "You're not serious."

"Yes, I am." He bent and brushed her mouth lazily with his. "You want me, Kit. And I want you. The rest will come naturally. We'll get married and make babies and raise cattle."

Her pulse was going wild. "But—"

His mouth opened on hers. His chest came down over her breasts, crushing them gently, his hands smoothing down her sides to her hips. Abruptly he turned on his side, jerking her body completely against his.

She gasped, her eyes wide open in shock at the contact with his hard body, only the flimsy film of her gown between them.

"Kit," he breathed, his eyes dark as she'd never before seen them, a tremor in the arms that urged her even closer. "God, you're so soft. Velvet and silk and magic in my arms."

"Matt, you don't…have any clothes on," she faltered.

He searched her eyes. "We could take your gown off," he whispered. "We could feel each other like this."

Her lips trembled. "No."

"You want to," he whispered, leaning nearer to brush her eyes closed with his mouth. "Don't you?"

His hands were on her body, on the long line of her back, her hips, her upper thighs. She trembled, and he smiled against her forehead, nudging her body against his in a slow, torturous rhythm, letting her feel what she already knew, that he wanted her obsessively.

"Oh… Matt…" Her voice broke as the sensations grew unmanageable. Her hands went to his chest, trembling as they pressed into thick hair and hard muscle.

"Don't stop there," he whispered at her mouth. "Touch me. Learn my body, as I'm learning yours."

She started to protest, but he moved, guiding her hands, watching her face as she learned the most private things about him. Her eyes grew enormous, but she didn't fight him.

He smiled at her shocked fascination, laughing even as he trembled with pleasure. "Marry me, Kit," he breathed, "and I'll let you have me."

"Tease," she returned, barely able to manage laughter herself.

"Don't you want me, honey?" He brushed his mouth lazily over hers, feeling it open and warm to his kisses. "Don't you want to lie in my arms every night in the darkness and be warmed by my body in the chill of dawn?"

"But, marriage…" she protested.

"Say yes, Kit," he murmured.

"Not…not now," she forced herself to say. "Not yet. I need time."

"Okay. I'll give you five seconds."

"No! Time, Matt."

He lifted his head with a sigh, and his hands stilled. He studied her flushed face quietly, his hair mussed, his mouth swollen, his dark eyes intent and warm. "Okay. But until you make up your mind, honey, we're engaged. I'm not throwing myself into that barracuda pack downstairs without protection."

She smiled at the phrasing. "Do you suppose Mother was charging admission?"

"If she was, I want my cut." Matt grinned. "Come on, get up, you seductive little thing, and let me get back to work."

"Who's stopping you?" she teased.

"Well, if you don't mind, I sure as hell don't." And it was then that she realized he'd given her a chance to get out of bed before he did. But it was too late because he was standing by the bed, magnificent in his nudity, smiling at the confused shock in her eyes as she stared at him helplessly.

"This is a first," he murmured. "Remember you said once that you'd been saving yourself for me?"

She nodded, dazed.

"Well, I figured I could save at least one first for you, so I always made love in the dark. I've never let another woman see me like this."

Her eyes lifted to his. "I'm glad," she said in a stranger's husky voice.

"So am I. Now," he added, winking at her, "get dressed before you drive me to drink again." He turned and started to dress himself as she unwound herself from the tangle of the sheet and got up.

"Again?" She caught on as she reached the door and turned.

He was just snapping his jeans. He grinned at her. "Hal got me drunk last night. I staggered in here half-blind and never noticed the bed was occupied. He did a job on both of us."

"Why, do you suppose?" she asked, puzzled. "Revenge?"

He searched her eyes quietly. "No," he replied after a minute. "I think he was trying to make amends."

"For what?"

"Never mind, honey. We've got some music to face." He let his eyes wander down her body, and he smiled wickedly. "Better wear something terribly unrevealing while we try to explain our way out of this."

"I've got a great idea," she said. "I found you on a lily pad and kissed you—"

"That's been tried before, and I'll bet the princess's father didn't fall for it any more than the family would." He chuckled, reaching in his closet for a clean shirt. "Move, woman!"

"Yes, Your Grace." She curtsied and jerked away just in time to avoid his swinging palm.

WHEN SHE'D DRESSED in a becoming wine pantsuit, she found him waiting in the hall for her, and her heart jumped at the sight of him in a brown patterned shirt and tight jeans. He always looked good, but after this morning she felt possessive about him. It would be insane to pretend that he really wanted to marry her, that this engagement was anything more than a ruse to keep the family from being upset about this morning's revelation. But she wanted it to be real. She wanted to marry Matt and have his children. And even though she knew he didn't love her, that he was still involved with Layne, perhaps if they were living together, she could make him love her. She'd work so hard at it!

"Why the frown, baby?" he murmured as she came out of her room.

"Just thinking," she sidestepped, smiling up at him.

He bent and kissed her softly. "Don't think. Just let things happen." He put an arm around her shoulders and led her down the stairs.

All eyes turned toward them when they walked into the dining room.

Matt stared back, cocking his dark head to one side. "Okay, it's like this," he began. "I was sitting on a lily pad, minding my own business, when—"

"Cut that out," Catherine grumbled. "You were the one who told me they'd never fall for it."

"In that case, Kit and I are engaged," he told Betty. "Hal, go break out a bottle of champagne, and we'll start a new breakfast tradition."

"You bet!" Hal chuckled, rising. "Congratulations!"

Betty echoed that, hugging Catherine and then Matt. "I saw the way you two have been watching each other lately, and I had a feeling this announcement wouldn't be far off."

"Mother, about last night—" Catherine began.

"Now, now, no need to worry about it," Betty said, patting her hand affectionately as she led her to the table. "You're engaged, and these things happen."

There went Catherine's fragile hope that Hal had confessed all. She sighed and smiled at Angel and Mr. Bealy and Jerry and Barrie as she sat down next to Matt at the table and received the mingled congratulations.

"It's been a long, hard, uphill battle," Matt told them as he reached for his coffee cup. "But I won."

"I am not a conquest," Catherine teased, and then remembered how they'd been found this morning, and she turned red.

Matt laughed uproariously. "Liar," he murmured.

"Come down and look at my herd, Matt," Barrie invited. "You and Catherine can cuddle in the backseat."

"You drive an MG Midget," Catherine reminded her. "There is no backseat."

"Well, in that case, Matt, I'll let Jerry drive us in the Oldsmobile."

"Okay," Matt agreed. "Pick us up after church."

Catherine gaped at him. "You're going to church with me?"

"I do go occasionally," he reminded her.

"Once a year."

"So I'll reform," he promised. "After all, a man has to be responsible when he has a family."

"We don't have one."

"We will have." He grinned and stared at her until she dropped her eyes in embarrassment.

Hal came back with champagne, which he opened and poured into delicate champagne glasses, then toasted the happy couple.

AFTER CHURCH, WHICH had been a really delicious event— Catherine had been so proud to have Matt beside her and Betty in the family pew—they rode over to see Barrie's new Santa Gertrudis cattle.

Matt stood at the fence beside Catherine, and his eyes widened as he stared. There were six heifers and a bull, and as he studied the bull closely, he burst out laughing.

"He isn't funny," Barrie muttered. "What are you laughing at?"

"My God, are you planning to breed him?" Matt asked.

"Of course, that's why I have six cows. I want lots of calves." Barrie sighed, smiling dreamily, her red curls wafting on the breeze.

"How much did you pay for that bull?"

"Four hundred dollars," she said.

"Didn't it occur to you," he said gently, "that a purebred champion bull that age would bring at least fifty grand?"

Barrie cocked her head, glancing from the bull to Matt. "Is something wrong with him, do you think?"

Matt drew his straw hat low over his eyes. "No, as long as you only want him to pet."

"I don't understand."

"He's a steer," Matt explained.

"Yes, I know," Barrie agreed blankly. "So what's that got to do with breeding him?"

Catherine had to bite her lip. Barrie did love cattle, but mostly as pictures in magazines. She had a lot to learn about technicalities.

"Barrie," Matt said quietly, "a steer is a bull that's been fixed. Sterilized. Like a gelding horse. You can't breed him. He's hamburger beef, not stud material."

Barrie cleared her throat. She stared at Jerry, who was turning purple trying not to burst out laughing. "You!" she growled at him. "You knew that! You bought me this super bull, and all the time you knew he was a steer!"

"Not my fault," Jerry choked. "I thought you could look at him and tell."

"I'm so used to looking at beef cattle, I didn't realize," Barrie wailed. "Now what will I do?"

"Well, we can have steaks every night..." Jerry suggested.

Barrie's eyebrows shot up. "Eat Beauregard?"

"Sure, with lots of steak sauce."

"Never!" She bit her lip. "Oh, poor old thing," she murmured. "Poor old bull."

"Don't break your heart over it," Matt told her, smiling. "I know a man who runs purebred Santa Gertrudis. You can get a young bull for around a thousand and raise him up the way you want to. Okay?"

"Oh, Matt, that would be lovely!"

"A thousand dollars?" Jerry asked, all eyes.

"Don't you fuss, either," Barrie challenged. "It's your fault that we bought that silly bull anyway, and you're not going to eat him, either. We're going to put him in a pasture and let him grow old gracefully."

"I'll grow old gracefully, trying to pay off your new bull." Jerry sighed.

"I slave over hot stoves, I break my back washing clothes and cleaning house..." Barrie began.

Jerry turned with a sigh and walked away. She followed him, still raging.

Catherine laughed softly. "Poor Barrie."

"She'll learn," he said. He put a comfortable arm around her and drew her close as he studied the heifers. "They aren't bad," he murmured. "Good conformation. Pity she bought them open though."

"Open?" She stared up at him.

He searched her eyes slowly. "An open heifer is one that hasn't been bred."

"Oh."

His hand came up to her cheek and traced its softness. "I go hot all over when I think about babies," he whispered. "You've got wide hips, Kit. You wouldn't have a hard time."

Her heart shot up into her throat. "It's too soon to be... to be thinking about that," she said, her voice faltering.

"I think about it all the time," he said, bending to brush

a tender kiss against her forehead. "I think about having you in my bed and loving you in the darkness."

"Matt!" Her cheeks burned, and she glanced toward Jerry and Barrie, who were oblivious to them, still arguing.

"They can't hear," he breathed. He lifted his head and searched her eyes intently, unblinking. "Marry me, Kit."

Her legs felt like rubber. It was a terrible chance to take, a risk. But the thought of not marrying him was worse. He only wanted her, but she could change that. Somehow, she'd make him care.

"All right," she said softly.

"No backing out," he warned, his voice deep and low.

"No backing out."

He bent and put his mouth tenderly to hers, warming it, cherishing it. He lifted his dark head. His hand pressed against her cheek, his fingers brushing back a stray wisp of chestnut hair from her mouth. "I'll take care of you all my life," he whispered.

He looked and sounded solemn, and she wondered for one wild, sweet second if he really meant what he said. But suddenly he grinned, and the spell was broken.

"Now that I've overcome your resistance, what kind of ring do you want?" he asked.

She hadn't thought about it. "I don't want a diamond," she said absently.

"Okay. How about an emerald?"

"I've never seen an emerald set as an engagement ring. It would be different, wouldn't it?"

"We could get a band to match," he said. "Diamonds and emeralds in a wide band."

"I love it!"

"We'll go into town first thing tomorrow," he promised.

"But we can't," she moaned. "I have to take the ads to the newspaper."

"We'll drop them off on the way," he soothed. "Stop worrying."

But she couldn't help it, and it wasn't work that worried her. It was Matt. He was marrying her only because he couldn't have her any other way, because the family was so close-knit. But what would it be like when the newness wore off? Would he go back to Layne? She couldn't believe he would; Matt always kept his word. But would he be happy with her? The thought tormented her for the rest of the day, leaving her unusually quiet and reserved.

CHAPTER ELEVEN

MATT TOOK HER to an exclusive Fort Worth jeweler to buy the emerald. Fortunately they arrived during a remounting, so he was able to buy the flawless clear stone and the mounting and have the emerald set at the same time. Not one of the set emeralds in the store would have done for an engagement ring. There was a diamond and emerald wedding band that matched the stone perfectly, so he bought that, too.

Catherine sighed and sighed over the rings, smiling up at Matt with her eyes full of dreams.

"How about a wedding ring for you?" she exclaimed when he paid for hers and said it was time to go.

He smiled indulgently. "If you want me to wear one. As long as it goes on my finger, and not through my nose."

"I can see me now, leading you around by your nose," she scoffed.

He ran a lean finger down her pert nose. "Don't you think you could, honey?" he murmured sensuously.

She averted her eyes. No, she didn't. Because somewhere in the background was Layne, and that specter hung over her head like a sword.

"What's wrong?" he asked gently.

"Not a thing," she murmured, and forced herself to smile.

Matt liked a wide gold band, and since her emeralds and

diamonds were set in yellow gold, the two rings matched very well.

"Now it's official," he remarked as they drove home. "No more searching looks from the family."

She leaned her head back against the seat. "It's all Hal's fault," she murmured. "If he hadn't lied about it…"

"Never mind," he said pleasantly. "By the time the wedding rolls around, everyone will have forgotten anyway. Do you fancy a short engagement, Kit? I do."

"You just want to get me into bed," she grumbled.

His eyes shot to her face. "Is that what you think?" he asked.

"You haven't made any secret of it, have you?"

He drew his gaze back to the road and lit a cigarette. His brows came together as he smoked it. "No, I suppose not," he said absently. "Maybe I'll have to change tactics again, Kit."

That didn't make sense, but she didn't question it. She gazed at the long horizon instead, and wondered for the hundredth time if she was doing the right thing.

MATT'S BEHAVIOR IN the following days didn't make her any more confident. He suddenly became the friendly companion of the days past, and the tempestuous kisses she'd gotten used to disappeared. Now there was nothing more between them than holding hands and a brush of his lips against her cheek at bedtime. That worried her most of all, that he didn't seem interested in her physically anymore. Her mind was so occupied with the sale that she'd forgotten the conversation they'd had after they'd bought the rings. Of course, they did talk: about his plans for the ranch; about her own need to be doing something besides collecting dividend checks; about politics and religion and family. She got to know him on a different plane. She got to know him as a person as well as a man, and she loved what she learned. But would he really be interested in her as a person, if all he wanted was her body? It puzzled her, more and more.

THE NEWSPAPER ADS were out, the invitations accepted and the caterers arrived on schedule with truckloads of food.

Catherine wrung her hands, shooting worried glances in Matt's direction as the buyers started arriving.

"Stop turning your hair gray," he chided during a quiet moment. He tugged playfully on a lock of her waving short hair. "Everything's going great. You've done a magnificent job."

Her wide eyes searched his. "Do you really think so?"

"I really do." He touched her cheek gently. "After this is over, you and I are going to spend some time together. We have some plans of our own to finalize."

"It's been so hectic," she remarked.

"Yes." He touched his mouth to her forehead. "Want to come down to the auction?"

She shook her head. "I've got too much to do here. See you later."

He winked. "Save me some barbecue. These cattlemen eat the way they spend money."

"Don't you hope." She laughed.

His dark eyes beheld her radiant face. Her green eyes were like dew-kissed grass, her complexion all peaches and cream in its frame of chestnut hair. She was wearing a floral sundress with a halter top and she looked gorgeous.

"I've never seen anything as lovely as you look right now," he said quietly. "Beautiful little Kit, you've done a lot of growing up since you've come home."

She smiled at him. "Aren't you pleased?" she asked. "I was a thorn in your side for a while there."

He shook his head. "Never a thorn in my side. In my heart, maybe," he said enigmatically. "See you, pretty girl." He turned and strode off toward his buyers, dignified and urbane in his expensive light denim suit and his boots and Stetson, towering over the other men. He looked as Western as a spur, and Catherine's eyes adored him. With a sigh, she turned away and got back into organizing the tables.

The sale lasted until well after dark, with the last of the barbecue being divided equally among the lingering out-of-town cattlemen. Catherine felt very proud of the outcome. Matt had sold all his purebreds except for one lone heifer, and he wasn't complaining about that. A Western band played waltzes, and some of the men who'd come with their wives were dancing lazily to the music.

Matt finished off a neat whiskey and smiled down at Catherine. "Feel like dancing?" he asked.

He'd taken off his jacket and unbuttoned his shirt, and he looked as wickedly male as a movie star. Catherine went into his arms without a word, loving the feel of his hard, strong body against her. She slid both her hands around his waist and up his back to let them flatten on his shoulder blades.

"Was it a success?" she asked tiredly.

"Very much a success," he agreed. "Have you seen anything of the family?"

"Mother's around somewhere with Barrie and Jerry. Mother was hostessing while I ate. Hal and Angel were here for a while, but I think they've gone."

"The band will go soon," he murmured. "And I've already said my goodbyes. So suppose," he added under his breath, drawing her closer, "you and I find a nice dark spot and make love until we can't stand it anymore?"

Her body tingled. "Could we?" she whispered.

He went rigid for a minute. "I thought you were tired of all that," he said, lifting his head. "You seemed to have the idea that it was the only thing on my mind."

"We are engaged," she murmured, dropping her eyes. "And you haven't touched me for days..."

Suddenly he caught her hand and led her off, away from the crowd, into the study by way of the patio. He left her standing by the open window, and without turning on a light, he went and locked the door.

"What are you doing?" she asked as he came back to her, stripping off his shirt on the way.

"Striking a blow for male domination," he said under his breath. He caught her to him, and before she realized what he intended, he had stripped the halter of her dress down to the waist and pulled her against his hard, warm chest.

"Matt!" she gasped.

"God, that's good," he breathed. He moved her against him, letting her feel the crisp hair on his chest, rough against her taut breasts. "Lift up."

She slid her arms hesitantly around his neck and went on tiptoe, throbbing with hunger. He half lifted her, so that she was against him, breast to breast, hip to hip, thigh to thigh.

"Now," he whispered, holding her there so that it felt as if an electric current joined them. "Now, we dance."

But it was more like making love. She clung, feeling the roughness of his skin against her own, loving the intimate contact of their bodies. Her breath caught in her throat as she moved lazily to the beat with him, loving the feel of his lean, callused hands against her bare back, the sound of his voice whispering in her ear.

"I love touching you, Kit," he said softly. "I love the way my body throbs when it feels yours this way."

"I never dreamed anything would be so sweet," she confessed, pressing soft kisses against his collarbone, his bare shoulder.

"Do it here, honey," he whispered, shifting so that he could press her face against a hard male nipple.

She looked up at him, questioning.

"Men like it, too," he said, smiling as he coaxed her mouth down to him.

She remembered how he'd done it with his whole mouth, his teeth, his tongue and that was how she did it. He stiffened and caught the back of her head, forcing her closer. She drew him into her mouth, and he groaned roughly and shuddered.

"Matt," she whispered. Her hands adored him as she moved to the other side of his chest and repeated the seductive touch. Her lips learned him slowly, sweetly, from his collarbone to the thick muscles at his narrow waist, and he trembled.

"Oh, can't we lie down?" she whispered achingly, looking up at him with eyes that smoldered.

"If we do, I'll take you," he said unsteadily. "Can't you feel what's happening to me?"

She could, and she delighted in the knowledge that she could rouse him so easily.

"You said you wanted babies," she reminded him in a husky, aching tone.

"I do," he said, his voice rough with passion. "I want you, too. But not like this."

He caught her waist and moved her gently away from him, letting his eyes feast on her bareness. "So pretty," he whispered, touching the hard tips of her breasts with reverent hands, then rubbing them with his thumbs so that she gasped. "Mauve and cream. Kit…"

He bent and opening his mouth on them, tasted them in a silence that blazed with helpless longing.

"Please," she whispered, eyes closed, body yielding. "Please."

He scooped her up in his arms, looked down at her with dark, frightening passion in his eyes, his face. His arms trembled; his eyes ate her. "It won't be perfect this time," he said in an uneven tone. "I may hurt you."

"I don't care," she moaned, reaching up to find his mouth and tease it with hers. "I want to belong to you all the way."

She shuddered. His mouth opened on hers. "I want it, too," he whispered. "I want to show you how bodies join, lock together like two living puzzles. I want that intimacy with you. Only with you. Kit, Kit, I haven't had a woman in so long…" He moaned against her hungry mouth.

The kiss was endless, and during it he began to move toward the sofa. At first it only registered vaguely, what he'd said about its being so long. But surely he'd had Layne? Her dizzy mind went under in a blaze of fire so hot that her skin felt inflamed by it; her arms trembled as they held him. And somewhere in the distance, someone was calling his name…

He stopped at the sofa, shuddering still. He listened, frowning. "Hal," he bit off.

Her fingers touched his face. "Don't answer him," she whispered urgently, shamelessly. She wanted him so much it was almost a pain.

"I have to," he said huskily, "or he might walk in on us."

He put her down gently, his hands reluctant as they left her. With a muffled curse, he lifted his head. "What is it, Hal?" he yelled.

There was a pause. "Mr. Murdock needs to confirm something!"

Matt consigned Mr. Murdock to the fiery reaches, but even as he muttered, he was buttoning his shirt and tucking it back into his slacks. "I'm coming!" he yelled.

Catherine stood helplessly as he turned and looked down at her. He lifted the bodice back into place and fastened it behind her neck.

"I'm sorry," he said gently. "It's just as bad for me as it is for you, maybe worse."

"Want a whiskey?" she asked softly.

He laughed. "You didn't knock me completely off balance—not so far, anyway," he murmured. "I'll survive. But I could use that whiskey."

She turned on the light and fetched him a shot glass full. Handing it to him, she looked up at his tousled dark hair and swollen mouth. She looked as disheveled herself. He took the glass and downed the amber liquid.

"Thanks." He handed it back, loving her with his dark eyes. "One day it will happen," he said then. "One day, I won't be able to draw back. If Hal hadn't called me just now, we'd already be in too deep to stop."

"I know," she whispered, looking up with her regret clear in her eyes. "It was never that bad before."

"It gets worse, honey," he replied. His face was solemn now, serious. "It's now or never, Catherine. We have to get married soon."

She frowned, uncertain. "Matt...what about Layne?" she asked gently.

"Matt!" Hal yelled again.

Matt sighed impatiently. "We'll talk about it later," he said, bending to kiss her, very softly. "Wait up for me."

"I wouldn't dare," she replied, touching his mouth with her fingers.

"Well, you may have a point," he agreed ruefully. "We'll talk tomorrow, then."

She nodded. "Good night."

"Good night, little one." He smiled at her, turned and went out. Catherine stared after him for a long, long time before she could get her legs to take her upstairs.

So now there was no more time. She either married him or ran. She went to sleep wondering which was the more sensible.

CHAPTER TWELVE

THE BRIGHT SUN streamed into the dining room, and Catherine found herself eating breakfast alone. Betty was still sound asleep. Hal and Matt had gone to work. It was curious that Matt hadn't waited for her, she thought, especially after last night. She could feel her cheeks burn at just the memory of how it had been, how close they'd come. And if she'd been stupid enough to let it happen, how would she be feeling now? Matt would have no choice but to marry her. Did he really want that kind of commitment? Or did he just have a hunger for her that was so strong that he wasn't rational anymore?

The more she thought about it, the more worried she became. She got up and paced, hating her inactivity. She'd gotten used to going into the office every morning, but now the sale was over and she'd worked herself out of a job. Dressed in jeans and a yellow tank top, she wandered around the house like a lost soul. Soon it would be autumn, and how much would her life have changed by then?

Should she marry Matt and take a chance? Or should she go on to New York? She was at the point of tossing a coin. So much was at stake. She loved him, now more than ever. She wasn't sure anymore that she had enough willpower to walk away from him. At least he still wanted her. Wasn't that enough to start with?

The sudden opening of the front door startled her. She

whirled around in the hall, wide-eyed, to find Matt standing just inside the screen door.

"Good morning," she said hesitantly. She felt shy with him all of a sudden, girlish.

"Good morning," he replied. "Have you eaten?"

"Yes."

He held out his hand. "Come for a ride, Catherine."

She took the outstretched fingers, letting him lock them with hers, and followed him out into the warm sunshine.

"Where are we going?" she asked when he'd put her into the front seat of the Lincoln and climbed in behind the wheel.

"To the Comanche Flats airstrip. From there we fly to the Dallas-Fort Worth airport."

"And from there?" she persisted.

"We aren't going anywhere. We're going to meet somebody there."

"Oh." She felt vaguely disappointed. She liked shooting off into the sky with Matt, but this short hop seemed less than thrilling. She fingered the leather upholstery. "Did you arrange for all those shipments?" she murmured.

"From the sale?" He nodded. He lit a cigarette, glancing at her curiously with his black, black eyes. He took a draw on the cigarette and stared ahead at the long highway. "Catherine, about last night..."

And here it comes, she told herself, stiffening. He was going to apologize for what had happened. Or admit that he'd suddenly realized he couldn't go through with the wedding. Or...

"I didn't sleep much," he continued quietly. "I've been thinking about us. About the way this engagement happened."

"If you want to call it off..." she began hesitantly.

He glanced at her. "Is that what you want, honey?" he asked gently. "What you really want? Have I pushed you into a corner?"

She studied his hard face. Yes, here it is. Her chance to escape. To be free. She gnawed on her lower lip. Why was it so hard to say the words?

"You don't have to say it," he said then. "I think I understand how you feel. I haven't really given you a chance to make up your own mind, to sort out how you feel about me. Catherine, if you'd rather not marry me, I'll let you go—to New York, if that's what you want."

He looked strange this morning. Hard-eyed and stiff and unapproachable. "How do you feel about it?" she asked.

He laughed curtly and took another draw on the cigarette. "We're not discussing me."

"No, we never do," she said abruptly, glaring at him. "I never know how you feel or what you think. You're a stranger half the time."

"How can I be anything else at this point?" he asked, glancing at her pointedly. "You're as much a clam as I am."

She started to speak but closed her mouth on a heavy sigh. She didn't know what he wanted, but she had a cold feeling that he'd had second thoughts.

"If I asked you to let me break the engagement?" she probed.

"I would," he replied.

"Gladly, it sounds," she said lightly. "You don't want a noose around your neck anyway, do you?"

He studied her for a long moment, his eyes quiet, haunted, then he turned his gaze to the road. "If New York is what you really want, tell me!" he bit off.

She took a deep breath. "All right. It's what I really want!" she lied.

He didn't say a word for another mile. "Okay," he said then. "We're quits."

Her eyes filled with tears that she was too proud to let him see. It was no good telling herself this was the best way. She was hurting too much. She started to take off the emerald ring, but her fingers wouldn't cooperate. Soon, she promised. Soon I'll do it; I'll give it back.

Sitting beside him in the small private plane as he flew them to the airport, she refused to speak until they'd taxied to a stop and were walking into the terminal.

"Why are we here, anyway?" she asked in a husky tone.

"To meet Layne. She's agreed to meet me here so I can sign some papers."

"Layne!" She glared at him, lips trembling, eyes flashing. "You brought me here, knowing that…that woman is coming?" she demanded. "How could you!"

His eyebrows shot straight up. But before he could say anything, he was being paged to the information desk.

"This way," he said, propelling her with a steely hand. He glanced down at her. "When we're through here, you're going to explain that outburst."

"Don't hold your breath, big man," she retorted.

He dragged her to the desk, where a tall, heavyset woman with black hair waited, smiling down at a young boy about six years old.

"Hello, Layne," a grinning Matt greeted her, holding out a hand to shake hers. After introducing the two women, he said to Layne, "Thanks for making this rushed trip."

"No problem." Layne laughed. "My youngest wanted to ride with Mama, so I let him come along. I have three, you know," she confided to a thunderstruck Catherine. "My husband and I work all hours just to pay the grocery bills. You should see how much food they can put away!"

Matt smiled, but without much feeling. He signed the necessary papers while Catherine stood stock-still nearby, her heart as cold as November snow. She'd really done it now. She'd lied, telling Matt she didn't want to marry him, only because she was sure he was involved with Layne. And here was Layne, a very married lady who obviously loved her family and whose only interest in Matt was making a sale. Catherine wanted to die. How could she have misread the situation so horribly? And worse, why had Matt deliberately misled her?

She waited until he finished, then said goodbye to Layne and followed Matt back out to the airplane. Stony silence prevailed until after they'd landed at the Comanche Flats airstrip.

"She's married," she said dully after he'd put her in the car and gotten in beside her.

"Yes," he said quietly.

"Angel said she called you all the time."

"Of course. We've been working on this deal for a long time. There were days when I wouldn't even let Angel put her through to me, I was so sick of the wrangling." He lit a cigarette with a hard sigh. "We closed the deal this morning."

"I... Hal said she was your latest," she murmured. "And you let me think she was. Why?"

He shrugged. "It was all part of the game, honey. I thought I was winning, for a while there."

So she'd been right. Layne was fiction, but the game wasn't. He'd only been amusing himself. Tears stung her eyes as she stared out at the landscape.

They drove back to the ranch in a stark kind of silence, and as she glanced at Matt, she found the stranger there— a cold, unsmiling man who looked as if he'd lost his whole world. Where was the pleasant, teasing, laughing man of weeks past? And then she began to wonder if that hadn't been a mask he'd worn to keep her from seeing the very serious man underneath. She felt as if she'd never really known Matt at all. Now New York was more a terror than an anticipated delight.

He stopped at the front porch and waited for Catherine to get out. And she had a premonition that if she did, it would be the end of everything between them. Outside, clouds had formed overhead and it was just beginning to sprinkle rain. But she felt much more stormy than the weather.

She turned to him, but he wouldn't even look at her. His face was harder than she'd seen it in weeks.

"Matt?" she began softly.

"There's nothing more to say, Catherine," he replied quietly. "It's all over."

"I should have trusted you, shouldn't I?" she asked, as the puzzle pieces began to fall into place. "I should have realized that you aren't the kind of man who'd court one woman and keep another on the side. And I didn't even begin to see it."

His head turned slowly, his eyes solemn and even as he studied her. "Perhaps you didn't want to see it," he remarked, and drew on his cigarette. "You're very young, Catherine. I should have taken that into account. You didn't have the experience to understand what was happening."

She smiled wistfully. "I feel pretty old right now, if you want to know."

He shook his head. "You needed time, and I couldn't give it to you. Patience isn't one of my virtues." He finished the cigarette and put it out. "Go to New York, honey. Get your wanderlust out of your system. Maybe you'll find someone up there who's closer to your own age—"

"No!"

She hadn't meant to do that, to put quite so much feeling into that one word. But her voice broke on it, and Matt's head jerked around when he heard her. He searched her anguished face, and his chest was still, as if he'd stopped breathing.

Her eyes locked into his, helpless, hungry. Her lips trembled as she tried to find words and failed.

His face hardened even more; his eyes blazed as they returned her hungry stare. "I love you," he said roughly. "Is that what you want to hear, Kit?"

Tears came down her cheeks like silver rain, and she managed a watery smile. Rainbows. All her dreams coming true at once. Heaven.

"Oh, God. Come here!" he whispered unsteadily and reached for her.

She felt his mouth devouring hers, his arms crushing her against his hard chest. And outside, the rain beat on the metal roof while she got drunk on Matt's warm mouth and slid her hands lovingly into his dark, cool hair.

"Love me," she whispered as his mouth opened and brushed lovingly against hers. "Love me, Matt."

His hands made magic on her body, finding their way under her blouse to warm, soft curves that he quickly made bare and caressed with aching tenderness. His mouth pressed her head back into his shoulder with its hungry, ardent pressure and he made a rough sound under his breath, a groan.

"I was jealous," she whispered breathily in his ear as she pressed closer. "I loved you, and there was Layne, and I was so afraid to take you seriously. I couldn't have gone on living if it hadn't been true, if you'd only been playing."

He laughed gruffly and his arms contracted lovingly,

pressing her yielding body against his own as the rain made a veil between them and the world. "That was the biggest joke of all," he whispered, "that I was amusing myself with you. My God, I've been out of my mind waiting for you, waiting for you to see me as a man. You came out on the flats and announced you were going to New York, and I felt my world crashing down on my head! And Hal didn't help. I could have shot him for interfering."

"I could have, too," she breathed, nuzzling her face into his throat. "But with all the women you had running after you, I couldn't believe you'd ever wanted me."

"Window dressing," he confessed, lifting his head to pin her with his dark, warm eyes. "Kit, do you remember the night we almost went too far, at the barbecue? And I told you it had been so long since I'd had a woman?"

She nodded, coloring a little with the fierce sweetness of the memory.

He touched her mouth with fingers that had a fine tremor. "I haven't had a woman in two years, Kit," he whispered huskily. "Not since the day I opened my eyes and realized that I'd been possessed by soft green eyes and a laughing young face that were all I wanted to see for the rest of my life."

She didn't know what to say. She touched his face, wondering at the love she could read in it so plainly. "How could I have been so blind?" she whispered.

"How could I?" he replied. "All the signs were there, but I was too strung out worrying about losing you to read them. Kit, I tricked you into this engagement, but I wanted it so desperately. I want to marry you. To have children with you. To lie in the darkness with you and love you all the days of my life. If you leave me, I might just as well lie down and die," he murmured fervently against her warm mouth. "I love you...!"

She felt the wetness of her tears in the kiss and lifted her body against him, savoring the newness of belonging, smiling breathlessly as his searching hands went under her shirt and took possession of the soft weight of her breasts.

"Did you know I was in bed with you the night Hal tricked me?" she whispered shakily, then caught her breath as his thumbs edged out and found the evidence of her arousal.

"I knew," he confessed with a faint smile. "But it was too good an opportunity to miss. For once, old Hal did the right thing and tried to make amends, and it didn't backfire. I took shameless advantage of it. I thought if I could get you to marry me, I could teach you to love me."

"And I didn't need teaching," she murmured softly.

"Well, not in that," he agreed. "But in other ways..."

"You'll have to marry me, then," she told him. "And..." She gasped, lifting herself closer to his searching hands. "Oh, Matt, it had better be soon!"

"I feel the same way," he murmured at her mouth. "I want you so badly, Kit. I want the physical expression of love, the joining, the oneness. I've never had that because, until now, I've never loved."

He made it sound so beautiful, so much a part of loving and being loved. She looked up at him with her heart in her eyes, feeling already that bonding of skin on skin, of voices urgent and hungry, of hands touching, bodies locking together in a rhythm that was already familiar. Her face reddened at the vivid images, and he saw that look and crushed her mouth with his, groaning.

"I can picture it, too," he whispered unsteadily, holding her even closer. "Picture it, feel it, the way you'll be with me. Your body under mine, your voice breaking, your hands clutching at my hips—"

"Matt!" She shuddered with the sweetest kind of pleasure and hid her face against his pounding chest.

"I'll be so damned tender, Kit," he breathed. "I'll cherish you."

"Yes, I know," she whispered, closing her eyes. "I love you so."

"Hush, and kiss me."

By the time he'd had enough, the windows were fogged up all over, closing out the world, and she lay in his arms looking up at him with lazy, seductive eyes.

"I guess you won't let me work?" she teased.

"If you want to," he replied surprisingly. "You can publicize all my sales."

"You'll have to pay me a good salary," she added.

He smiled slowly, looking dark and handsome and wildly possessive. "Oh, I'll do that. And you get great fringe benefits."

"Like insurance and retirement?"

"Plus you'll get to sleep with the boss," he added, grinning from ear to ear.

She peeked up at him through her lashes. "Nice benefits."

"Reciprocal, too," he murmured, letting his eyes run slowly over her body.

He bent to her mouth again, and just as he started to draw her closer, they heard voices outside the car.

"Are you sure they're in there?" Hal was asking. "Windows sure are foggy."

"That's why I'm sure they're in there," Betty replied. "Go on, knock on the window."

"I don't know. Matt's got a pretty hard right cross."

Smiling at Catherine, Matt sighed as he reached over and flicked on the ignition. He let the power window down a couple of inches.

"Well?" he asked Hal and Betty, who were standing huddled under an umbrella.

They took in the picture: swollen mouths, dreamy looks, Catherine's crumpled shirt, Matt's shirt half unbuttoned. They grinned.

"How about some champagne?" Hal offered.

"Get it out," Matt agreed. "It feels like a champagne morning, all right."

Catherine looked up into the warmly possessive eyes of her husband-to-be, the laughter soft and loving on her face. Yes, it felt like a champagne morning. And it would, all the mornings of their lives. She told him so as the others disappeared, and she watched him smile slowly as he eased the window back up and bent again to her mouth.

* * * * *

SPECIAL EXCERPT FROM

HQN

To gain her rightful inheritance, Gaby Dupont takes a job with attorney Nicholas Chandler. She's shocked when sparks fly with the infuriating lawyer, but can Gaby risk her legacy for forever love?

Read on for a sneak preview of
Notorious,
by New York Times *bestselling author Diana Palmer.*

He gave her a long-suffering look. "I want to know if you have entanglements that will interfere with the work you do here," he returned. "I also need references."

"Oh. Sorry. I forgot." She handed him another sheet of paper. "And no, I'm not involved with anyone. At the moment." She smiled sweetly.

He ignored the smile and looked over the sheet. His eyebrows arched as he glanced at her. "A Roman Catholic cardinal, a police lieutenant, two nurses, the owner of a coffee shop and a Texas Ranger?" he asked incredulously.

"My grandmother is from Jacobsville, Texas," she explained. "The Texas Ranger, Colter Banks, is married to my third cousin."

"And these others?"

"People who know me locally." She smiled demurely. "The police officers want to date me. I know them from the coffee shop. The owner…"

"Wants to date you, too," he guessed. He stared at her as if he had no idea on earth why any male would want to date her. The look was fairly insulting.

"I have hidden qualities," she mused, trying not to laugh.

"Apparently," he said curtly. His eyes went back to the sheet. "A cardinal?" He glowered at her. "And please don't tell me that he wants to date you."

"Of course not. He's a friend of my grandmother's."

He drew in a breath. Her comments about men who wanted to date her disturbed him. He studied her in silence. He was extremely wealthy, not only from the work he did but from an inheritance left to him by a late uncle.

"You don't want the job because I'm single?" he asked bluntly.

Now her eyebrows lifted almost to her hairline. "Mr...." She glanced at the paper in her hand. "Mr. Chandler," she continued, "I hardly think my taste would run to a man in his forties!"

His dark eyes almost exploded with anger. "I am not in my forties!"

"Oh, dear, do excuse me," she said at once. She had to contain a smile. "Honestly, you look very much younger than a man in his fifties!"

His lips made a thin line.

The smile escaped and her pale blue eyes twinkled.

Don't miss
Notorious *by Diana Palmer,*
available July 2021 wherever Harlequin books
and ebooks are sold.

HQNBooks.com

Copyright © 2021 by Diana Palmer

If you love
DIANA PALMER
then you'll love...

Available Now

**ROMANCE WHEN
YOU NEED IT**

H HARLEQUIN
SPECIAL EDITION

**Believe in love. Overcome obstacles.
Find happiness.**

Save **$1.00**

off the purchase of ANY
Harlequin Special Edition book.

Available wherever books are sold,
including most bookstores, supermarkets,
drugstores and discount stores.

Save $1.00

off the purchase of ANY Harlequin Special Edition book.

Coupon valid until June 30, 2022. Redeemable at participating outlets in the U.S. and Canada only.
Limit one coupon per customer.

52617182

Canadian Retailers: Harlequin Enterprises ULC will pay the face value of this coupon plus 10.25¢ if submitted by customer for this product only. Any other use constitutes fraud. Coupon is nonassignable. Void if taxed, prohibited or restricted by law. Consumer must pay any government taxes. Void if copied. Inmar Promotional Services ("IPS") customers submit coupons and proof of sales to Harlequin Enterprises ULC, P.O. Box 31000, Scarborough, ON M1R 0E7, Canada. Non-IPS retailer—for reimbursement submit coupons and proof of sales directly to Harlequin Enterprises ULC, Retail Marketing Department, Bay Adelaide Centre, East Tower, 22 Adelaide Street West, 40th Floor, Toronto, Ontario M5H 4E3, Canada.

5 65373 00076 2 (8100)0 12508

U.S. Retailers: Harlequin Enterprises ULC will pay the face value of this coupon plus 8¢ if submitted by customer for this product only. Any other use constitutes fraud. Coupon is nonassignable. Void if taxed, prohibited or restricted by law. Consumer must pay any government taxes. Void if copied. For reimbursement submit coupons and proof of sales directly to Harlequin Enterprises ULC 482, NCH Marketing Services, P.O. Box 880001, El Paso, TX 88588-0001, U.S.A. Cash value 1/100 cents.

® and ™ are trademarks owned by Harlequin Enterprises ULC.

© 2021 Harlequin Enterprises ULC

DPCOUP0721MAX

Love Harlequin romance?

DISCOVER.

Be the first to find out about promotions, news and exclusive content!

f Facebook.com/HarlequinBooks

Twitter.com/HarlequinBooks

Instagram.com/HarlequinBooks

Pinterest.com/HarlequinBooks

You Tube YouTube.com/HarlequinBooks

ReaderService.com

EXPLORE.

Sign up for the Harlequin e-newsletter and download a free book from any series at
TryHarlequin.com

CONNECT.

Join our Harlequin community to share your thoughts and connect with other romance readers!
Facebook.com/groups/HarlequinConnection

HARLEQUIN

HARLEQUIN

Heartfelt or thrilling, passionate or uplifting—Harlequin is more than just happily-ever-after.

With twelve different series to choose from and new books available every month, you are sure to find stories that will move you, uplift you, inspire and delight you.

SIGN UP FOR THE HARLEQUIN NEWSLETTER

Be the first to hear about great new reads and exciting offers!

Harlequin.com/newsletters